Nov. 28/15
Dec 16/15

FRIEND OF THE DEVIL

PETER ROBINSON

FRIEND OF THE
DEVIL

McCLELLAND & STEWART

Library and Archives Canada Cataloguing in Publication

Robinson, Peter, 1950 –
Friend of the devil : an Inspector Banks novel / Peter Robinson.

ISBN 978-0-7710-7610-7

I. Title.

PS8585.035176F75 2007   c813'.54   C2007-901440-2

We acknowledge the financial support of the Government of Canada through the
Book Publishing Industry Development Program and that of the Government of
Ontario through the Ontario Media Development Corporation's Ontario Book
Initiative. We further acknowledge the support of the Canada Council for the Arts
and the Ontario Arts Council for our publishing program.

Typeset in Minion by M&S, Toronto
Printed and bound in Canada

This book is printed on acid-free paper that is 100% recycled,
ancient-forest friendly (100% post-consumer recycled).

McClelland & Stewart Ltd.
The Canadian Publishers
75 Sherbourne Street
Toronto, Ontario
M5A 2P9
www.mcclelland.com

1 2 3 4 5   11 10 09 08 07

To my agent, Dominick Abel, with thanks

1

She might have been staring out to sea, at the blurred line where the grey water meets the grey sky. The same salt wind that rushed the waves to shore lifted a lock of her dry hair and let it fall against her cheek. But she felt nothing; she just sat there, her expressionless face pale and puffy, clouded black eyes wide open. A flock of seagulls quarrelled over a shoal of fish they had spotted close to shore. One of them swooped low and hovered over the still shape at the cliff edge, then squawked and headed back to join the fray. Far out to sea, a freighter bound for Norway formed a red smudge on the horizon. Another seagull flew closer to the woman, perhaps attracted by the movement of her hair in the wind. A few moments later, the rest of the flock, tired of the squabble over fish, started to circle her. Finally, one settled on her shoulder in a grotesque parody of Long John Silver's parrot. Still, she didn't move. Cocking its head, it looked around in all directions like a guilty schoolboy in case someone was watching, then it plunged its beak into her ear.

Sunday mornings were hardly sacrosanct to Detective Chief Inspector Alan Banks. After all, he didn't go to church, and he rarely awoke with such a bad hangover that it was painful to move or speak. In fact, the previous evening he had watched *The Black Dahlia* on DVD and had drunk two glasses of Tesco's finest Chilean Cabernet with his reheated pizza funghi. But he did appreciate a lie-in and an hour or two's peace with the newspapers as much as the next man. For the afternoon, he planned to phone his mother and wish her a happy Mother's Day, then listen to some of the Shostakovich string quartets he had recently purchased from iTunes and carry on reading Tony Judt's *Postwar*. He found that he read far less fiction these days; he felt a new hunger to understand, from a different perspective, the world in which he had grown up. Novels were all well and good for giving you a flavour of the times, but he needed facts and interpretations, the big picture.

That Sunday, the third in March, such luxury was not to be. It started innocently enough, as such momentous sequences of events often do, at about half past eight, with a phone call from Detective Sergeant Kevin Templeton, who was on duty in the Western Area Major Crimes squad room that weekend.

"Guv, it's me. DS Templeton."

Banks felt a twinge of distaste. He didn't like Templeton, would be happy when his transfer finally came through. There were times when he tried to tell himself it was because Templeton was too much like him, but that wasn't the case. Templeton didn't only cut corners, he trampled on far too many people's feelings and, worse, he seemed to enjoy it. "What is it?" Banks grunted. "It had better be good."

"It's good, sir. You'll like it."

Banks could hear traces of obsequious excitement in Templeton's voice. Since their last run-in, the young DS had tried to ingratiate himself in various ways, but this kind of phony breathless deference was too Uriah Heep for Banks's liking.

"Why don't you just tell me?" said Banks. "Do I need to get dressed?" He held the phone away from his ear as Templeton laughed.

"I think you should get dressed, sir, and make your way down to Taylor's Yard as soon as you can."

Taylor's Yard, Banks knew, was one of the narrow passages that led into the Maze, which riddled the south side of the town centre behind Eastvale's market square. It was called a yard not because it resembled a square or a garden in any way, but because some bright spark had once remarked that it wasn't much more than a yard wide. "And what will I find there?" he asked.

"Body of a young woman," said Templeton. "I've checked it out myself. In fact, I'm there now."

"You didn't —"

"I didn't touch anything, sir. And between us, Police Constable Forsythe and me have got the area taped off and sent for the doctor."

"Good," said Banks, pushing aside the *Sunday Times* crossword he had hardly started and looking longingly at his still-steaming cup of black coffee. "Have you called the super?"

"Not yet, sir. I thought I'd wait till you'd had a butcher's. No sense in jumping the gun."

"All right," said Banks. Detective Superintendent Catherine Gervaise was probably enjoying a lie-in after a late night out to see *Orfeo* at Opera North in Leeds. Banks had seen it on Thursday with his daughter, Tracy, and enjoyed it very much. He wasn't sure whether Tracy had. She seemed to have turned in on herself these days. "I'll be there in half an hour," he said. "Three-quarters at the most. Ring DI Cabbot and DS Hatchley. And get DC Jackman there, too."

"DI Cabbot's still on loan to Eastern, sir."

"Of course. Damn." If this was a murder, Banks would have liked Annie's help. They might have problems on a personal level, but they still worked well as a team.

Banks went upstairs and showered and dressed quickly, then back in the kitchen he filled his travel mug with coffee to drink on the way, making sure the top was pressed down tight. More than once he'd had a nasty accident with a coffee mug. He turned everything off, locked up and headed for the car.

He was driving his brother's Porsche. Though he still didn't feel especially comfortable in such a luxury vehicle, he was finding that he liked it better each day. Not so long ago, he had thought of giving it to his son, Brian, or to Tracy, and that idea still held some appeal. The problem was that he didn't want to make one of them feel left out, or less loved, so the choice was proving to be a dilemma. Brian's band had gone through a slight change of personnel recently, and he was rehearsing with some new musicians. Tracy's exam results had been a disappointment to her, though not to Banks, and she was passing her time rather miserably working in a bookshop in Leeds and sharing a house in Headingley with some old student friends. So who deserved a Porsche? He could hardly cut it in half.

It had turned windy and cool, so Banks went back to switch his sports jacket for his zip-up leather jacket. If he was going to be standing around in the back alleys of Eastvale while the SOCOs, the photographer and the police surgeon did their stuff, he might as well stay as warm as possible. Once snug in the car, he started the engine and set off through Gratly, down the hill to Helmthorpe and on to the Eastvale Road. He plugged his iPod into the adapter, on shuffle, and Ray Davies's "All She Wrote" came on, a song he particularly liked, especially the line about the big Australian barmaid. That would do for a Sunday-morning drive to a crime scene, he thought; it would do just fine.

Gilbert Downie didn't particularly like walking the dog. He did it, but it was a chore. The whole thing was one of those typical family decisions gone wrong. His daughter, Kylie, had wanted a puppy, had talked about nothing else since she was eight. Finally, Gilbert and Brenda had given in and bought her one for her birthday, though Brenda wasn't especially fond of dogs, and they sometimes made her sneeze. A few years later, Kylie had lost interest and moved on to boys and pop music, so it was now left to him, Gilbert, to take care of Hagrid.

That Sunday morning, the weather was looking particularly nasty, but Gilbert knew he shouldn't complain. At least Hagrid gave him an excuse to get out of the house while Brenda and Kylie, now fourteen, had their usual Sunday-morning row about where she'd been and what she'd been doing out so late on Saturday night. There weren't any decent walks near the village, at least none that he wasn't already sick to death of, and he liked the sea, so he drove the short distance to the coast. It was a bleak and lonely stretch, but he enjoyed it that way. And he would have it all to himself. More and more these days, he preferred his own company, his own thoughts. He wondered if it was something to do with getting old, but he was only forty-six. That hardly qualified as old, except to Kylie and her deadbeat friends.

Gilbert pulled up the collar of his waxed jacket and shivered as the damp wind hit him. The grass was slippery from a previous shower. Hagrid didn't seem to mind. In no time he was off sniffing clumps of grass and shrubbery, Gilbert ambling behind, hands in pockets, glancing out at the choppy water and wondering what it must have been like to go out on the whaling ships from Whitby. The crews were gone for months at a time, the women waiting at home, walking along West Cliff day after day watching for signs of a sail and hoping to see the jawbone of a whale nailed to the mast, a signal that everyone was safe.

Then Gilbert saw a distant figure sitting at the cliff edge. Hagrid, ever gregarious, dashed towards it. The odd thing, as far as Gilbert was concerned, was that a seagull perched on each shoulder. The scene reminded him of an old woman he had once seen on a park bench, absolutely covered by the pigeons she was feeding. When Hagrid got close enough and barked, the seagulls launched themselves languidly and floated out over the sea, making it clear from their close circling and backward glances that this was only a temporary setback. Gilbert fancied they squawked in mockery that mere earthbound animals, like him and Hagrid, couldn't follow where they went.

Hagrid lost interest and edged towards some bushes away from the path, where he probably sniffed a rabbit, and Gilbert walked towards the immobile figure to see if he could offer any assistance. It was a woman, he thought. At least something about the way she sat and the hair curling over her collar indicated that she was. He called out but got no response. Then he realized that she was sitting in a wheelchair, wrapped in a blanket, her head propped up by something. Perhaps she couldn't move? There was nothing unusual about seeing a woman in a wheelchair around Larborough Head – the care home wasn't far away, and relatives occasionally took parents or grandparents for walks along the coast – but what on earth was she doing there all by herself, especially on Mother's Day, abandoned in such a precarious position? It wouldn't take much for the chair to slip over the edge, just a change in the wind. Where the hell was her nurse or relative?

When he arrived at the figure, Gilbert was struck almost simultaneously by two odd things. The first, bloodless scratches around her ears, he noticed because he approached her from behind, and when he moved around to the front, he saw the second: the upper half of her body, including the blanket, from her neck to her thighs, was absolutely drenched in blood. Before he even looked into her eyes, he knew that she was dead.

Holding back the bitter taste of bile that surged in his throat, Gilbert whistled for Hagrid and started running back to the car. He knew from experience that his mobile wouldn't get a signal out here, and that he had to drive at least a couple of miles inland before calling the police. He didn't want to leave her just sitting there for the gulls to peck at, but what else could he do? As if reading his mind, two of the boldest gulls drifted back towards the still figure as soon as Gilbert turned his back and ran.

Banks unplugged the iPod and stuck it in his pocket halfway through Tom Waits's "Low Down" and climbed out of the warm Porsche into the wind, which now seemed to be whipping sleet in his direction. The market square was busy with locals in their Sunday best going to the Norman church in the centre of the square, the women holding their hats fast against the wind, and the bells were ringing as if all were well with the world. One or two sightseers, however, had gathered around the taped-off entrance to Taylor's Yard. On one corner stood a pub called the Fountain, and on the other Randall's leather goods shop. Between them, the narrow, cobbled street led into the Maze, that labyrinth of alleys, called ginnels and snickets locally, tiny squares, court-yards, nooks and crannies and small warehouses that had remained unchanged since the eighteenth century.

Short of knocking the whole lot down and starting again, there was nothing much anyone could do with the cramped spaces and awkward locations other than use them for storage or let them lie empty. The alleys weren't really a shortcut to anywhere, though if you knew your way, you could come out into the castle car park above the terraced gardens that sloped down to the river, below Eastvale Castle. Apart from a row of four, tiny occupied cottages near the end of the car park, the buildings were mostly uninhabitable, even to squatters, and as they were also listed, they couldn't be knocked down, so the Maze stayed as it was, a handy hideaway for a quick knee-trembler, a hit of crystal meth or skunk weed before a night on the town.

The street-cleaners had complained to the police more than once about having to pick up needles, roaches, used condoms and plastic bags of glue, especially around the back of the Bar None Club or down Taylor's Yard from the Fountain, but even though the Maze was just across the square from the police station, they couldn't police it twenty-four hours a day. Detective Constable Rickerd and his community support officers, the "plastic policemen," as the townsfolk called them, did the best they could, but it wasn't enough. People kept out of the Maze after dark. Most law-abiding folks had no reason to go there, anyway. There were even rumours that it was haunted, that people had got lost in there and never found their way out again.

Banks took his protective clothing from the boot of the car, signed the log for the constable on guard duty and ducked under the blue and white police tape. At least the sleet barely penetrated the Maze. The buildings were so high and close, like the Shambles in York, that they blocked out the sky, except for a narrow grey strip. If anyone had lived on the upper floors, they could easily have reached out and shaken hands with their neighbours across the street. The blocks of limestone from which the Maze was built were dark from the earlier rain, and a hint of peat smoke drifted through the air from the distant cottages. It made Banks think of Laphroaig, and he wondered if he might regain his taste for Islay malt whisky before long. The wind whistled and moaned, changing pitch, volume and timbre like breath blown through a wood-wind. The Maze was a stone wind, though, Banks reckoned.

As promised, DS Kevin Templeton was keeping a watch on the building where the body had been found, where Taylor's Yard crossed Cutpurse Wynde. It wasn't much more than an outbuilding, a stone-built shed, used for storing swatches and remnants by Joseph Randall, the owner of the leather goods shop. The frontage was limestone, and there were no windows. Usually, if a building did have any ground-floor windows in the Maze, they were boarded up.

Templeton was his usual suave self, gelled black hair, expensive tan chinos, damp around the knees, and a shiny leather jacket slick with

rain. His eyes were bloodshot from the previous night's excess, and
Banks imagined him at a rave or something, twitching away to a techno-
pop beat or some DJ mixing Elvis with Eminem. Whether Templeton
took drugs or not, Banks wasn't sure. He had noticed no evidence, but
he was certainly keeping an eye on him ever since the overambitious
DS's attempt to ingratiate himself as the new super's toady. That had
backfired, with a little help from Banks and Annie, but it hardly seemed
to have dampened Templeton's ardour for advancement or his apparent
taste for arse-licking. The man wasn't a team player; that was for certain.

"What have we got?" Banks asked.

"Doc Burns is in with her now," Templeton answered.

"SOCOs?"

"On their way."

"Then we'd better have a look now before the little Hitlers take
over."

Templeton grinned. "It's not very pretty in there."

Banks stared at him. In the ranks of pointless comments he had
heard in his time, it didn't rate particularly high, but it had its place.
Templeton shrugged, didn't even have the awareness to be embarrassed.
Banks wondered if that was a psychopath's trait, along the lines of lack
of conscience, no sense of humour and zero human empathy.

Kitted out in protective overalls and gloves, Banks pushed the green
wooden door. It creaked on rusty hinges as it opened to reveal Dr. Burns
kneeling over a body in the light of a naked bulb. For a split second,
Banks was reminded of an image from a film he had seen, something to
do with Jack the Ripper bending over one of his victims. Well, the Maze
certainly had its similarities to the Ripper's Whitechapel, but Banks
hoped that was where the comparison ended.

He turned back to Templeton. "Do you know whether the door was
locked before the girl was put in there?"

"Hard to say, guv. The wood's so old and rotten, a quick, hard shove
would have done for it. It could have been broken for ages."

Banks turned back to the storeroom. The first thing he noticed, other
than the dust, whitewashed walls and spiderwebs, were the mingled
smells of leather, vomit and blood, the latter faint, a distant sweet metallic
undertone, but nevertheless discernible. The victim was lying on a pile of

leather scraps and remnants. From what Banks could see in the dim light, they were of various colours – green, blue, red, brown – and mostly triangular or rectangular. Banks picked one up. It was very soft, pliable leather that might be useful for something down the line: an elbow-patch, say, or a small item, like a change purse.

Dr. Burns glanced over his shoulder and moved back to stand beside Banks. The room was just high enough for them both to stand upright. "Ah, Alan. I've disturbed things as little as possible. I know what the SOCOs are like."

Banks knew, too. The scenes-of-crime officers were very territorial about their work, and woe betide anyone who got in their way, DCI or not. "Have you had a chance to determine cause of death?" he asked.

"Looks like manual strangulation to me, unless there are any hidden causes," Burns said, stooping and carefully lifting a strand of blonde hair, gesturing towards the dark bruising under her chin and ear.

From what Banks could see, she was young, no older than his own daughter, Tracy. She was wearing a green top and a white miniskirt with a broad pink plastic belt covered in silver glitter. The skirt had been hitched up even higher than it was already to expose her upper thighs. The body looked posed. She lay on her left side, legs scissored, as if she were running in her sleep. Something glistened on her pale flesh lower down, just above her knee, and Banks thought it might be semen. If so, there was a good chance of DNA. Her red knickers, skimpy as string, had snagged on her left ankle. She was wearing black patent-leather high heels and a silver chain around her right ankle. Just above it was a tattoo of a tiny butterfly. Her top had been pushed up to expose the profile of her small breasts and swollen nipples, and her eyes were open, staring at the far wall. Two or three of the leather remnants protruded from her mouth.

"Pretty young thing," said Dr. Burns. "Damn shame."

"Is that all she was wearing? It's bloody freezing."

"Kids today. You must have seen them."

Banks had. Whole groups of them, girls in particular, though plenty of boys wore nothing but T-shirts and jeans, running around town from pub to pub in the middle of winter wearing thin sleeveless tops and short skirts. No tights. He had always assumed it was because they wanted to show off their bodies, but perhaps it was a simple practical matter. It just made things easier when you were on the move: no clutter, nothing to remember, or forget, except your handbag. It made coming and going from places easy, and perhaps it was a mark of youth too, indifference to the cold, thumbing one's nose at the elements.

"She wouldn't have ended up in that position naturally, would she?" Banks asked.

"Not if she was raped and strangled," said Burns. "She would have been on her back with her legs open, but there's no sign of lividity there."

"So he moved her when he'd finished, turned her on her side, turned her face away, made her appear a bit more decent, as if she was sleeping. Perhaps he cleaned her up, too."

"Well, if he did, he missed something, didn't he?" said Dr. Burns, pointing to the glistening spot.

Dr. Burns moved and accidentally bumped his head against the light bulb, which started swinging back and forth. In the corner, beside the door, Banks glimpsed something catching the light. There, on the dusty stone floor, lay a gold lamé bag with a thin shoulder strap. Carefully, with his gloved hands, Banks picked it up and opened it. Lipstick, compact with mirror, three condoms, four Benson & Hedges, purple Bic cigarette lighter and a book of matches from the Duck and Drake, facial tissues, paracetamol, nail file and clipper, a tampon, cheap turquoise gel pen, iPod Shuffle in a pink skin, driver's licence, an unmarked bottle with four white pills in it, Ecstasy, each stamped with a crown, a small purse with twenty pounds in notes and sixty-five pence in coins. Finally, an address book with a William Morris cover, and in the front a name, Hayley Daniels, the same name that appeared with the photograph on her driver's licence, and an address in Swainshead, a village about thirty miles west of Eastvale.

Banks made a note of the details in his notebook and put everything back in the handbag for the SOCOs. He called Kevin Templeton into the doorway and told him to phone the local police station in Swainshead and have the constable there break the news to the girl's parents. Arrangements would then be made for them to come to Eastvale to identify the body. No more than the necessary details to be given.

Then Banks glanced back towards the girl's twisted body. "Anything on the sexual element?" he asked Dr. Burns. "Apart from the obvious."

"Nothing certain yet, but it looks as if she's been brutally raped," said Burns. "Vaginal and anal. Dr. Wallace will be able to tell you more when she gets her on the table. One odd thing."

"Yes."

"Well, she's been shaved. Down there."

"The killer?"

"It's possible, I suppose. But some girls do it . . . I mean, so I've heard. And there's a tattoo, where the hair would have been. You can't see it well at all from this position, and I don't want to disturb the body any more than necessary until the SOCOs have had their turn. But it would seem to indicate maybe she had it done herself some time ago. You can see the tattoo on her ankle, too."

"Yes."

Dr. Burns was the local police surgeon and, as such, his job usually stopped with attending the scene, declaring death and releasing the body for the coroner. After that, Dr. Wallace, the new Home Office pathologist, usually performed the post-mortem. Banks had found Burns useful in the past, though. Like all doctors, he didn't like to commit himself, but he could be led into a speculation or two on cause and time of death, which usually proved accurate enough to save Banks some time. That was what he asked about next.

Burns checked his watch. "It's half past nine now," he said. "The cold would slow down rigor, and she seems young and healthy enough. I mean . . . you know."

Banks knew. Over the years he had got used to dead people being described as "in good health."

"I'm only guessing, of course," Burns went on, "but I'd say after midnight, maybe as late as two in the morning, but not likely later than that."

"Was she killed here?"

"It seems that way," said Burns.

Banks scanned the room. "It's a pretty isolated spot," he said. "Insulated, too. Thick walls. I doubt anybody would hear anything, if

there were anything to hear." He looked at the swatches of leather that
filled the girl's mouth. "Even if she got off one good scream to start with,
that would have soon silenced her."

Dr. Burns said nothing. He took out his notebook and made a
number of jottings, which Banks assumed to be time, temperature,
position of body and such. They needed the photographer here soon.
The SOCOs would have to wait until he had finished, of course, but they
wouldn't like it. They'd be straining at their chains like a pack of
Dobermans who hadn't been given a lump of meat in a month.

The hinges creaked and Peter Darby, the police photographer,
arrived with his old Pentax and new digital videocam. The room was
small, so Banks and Burns edged out and left him to it. Banks felt an
urge for a cigarette. He didn't know why, as nobody around him was
smoking. Perhaps it was the Benson & Hedges he had seen in the
victim's handbag. Or the rain that had now replaced the sleet. He had a
memory of a cigarette tasting so good in the rain once, when he had
been a very young smoker, and it had stuck with him for some reason.
He let go of the thought, and the urge faded. From the church in the
market square he thought he could hear the congregation singing
"There Is a Green Hill Far Away," and it reminded him that Easter was
coming up in only a few weeks.

"She'd also been sick," Dr. Burns added. "I don't know if it's
significant, but I noticed traces of vomit both inside and on the wall
outside."

"Yes," said Banks. "I smelled it, too. There's also a chance it could
have been the killer's. Not everyone has the stomach for this sort of thing,
thank God. I'll make sure the SOCOs pay close attention. Thanks, doc."

Dr. Burns nodded and walked away. Templeton came over and
shifted from foot to foot, rubbing his hands together. "Juicy one, isn't it,
guv?" he said. "Just like I told you."

Banks closed his eyes, turned his head up to the strip of grey sky,
feeling a few drops of rain on his eyelids, and sighed. "It's a dead girl,
Kev," he said. "Raped and strangled. Now, I appreciate a bit of crime
scene humour as much as the next copper, but can you just hold back
your glee for a while longer, do you think?"

"Sorry, guv," said Templeton, his tone indicating that he had absolutely no idea what he had to apologize for.

"And we'll want to interview all local sex offenders, everyone on the books, and those we think should be."

"Yes, guv."

"And ring the super," Banks said. "She'll have to know."

Templeton reached for his mobile.

Banks enjoyed the quiet for a moment, the music of the wind, water dripping from a gutter somewhere, and the distant choir singing a hymn. It was so long since he had been to church. Then he heard new sounds and noticed Detective Constable Winsome Jackman and Detective Sergeant Stefan Nowak, crime scene coordinator, come bustling down Taylor's Yard with a gaggle of SOCOs kitted out like spacemen. Soon, they would have the storeroom as brightly lit as a film studio, and their various tools and gadgets would be sucking up or illuminating tiny traces of the most unusual and practically invisible substances. Everything would be carefully bagged, labelled and stored to be used in the event of a court case down the line, and some of it might even be of use in tracking down the girl's killer. If they got lucky, they would find DNA, and it would match a sample they already had in the DNA National Database. *If.*

Banks welcomed Stefan Nowak and explained what he knew of the situation. Nowak had a few words with his team, and when Peter Darby came out, they went in. They'd be a while setting up and getting started, Nowak explained, and they wanted everyone out of their way. Banks checked the time. Pity, he thought, that with all these new liberal opening hours, none of the local pubs extended them to as early as ten o'clock on a Sunday morning.

Banks sent Winsome off to Swainshead to interview the girl's parents before bringing them back to Eastvale General Infirmary to identify the body. He needed to know as much as she could find out about where the girl had been last night, and with whom. There was a lot to set in motion, and the sooner the better. Leads had a habit of vanishing very quickly.

After about three-quarters of an hour, Banks had another brief period of peace in which to assess the situation. By the looks of her, the girl had been out on the town, most likely with a boyfriend or with a group of friends. They needed to be tracked down and interviewed. Someone would have to get hold of all the closed-circuit television footage, too. Most of the market square was covered by CCTV these days, though there were blind spots. How had she ended up alone? Had she gone off with someone, or had the killer been lurking in the Maze, waiting for a victim? Why had she wandered in there alone? Unfortunately, there was no CCTV in the Maze itself.

Then a voice cut through his reverie. "This had better be bloody important, DCI Banks. I've had to cut short my morning gallop, and my son and his wife are expecting me for lunch." And down the alley strutted the diminutive but svelte and powerful figure of Detective Superintendent Catherine Gervaise, resplendent in jodhpurs, cap and boots, slapping her riding crop gently against her thigh as she approached.

Banks smiled. "I must say, ma'am, you cut quite a dashing figure. Fancy a coffee? We can have a chat and leave DS Nowak to watch over things here."

Was Banks imagining it or did Superintendent Gervaise actually blush at the compliment?

Somewhere in the distance, beyond the pain screaming in her head and the sound of the seagulls and church bells, Detective Inspector Annie Cabbot could hear her mobile ringing. They don't really ring these days, she thought, as she strained towards consciousness; they have ringtones; they tinkle; they play tunes. Hers was playing "Bohemian Rhapsody" and it was driving her crazy. The phone salesman's little joke. She would have to learn how to change it. Just when she managed to half open an eye and reach for the bedside table, the sound stopped. Damn, she thought, as her hand reached into empty space. There *was* no bedside table. Where had the bloody thing gone? She had a moment of absolute panic, not knowing where, or even who, she was. She certainly wasn't at Mrs. Barnaby's B & B, where she should have been. Then she became aware of a warm, heavy object resting on her hip.

When she got both her eyes open and looked around, she became immediately aware of three things: she was not in her own bed, hence no bedside table; she had a splitting headache; and the warm, heavy thing lying across her hip was a man's arm. Fortunately – or not, as the case may be – it was still attached to a man.

Piece by piece, like flipping through cards to make a moving picture, but with cards missing, fragments of the previous evening came back to her. It was vague and fuzzy, and there were big gaps, but she did remember beer, loud music, dancing, fizzy blue drinks with umbrellas, flashing lights, a live band, people laughing, stumbling through winding, dimly lit streets, up a long hill, a steep staircase . . . then things got more blurred. Another drink or two, perhaps, drunken fumblings and a tumble on the bed. This bed. Gently, Annie disengaged the arm. Its owner stirred and grumbled in his sleep, but thankfully he didn't awaken. Then Annie sat up and took stock.

She was naked. Her clothes lay strewn across the hardwood floor with the kind of carelessness that suggested desperate and wanton abandon, her black silk knickers hanging on the bed knob like some obscene sort of trophy. She snatched them off, swung to the side of the bed and slipped them on, then ran her hands through her tousled hair. She felt like shit. Idiot, she said to herself. *Idiot.*

She glanced at his body, where the sheet had slipped off. Short black hair sticking up here and there where he had slept on it, one lock over his right eye, a strong jaw, broad shoulders, a nice chest, not too hairy, but masculine enough. Thank God he wasn't a colleague, someone from the station. She couldn't see what colour his eyes were because they were closed, and it shamed her that she couldn't remember. He needed a shave, but not too many years ago he wouldn't have. How old was he? Twenty-two, twenty-three at the most, she guessed. And how old was she? Just turned forty. At least he wasn't married, not as far as she could tell from the appearance of the flat. It was usually the older ones, the married ones, that she fell for.

With a sigh, she began to gather up the rest of her clothes and get dressed. The room was pleasant enough, with pale blue walls, a poster of a Modigliani nude, and a Venetian blind that didn't keep out very much light. There was also a poster of some rock band she didn't recognize on the opposite wall. Worse, there was an electric guitar propped up beside a small amplifier. She remembered him telling her that he played in a band. Christ, had she really gone home with a musician? Look on the bright side, she told herself; at least it was the guitarist, not the drummer or the bass player, as her old friend Jackie would have said, and especially not the saxophone player. "Never go with a sax player, sweetie," Jackie had told her. "The only thing he's thinking of is his next solo." Still, what a cliché.

In the cold light of day, was he even younger than she thought? She checked him out again. No. At least twenty-two. Younger than Banks's rock-star son, Brian, though. Perhaps it should make her feel good, she tried to tell herself, that someone so young and attractive had fancied her, that she still had such pulling power, but somehow it didn't; it made her feel like an old whore. Perfectly all right for older men and younger women – a man would feel proud of himself – but not for her. She zipped up her jeans. Christ, they felt tight. She'd been putting on weight like nobody's business lately, and it didn't make her feel any better to see that little bulge of fat where her flat belly used to be. Time for more exercise and less ale.

Annie found her mobile in her shoulder bag and checked the call. It was from the station. She didn't know if she could face work feeling the way she did. She took her bag with her into the bathroom and closed the door. She used the toilet first, then found some Aspirin in the cabinet above the sink, washed herself as best she could – was that what they called a "whore's bath"? – and applied some makeup. He didn't have a shower, and she didn't feel like undressing again and getting in the bath. Best just to leave. Find her car, answer the message, then go home, or what passed for home these days, for a good long soak and self-flagellation. Write out a thousand times: "I must not go home with strange young guitarists I meet in nightclubs." At least she knew she had left her car somewhere near the club. She hadn't been stupid enough to drive. She'd had *some* sense, then. And she thought she could even remember which club they had ended up in.

The air in the bedroom smelled of stale smoke and worse, and Annie saw on a small table by the door an ashtray with cigarette butts and a couple of roaches. Beside it lay a small plastic bag of marijuana and her hoop earrings. God, she had had the presence of mind to take her earrings off and yet she had smoked a couple of joints and . . . well, what else had she done? It didn't bear thinking about. She fumbled with the earrings and got them on.

He stirred as she opened the door, but just enough to pull the sheet up, wrap it around him and curl up like a child. Annie shut the door behind her and walked down the stairs to a strange new day in a strange place. She could smell the fresh sea air as soon as she got outside, feel the cold wind and hear the seagulls squealing. At least she had a warm jacket.

While she headed back down the hill in the direction of the club to her car, she fumbled with her mobile and accessed her voice mail. She was finally rewarded by the stern voice of Detective Superintendent Brough from Eastern Area headquarters telling her to get down to Larborough Head immediately. There'd been a murder and the locals needed her. Being on loan, she thought, ending the call, sometimes felt like being a whore. Then she realized she had had the same thought twice in the space of about half an hour, under different circumstances, and decided it was time to change metaphors. Not a whore at all but an angel of mercy. That's what she was: Annie Cabbot, *Angel of Mercy*, at your service. She found the purple Astra in the public car park beside the club, thinking for the hundredth time that it was about time she got a new car, consulted her AA road map and, with a crunch of gears, set off for Larborough Head, at the far northern edge of Eastern's territory.

At least the cafés in the market square were open. Banks chose one only three doors down from Taylor's Yard, on the upper level above the Age Concern shop, where he knew the coffee was good and strong, and sat down with Superintendent Gervaise. She appeared quite attractive, he noticed, with the pert nose, blue eyes, cupid's bow lips and the slight glow her morning's exercise had given to her pale complexion. The faint scar beside her left eye was almost a mirror image of his own. She was probably a good ten years younger than him, which put her in her early forties. Once they had given their orders, his for coffee, hers for a pot of Earl Grey tea, and toasted teacakes for both of them, they got down to business.

"It looks like we've got a particularly nasty murder on our hands," Banks said.

"And things have been so quiet lately," said Gervaise. She lay her riding crop on the table, took off her helmet, gave her head a shake and ran her hand over her short fair hair, which lay flattened against her skull. "Ever since that business with the rock group." She gave Banks a look.

Banks knew that, even though she had given him the freedom he needed to solve his previous murder case, she had still been unhappy with its conclusion. Banks had, too. But that couldn't be helped. Sometimes things just don't work out the way you hope they will. Banks moved on quickly, telling her what he had found out from DS Templeton and Dr. Burns. "The body was discovered at quarter past eight this morning by a Mr. Joseph Randall, age fifty-five, of Hyacinth Walk."

"And what was he doing in the Maze at that time on a Sunday morning?"

"He's the owner of the leather goods shop on the corner," Banks explained. "It's his storeroom. He said he went around there to search for some samples, found the lock broken and saw her just lying there. Swore he didn't touch anything. Said he backed out and ran straight across the square to the station."

"Do we believe him?"

"He says he opened the storeroom door at quarter past eight, but one of the people in the market square told DS Templeton she saw Randall go into the Maze at ten past eight by the church clock, which is pretty accurate. She remembers because she was late for church and glanced up to see the time. The desk sergeant logged the report from Randall at eight twenty-one."

"That's eleven minutes." Gervaise pursed her lips. "Sounds rather thin," she said. "Where is he now?"

"DS Templeton sent him home with a constable. Apparently Mr. Randall was very upset."

"Hmm. Interview him yourself. Go in hard next time."

"Yes, ma'am," said Banks, making a doodle in his notebook. Ever one for stating the obvious, was Gervaise. Still, it was best to let her think she was in control. Their order arrived. The coffee was as good as he remembered, and the teacakes had plenty of butter on them.

"What was the girl doing in the Maze by herself?" Gervaise asked.

"That's one thing we have to find out," said Banks. "But, for a start, we don't know that she was by herself. She could have gone in there with someone."

"To take drugs perhaps?"

"Perhaps. We found some pills in her handbag. Ecstasy. Or maybe she just got separated from her friends and someone lured her there with the promise of drugs? Still, you hardly need to hide away in the Maze to pop E. You can do it in any pub in town. She could have been taking a shortcut to the car park or the river."

"Did she have a car?"

"We don't know yet. She did have a driver's licence."

"Follow it up."

"We will. She was probably drunk," Banks said. "At least tipsy. There was a whiff of vomit in the storeroom, so she may have been sick, if it wasn't our killer's. Forensics should solve that one, anyway. She most likely wouldn't have been thinking about safety, and I doubt there's any great mystery as to how or why she came to be in the Maze alone. There are any number of possibilities. She could have had an argument with her boyfriend, for example, and run off."

"And someone was lying there in wait for her?"

"Or the chance of someone like her. Which indicates it might be a killer who knows the habits of the locals on a Saturday night in Eastvale after closing time."

"Better round up the usual suspects, then. Local sex offenders, known clients of sex workers."

"It's being done."

"Any idea where she'd been?"

"Judging by the way she was dressed," Banks said, "it seems as if she'd been doing the rounds of the market square pubs. Typical Saturday-night getup. We'll be canvassing all the pubs as soon as they open." He glanced at his watch. "Which won't be long now."

Gervaise squinted at him. "Not personally, I hope?"

"Too much of a job for me, I'm afraid. Thought I'd put Detective Sergeant Hatchley in charge of it. He's been housebound lately. Do him good to get out and about."

"Keep him on a tight leash, then," said Gervaise. "I don't want him offending every bloody minority group we've got in town."

"He's mellowed a lot."

Gervaise gave him a disbelieving look. "Anything else?" She dotted her mouth with a paper serviette after a couple of dainty nibbles of teacake.

"I'll get a couple of officers to work on reviewing all the CCTV footage we can find of the market square last night. A lot of the pubs have CCTV now, and I know the Bar None does, too. There should be plenty, and you know what the quality's like, so it'll take time, but we might find something there. We'll also conduct a thorough search of the Maze, adjacent buildings, the lot, and we'll do a house-to-house of the immediate area. Trouble is, there are ways in and out that don't show up on any CCTV cameras. The exit into the car park above the river gardens, for example."

"Surely there must be cameras in the car park?"

"Yes, but not covering it from that angle. They're pointing the other way, *into* the car park *from* the alley. Easy to slip under them. It's only a snicket, and hardly anyone uses it. Most people use the Castle Road exit, which *is* covered. We'll try our luck, anyway."

"Check them all out as best you can."

Banks told her what Dr. Burns had said about cause and approximate time of death.

"When will Dr. Wallace be available to do the post-mortem?" she asked.

"Tomorrow morning, I should hope," said Banks. Dr. Glendenning had retired, in his own words, "to play golf," about a month ago, and Banks hadn't really seen his replacement at work, since there hadn't been any suspicious deaths in that period. From what he could gather from his brief meetings with her, she seemed to be a dedicated professional and efficient pathologist.

"The picture on the driver's licence I found in the handbag matches the victim," Banks said, "and we've got an address from the flyleaf of her address book. Hayley Daniels. From Swainshead."

"Reported missing?"

"Not yet."

"So perhaps she wasn't expected home," said Gervaise. "Any idea how old she was?"

"Nineteen, according to the licence."

"Who's following up?"

"DC Jackman's gone to Swainshead to talk to the parents. She ought to be arriving there about now."

"Rather her than me," said Gervaise.

Banks wondered if she had ever been given the job of breaking bad news to a victim's parents.

"I know what you're thinking," Gervaise said with a smile. "You're thinking me, with all my nice upper-middle-class upbringing, university degrees, accelerated promotion and the rest, what would I know about it, aren't you?"

"Not at all," said Banks with a straight face.

"Liar." Gervaise sipped some tea and stared at a spot just over Banks's head. "My first week as a probationary PC," she said, "I was working at Poole, Dorset. Mostly making tea and coffee. Friday morning they found the body of an eleven-year-old schoolboy on a tract of wasteland at the edge of town. He'd been raped and beaten to death. Working-class family. Guess who they sent?"

Banks said nothing.

"Christ, I was sick to my stomach," Gervaise said. "Before I went out there. Really, physically sick. I was convinced I couldn't do it."

"But you did?"

She looked Banks in the eye. "Of course I did. And do you know what happened? The mother went berserk. Threw a plate of eggs, beans and chips at me. Cut my head open. I had to put the bloody handcuffs on to restrain her in the end. Temporarily, of course. She calmed down eventually. And I got ten stitches." Gervaise shook her head. "What a day." She looked at her watch. "I suppose I'd better ring my son and tell him lunch is off."

Banks glanced out the window. The wind was blowing harder, and the people coming out of church were having a difficult time keeping their hats on. He thought of the body on the pile of leather. "I suppose so," he said. "Today isn't looking too good so far, either." Then he went to the counter to pay.

Swainshead, or the Head as the locals called it, started with a triangular village green that split the main road at the T-junction with the Swainsdale Road. Around the triangle were the church, the village hall and a few shops. This, Winsome knew, was called Lower Head, and was the part most frequently visited by tourists. The Daniels family lived in Upper Head, where the two branches of the road joined into one and separated two rows of stone cottages facing one another. Behind the cottages on both sides, the pastures rose slowly, criss-crossed by drystone walls, and finally gave way to steep fells ending in moorland.

The area was so named because the source of the River Swain was to be found in the surrounding hills. It began as a mere puddle bubbling forth from the earth, overflowing into a thin trickle and then gaining strength as it went, finally plunging over the edge of a hanging valley at Rawley Force to cut its main course along the dale. Banks had once told Winsome about a case he'd worked on there, long before her time in Eastvale. It had taken him as far as Toronto in search of a missing expatriate. As far as Winsome knew, none of the people involved still lived in Swainshead, but those who did live there remembered the incident; it had become part of village folklore. Years ago, people would have written songs about it, the kind of old broadsheet folk ballads that Banks liked so much. These days, when the newspapers and TV had picked the bones clean, there was nothing left for anyone to sing about.

The sound of Winsome's car door closing shattered the silence and sent three fat crows soaring up into the sky from a gnarled tree. They wheeled against the grey clouds like black umbrellas blowing inside out.

Winsome checked the address as she walked past a pub and a couple of houses with BED AND BREAKFAST signs swinging in the wind, VACANCIES cards displayed in their bay windows. Three grizzled old men leaning on their walking sticks and chatting on the old stone bridge, despite the weather, fell silent and followed her with their eyes as she walked by. Winsome supposed they didn't often see a six-foot black woman in Swainshead.

The wind seemed to be blowing from all directions and with it, like a part of it, came the sleet, stinging her eyes, seeping through her black denim jeans, tight around the thighs, where her jacket ended. It wouldn't do the suede jacket much good, either, she realized, thinking she ought to have worn something more practical. But she'd been in a hurry, and it was the first thing she touched in the hall cupboard. How was she to know it was going to be like this?

Winsome found the house and rang the doorbell. A dour constable answered, tried unsuccessfully to cover up his surprise at the sight of her, and led her into the front room. A woman who looked far too young to have a daughter the victim's age sat there, staring into space.

"Mrs. Daniels?" Winsome asked.

"McCarthy," the woman said, glancing up. "Donna McCarthy. But Geoff Daniels is my husband. I kept my maiden name for professional reasons. I was explaining to the constable here that Geoff's away at the moment on business."

Winsome introduced herself. She noticed with approval that Donna McCarthy showed neither surprise nor amusement at her appearance.

Mrs. McCarthy's eyes filled up. "Is it true, what he told me? About our Hayley?"

"We think so," Winsome said, reaching for the plastic bag that held the address book Banks had given her. "Can you tell me if this belonged to your daughter?"

Donna McCarthy examined the cover, with its William Morris pattern, and the tears spilled over. "She's not my real daughter, you understand," she said, voice muffled through a handkerchief. "I'm Geoff's second wife. Hayley's mother ran off twelve years ago. We've been married for eight."

"I see," said Winsome, making a note. "But you can definitely identify that address book as belonging to Hayley Daniels?"

Donna nodded. "Can I have a peek inside?"

"I'm afraid you can't touch it," said Winsome. "Here, let me." She took out the latex gloves she had brought for just such an eventuality, slipped the address book out of its bag and opened it to the flyleaf. "Is that Hayley's handwriting?"

Donna McCarthy put the handkerchief to her face again and nodded. Winsome flipped a few pages, and she kept on nodding. Finally, Winsome put the book away again and took off her gloves and crossed her wet legs. "Any chance of rustling up some tea?" she asked the constable. He gave her a look that spoke volumes about a man like him being asked to do such a menial task by a black woman of equal rank, albeit a detective, and sloped off, presumably towards the kitchen. Miserable bugger. Winsome touched the woman's hand gently with her own. "I'm so sorry," she said. "But I do need to ask you a few questions."

Donna McCarthy blew her nose. "Of course," she said. "I understand." She seemed a slight, desolate figure alone on the sofa, but Winsome could see that she was also fit, almost muscular in her shoulders and arms. She had pale green eyes and short light-brown hair. Her clothes were casual, jeans and a plain white T-shirt showing the outline of her bra over small, firm breasts. It stopped just short enough to show an inch or so of flat stomach.

"Do you have a recent photograph of Hayley?" Winsome asked.

Donna McCarthy got up and rummaged through a drawer, coming back with a snapshot of a young girl standing by the market cross. "That was taken about a month ago," she said.

"Can I borrow it?"

"Yes. I'd like it back, though."

"Of course. When did you last see Hayley?" Winsome asked.

"Yesterday evening. It must have been about six o'clock. She was going to catch the bus to Eastvale to meet some friends."

"Was this something she did often?"

"Most Saturdays. As you probably noticed, there's not a lot to do around here."

Winsome remembered the village where she had grown up, high in Jamaica's Cockpit Mountains above Montego Bay. *Nothing to do* had been an understatement there. There was a one-room schoolhouse and a future in the banana-chip factory, like her mother and grandmother, unless you went down to the bay, like Winsome did at first, and worked at one of the tourist resorts. "Can you give me the names of her friends?" she asked.

"Maybe a couple of them. First names. But she didn't talk about them to me, and she didn't bring them back here to meet us."

"Were they friends from work? School? College? What did Hayley do?"

"She was a student at Eastvale College."

"She went by bus every day? It's a long way."

"No. She drove. She's got an old Fiat. Geoff got it for her second-hand. It's his business."

Winsome remembered the driver's licence Banks had found in the girl's handbag. "But she didn't drive last night?"

"Well, no, she wouldn't, would she? She was off drinking. She was always careful that way. Wouldn't drink and drive."

"How did she plan on getting home?"

"She didn't. That's why ... I mean, if I'd expected her home, I'd have reported her missing, wouldn't I? I might not be her birth mother, but I did my best to love her as if I was, to make her feel ..."

"Of course," said Winsome. "Any idea where she planned on staying?"

"With one of her college friends, as usual."

"What was she studying?"

"Travel and tourism. National diploma. It was all she wanted to do, travel the world." Donna McCarthy started crying again. "What happened to her? Was she ...?"

"We don't know," Winsome lied. "The doctor will be examining her soon."

"She was such a pretty girl."

"Did she have a boyfriend?"

The constable returned bearing a tray, which he plunked down on the table in front of the two women. Winsome thanked him.

"Anything else?" he asked, voice dripping with sarcasm.

"No," Winsome said. "You can go now, if you like. Thanks."

The constable grunted, ignored Winsome, made a bow towards Donna McCarthy, then left.

Donna waited a moment until she heard the front door shut, then said, "No one in particular. Not that I know of. A lot of kids today like to hang around with a group rather than hitch themselves up to just one lad, don't they? I can't say I blame them. Having too much fun to start going out with anyone seriously, aren't they?"

"I don't mean to pry," said Winsome, "but had there been anyone . . . ? I mean, was Hayley sexually active?"

Donna McCarthy thought for a moment, then said, "I'd be surprised if she wasn't, but I don't think she was promiscuous or anything. I'm sure she tried it. A woman can tell these things." The central heating was turned up, and it was too warm in the small room. A sheen of moisture glistened on Donna's brow.

"But you don't know the name of the boy?"

"No. I'm sorry."

"Never mind." Winsome thought she probably had enough to go on. She'd track Hayley's friends through the college's travel and tourism department and take it from there. "You said earlier," she went on, "that you kept your maiden name for professional reasons. Might I ask what they were?"

"What?" She wiped the back of her hand across her eyes, smearing some mascara. "Oh, I was a personal trainer. Fitness. Nothing special. But people knew me by that name, I had cards printed, the business logo, everything. It just seemed easier to keep it. And Geoff didn't mind. That's how I met Geoff in the first place, actually. He was a client."

"What happened to the business?"

"I packed it in six months ago. Geoff makes more than enough for us all to live on, and I've got plenty of other things to occupy my time. Besides, I'm getting a bit old for all those hard workouts."

Winsome doubted that. "What did you do last night, all on your own?" she asked casually.

Donna shrugged. If she felt that Winsome was prodding her for an alibi, she didn't show it. "Just stayed in. Caroline from across the road came over with a DVD. *Casino Royale*. The new one, you know, with that dishy Daniel Craig. We drank a few glasses of wine, ordered a pizza, got a bit giggly . . . you know."

"Girls' night in, then?"

"I suppose so."

"Look, do you know how to get in touch with your husband?" Winsome asked. "It's important."

"Yes. He's staying at the Faversham Hotel, just outside Skipton. A convention. He should be back home sometime tomorrow."

"Have you rung him?"

"Not yet. I . . . the policeman was here and . . . I just don't know what to say. Geoff dotes on Hayley. He'll be devastated."

"He has to be told," Winsome said gently. "He *is* her father. Would you like me to do it?"

"Would you?"

"Have you got the number?"

"I always just ring his mobile," Donna said and gave Winsome the number. "The phone's in the kitchen, on the wall."

Winsome walked through and Donna followed behind her. The kitchen looked out on the sloping hillside at the back of the house. There was a large garden with a small wooden tool shed leaning against the green fence. Hail pellets now pattered against the windowpanes behind the net curtains. Winsome picked up the handset and dialled the number Donna had given her. As she waited for an answer, she tried to work out what she was going to say. After a few rings, the call went through to Geoff's answering service.

"Have you got the hotel's number?" Winsome asked.

Donna shook her head.

"It's okay." Winsome rang directory inquiries and got connected to the Faversham. When someone from reception answered, she asked to be put through to Geoffrey Daniels. The receptionist asked her to please hold. There was a long silence at the other end, then the voice came back on. "I'm sorry," the woman said, "but Mr. Daniels isn't answering his telephone."

"Perhaps he's at a session?" Winsome said. "He's with the convention. The car salesmen. Can you check?"

"What convention?" the receptionist said. "There's no convention here. We're not a convention hotel."

"Thank you," said Winsome, hanging up. She looked at Donna McCarthy and the hopeful, expectant expression on her face. What the hell was she going to say now? Well, whatever it was, she would have a bit of time to think while she drove Donna to Eastvale General Infirmary to identify her stepdaughter's body.

2

It didn't take Annie long to drive to Larborough Head from Whitby, where she was temporarily on loan to Spring Hill police station, District of Scarborough, Eastern Area, their rank of detectives being decimated by illness and holidays. Usually she slept in Mrs. Barnaby's B & B on West Cliff, special rates for visiting police officers, a nice but small third-floor room whose luxuries consisted of an ensuite bathroom, sea view, telephone and tea-making facilities, but last night . . . well, last night had been different.

It was a Saturday, she'd been working late, and she hadn't had a good night out in ages. At least that was what she had told herself when the girls in the station invited her for a drink at the local watering hole and then on to a club or two. She'd lost contact with the rest of the girls sometime during the evening and only hoped they hadn't seen what had become of her. The guilt and shame bit away at her stomach almost as badly as the heartburn as she pulled up at the side of the unfenced road about a hundred yards from the edge of the cliff. Her heart sank when the first figure she saw was the bulky shape of Detective Superintendent Brough heading over to her.

"Good afternoon, DI Cabbot," he said, though it was still morning. "Glad you could join us."

Considering how quickly Annie had got there, she thought that was a stupid and insensitive remark, but she let it pass. She was used to those coming from Brough, well-known as a lazy, time-serving sod with both eyes fixed on retirement six months down the road, endless rounds of golf and long holidays in Torremolinos. Even as a working copper, he hadn't had the energy or gumption to line his pockets like some, so there was no villa, just a rented flat with Polyfilla walls and an aging Spanish floozy with a predilection for flashy jewellery, cheap perfume and even cheaper booze. Or so rumour had it.

"I'm surprised to find you up and about on a Sunday morning, sir," Annie said as brightly as she could manage. "Thought you'd be in church."

"Yes, well, needs must. Duty, Cabbot, duty," he said. "The magic word. And something we would all do well to embrace." He gestured over to the cliff edge, where Annie could see a seated figure ringed by police. "It's over there," he said as if washing his hands of the entire scene. "Detective Sergeant Naylor and Detective Constable Baker will fill you in. I'd better get back to the station and start coordinating. We've had to shoo off a couple of local reporters already and there's bound to be more media interest. You'll know what I mean when you've seen it. Bye for now, DI Cabbot. And I expect 120 per cent on this. 120 per cent. Remember."

"Yes, sir. Bye, sir," Annie said to his retreating back. She mumbled a few curses under her breath and started walking with difficulty against the wind over the slippery clumps of grass to the cliff. She could taste salt on her lips and feel its sting in her eyes. From what she could make out as she squinted, the figure was sitting in a wheelchair staring out to sea. When she got closer and saw it from the front, she noticed that it was a woman, her head supported by a halo brace. Below her chin, a broad, deep bib of dark blood had spread all the way down to her lap. Annie had to swallow an ounce or so of vomit that rose up into her mouth. Dead bodies didn't usually bother her, but a few pints of Sam Smith's the night before, followed by those fizzy blue drinks with the umbrellas, didn't help.

Naylor and Baker were standing beside the body while the police surgeon examined her and the photographer hovered and snapped. Annie greeted them. "What have we got here?" she asked Naylor.

"Suspicious death, ma'am," said Naylor in his usual laconic manner. DC Baker smiled.

"I can see that, Tommy," said Annie, taking in the ear-to-ear cut, exposed cartilage and spilled blood. "Any sign of a weapon?"

"No, ma'am."

Annie gestured to the cliff edge. "Anyone checked down there?"

"Got a couple of PCs doing a search right now," said Naylor. "They'll have to hurry up, though. The tide's coming in fast."

"Well, in the absence of a weapon, I think we can assume she didn't top herself," said Annie. "Think the seagulls did it?"

"Might have done, at that," said Naylor, glancing up at the noisy flock. "They're getting bolder, and they've definitely been at the body." He pointed. "See those marks in and around the ear? My guess is there's no blood because she'd already bled out by the time they started pecking at her. Dead bodies don't bleed."

The doctor glanced up. "We'll make an MD out of you yet, Tommy," he said.

Annie's stomach gave another unpleasant lurch and again she tasted sick in the back of her throat. No, she wasn't going to do it. She wasn't going to be sick in front of Tommy Naylor. But seagulls? She had always hated them, feared them even, ever since she was a kid in St. Ives. It didn't take *The Birds* to make Annie aware of the threat inherent in a flock of gulls. They had once swarmed her when she was in her pram and her father was off about twenty yards away sketching a particularly artistic group of old oaks. It was one of her earliest memories. She shivered and pulled herself together.

"Anything for us yet, doc?"

"Not much, I'm afraid. She's been dead for an hour or two, and the cause is most likely exsanguination, as you can see. Whoever did this is a very sick bastard. The woman was seriously disabled, by the looks of it. Probably couldn't even lift a bloody finger to defend herself."

"Weapon?"

"Some sort of very thin, very sharp blade, like a straight-blade razor or even a surgical instrument. The pathologist will no doubt be able to tell you more later. Anyway, it was a clean, smooth cut, no sawing or signs of serrations."

"Right- or left-handed?"

"It's often impossible to say with slash wounds, especially if there are no hesitation cuts, but I'd say perhaps left to right, from behind."

"Which makes the killer right-handed?"

"Unless he was faking it. Only *probably*, mind you. Don't quote me on it."

Annie smiled. "As if I would." She turned to Naylor. "Who found the body?"

Naylor pointed to a bench about two hundred yards away. "Bloke over there. Name's Gilbert Downie. Walking his dog."

"Poor sod," said Annie. "Probably put him right off his roast beef and Yorkshire pud. Anyone know who she is?"

"Not yet, ma'am," said DC Baker. "No handbag, purse or anything." Helen Baker was a broad, barrel-shaped woman, built like a brick shithouse, as the saying went, but she was remarkably nimble and spry for someone of her shape and build. And she had flaming-red spiky hair. Among her friends and colleagues she was known affectionately as "Ginger" Baker. She glanced around. "Not even a wristband, like they sometimes wear. This is a pretty isolated spot, mind you, especially at this time of year. The nearest village is four miles south and half a mile inland. About the only place in any way close is that residential care home about a mile to the south. Mapston Hall."

"Residential care home for what?"

"Don't know," Ginger glanced at the wheelchair. "For people with problems like hers, I'd hazard a guess."

"But there's no way she could have made it all the way here by herself, is there?"

"Doubt it," Naylor chipped in. "Unless she was doing an Andy."

Annie couldn't help but smile. She was a big fan of *Little Britain*. Banks, too. They had watched it together a couple of times after a long day at work over an Indian take-away and a bottle of red. But she didn't want to let herself think of Banks right now. From the corner of her eyes, she saw the SOCO van turn onto the grass verge. "Good work, Tommy and Ginger," she said. "We'd better get out of the way and let the SOCOs do their stuff. Let's sit in the car and get out of this bloody wind."

They walked over to Annie's Astra, stopping for a brief chat on the way with the crime scene coordinator, Detective Sergeant Liam McCullough, and sat in the car with the windows open an inch or two to let in some air, Ginger in the back. Annie's head throbbed and she had to force herself to pay attention to the matter at hand. "Who'd want to murder some defenceless old woman confined to a wheelchair?" she asked out loud.

"Not that old," said Naylor. "I reckon that sort of injury ages a person prematurely, but if you can see past the hair and the pasty complexion, you'll see she's probably not more than forty or so. Maybe late thirties. And she was probably quite a looker. Good cheekbones, a nice mouth."

Forty, Annie thought. My age. Dear God. Not old at all.

"Anyway," Naylor added, "it takes all sorts."

"Oh, Tommy, don't come the world-weary cynic with me. It might suit your rumpled appearance, but it doesn't get us anywhere. You saw her, the chair, halo brace and all, and you heard what the doc said. She probably couldn't move at all. Maybe even couldn't talk, either. What kind of a threat could she have posed to anyone?"

"I'll bet she wasn't always in a wheelchair," said Ginger from the back seat.

"Good point," said Annie, turning her head. "Very good point. And as soon as we find out who she was, we'll start digging into her past. What do you think of the bloke who found her, Tommy?"

"If he did it, he's a damn good actor. I think he's telling us the truth." Tommy Naylor was a solid veteran in his early fifties with no interest in the greasy poles of ambition and promotion. In the short while they had been working together, Annie had come to respect his opinions. She didn't know much about him, or about his private life, except rumour had it that his wife was dying of cancer. He was taciturn and undemonstrative, a man of few words, and she didn't know whether he approved of her or not, but he got the job done without question, and he showed initiative when it was called for. And she trusted his judgment. That was as much as she could ask.

"So someone took her walkies out there, cut her throat and just left her to bleed to death?" she said.

"Looks that way," said Naylor.

Annie mulled that over for a moment, then said, "Right. Ginger, you go see about setting up the murder room. We'll need a manned mobile unit out here, too. And, Tommy, let's you and me get down to Mapston

Hall and see if we can find out if that's where she came from. Maybe if we're lucky they'll even offer us a cup of tea."

While Superintendent Gervaise went to the station to set up the mechanics of the murder investigation and deal with the press, the various experts performed their specialist tasks, and DS Hatchley organized a canvassing of the town centre pubs, Banks decided to pay a visit to Joseph Randall, the leather-shop owner who had discovered Hayley Daniels's body.

Hyacinth Walk was an unremarkable street of rundown pre-war red-brick terraces just off King Street, about halfway down the hill between the market square and the more modern Leaview Estate, a good fifteen- or twenty-minute walk from the Maze. Inside, Joseph Randall's house was starkly furnished and neat, with plain coral wallpaper. A large TV set, turned off at the moment, held centre stage in the living room.

Randall seemed still dazed by his experience, as well he might be, Banks thought. It's not every day you stumble across the partially clad body of a young girl. While everyone else was no doubt eating their Sunday lunch, Randall didn't seem to have anything cooking. Radio 2 was playing in the background: Parkinson interviewing some empty-headed celebrity on his *Sunday Supplement* program. Banks couldn't make out who it was, or what was being said.

"Sit down, please," said Randall, pushing his thick-lensed glasses up on the bridge of his long, thin nose. Behind them, his grey eyes looked bloodshot. His wispy grey hair was uncombed, flattened to the skull in some places and sticking up in others. Along with the shabby beige cardigan he wore over his round shoulders, it made him appear older than his fifty-five years. And maybe this morning's trauma had something to do with that, too.

Banks sat on a brown leather armchair that proved to be more comfortable than it looked. A gilt-edged mirror hung at an angle over the fireplace, and he could see himself reflected in it. He found the image distracting. He tried to ignore it as best he could while he spoke to Randall.

"I'd just like to get a bit of clarification," he began. "You said you discovered the body when you went round to the storeroom to pick up some samples. Is that correct?"

"Yes."

"But it was Sunday morning. What on earth could you possibly want with a few swatches of leather on a Sunday?"

"When you run your own business, Mr. Banks, you find yourself working the oddest hours. I'm sure it must be the same for you."

"In a way," said Banks, thinking that he had little choice in the matter, especially when it came to murder. "Who were the samples for?"

"For me."

"Why?"

"Someone asked me to make a woman's handbag for his wife's birthday, wanted to know what the options were."

"You didn't have samples in the shop?"

"Some, but not the ones I wanted."

"Why were you in such a hurry?"

"The birthday is on Tuesday. It was a rush job. I thought if I got off to a quick start . . ." He paused and adjusted his glasses again. "Look, Mr. Banks, I can see why this might seem odd to you, but it isn't. I don't go to church. I'm not married. I have no hobbies. Outside of my work, I don't have a great deal to do with my time except watch television and read the papers. This project was on my mind, the shop isn't far away, so I thought I'd get started rather than idle around with the *News of the World*."

That wouldn't take long, Banks thought, but he could see Randall's point. "Very well," he said. "Can you give me the woman's name and address? The one whose birthday it is on Tuesday?"

Randall frowned but gave Banks the information.

"Is there a back or side entrance to your shop?"

"No, just the front."

"Is there a way from the shop to the storeroom from the inside?"

"No. You have to go down Taylor's Yard. I rent it very cheaply, and that's one of the minor inconveniences."

"Okay. Now tell me exactly how it happened," Banks went on. "How did you approach the building? What did you see?"

Randall paused and glanced at the rain-splattered window. "I approached the place as I usually would," he said. "I remember being annoyed about the weather. There was a sudden shower. My umbrella had broken near the top of King Street, blown inside out, and I was getting wet."

"Did you notice anything unusual in the market square, anyone behaving oddly?"

"No. Everything was normal. You surely don't think . . . ?"

Banks had a pretty good idea from Dr. Burns that Hayley Daniels had been killed late the previous night, but that didn't rule out the killer returning to the scene, or leaving it, having revisited. "Anyone heading out of the Maze?"

"No. Only people going to church, late for the service. And a small queue waiting for the Darlington bus."

"That's all?"

"Yes."

"All right. Go on."

"Well, as I said, I was put out by the weather, but there was nothing I could do about that. Anyway, the rain had stopped when I got to the storeroom –"

"What did you notice first?"

"Nothing."

"You weren't aware that it had been broken into?"

"No. The door looked closed as usual. It opens inwards. There's only a Yale lock and a handle to pull it shut."

"And it was shut?"

"As far as I could see, yes, but I wasn't really paying much attention. This was something I'd done hundreds of times before. I was just on automatic pilot, I suppose. There must have been a small gap, if the lock had been broken, but I didn't notice it."

"I understand," said Banks. "Carry on."

"When I went to unlock the door, it just started to swing open. Obviously it couldn't have been pulled all the way shut, because the lock was broken, as if someone had forced it from the outside."

"In your opinion, would that have taken much pressure?"

"No. The wood was old, the screws loose. I never really worried about it as I . . . well, all I kept there were scraps and remnants, really. They weren't valuable. Who'd want to steal them? As I think I've told you, they're usually the bits left over from various projects, but they're often useful for patchwork and as samples, so I just throw them in there whenever the basket gets full. I've got a workshop in the back of the shop where I do most of the cutting and sewing and repairs."

"Do you have any employees?"

Randall barked. "Ha! You must be joking. Most of the time I hardly have enough work to pay the rent, let alone hire an employee."

"Enough work to get you there very early on a Sunday morning, though."

"I told you. That was a special commission. A rush job. Look, I'm getting tired of this. I had a hell of a shock to my system a few hours ago, and now here you are practically accusing me of attacking and killing that poor girl. By all rights I should be under sedation. My nerves are bad."

"I'm sorry if I gave you the wrong impression," said Banks. "Calm down. Take it easy. I'm just trying to find out as much as I can about what happened this morning."

"Nothing happened this morning! I went to the storeroom and I saw . . . I saw . . ." He put his hands to his head and his chest started heaving, as if he were having difficulty breathing. "Oh God . . . I saw . . ."

"Can I get you anything?" Banks asked, afraid that Randall was having a heart attack.

"Pills," he gasped. "They're in my jacket pocket." He pointed, and Banks saw a navy sports jacket hanging on the back of the door. He took out a small bottle of pills, noting that it was labelled Ativan sublingual, prescribed by a Dr. Llewelyn, and passed it to Randall, who opened it with shaking hands and placed a tiny tablet under his tongue.

"Water?" Banks asked.

Randall shook his head. "See what I mean?" he said a few moments later. "It's my nerves. Shattered. Never been strong. I get anxiety attacks."

"I'm sorry, Mr. Randall," said Banks, feeling his patience running out. It wasn't that he didn't feel compassion for anyone who found a dead body, but Randall seemed to be pushing everything just a little over the top. "Perhaps we can get back to your account of what happened next, if it isn't too painful."

Randall gave him a glare to indicate that the sarcasm wasn't lost on him. "It *is* painful, Mr. Banks. That's what I've been trying to tell you. I can't get the image out of my mind, out of my memory. That poor girl. As if she were just . . . asleep."

"But you knew she was dead?"

"Yes. You can tell. I mean, there's something . . . something missing, isn't there? Nobody home. Just a shell."

Banks knew the feeling and had often put it that way himself. "The image will fade in time," he said, though he doubted that it would. None of his had. "Just tell me exactly what happened. Try to visualize it. Concentrate on the details. There might be something important you've overlooked."

Randall seemed to have calmed down. "All right," he said. "All right, I'll try."

"How dark was it in the room?"

"Quite dark. I mean, I couldn't really make anything out until I turned on the light. It's just a bare bulb, as you probably know, but it was enough."

"And you saw her straight away?"

"Yes. On the pile of remnants."

"Did you know her?"

"Of course not."

"Ever seen her before?"

"No."

"Did you touch her at all?"

"Why would I touch her?"

"To check if she was still alive, perhaps?"

"No, I didn't. It never really occurred to me."

"So what did you do next?"

Randall shifted in his chair and tugged at his collar. "I just . . . I suppose I just stood there a few moments, in shock, taking it all in. You have to understand that at first it seemed so unreal. I kept thinking she would get up and run out giggling, that it was some sort of practical joke."

"Have any of the local young people played practical jokes on you before?"

"No. Why?"

"Never mind. You said earlier that you knew she was dead."

"That was later. These things can run through your mind at the same time. It was the shock, I suppose."

"Did you touch anything in the room?"

"Only the door. And the light switch. I never got beyond the doorway. As soon as I saw her I stopped where I was."

"And when you'd got over the shock?"

"I thought I'd go into the shop and dial 999, then I realized the police station was just across the square, and it would probably make more sense to go over there. So I did."

"Can you give me any idea of how long it was, between your finding the body and getting to the station?"

"Not really. I had no concept of time. I mean, I just acted. I ran across the square."

"You said you found the body at quarter past eight."

"That's right. I checked my watch when I got there. Habit."

"And you reported it at eight twenty-one. Does that sound right?"

"If you say so."

"Six minutes, then. How accurate is your watch?"

"It's accurate as far as I know."

"You see," said Banks, shifting in his chair, "we have a witness who saw you enter the Maze at *ten past* eight by the church clock, and we know it's no more than thirty seconds or so from the entrance on Taylor's Yard to your storeroom. What do you make of that?"

"But that would mean . . . eleven minutes. I surely can't have been that long?"

"Could your watch have been fast?"

"I suppose so."

"Mind if I see it?"

"What?"

Banks gestured towards his wrist. "Your watch. Mind if I have a look?"

"Oh, not at all." He turned the face towards Banks. Twelve twenty-seven, the same as his own and, he knew, the same as the church clock.

"Seems to be accurate."

Randall shrugged. "Well . . ."

"Have you any explanation for those eleven minutes?"

"I didn't even know there *were* eleven minutes," said Randall. "As I told you, I have no conception of how long it all took."

"Right," said Banks, standing. "That's what you said. And it's only five minutes' difference from what you told us, after all, isn't it? I mean, what could possibly happen in five minutes?" Banks held Randall's eyes, and the latter broke away first. "Stick around, Mr. Randall," Banks said. "I'll be sending someone along to take your official statement later this afternoon."

Mapston Hall was an old pile of dark stone squatting on its promontory like a horned toad. Beyond the high gates in the surrounding wall, the gravel drive snaked through a wooded area to the front of the building, where there was parking for about ten cars. Most spots were already taken by staff or visitors, Annie guessed, but she found a place easily enough and approached the imposing heavy wooden doors, Tommy Naylor ambling beside her, nonchalant as ever, taking in the view. Despite the Aspirins, Annie's headache was still troubling her, and she felt in desperate need of a long, regenerative soak in the tub.

"Must cost a bob or two to run this place," Naylor speculated. "Wonder who pays the bills."

"Not the NHS, I'll bet," said Annie, though the sign outside had mentioned that the National Health Service had a part in running the place and that Mapston Hall specialized in care for people with spinal cord injuries.

"Rich people in wheelchairs," said Naylor. "Where there's a will . . . Just a thought. Some relative couldn't wait for the cash? Or a mercy killing?"

Annie glanced at him. "Funny way to go about it, slitting her throat," she said. "But we won't forget those angles." How aware would the victim have been of her life slipping away from her? Annie wondered. Perhaps her body had been incapable of sensation, but what emotions had she felt during those final moments? Relief? Horror? Fear?

Though the inside of the hall was as old and dark as the exterior, like a stately home, with its parquet floor, wainscoting, broad, winding staircase, high ceiling complete with crystal chandelier, and oil paintings of eighteenth-century dignitaries on the walls – the Mapston clan, no doubt – the computer set-up behind the reception desk was modern enough, as was the elaborate stairlift. The place was surprisingly busy, with people coming and going, nurses dashing around, orderlies pushing trolleys. Controlled chaos.

Annie and Naylor presented their warrant cards to the receptionist, who looked like a frazzled schoolgirl on her weekend job, and told her they were making inquiries about a patient. The girl probably wanted to work with handicapped people and was getting some work experience, Annie thought. She certainly seemed earnest enough and had that slightly bossy, busybodyish, passive-aggressive way about her that so often indicated a social worker. Her name badge read, Fiona.

"I can't tell you anything," she said. "I'm only part-time."

"Then who should we talk to?"

Fiona bit her lip. "We're short-staffed. And it's a Sunday. Mother's Day, in fact."

"Meaning?" Annie asked.

"Well, it's a very busy day for us. Visitors. Most of them come on the weekends, you see, and Sunday morning's the most popular time, especially as it's –"

"Mother's Day. Yes, I see," said Annie. "Is there *anyone* who can help us?"

"What is it exactly you want to know?"

"I told you. It's about a patient, a possible patient."

"Name?"

"That's one thing we're trying to find out."

"Well, I don't –"

"Fiona," Annie cut in. "This is really important. Will you please page someone who knows what they're doing?"

"You don't have to take –"

"Please!"

Fiona held Annie's gaze for just a moment. Annie felt her head throb. Fiona sniffed and picked up the phone. Annie heard her page someone called Grace Chaplin over the PA system. In a few moments, a woman of about the same age as Annie, looking elegant and handsome in a crisp white uniform, came striding in a no-nonsense way along a corridor, clipboard under her arm. She stepped over to Fiona and asked what the problem was. Fiona looked nervously towards Annie, who proffered her warrant card. "Is there somewhere we can talk, Ms. Chaplin?"

"Grace, please," the woman said. "By the way, I'm director of patient care services."

"Sort of like a matron?" Annie said.

Grace Chaplin gave her a tiny smile. "Sort of like that," she said. "And the conference room is over here, if you would just follow me. It should be free."

Annie looked at Tommy Naylor and raised her eyebrows as Grace Chaplin turned and led them towards a set of double doors. "Have a nose around, Tommy," she said softly. "I'll deal with this. Chat up some of the nurses. Patients, too, if you can. Use your charm. See if you can find anything out."

"Am I after anything in particular?"

"No. Just have a wander around and try to develop a feel for the place. See how people react to you. Make a note of anyone who strikes you as useful – or obstructive. You know the drill."

"Right, ma'am," said Naylor, heading off across the tiled hall.

The conference room had a large round table upon which sat a jug of water and a tray of glasses. Grace Chaplin didn't offer, but as soon as Annie sat down, she reached for a glass and filled it. The more water she could get into her system the better.

"You look a bit under the weather, Inspector," said Grace. "Is every- thing all right?"

"I'm fine," said Annie. "Touch of flu, maybe."

"Ah, I see. What is it I can help you with?"

Annie explained a little about the body in the wheelchair, and Grace's expression became more serious as she spoke. "In the end," Annie said, "this place seemed a natural one to start asking questions. Any idea who it might be?"

"I'm afraid I don't," said Grace. "But if you don't mind staying here a moment, I might be able to find out for you."

"Thank you."

Annie topped up her water. Through the large window, she could see Grace go back to the reception desk and talk to Fiona, who seemed flustered. Eventually, Fiona picked up a large ledger from her desk and handed it to Grace, who looked at the open page and returned to the conference room carrying the book.

"This should help," she said, placing it on the table. "It's a log of all patient comings and goings. Anyone who leaves the building with a friend or relative has to be signed out."

"And is anyone?" asked Annie.

"Only one. Usually we have far more out on a Sunday morning, but today the weather has been so unsettled, hail one minute, sleet and gale-force wind the next, that most visitors either didn't stay out long or decided simply to stop in with their loved ones. We've organized a special Mother's Day lunch, and most people will be staying indoors for that."

"And the one who's signed out?"

Grace slid the book around so Annie could read the single entry: KAREN DREW, taken out at 9:30 a.m. No return time filled in. And next to her name was an unintelligible signature, the first part of which might just, at a stretch of the imagination, have been Mary.

"Are you sure she's not back?" Annie asked.

"I don't know. Mistakes do happen. I'll have to have someone check her room to make certain."

"Would you do that, please?"

"Just a moment. I'll get Fiona to page Mel, her carer. You'll want to talk to her, anyway, I presume?"

"Yes, please," said Annie, reaching for the water jug again as Grace went back to see Fiona.

When Banks arrived at the Queen's Arms for a working lunch, Detective Sergeant Hatchley and the new probationary Detective Constable, Doug Wilson, were already there and had been lucky to snag a dimpled, copper-topped table by the window looking out on the church and market cross. The pub was crowded already, and people were crossing the market square carrying bouquets of flowers or potted plants. It reminded Banks that he had yet to phone his mother.

The detectives were still on duty, at the very beginning of a serious inquiry, so under Detective Superintendent Gervaise's new totalitarian regime, alcohol was strictly out of the question. Food, though, was another matter entirely. Even a working copper has to eat. Sipping a Diet Coke when Banks arrived, Hatchley ordered roast beef and Yorkshire pudding all round, and they settled down to business.

Hatchley was starting to appear old, Banks thought, though he was only in his forties. The cares of fatherhood had drawn lines around his eyes and bags under them. Lack of exercise had put on pounds that sagged around the waist of his suit trousers. Even his thatch of strawlike hair was getting thin on top, not helped at all by a very precarious combover. Still, Hatchley was never a man who had taken great pride in his appearance, though perhaps the saddest thing about him now was that he would hardly scare even the most mouselike of villains. But he remained a stubborn and dogged copper, albeit slow on the uptake, and Banks valued his presence on the team, when they could steal him away from his teetering piles of paperwork in CID. DC Wilson was fresh from detective training school and looked as if he'd be happier out playing football with his mates.

Hayley Daniels, it seemed, had been around. A number of landlords and bar staff recognized her from the picture Winsome had got from Donna McCarthy, though nobody admitted to actually knowing her. She had been part of a large mixed group of Saturday-night regulars, mostly students from the college. At some times there were eight or nine of them, at others five or six. Hayley had been drinking Bacardi Breezers, and towards the end of the evening at least one landlord had refused to serve her. Nobody remembered seeing her enter the Maze.

"The barmaid from the Duck and Drake recognized her," DC Wilson said. "In fact, she's a student at the college herself, working part-time, like a lot of them, and she said she's seen Hayley around on campus. Doesn't know her especially well, though."

"Anything else?" Banks asked.

"She was able to give me a couple of names of people who were with Hayley on Saturday night. She thought there were about eight, maybe nine of them in all, when she saw them. They met up at the Duck and Drake around seven o'clock, had a couple of drinks and moved on. They weren't particularly boisterous then, but it was early."

"Did you ask if she noticed anyone paying them much attention?"

"I did. She said it was pretty quiet around then, but there was one bloke by himself in a corner giving the girls the eye. In all fairness, the barmaid said she didn't blame him, given how little they were wearing."

"Name?"

"Didn't know," said DC Wilson. "Said he was vaguely familiar, thought she'd seen him before but couldn't think where. Thought he might be one of the local shopkeepers having a quiet drink after work. Anyway, I gave her my mobile number in case she remembered."

"That's good work, Doug," said Banks. The pub was filling up and getting noisy around them. It was hardly a day for tourists, but a coach had pulled up in the market square nevertheless, and they all came dashing towards the Queen's Arms, plastic macs over their heads, mostly aging mothers led by their sons and daughters.

"So DC Wilson found one place they had drinks at, and I found three," Hatchley said. "Did we miss anywhere, lad?" Hatchley glanced at Wilson, who didn't need telling twice. He shot up from his seat and hurried to the bar ahead of the tourists.

"He'll be all right," said Hatchley, winking at Banks.

"Find out anything else about Hayley?" Banks asked.

"Well," said Hatchley, "she had quite a mouth on her, according to Jack Bagley at the Trumpeter's, especially when he refused to serve her. Wouldn't believe the stream of foul language that came out of such a pretty young thing, Jack wouldn't, and there's not much he hasn't heard."

"It's the drink," said Banks. "Lord knows, I don't mind a drop or two myself, but some kids don't know when to stop these days."

"It's not just these days," said Hatchley, scratching the side of his nose. "I could tell you a rugby club tale or two that would curl your toes. And what's binge drinking, anyway, when you get right down to it? Five or more drinks in a row, three or more times a month. That's how the so-called experts define it. But you tell me which one of us has never done that. Still, you're right. Drinking's quite the social order problem these days, and Eastvale's up there with the worst, for a town its size. And it was St. Paddy's Day yesterday, too. You know the Irish. Couple of drinks, a punch-up, a few songs and another drink."

"Come on, Jim," said Banks. "I promised Superintendent Gervaise you weren't going to offend anyone."

Hatchley looked hurt. "Me? Offend?"

DC Wilson rejoined them, looking pleased with himself. "Seems they were here later on in the evening," he said.

"And Cyril served them?"

"Cyril wasn't here last night. The young lad at the far end was, though. He said they were quiet enough by then. Maybe a bit the worse for wear, but nobody was acting so drunk he thought he ought to refuse to serve them. They had a drink each, just the one, and left in an orderly fashion half an hour or so before closing time."

"That would be about half past eleven, then," said Banks.

"Did he see where they went?" Hatchley asked.

"Over to the Fountain."

The Fountain was the pub on the far side of the square, on the corner of Taylor's Yard, and it was known to stay open until about midnight, or not long after. "The others must have quietened Hayley down after that fracas in the Trumpeter's so they could get more drinks," Hatchley said. "I wonder if they went to the Bar None when the Fountain closed? They've been stricter about who they serve in there since the last time they were in trouble, but it's the only place in town you can get a drink after midnight, unless you fancy a curry and lager at the Taj."

DC Wilson's mobile buzzed and he put it to his ear. When he had asked a couple of questions and listened for a while, the frown deepened on his brow.

"What is it?" Banks asked when Wilson turned the phone off.

"It was that barmaid at the Duck and Drake," he said. "She remembered where she'd seen the bloke sitting by himself. Got a tear in her leather jacket a couple of months ago and someone recommended that shop on the corner of Taylor's Yard for invisible mending. Said she didn't know the bloke's name, but it was him, the bloke from the leather shop."

Mel Danvers, Karen Drew's assigned carer, was a slender young thing of twenty-something with doe eyes and a layered cap of chocolate brown hair. Grace Chaplin seemed in control, but Mel seemed nervous, fiddling with a ring on her finger, perhaps because she was in front of her supervisor. Annie didn't know if the nervousness meant anything, but she hoped she would soon find out. Someone had managed to get their hands on an assortment of sandwiches, she noticed, along with some digestive biscuits and a pot of tea. Things were looking up in the conference room.

Mel turned from Annie to Grace. "I can't believe it," she said. "Karen? Murdered?"

She had checked Karen's room, and her colleagues had searched the rest of Mapston Hall, just in case Karen had somehow returned without anyone knowing, but she was nowhere to be found. And Karen fit the description that Annie gave Grace and Mel. Tommy Naylor was busy searching her room.

"Tell me what happened." Annie said. "Were you there when she left?"

"Yes. I even advised her against it. The weather . . . but her friend was quite adamant. She said a bit of wind and rain never bothered her, and it would be a long time before she could come again. I couldn't stop her from going. I mean, she wasn't a prisoner or anything."

"It's all right," said Annie. "Nobody's blaming you. What was her friend's name?"

"Mary."

"No surname?"

"She didn't give me one. It should be in the log," Mel said with a glance at Grace. "They have to sign the log."

Annie showed her the signature. Mel narrowed her eyes and shook her head. "I can't read it," she said.

"Nobody can," said Annie. "I think that was the intention."

"But you can't mean . . . Oh, dear God!" She put her hand to her mouth.

Grace touched her shoulder gently. "There, there, Mel," she said. "Be strong. Answer the inspector's questions."

"Yes," said Mel, stiffening and straightening her uniform.

"Is the time right? Half past nine?" Annie asked.

"Yes," Mel answered.

Well, that was something, Annie thought. "Do you require any sort of identification from people signing patients out?" she asked.

"No," said Grace. "Why would we? Who would want to . . ." She let her words trail off when she realized where she was heading.

"I understand," said Annie. "So basically anyone can walk in and take any one of your patients out?"

"Well, yes," said Grace. "But usually they're friends or relatives, unless they're social workers or volunteers, of course, and then they take whoever requires them." She paused. "Not all our patients have relatives who recognize their existence."

"It must be difficult," Annie said, not entirely sure what she meant. She turned to Mel again. "Had you ever seen this Mary before?" she asked.

"No."

"Are you certain it was a woman?"

"I think so," Mel said. "It was mostly her voice, you know. I couldn't see much of her face because she was wearing a hat and glasses, and she had a long raincoat on with the collar turned up so, you know, it sort of hid her shape, her figure and her neck. I'm pretty sure, though."

"What was her voice like?"

"Just ordinary."

"Any particular accent?"

"No. But not Yorkshire, like, or Geordie. Just sort of neutral. She didn't say very much, just said she was a friend and had come to take Karen for a walk."

"What *did* you notice about her?"

"She was quite slight. You know, wiry. Not very tall."

"Did you catch a glimpse of her hair colour at all?"

"Not really. I think it must have been under the hat."

"What kind of hat?"

"I don't know. A hat. With a brim."

"What colour?"

"Black."

"Any idea what age she was?"

"Hard to say. I didn't get a real look at her face. Old, though. From the way she moved and her general appearance, I'd say maybe late thirties or forty."

Annie let that go by. "Anything distinguishing about her?"

"Just ordinary, really."

"Okay. Did you see her car? She couldn't have walked here."

"No," said Mel. "I mean, I was inside all the time. Someone might have seen it in one of the parking spots."

"Do you have CCTV in the car park?"

"No. We don't have it at all here. I mean, it's not as if the patients are under guard or they're going to do . . . you know, run away or anything."

"How did Karen react to the idea of a walk with Mary?"

Mel fiddled with her ring and reddened. "She didn't. I mean, sh-she couldn't, could she? Karen was a quadriplegic. Plus, she couldn't communicate."

"Did she have any particular friends here?" Annie asked. "Anyone she spent a lot of time with?"

"It's difficult when a person can't communicate," Mel said. "You tend to be confined to a pretty solitary existence. Of course, the staff here make sure she has all she needs. They talk to her, tell her what's going on. They're all truly wonderful people. And she has her television, of course. But . . . well, it all goes in, but nothing comes out." Mel shrugged.

"So you had no way of knowing whether she recognized Mary? Or, indeed, *wanted* to go with her?"

"No. But why would this Mary . . . I mean . . ." Mel started crying. Grace passed her a handkerchief from her pocket and touched her shoulder again. "Why would anybody want to take Karen out if they didn't know her?" Mel went on. "What would be the point?"

"Well, I think we know the answer to that," Annie said. "Someone wanted to get her alone in an isolated spot and kill her. The puzzle that remains is why. Was Karen wealthy?"

"I believe she had some money from the sale of her house," Grace said, "but that would all have been put towards her care. I wouldn't say she was wealthy, no."

"How did she end up here, by the way?" Annie asked.

"Drink driver," said Grace. "Broke her back. Awkward area. Spinal cord damage. It happens far more often than you would imagine. Tragic case."

"There'd be insurance, then?"

"Whatever there was, it would have also gone towards her care."

"How long had she been here?"

"About three months."

"Where did she come here from?"

"A hospital called Grey Oaks, just outside Nottingham. Specializes in spinal injuries."

"How did she end up here? What's the process?"

"It varies," said Grace. "Sometimes it's people's families who've heard of us. Sometimes it comes through social services. Karen's stay in the hospital was up – there was nothing more they could do for her there, and they need all the beds they can get – so social services helped and came up with us. We had a room available, and the details were worked out."

"Do you know the name of the social worker involved?"

"It should be in the file."

"Does Karen have any relatives?"

"None that I know of," said Grace. "I'd have to check the files for the information you want."

"I'd like to take those files."

Grace paused, then said, "Of course. Look, do you seriously think the motive was money?"

"I don't know what it was," said Annie. "I'm just covering all the possibilities. We need to know a lot more about Karen Drew and the life she lived before she ended up here if we hope to get any further. As nobody seems to be able to help us very much on that score, perhaps we'd better concentrate our efforts elsewhere."

"We've told you all we can," said Grace. "You should find more information in her files."

"Maybe." Annie looked at Mel, who seemed to have pulled herself together and was nibbling on a digestive biscuit. "We'll need a description of this Mary as soon as possible. Someone might have seen her locally. Mel, do you think you could work with a police artist on this? I don't know how quickly we can get someone here at such short notice, but we'll do our best."

"I think so," said Mel. "I mean, I've never done it before, but I'll have a try. But like I said, I never got a good look at her face."

Annie gave her a reassuring smile. "The artist's very good," she said. "Just do your best. He'll help steer you in the right direction." Annie stood up and said to Grace, "We'll be sending some officers over to take statements from as many staff members and patients as possible. DS Naylor will be picking up the files before we leave. I hope you'll be cooperative."

"Of course," said Grace.

Annie remained in the conference room and ate a potted-meat sandwich, washed down with a glass of water, until Tommy Naylor came in with the files, then they left together. "What do you think?" she asked Naylor when they got outside.

"I think we've got our work cut out," he said, waving a file folder about half an inch thick. "I've had a quick glance, and there's not a lot here except medical mumbo-jumbo, and we don't even have a next of kin to go on."

Annie sighed. "These things are sent to try us. See if you can get the artist organized, not that it'll do much good, by the sound of things, and I'll find out if DS McCullough and the SOCOs have anything for us."

3

Winsome wondered if she was doing the right thing as she parked outside the Faversham Hotel that afternoon. She had told Donna McCarthy that Geoff was at a meeting and unavailable over the telephone. Rather than try to reach him later, leave a message, or wait for him to come back to Swainshead, she said she would go to find him and break the news herself. Donna had been grateful and relieved that someone else was going to tell Geoff about his daughter. Winsome had tried his mobile and the hotel switchboard a couple more times on her way to Skipton, but with no luck.

The hotel lay just outside the town, not far from where the wild millstone grit of the Brontë moorland metamorphosed into the limestone hills and valleys of the Yorkshire Dales National Park. Winsome knew the area reasonably well, as she had been pot-holing with the club in the Malham area on several occasions, but she didn't know the Faversham. It resembled a big old manor house with a few additions tacked on. A stream ran by the back, and Winsome could hear it burbling over the rocks as she went in the front door. Very rustic and romantic, she thought.

She showed her warrant card at the front desk and explained that she needed to talk to Mr. Daniels. The receptionist rang the room but got no answer. "He must be out," she said.

"What's his room number?"

"I can't –"

"This is police business," Winsome said. "He forgot to bring his medicine, and without it he could die. Bad heart." It was a quick improvisation, but the word *die* did the trick. You didn't have to see *Fawlty Towers* to know what problems a dead body in a hotel room could cause.

"Oh, my God," said the receptionist. "He hasn't been answering his phone all morning." She called someone in from the back room to take over for her, then asked Winsome to follow her. They made their way in silence on the lift to the second floor and along the corridor where trays of empty plates and cups sat outside doors.

Outside number 212 was a tray with an empty bottle of champagne in a cooler – Veuve Clicquot, Winsome noticed, the ice long melted to water – and a couple of plates bearing the discarded translucent pink shells of several prawns. A DO NOT DISTURB sign hung on the door handle.

Winsome was immediately transported back to the time when she worked at the Holiday Inn outside Montego Bay, cleaning up after the American and European tourists. She had hardly been able to believe the state of some of the rooms, the things people left there, shamelessly, for a young impressionable girl, who went to church in her best frock and hat every Sunday, to clean up or throw away. Winsome remembered how Beryl had laughed the first time she held up a used condom and asked what it was. Winsome was only twelve. How could she be expected to know? And sometimes people had been in the rooms, doing things, though they hadn't posted a sign. Two men once, one black and one white. Winsome shuddered at the memory. She had nothing against gays, but back then she had been young and ignorant and hadn't even known that such things happened.

Winsome looked at the receptionist, who held the pass card, and nodded. Reluctantly, the receptionist stuck the card in the door, and when the light turned green, she pushed it open.

At first Winsome found it hard to make out what was what. The curtains were drawn, even though it was past midday; the air was stale and filled with the kind of smells only a long night's intimacy imparts to an enclosed space. The receptionist took a step back in the doorway and Winsome turned on the light.

A man lay spread-eagled on the bed, tied to the frame by his ankles and hands with black silk scarves, wearing a thick gold chain around his neck, and nothing else. A woman in the throes of ecstasy squatted on his mid parts, wearing a garter belt and black stockings. When the light came on, she screamed and wrapped a blanket around herself.

"What the fuck's going on?" the man yelled. "Who the fuck are you?"

The receptionist headed off down the corridor muttering, "I'll leave this to you then, shall I?"

"Police." Winsome showed her warrant card. She didn't think of herself as a prude, but the scene shocked her so much that she didn't even want to look at Daniels lying there with his drooping manhood exposed. It also made her angry. Maybe Geoff Daniels couldn't have known that his daughter was going to die a terrible death while he was playing sex games with his mistress, but she was damn well going to make him feel the guilt of it. She asked the woman her name.

"Martina," she said. "Martina Redfern." She was a thin, pouty redhead who looked about the same age as Hayley Daniels but was probably closer to Donna McCarthy's age.

"Okay, Martina," Winsome said. "Sit down. Let's have a little chat."

"What about me?" said Daniels from the bed. "Will someone fucking untie me and let me go?"

Martina looked towards him anxiously, but Winsome ignored him and took her aside. She knew she should break the bad news to Daniels, but how do you tell a naked man tied to a bed by his mistress that his daughter has been murdered? She needed time to take in the situation, and it wouldn't do any harm to put a few dents in his dignity along the way. "Care to tell me about your evening?" she said to Martina.

"Why?" Martina asked. "What is it?"

"Tell me about your evening first."

Martina sat in the armchair by the window. "We had dinner at the Swan, near Settle, then we went to a club in Keighley. After that we came back to the hotel, and we've been here ever since."

"What club?"

"The Governor's."

"Would they remember you? We can check, you know."

"Probably the barman would," she said. "Then there's the taxi driver who brought us back here. And they'd remember us at the Swan, too. They weren't very busy. But what are we supposed to have done?"

Winsome was more interested in the time after midnight, but any sort of an alibi for last night would be a help for Martina and Daniels. It would take at least an hour to drive from Skipton to Eastvale. "What time did you get back here?" she asked.

"About three o'clock."

"No wonder you needed a lie-in," said Winsome. "Long past bedtime. And you were together all that time?"

Daniels cursed and thrashed around on the bed. "That was the whole point of the exercise," he said. "And this is police brutality. Untie me right now, you fucking black bitch."

Winsome felt herself flush with anger and shame as she always did when someone insulted her that way. Then she calmed herself down, the way her mother had taught her.

"Can I get dressed now?" Martina asked, gesturing towards the bathroom.

Winsome nodded and looked at the naked man on the bed, the man who had just called her a black bitch. His daughter had been raped and murdered last night, and she had to tell him now. She couldn't just leave him there and keep putting it off, much as she would like to.

Courses taught you only so much about dealing with unusual situations, and simulations even less. When it came right down to it, Winsome thought, there was no book to go by, only instinct. She wanted to hurt him, but she didn't want to hurt him in the way she knew she was going to do. The image of Hayley Daniels lying there on the pile of leather like a fallen runner caused her breath to catch in her throat. Winsome took a deep breath. "I'm very sorry I have to tell you this, Mr. Daniels," she said, "but I'm afraid it's about your daughter."

Daniels stopped struggling. "Hayley? What about her? What's happened to her? Has there been an accident?"

"Sort of," said Winsome. "I'm afraid she's dead. It looks very much as if she was murdered." There, it was said, the dreaded word that would change everything, and its weight filled the room and seemed to suck out all the air.

"Murdered?" Daniels shook his head. "But . . . she can't be. It must be someone else."

"I'm sorry, sir. There's no mistake. She was carrying her driver's licence and an address book with her name in it."

"Was she . . . ? I mean, did he . . . ?"

"I'd rather not say anything else until we get back to Eastvale," Winsome said. "Your wife's waiting for you there."

Martina came out of the bathroom in time to hear this. She looked at Winsome. "Can I untie him now?" she asked.

Winsome nodded. Since she had told Daniels the news about Hayley, she had forgotten that he was still naked and tied to the bed. He seemed to have forgotten it, too. And humiliating Daniels didn't matter any more. She wasn't a cruel person; she had simply wanted to quash his arrogance and hear an alibi from Martina before the two of them had time or reason to make anything up. In both these matters, she thought she had succeeded, but now she felt a little ashamed of herself.

Martina got to work on the scarves as Daniels just lay there, staring at the ceiling. Finally freed, he sat up and wrapped the bedsheet around him and cried. Martina sat beside him, glum and flushed. She tried to touch him, but he flinched. He had curly dark hair, a Kirk Douglas cleft in his chin and sideburns reaching the line of his jaw. Perhaps he was the kind of man some white women liked to mother, Winsome thought, but he did less than nothing for her. He looked up at her through his tears. "I'm sorry," he said. "That remark I made earlier . . . it was uncalled for. I –"

"I'm sorry, too," said Winsome, "but untying you wasn't my first priority. I needed to know why you were lying to your wife and where you were last night." She pulled up a chair and sat down. "I've been trying to reach you all morning."

Daniels got to his feet and pulled on his underpants and trousers. Then he put on a shirt and started tossing socks and underwear from the drawers into an overnight bag. "I must go," he said. "I must get back to Donna."

"Donna?" said Martina. "What about me? You told me you were going to leave her and get a divorce. We were going to get married."

"Don't be stupid. Didn't you hear? I've got to get back to her."

"But, Geoff . . . What about us?"

"I'll ring you," Daniels said. "Go home. I'll ring you."

"When?"

"When? When I've buried my bloody daughter! Now bugger off, won't you, you stupid cow. I don't think I can stand the sight of you any more."

Sobbing, Martina picked up her bag, not bothering to get her toiletries from the bathroom, or anything she may have put in the wardrobe, and headed for the door. Winsome cut her off. "I need your name, address and phone number," she said.

Martina glared over at Daniels. "Ask *him*, why don't you?" She edged forward.

Winsome stood her ground. "I want you to tell me."

Martina paused, then gave Winsome the information. Next she opened the wardrobe and took out a three-quarter-length suede jacket. "Mustn't forget my birthday present," she said to Daniels, then she was out the door and down the corridor.

Daniels stood with his grip in his hand. "All right," he said. "What are we waiting for? Let's go."

Winsome looked at him, shook her head slowly and led the way out.

Karen Drew's body had been removed according to the coroner's instructions, but the SOCOs were still clustered around the wheelchair at the cliff edge when Annie and Tommy Naylor got back after their visit to Mapston Hall.

The wind had died down a little, leaving a light tepid drizzle. The SOCOs had tented the area to protect it from the elements while they worked, collecting samples and bagging them for evidence. The surrounding area had been thoroughly searched in a grid pattern, yielding nothing of immediate interest, and no weapon had been found at the bottom of the cliff or anywhere else. It could have drifted out to sea, or Mary, if she was the killer, could have taken it away with her.

Somehow or other, Annie thought, the mysterious Mary had slipped away into the morning and disappeared. She could be anywhere by now: anonymous in the London crowds, on a train to Edinburgh or Bristol. Had the murder been premeditated? If so, the odds were that she had worked out an escape route. If not, then she was working off her wits. But a stranger doesn't just walk into a care home, ask to take out a specific patient and then slit her throat. She had said she was a friend, and whether that was true, there had to be some connection between this Mary and Karen Drew. To have any hope of finding Mary, they first had to discover as much as they could about Karen and the people she had known before her accident. It was best not to assume too much yet. While there were no signs of a struggle, it was also possible that Mary wasn't the killer but had been another victim. What if Karen had been killed and Mary abducted, or killed and dumped in the sea, or somewhere else?

Annie cursed the lax security at the care home, but to be realistic about it, Grace Chaplin had been right. What, or whom, did their patients need protecting from? They were harmless, incapable of moving and, some of them, of even speaking. Why on earth would anyone want to kill one of them? That was what Annie and her team had to find out.

Annie noticed DS Liam McCullough, the crime scene coordinator, detach himself from the group of white-suited figures, and she called him over. They had met on several occasions before they started working together, as Liam was a close friend of the Western Area coordinator, Stefan Nowak, which made for a less strained relationship, Annie found. SOCOs could be annoyingly possessive of their crime scenes and tight-arsed about any information they gave out, but with Liam in charge, Annie's job was just that little bit easier.

"Nearly finished," McCullough said, walking over to her, that lopsided grin on his face showing a mouthful of ill-fitting teeth.

"Find anything useful?"

"We won't know what's useful until later," McCullough said.

"We think the killer might be a woman," Annie told him. "At least it was a woman who took the victim out of Mapston Hall, so that's the theory we're working on at the moment."

"Thanks for letting me know. It doesn't make much difference now, but it's good to bear in mind."

"I don't suppose you found any footprints?"

"In this grass?"

"Thought not. Fingerprints?"

"Plenty on the wheelchair. Don't worry, we'll be every bit as thorough as Western Area."

"I have no doubt," Annie said. "Any traces of a car parked in the vicinity?"

"None that we could find."

"Okay," said Annie. "I didn't expect anything. We'll have to send out a house-to-house team." She looked around the bleak, windswept stretch of coast. "Not that there's really anywhere for them to go."

"We did find several hairs on the victim's blanket," McCullough said. "No doubt some belong to the staff at the care home, and perhaps some to other patients, but you never know, the killer's might be among them."

"The person who dealt with our suspect at Mapston said her hair was hidden under a hat."

McCullough smiled. "Haven't you ever noticed how hair gets just everywhere?"

"I suppose you're right," said Annie, who had noticed a short black hair on her sleeve on her way there, as if she needed reminding about last night. "What about the marks on her ears and neck?"

"Seagulls," McCullough said. "Post-mortem, thank God. That's why there's no blood."

"I suppose that she was killed here, in the wheelchair?"

"Yes. I consulted with the doc on that. Lividity is as you'd expect if that were the case, and there's enough blood on the grass around the chair to bear it out. She was killed where she sat. We haven't finished blood spatter analysis yet – the grass makes it difficult – but we've photographed and videoed every square inch."

"Okay. Well, carry on, Liam. And thanks for the update."

McCullough doffed his imaginary cap. "No problem. I trust you're in charge of this inquiry?"

"Detective Superintendent Brough's the official SIO."

"So we send everything to you?" McCullough smiled.

Annie smiled back. "Might as well. But do it discreetly."

"My middle name, discretion. Bye, ma'am."

"See you," said Annie. She shivered as a gust of wind blew in from the sea and a seagull glided over her. She walked to the edge of the cliff and stood as close as she dared on the treacherous, slippery grass, looking down. The tide was well up now, the crashing waves dizzying and magnetic. She could understand how people had been drawn to jump into moving water, hypnotized and seduced by its sinuous, swirling motion. Feeling a twinge of vertigo, she glanced at the empty wheelchair. It would have been so easy just to push it that extra foot or so, onto the rocks. No fuss. No blood. Why go to the trouble and mess of slitting Karen Drew's throat?

Unless, Annie thought with a sinking feeling, it was done to make some kind of statement. In her experience, killers who wanted to make statements were like bores at a party: a bugger to shut up until they'd finished what they had to say.

While Joseph Randall waited in an interview room, Banks sat in his office enjoying his first few moments of peace and quiet since Templeton's phone call that morning. He had remembered to phone his mother, who thanked him for the card, and he was pleased to hear that all was well in the Banks household. His parents were going on a Mediterranean cruise in June, she had told him – their first time abroad, except for the time his father was in the army towards the end of the war. They were leaving from Southampton so they didn't have to fly.

Now Banks was sipping a cup of tea, eating a KitKat and listening to Anna Netrebko's *Russian Album* as he jotted down a list of actions and TIEs – Trace, Interview and Eliminate – he thought should be carried out as quickly as possible in the Hayley Daniels murder investigation.

Winsome had questioned the father, Geoff Daniels, and the hotel staff at the Faversham confirmed his alibi. No one had seen him leave his room since he arrived with his girlfriend, Martina, rather the worse for wear around three o'clock in the morning. The barman and doorman at the club in Keighley also remembered the couple, who had been there the whole time between about midnight and half past two. They had had more than enough to drink, he said, and at one point they were practically doing it right there on the dance floor. The bouncer even had to step in and ask them to cool it. There was no way either, or both, of them could have driven to Eastvale and killed Hayley. Winsome hadn't tracked down the taxi driver yet, but it was just a matter of time.

Also, mostly for form's sake, Winsome had checked Donna McCarthy's alibi with her friend and neighbour, Caroline Dexter. They had indeed spent the evening together eating pizza and watching *Casino Royale*, until well after midnight.

Officers were already reviewing as much CCTV footage as they had been able to gather, and forensics experts were still busy in Taylor's Yard, while most of the samples the SOCOs had collected were being prepared for analysis. Nothing would happen until Monday, of course, and results wouldn't start coming until Tuesday, or even later in the week, depending on the tests and workloads of the labs involved. If only DNA results came as quickly as they seemed to do on television, Banks thought, his job would be a lot easier. Sometimes waiting was the worst part.

Banks put the writing pad aside. He'd enter it all into the computer later. He glanced out the window and was surprised to see snowflakes blowing horizontally in the wind, obscuring the market square. He watched for a few moments, hardly believing what he saw, then it stopped and the sun came out. Strange weather, indeed.

He glanced at the map of the Maze he had had enlarged and pinned to his cork board. There were far more ways in and out than he had realized, and it covered a greater area. Next to the map hung his Dalesman calendar. The month of March lay in neat columns below a photograph of Settle marketplace on a busy day. He had check-up appointments with both his dentist and his GP, having thought at the time it was best to get both unpleasant duties out of the way simultaneously. Now, he was beginning to wonder. Perhaps he should postpone the dentist until next month. Or the doctor.

His only upcoming social engagement was a dinner party at Harriet Weaver's, his old next-door neighbour in Eastvale, the following Saturday. Informal, Harriet had said, about ten or twelve people, bring a bottle, he would enjoy himself. Her niece Sophia was up from London and might drop by. Every man fell in love with Sophia, Harriet said. Banks thought it would be a very foolish thing to do, in that case, and determined not to. It was all very well for middle-aged writers, artists or rock stars to go around falling in love with younger women, but most irresponsible for a police detective with as much baggage as he was carrying.

Banks hated dinner parties anyway, and he was only going because he felt guilty about not having kept in touch with Harriet and her husband since he had split up with Sandra. And she had had the good grace to invite him. Well, he'd go, then he'd leave as quickly as he decently could. It shouldn't be too hard to get Winsome or someone to call his mobile on some pretext or other. It would save him from having to explain the latest crime statistics, or why so many obvious rapists and murderers got off, the usual sort of stuff you get at parties when people know you're a policeman. One woman had even had the nerve to ask Banks to put a tail on her husband, whom she suspected of having an affair with a local estate agent. After Banks explained that he wasn't Sam Spade or Philip Marlowe, the woman lost all interest in him and started making eyes at the host.

Banks got up. It was time to have a chat with Joseph Randall, who didn't seem too happy at being dragged down to Western Area Headquarters that afternoon and left to stew in an interview room accompanied only by a taciturn constable who wouldn't tell him why he was there. There was no reason for the delay other than to make Randall nervous and angry. In that state, he might make a slip. He had his Ativan with him if he needed it, and the constable had been warned to watch out for any signs of a panic attack, so Banks hadn't been worried on that score.

The interview room was cramped, with one high, barred window, a bare bulb covered by a rusty grille, metal table bolted to the floor, three foldup chairs and the recording equipment. The interview would be videotaped, and as Banks set it up, DC Doug Wilson sat facing a disgruntled Randall, who began by asking for his solicitor.

"You're not under arrest, Mr. Randall, and you haven't been charged with anything," Banks explained, sitting down. "You're simply here to help us with our inquiries."

"Then I don't *have* to talk to you?"

Banks leaned forward and rested his forearms on the table. "Mr. Randall," he said. "We're both reasonable men, I hope. Now this is a serious case. A young girl has been raped and murdered. On your property. I'd think you'd be as interested as I am in getting to the bottom of it, wouldn't you?"

"Of course I am," said Randall. "I just don't understand why you're picking on me."

"We're not picking on you." Banks turned to DC Wilson. Might as well give the new kid a chance. "Detective Constable Wilson, why don't you tell Mr. Randall here what you found out from the barmaid at the Duck and Drake?"

Wilson shuffled his papers nervously, played with his glasses and licked his lips. Banks thought he looked rather like a frightened schoolboy about to translate a Latin unseen for the class. The blazer he wore only enhanced the image. "Were you in the Duck and Drake around seven o'clock yesterday evening?" Wilson asked.

"I had a couple of drinks there after I closed the shop, yes," said Randall. "As far I was aware that's not against the law."

"Not at all, sir," said Wilson. "It's just that the victim, Hayley Daniels, was also seen in the pub around the same time."

"I wouldn't have recognized her. How could I? I didn't know her."

"But you'd remember her now, sir, wouldn't you?" Wilson went on. "Since you saw her in the storeroom. You'd remember how she looked, what she was wearing, wouldn't you?"

Randall scratched his forehead. "I can't say I do, as a matter of fact. There are always a lot of young people in the Duck and Drake at that time on a Saturday. I was reading the paper. And in the room it was all such a blur."

"Is it your local, then, the Duck and Drake?"

"No. I don't have a local, really. I just go where it strikes my fancy if I want a drink after shutting up. It's not very often I do. Usually I just go home. The drinks are cheaper."

"Where were you between the hours of midnight and two this morning?" Wilson asked.

"At home."

"Can anybody corroborate that?"

"I live alone."

"What time did you go to bed?"

"About a quarter to one, shortly after I'd put the cat out."

"Anybody see you?"

"I don't know. The street was quiet. I didn't see anybody."

"What were you doing before that?"

"After I left the pub, about eight, I picked up some fish and chips on my way home and watched television."

"Where did you get the fish and chips?"

"Chippy on the corner. Now, look, this is –"

"Let's go back to the Duck and Drake, shall we?" Wilson persisted.

Randall crossed his arms and sat in a rigid position, lips set in a hard line.

"Now you've had a chance to think back, sir," Wilson went on, "do you remember seeing Hayley Daniels in the pub?"

"I suppose I might have."

"Did you or didn't you?"

"If she was there, I suppose I must have seen her. I just don't remember her in particular. I wasn't really interested."

"Oh, come off it," said Banks. "A beautiful girl like her. A lonely old pervert like you. You were giving her the eye. Why don't you admit it? You want us to think you'd never seen her before because you set your sights on her right from the start. I'm right, aren't I?"

Randall glared at him and turned back to DC Wilson, his ally. Sometimes, Banks thought, good cop, bad cop was that easy. They hadn't even decided to play it this way; it just worked out as the interview went on. For all the courses he'd done and all the books he'd read on interview techniques over the years, Banks found that a spontaneous approach often worked best. Go in with a general, vague outline and play it by ear. The most revealing questions were often the ones that just came to you as you sat there, not the ones you had worked out in advance. And when there were two of you doing the interviewing, a whole new dynamic sprung up. Sometimes it worked; sometimes it didn't. Then you ended up with egg on your face. But young Wilson didn't seem to need telling what his role was, and that was good.

"She was with a group of people about her own age, and they were laughing and talking and drinking at the bar. Is that right?" Wilson went on.

"Yes."

"Did you see anybody touch her? If she had a special boyfriend, he might touch her on the shoulder, let his hand linger, hold hands, sneak a quick kiss, that sort of thing."

"I didn't see anything like that." Randall glared over at Banks. "But as I've been trying to explain, I wasn't paying much attention."

"Who left first?"

"They did. One minute they were there, noisy and full of themselves, the next minute they were gone and it was nice and quiet."

"Full of themselves? What do you mean by that?"

Randall shifted in his chair. "You know what I mean. Preening, showing off for one another, laughing at their own jokes, that sort of thing."

"Don't you like young people?"

"I don't like ruffians."

"And you think they were ruffians?"

"Well, I wouldn't have wanted to get on the wrong side of them. I know how things get around here on a weekend when they all go binge drinking. It's got so a decent person can't go out for a drink in town on a Saturday night. Sometimes I wonder what you police are here for. I've seen the vomit and the rubbish outside my shop the morning after."

"But this morning it was something different, wasn't it?" Banks said.

"The thing is, sir," Wilson cut in, so gently Banks admired him for it, "that the barmaid in the Duck and Drake distinctly remembers you ogling Hayley Daniels."

She hadn't actually used the word *ogling*, Banks knew, but it showed inventiveness on the new kid's part. It had so much more impact than "looking at" or even "eyeing up."

"I was doing no such thing," Randall replied. "As I told you, I was sitting there quietly with my drink, reading the paper."

"And you didn't even notice Hayley Daniels?"

Randall paused. "I didn't know who she was," he said, "but I suppose one couldn't help but notice her."

"Oh?" said Wilson. "In what way, sir?"

"Well, the way she was dressed, for a start. Like a common trollop. All that bare leg and tummy. If you ask me, girls who dress like that are asking for trouble. You might even say they deserve what they get."

"Is that why you lied about ogling her in the first place?" Banks said. "Because you thought if you admitted it, it would seem suspicious that you also found her body? Was it you who gave her what she deserved?"

"That's an impertinent question, and I won't dignify it with an answer," said Randall, red-faced. "I've had enough of this. I'm leaving."

"Are you sure you didn't follow Hayley Daniels around for the rest of the evening and somehow lure her into your storeroom, where you knew you'd be able to have your way with her?" said Wilson, an innocent and concerned expression on his young face. "Maybe you didn't mean to kill her, but things just went too far? It could go in your favour if you told us now."

Randall, half standing, gave him an *et tu, Brute* look and collapsed back into the chair. "What I've told you is the truth," he said. "She was in the pub with a group of friends. That was the first and last time I saw her. I didn't pay her any special attention, but now you mention it, I'll admit she stood out from the crowd, though not in a way I approve of. I didn't mention it at first because I know the way your minds work. That's all I have to say on the matter." He glared at Banks. "And I *am* leaving now."

"As you wish," said Banks. He let Randall get to the door, then said, "I'd appreciate it if we could get a set of your fingerprints and a DNA sample. Just for the purposes of elimination, you understand. At your own convenience. DC Wilson will sort out the consent forms."

Randall slammed the door behind him.

4

Annie was in her office at the squat brick-and-glass building on Spring Hill early on Monday morning feeling a lot better than she had on Sunday. Even the weather seemed to echo her lift in spirits. The rain had passed and the sky was bright blue dotted with fluffy white clouds. The usually grey North Sea had a bluish cast. There was a chill in the wind, but by mid-afternoon people would be taking their jackets off on the quays and piers and sitting outside at the pubs. It was almost spring, after all.

The "Wheelchair Murder" had hit the local papers and TV breakfast news, and Superintendent Brough had scheduled a press conference for later that morning. Luckily, Annie wouldn't have to attend, but he would expect her to give him something to feed the hungry mob with.

Annie felt another quiver of guilt and self-loathing when she thought about Saturday night. Behaving like a randy teenager at her age was hardly becoming, she felt. But it had happened; now it was time to follow the old Zen lesson and let go with both hands. Life is suffering, and the cause of suffering is desire, so the Buddhists say. You can't stop the desires, memories, the thoughts and the feelings, the teaching went, but you didn't have to grasp them and hang on to them to torture yourself; you could simply let them go, let them float away like balloons or bubbles. That was what she did when she meditated, concentrated on one fixed thing, her breathing or a repeated sound, and watched the balloons with her thoughts and dreams inside them drift away into the void. She needed to get back to it regularly again. Anyway, it wasn't as if she didn't have plenty of other things to think about this morning.

Like Karen Drew, for a start.

The first detail Annie read from the files Tommy Naylor had brought from Mapston Hall shocked her: Karen Drew had been only twenty-eight years old when she died. Annie had thought her an old woman, and even Naylor had pegged her age at around forty. Of course, they only had the bloodless, shapeless lump under the blanket in the wheelchair with dry, greying hair to go by. Even so, Annie thought, twenty-eight seemed terribly young. How could the body betray one so cruelly?

According to the records, Karen's car had been hit by a driver losing control and crossing the centre of the road six years ago. She had been in a coma for some time and had had a series of operations and lengthy spells of hospitalization, until it became apparent to every medical expert involved that she wasn't going to recover, and that the only real option was full-time care. She had been at Mapston Hall for three months, as Grace Chaplin had said. That wasn't very long, Annie thought. And if Karen couldn't communicate, she could hardly have made any enemies so quickly. Passing psychopaths aside, it seemed all the more likely that the reason for her murder lay in her past.

Medically, the report suggested, there had been no change in her physical condition, and there never would be. When someone is as limited in self-expression as Karen Drew was, the slightest hint of progress tends to be hailed as a miracle. But nobody had really known what Karen was thinking or feeling. Nobody even knew whether she wanted to live or die. That choice had been taken out her hands, and it was up to Annie to find out why. Was it a mercy killing, as Naylor had hinted at, or did someone benefit in some way from Karen's death? And if mercy was the motive, who had shown it to her? These were the questions she would like answered first.

One thing Annie noticed about the files was that they told her very little of Karen's life before the accident. She had lived in Mansfield, Nottinghamshire, but there was no specific address listed, nor any indication as to whether she had grown up there or moved from somewhere else. Her parents were marked as deceased, again without details, and she apparently had neither siblings nor anyone especially close, like a husband, live-in partner or fiancé. All in all, Karen Drew hardly appeared to have existed before that fateful day in November 2001.

Annie was chewing on the end of her yellow pencil stub and frowning at this lack of information when her mobile rang shortly after nine o'clock. She didn't recognize the number but answered anyway. In the course of an investigation, she gave her card out to many people.

"Annie?"

"Yes."

"It's me. Eric."

"Eric?"

"Don't tell me you've forgotten so quickly. That hurts."

Annie's mind whizzed through the possibilities, and there was only one glaringly obvious answer. "I don't remember giving you my mobile number," she said.

"Well, that's a fine thing to say. Something else you don't remember, I suppose, like my name?"

Shit. Had she been that drunk? "Anyway," she went on, "it's my work number. Please don't call me on it."

"Give me your home number then."

"I don't think so."

"Then how am I supposed to get in touch with you? I don't even know your last name."

"You're not. That's the point." Annie ended the call. She felt a tightness in her chest. Her phone rang again. Automatically, she answered.

"Look," Eric said, "I'm sorry. We've got off to a bad start here."

"Nothing's started. And nothing's going to start," Annie said.

"I'm not proposing marriage, you know. But won't you at least allow me to take you out to dinner?"

"I'm busy."

"All the time?"

"Pretty much."

"Tomorrow?"

"Washing my hair."

"Wednesday?"

"Tenants' association meeting."

"Thursday?"

"School reunion."

"Friday?"

Annie paused. "Visiting my aging parents."

"Aha! But you hesitated there," he said. "I distinctly heard it."

"Look, Eric," Annie said, adopting what she thought was a reasonable but firm tone. "I'm sorry, but I don't want to play this game any more. It's not going to happen. I don't want to be rude or nasty or anything, but I'm just not interested in a relationship right now. End of story."

"I only asked you to dinner. No strings."

In Annie's experience, there were always strings. "Sorry. Not interested."

"What's wrong? What did I do? When I woke up, you were gone."

"You didn't do anything. It's me. I'm sorry. Please don't call again."

"Don't ring off!"

Against her better judgment, Annie held on.

"Are you still there?" he asked after a moment's silence.

"I'm here."

"Good. Have lunch with me. Surely you can manage lunch one day this week? How about the Black Horse on Thursday?"

The Black Horse was in Whitby's old town, on a narrow, cobbled street below the ruined abbey. It was a decent enough place, Annie knew, and not one that was frequented by her colleagues. But why was she even thinking about it? Let go with both hands.

"I'm sorry," she said.

"I'll be there at noon," Eric said. "You do remember what I look like?"

Annie remembered the young face with the slept-on hair, the stray lock, the night's growth of dark beard, the strong shoulders, the surprisingly gentle hands. "I remember," she said. "But I won't be there." Then she pressed the end call button.

She held the phone in her shaking hand for a few moments, heart palpitating, as if it were some sort of mysterious weapon, but it didn't ring again. Then a very unpleasant memory started surfacing into the light of consciousness.

She had only had her new mobile for a week. It was a BlackBerry Pearl, which combined phone, text and e-mail, and she was still learning all its bells and whistles, like the built-in camera. She remembered that Eric had the same model, and he had shown her how to work one or two of its more advanced features.

Hand trembling, she clicked on her recent saved photographs. There they were: her head and Eric's leaning towards one another, touching, almost filling the screen as they made faces at the camera with the club lights in the background. She remembered she had sent the photo to his mobile. That would be how he had got hold of her number. How could she be so stupid?

She put the phone in her handbag. What was she playing at? She ought to know she couldn't trust her judgment in these matters. Besides, Eric was just a kid. Be flattered and let go. Enough of this crap. Why did she even let her behaviour haunt her so? She picked up a slip of paper up from her desk. Time to talk to the social worker who had got Karen Drew placed in Mapston Hall. The poor woman had to have had some kind of life before her accident.

Dr. Elizabeth Wallace's post-mortem approach was far less flamboyant and flippant than Glendenning's, Banks discovered in the basement of Eastvale General Infirmary late that Monday morning. She seemed shy and deferential as she nodded to acknowledge Banks's presence and made her initial preparations with her assistant, Wendy Gauge. They made sure that the equipment she would need was all at hand and the hanging microphone on which she recorded her spoken comments was functioning properly. She seemed to be holding her feelings in check, Banks noticed, and it showed in the tight set of her lips and the twitching muscle beside her jaw. Banks couldn't imagine her smoking the way he and Glendenning had, or making bad jokes over the corpse.

Dr. Wallace first performed her external examination in a studied, methodical way, taking her time. The body had already been examined for traces and intimate samples, and everything the doctor and the SOCOs had collected from Hayley Daniels and her clothes had been sent to the lab for analysis, including the leather remnants that had been stuffed in her mouth, presumably to keep her quiet. Banks glanced at Hayley, lying on her back on the table, pale and naked. He couldn't help but stare at the shaved pubes. He had already been told about it at the scene, but seeing it for himself was something else entirely. Just above the mound was a tattoo of two small blue fishes swimming in opposite directions. *Pisces.* Her birth sign.

Dr. Wallace caught him staring. "It's not unusual," she said. "It doesn't mean she was a tart or anything. It's also not recent, not within the past few months, anyway, so the killer can't have done it. Tattoos like that are common enough, and a lot of young girls shave or get a wax these days. They call it a Brazilian."

"Why?" said Banks. "It must be painful."

"Fashion. Style. They also say it increases pleasure during inter-course."

"Does it?"

She didn't crack a smile. "How would I know?" she said, then went back to her examination, pausing every now and then to study an area of skin or an unusual mark closely under the magnifying lens and speaking her observations into the microphone.

"What's that brown discolouration below the left breast?" Banks asked.

"Birthmark."

"The arms, and between the breasts?"

"Bruising. Pre-mortem. He knelt on her." She called to her assistant. "Let's get her opened up."

"Anything you can tell me so far?" Banks asked.

Dr. Wallace paused and leaned forward, her hands on the metal rim of the table. A couple of strands of light brown hair had worked their way out of her protective head-cover. "It certainly appears as if she was strangled manually. No ligature. From the front, like this." She held her hands out and mimicked the motion of squeezing them around someone's neck.

"Any chance of fingerprints from the skin, or DNA?"

"There's always a chance that some of the killer's skin, or even a drop of blood, rubbed off on her. It looks as if he cleaned her up afterwards, but he might not have caught everything."

"There was something that might have been semen on her thigh," Banks said.

Dr. Wallace nodded. "I saw it. Don't worry, the lab has samples of everything, but it'll take time. You ought to know that. Fingerprints? I don't think so. I know it's been done, but there was so much slippage in this case. Like when you open a doorknob, your fingers slip on its surface and everything gets smeared and blurred."

"Did she struggle?"

Dr. Wallace glanced away. "Of course she bloody did."

"I was thinking of scratches."

Dr. Wallace took a deep breath. "Yes. There might be DNA in the samples the SOCOs took from under her fingernails. Your killer might have scratches on his forearms or face." She paused. "Frankly, though, I wouldn't hold out a lot of hope. As you can see, her fingernails were bitten to the quick."

"Yes, I'd noticed," said Banks. "And the bruising?"

"As I said, he knelt on her arms, and at one point on the centre of her chest, probably to hold her down while he used his hands to strangle her. She didn't have a chance."

"You're sure it's a man?"

Dr. Wallace gave him a scornful glance. "Take it from me, this is a man's work. Unless someone's girlfriend did the strangling after the boyfriend raped and sodomized her."

It had been done, Banks knew. Couples had acted in tandem as sexual predators or killers. Fred and Rosemary West. Myra Hindley and Ian Brady. Terry and Lucy Payne. But he thought Dr. Wallace was probably right to dismiss it in this case. "Were all the injuries inflicted while she was alive?"

"There's no evidence of post-mortem maltreatment, if that's what you mean. The bruising and tearing in the vagina and anus both indicate she was alive while he raped her. You can see the marks on her wrists where he held her. And you can see her upper arms, neck and chest for yourself, as well as the bruising on her thighs. This was a rough and violent rape followed by strangulation."

"How did he restrain her while he was raping her?" Banks mused out loud. "He couldn't have done it with his knees on her arms."

"He could have had a weapon. A knife, say."

"So why not stab her? Why strangle her?"

"I couldn't tell you. He may simply have used threats to control her. Isn't it often the case that rapists will threaten to kill their victims if they don't cooperate, or even to hunt them down later, harm their families?"

"Yes," said Banks. He knew his questions might sound crude and insensitive, but these were things he had to know. That was why it had always been so easy with Dr. Glendenning. Working with a woman pathologist was different. "Why kill her at all?" he asked.

Dr. Wallace looked at Banks as she might a specimen on her table. "I don't know," she said. "To shut her up, perhaps. Maybe she recognized him or could identify him. That's your job, isn't it, to figure out things like that?"

"I'm sorry. I was just thinking out loud. Bad habit of mine. I was also just wondering if there was any evidence that the strangulation was part of the thrill, rough sex gone wrong?"

Dr. Wallace shook her head. "I don't think so. Though he was certainly rough with her. As I said, it very much looks as if he had one knee pushing against her chest as he strangled her, and it would be difficult, if not impossible, in that position, to perform a sexual assault on her. I'd say in this case that he strangled her when he'd done with her."

"Dr. Burns estimated time of death at between midnight and two on Sunday morning. Do you agree?"

"I can't find anything that would argue against that estimate," Dr. Wallace said. "But it *is* just an estimate. Time of death is –"

"I know, I know," said Banks. "Notoriously difficult to establish. The one thing that can sometimes help us most. Just one more of life's little ironies."

Dr. Wallace didn't respond.

"Anything odd or unusual?"

"All perfectly normal so far, for this sort of thing." Dr. Wallace sounded weary and too old for her years, as if she'd seen it all too many times before. Banks stood back and kept quiet to let her get on with her work. She gripped the scalpel and started to make the Y incision quickly and precisely and Banks felt a shiver run up his spine.

Annie took Ginger with her to Nottingham to talk to Gail Torrance, Karen Drew's social worker, while Tommy Naylor held the fort back in Whitby. Annie liked Ginger's company, felt at ease with her. She was irreverent and funny, chewing gum constantly, talking a mile a minute, complaining about the other drivers, and she always seemed cheerful. Perhaps because of her rather butch appearance, many of the blokes at the station had first thought she was a lesbian, but it turned out that she had a stay-at-home husband and two young kids. For a moment, as Annie drove and listened to the hilarious tirade about the kids' weekend with a bouncy castle, she thought that Ginger might be someone she could talk to about Eric – there, he had a name now – but she realized it wouldn't be appropriate, that she didn't really know her well enough, and that she didn't want anyone to know, at least not right now. What did she expect? Advice? She didn't need any. She knew what to do. And if she talked to anyone about it, it would be Winsome, though they hardly saw one another these days.

Annie was driving because she didn't feel safe with Ginger behind the wheel. And Ginger knew that. Though she had somehow got her licence, driving was simply one of the skills she hadn't truly mastered yet, she apologized, and she was due for yet another training course in a month's time. But by the time they got lost in an area of desolate industrial estates, Annie was wishing she had handed the wheel over to Ginger, who was proving to be an even worse navigator than she was a driver.

They finally found the offices in West Bridgford. It was almost lunchtime when they arrived, and Gail Torrance was more than happy to join them in the nearest pub. The place was already busy with office workers, but they found a table cluttered with the previous occupants' leftover chips, salad and remains of scotch eggs, along with empty, lipstick-stained half-pint glasses with pools of pale warm lager in the bottom. The ashtray, too, was overflowing with crushed pink-ringed cigarette ends, one of them still smouldering slightly.

Ginger took the orders and went up to the bar. By the time she got back with the drinks, a sullen teenaged waitress had cleared away the debris, then brought knives and forks folded in paper serviettes. Annie and Ginger drank Slimline bitter lemon and Gail sipped a Campari and soda. She lit a cigarette. "Ah, that's better," she said, blowing out the smoke.

Annie managed to smile through the smoke. "As you know," she said, "we've come to talk about Karen Drew." She noticed Ginger take out her pen and notebook. Despite her size and her flaming-red hair, she had the knack of disappearing into the background when she wanted to.

"You're probably wasting your time," said Gail. "I mean, I can't really tell you very much about her."

"Why not?"

"Because I don't know anything."

"But you were her liaison between the hospital and Mapston Hall."

"Yes, but that doesn't mean anything. I mean, I handle all sorts of similar residential care cases all over the county."

"So tell us what you do know."

Gail tied her hair back behind her head. "About four months ago," she began, "the administration at Grey Oaks, the hospital where Karen had been for almost three years, got in touch with me – I've worked with them before – and told me about a woman they had been treating who needed special care. That's my area. I went out there and met Karen – for the first and only time, I might add – and talked to her doctors. They had assessed her needs, and from what I could see, I agreed with them – not that my opinion on the matter was required, of course." She flicked the ash off her cigarette. "There was nothing suitable available locally, and I'd dealt with the Mapston Hall people before, so I knew their area of specialization matched Karen's needs. It was just a matter of waiting for a bed, getting the paperwork done, dotting the i's and crossing the t's. I really had nothing more to do with it than that."

"What were your personal impressions of Karen?" Annie asked.

"That's a funny question."

"Why?"

"Well, what impression can you have of someone who just sits there and says nothing?"

"She must have had a life before the accident."

"I suppose so, but that wasn't any of my business."

"Didn't you have to contact her family at all?"

"She didn't have any. You must have read her file."

"Yes. It tells me nothing."

"Which is about as much as I can tell you, too." Gail stubbed out her cigarette as the food arrived. Burgers and chips for Gail and Ginger, the inevitable cheese-and-tomato sandwich for Annie. Maybe she should start eating meat again, she thought, then decided that her diet was probably the only part of her life she seemed to have much control over at the moment. The conversations ebbed and flowed around them. At one table, a group of women laughed loudly at a bawdy joke. The air was full of smoke tinged with hops.

"Karen lived in Mansfield before the accident according to her file," said Annie. "Do you know what her address was?"

"Sorry," said Gail. "But you should be able to find out from Morton's, the estate agents. They handled the sale for her. I do happen to know that. It was part of the financing."

"Okay," said Annie. "How do you know about the estate agent?"

"Her solicitor told me about them."

"Karen Drew had a solicitor?"

"Of course. Someone had to take care of her affairs and look after her interests. She couldn't do it herself, could she? And a proper bloody busybody she was, too. Always ringing about this, that or the other. Voice like fingernails on a blackboard. 'Gail, do you think you could just . . .' 'Gail, could you . . .'" She gave a shudder.

"Do you remember her name?"

"Do I? Connie Wells. That was her name. Constance, she called herself. Insisted on it. Right bloody smarmy stuck-up bitch."

"Do you have her phone number or address?"

"Probably, somewhere in my files. She worked for a firm in Leeds, that's all I can remember. Park Square."

It would be, thought Annie. Leeds. That was interesting. If Karen Drew lived in Mansfield, why was her solicitor with a firm in Leeds? It wasn't far away, true, just up the motorway, but there were plenty of lawyers in Mansfield or Nottingham. Well, she could google

FRIEND OF THE DEVIL

Constance Wells easily enough once she got back to Whitby. Maybe the solicitor would be able to tell them something about Karen Drew's mysterious past.

"Look, there she goes," said DS Kevin Templeton, pointing at the television screen. "Right there."

They were in the viewing room on the ground floor of Western Area Headquarters reviewing one of the CCTV tapes. It could have been a clearer image, Banks thought, and perhaps technical support could tidy it up, but even blurred in the dark, with flaws and light flares, there was no doubt that the tall, long-legged girl, a little unsteady on her pins, heading up the alley between Joseph Randall's leather shop and the Fountain pub was Hayley Daniels, teetering on her high heels, reaching her hands out to touch the walls on both sides as she made her way down Taylor's Yard.

She had come out the pub with a group of people at 12:17, said something to them and, after what looked like a bit of a heated discussion, waved them away and headed into the alley at 12:20. It was hard to make out exactly how many of them there were, but Banks estimated at least seven. He could see the backs of a couple of her friends as they lingered and watched her disappear, shaking their heads, then they shrugged and walked in the direction of the Bar None after the others. Banks watched as Hayley's figure was finally swallowed up by the darkness of the Maze. Nobody waited for her.

"Anyone go down there before or after her?"

"Not on any of the surveillance tapes we've seen," said Templeton. "It's her, though, isn't it, sir?"

"It's her, all right," said Banks. "The question is, was he waiting or did he follow her?"

"I've watched it through till half past two in the morning, sir, well after the doc's estimate of time of death," said Templeton, "and no one else went up Taylor's Yard earlier and no one goes up there after her. No one comes out, either. We've got some footage from the Castle Road cameras to view, but this is it for the market square."

"So whoever it was entered by some other way, an entrance not covered by CCTV," said Banks.

"Looks that way, sir. But surely no one could have known she was going to go into the Maze? And if no one followed her . . ."

"Someone was already there, waiting for just such a likelihood? Possibly," said Banks.

"A serial killer?"

Banks gave Templeton a long-suffering look. "Kev, there's only one victim. How can it be a serial killer?"

"*So far* there's only one victim," said Templeton. "But that doesn't mean it'll stop with one. Even serial killers have to start somewhere." He grinned at his own weak joke. Banks didn't follow suit.

Banks knew what he meant, though. Sexual predators who had done what this man had done to Hayley Daniels didn't usually stop at just one victim, unless the killer was a personal enemy of Hayley's, an area that remained to be explored. "What if she isn't his first victim?" he said.

"Sir?"

"Get on the National Database," Banks went on. "See if you can find any similar incidents in the last eighteen months, anywhere in the country. Get Jim Hatchley to help you. He's not much good with a computer, but he knows his way around the county forces."

"Yes, sir," said Templeton.

A few years ago, Banks knew, such information would not have been easily available, but a lot had changed in the wake of the Yorkshire Ripper investigation and other interforce fiascos. Now, belatedly, Banks thought, they had come kicking and screaming into the twenty-first century with the realization that criminals don't respect city, county or even country borders.

"I still wonder why she went into the Maze alone," Templeton said, almost to himself. "No one went in with her or waited for her to come back."

"She was well pissed," said Banks. "They all were. You could see that for yourself. People don't think straight when they're pissed. They lose their inhibitions and their fears, and sometimes it's only your fears that keep you alive. I'll send DC Wilson out to the college. He looks young enough to be a student there himself. We've got to find those people she was with, and the odds are that they were fellow students. She talked to them. You can see her doing it. They talked to her. It looked as if they were maybe trying to persuade her not to go. Someone must know something."

"She could have arranged to meet someone in there earlier. The Maze, that is."

"She could have," Banks agreed. "Again, we need to talk to her friends about that. We need to interview everyone she met that night from the time they set out to the time she went into that alley. We've let ourselves be sidetracked by Joseph Randall."

"I'm still not sure about him," said Templeton.

"Me, neither," Banks agreed. "But we have to broaden the inquiry. Look, before you get cracking on that database, have another word with the bartender who was on duty at the Fountain on Saturday night. Find out if there were any incidents in the pub itself. Any sign of him on the tapes?"

"Oddly enough, yes, sir," said Templeton.

"Why oddly?"

"Well, he wheeled his bicycle out of the front door and locked up."

"What's so strange about that?"

"It was nearly half past two in the morning."

"Maybe he's a secret drinker. What did he have to say?"

"He wasn't there when the lads canvassed the pubs yesterday. Day off. Nobody's talked to him yet."

"Interesting. If he's not there today, find out where he lives and pay him a visit. Ask him what he was doing there so late and see if he remembers anything more. We know Hayley and her friends left the Fountain, had a discussion in the market square, then three minutes later she left to go down Taylor's Yard. Maybe something happened in the pub? It's almost the last place she was seen alive in public."

"Yes, sir."

Templeton left the viewing room. Banks took the remote control and rewound the surveillance tape. He pressed play again and watched Hayley Daniels argue with her friends and head down Taylor's Yard. He couldn't read her lips; the tape was of too poor quality. There was also an annoying, flickering strip of light, like you get on old film prints, behind the group, beside Taylor's Yard. It disappeared. When Hayley stretched her arms out for balance, she could touch both sides of the alley easily. The glitter on the cheap plastic belt around her waist caught the headlights of a passing car.

After she had disappeared into the darkness, Banks rewound and watched the tape one more time. They might be able to isolate and enhance the licence plate of that car, he thought, reasoning that if the driver had seen a pretty girl walking into the Maze alone, he might have zipped around the back and entered from the car park, where there were no CCTV cameras, and seized his opportunity. It was a long shot, but in the absence of anything else, it was worth a try. Banks called DC Wilson down from the squad room.

There was no point in going all the way back to Whitby first, Annie realized, as she aimed the car towards Leeds on the M1. Not when she could ring Detective Inspector Ken Blackstone at Millgarth and find out exactly where on Park Square Constance Wells practised law.

"Annie," said Blackstone. "How nice to hear from you. How's things?"

"Fine, Ken."

"And Alan?"

Blackstone sometimes spoke as if Banks and Annie were still an item, or as if he wished they were, but it didn't bother her. "Haven't seen him for a while," she said. "I'm on loan to Eastern Area. Look, maybe you can help me?"

"Of course, if I can."

"Should be easy enough. I'm trying to track down a Park Square solicitor, name of Constance Wells. Ring any bells?"

"No, but give me a few minutes. I'll call you back."

Annie and Ginger passed close by the massive cooling towers near Sheffield, and around the bend Annie saw the sprawl of Meadowhall, the popular shopping mall, to her left, cars parked everywhere.

Annie's mobile rang and she answered immediately. "Ken?"

"Ken?" said the voice. "Who's that? Do I have a rival? Sorry to disappoint you, but it's me. Eric."

"What do you want?"

"I just wanted to check if you were still going to join me for lunch on Thursday."

"I'm expecting an important call. I can't talk now," Annie said.

"See you Thursday, then. Black Horse."

Annie pressed end. She felt her face flush as Ginger gave her a sideways look. "Boyfriend trouble?" she asked.

"I don't have a boyfriend."

Ginger held her hands up. "Sorry."

Annie glanced at her, then laughed. "Some blokes just won't take no for an answer, right?" she said.

"Tell me about it."

It wasn't an invitation, or Annie might have relented. As it was, the mobile saved her. Ken Blackstone this time.

"Yes?" Annie said.

"Constance Wells does indeed work in Park Square," he said. "Conveyancing."

"Makes sense," said Annie.

"Anyway, she's with the firm of Ford, Reeves and Mitchell." Blackstone gave an address on Park Square. "That help?"

"Very much," said Annie. "It even sounds familiar. Would that be *Julia* Ford's practice?"

"Indeed it would," said Blackstone.

Julia Ford was a hotshot solicitor who specialized in high-profile criminal cases. Annie had seen her name and picture in the newspapers from time to time, though they had never met. "Thanks, Ken," she said.

"My pleasure. And don't be a stranger."

"I won't."

"Say hello to Alan from me, and ask him to give me a ring when he has time."

"I'll do that," said Annie, not at all sure as to when she would get the chance. "Bye." She ended the call and concentrated on the road. They were coming to the eastern edge of Leeds, where the tangle of roads and motorways merging and splitting almost rivalled Birmingham's Spaghetti Junction. Annie followed the signs to the city centre as best she could and, with Ginger's help, ended up completely lost. Eventually, they found a car park near the back of City Station and, with only some vague idea of where they were, left the Astra there and walked the rest of the way. It was easy enough when they got to City Square, with its old post office turned into a restaurant, the statue of the Black Prince and torch-bearing nymphs, and a pedestrian area where people sat at tables eating and drinking when the weather was good. Even today, one or two brave souls had ventured out into the open.

They walked along Wellington Street for a short distance, then turned up King Street and made their way over to Park Square. The buildings were mostly Georgian, and the solicitors' offices hadn't been modernized that much inside. A receptionist sat clicking away at her computer in the high-ceilinged entrance hall and asked them what they wanted.

"We'd like to see Constance Wells, please," Annie said, showing her warrant card.

"Do you have an appointment?"

"I'm afraid not."

She picked up her telephone. "Let me see if Ms. Wells is available right now. Please take a seat." She gestured towards the L-shaped sofa with the table of magazines. Annie and Ginger looked at one another, then sat. Annie picked up *Hello!* and Ginger went for *Practical Mechanics*. They hadn't got very far when the receptionist called out. "She says she can see you in ten minutes, if you'd care to wait?"

"Of course," said Annie. "Thank you."

"Probably just sitting twiddling her thumbs making us wait," said Ginger.

"Or twiddling something else," Annie added.

Ginger laughed, a deep guffaw. The receptionist glared at her, then went back to her computer. The time passed quickly enough, and Annie was just about to find out the secrets of the latest megastar divorce settlement when the receptionist's phone buzzed and she directed them towards the first office at the top of the stairs.

Constance Wells appeared lost behind the huge desk. She was a petite woman with wispy dark curls, probably somewhere in her mid-thirties, Annie guessed. Filing cabinets and bookcases rested against the walls, and her window looked out over the square. A framed illustration of a scene from *Hansel and Gretel* hung on one wall. Annie admired the delicate colours and fluid lines. It was quality work. A couple of hard-backed chairs had been placed before the desk. "Please," she said, gesturing. "Sit down. How can I help you?"

"Karen Drew," Annie said.

Constance Wells blinked once. "Yes?"

"She's dead."

"Oh, I . . ."

"I'm sorry to be so abrupt," said Annie, "but it's why we're here. Karen Drew's death. Murder, rather. It raises a few questions."

Constance put her hand to her chest. "I do apologize," she said. "You took me quite by surprise. I'm not used to such things. Murder, you said?"

"Yes. Karen was murdered yesterday morning on the coast not far from Mapston Hall. Someone took her for a walk and didn't bring her back."

"But . . . who?"

"That's what we're trying to find out," said Annie. "So far we're not having a lot of luck."

"Well, I don't see how I can help you."

Annie turned to Ginger. "That's what everyone says, isn't it?"

"Yes, ma'am," said Ginger. "Quite frankly, I'm getting sick of it myself."

"I can't help that," said Constance Wells. "It happens to be true."

"We understand that you're her solicitor and that, among other things, you handled the sale of her house."

"Yes."

"An address would help, for a start."

Constance Wells managed a tight smile. "I think I can help you with that," she said, walking over to a cabinet. She was wearing a green pastel skirt and matching jacket over a white blouse with a ruffled front. She opened a drawer, extracted a file and gave them an address. "I can't really see how that will help you, though," she said, sitting down again.

"It's a start. Can you tell us anything else about her?"

"As Ms. Drew's solicitor," Constance said, "all communications between us are strictly privileged."

"Ms. Wells, you don't seem to understand. Karen Drew is dead. Someone slit her throat from ear to ear."

Constance Wells turned pale. "Oh . . . you . . ."

"I'm sorry if I shocked you," said Annie. "But believe me, it nearly shocked me right out of my breakfast." She hadn't had any breakfast yesterday, she remembered, having flown from Eric's flat like a bat out of hell, but Constance Wells wasn't to know that.

"Yes, well, I . . . look, I *really* can't help you. I'm bound by . . . I only acted for Karen in her business affairs, the house sale, but I think you should . . . would you excuse me for a moment?"

She got up and dashed out of the office. Annie and Ginger stared at one another.

"What's with her?" Ginger said. "Off to be sick? Taken short?"

"No idea," said Annie. "Interesting reaction, though."

"Very. What do we do?"

"We wait."

It was almost five minutes before Constance Wells came back, and by then she seemed more composed. Ginger had stayed in her chair, but Annie was standing by the window looking down on Park Square, people watching. She turned when she heard the door open.

"I'm sorry," said Constance. "I suppose that was rude of me, but it's, well, it's all rather unusual."

"What is?" Annie asked.

"Karen's case. Look, Julia, that's Ms. Ford, one of our senior partners, would like to see you. Can you spare her a few moments?"

Annie and Ginger exchanged another glance. "Can we?" Annie said. "Oh, I think so, don't you, DC Baker?" And they followed Constance down the corridor.

5

Templeton hated grotty old pubs like the Fountain. They were full of losers and tossers drowning their sorrows, and an atmosphere of failure hung in the air along with the stale smoke and ale. Just being in such a place made him cringe. Give him a modern bar, chrome and plastic seating, pastel walls and subdued lighting, even if the beer did come in bottles and the music was too loud. At least he didn't walk out smelling like a tramp.

The place was almost empty at three in the afternoon, only a few pathetic diehards with no lives worth living slobbering over their warm pints. A young man in jeans and a grey sweatshirt, shaved head and black-rimmed spectacles, stood at the bar polishing glasses. They still looked dirty when he'd finished.

"You the landlord?" Templeton asked, flashing his warrant card.

"Me? You must be joking," the man said. He had a Geordie accent. Templeton hated Geordie accents, and he heard far too many of them around Eastvale. "The landlord's away in Florida, like he is most of the time. I don't think he's set foot in the place more than twice since he bought it."

"What's your name?"

"Jamie Murdoch."

"Manager, then?"

"For my sins."

"You look too young."

"And you look too young to be a detective."

"I'm a quick study."

"Must be."

"Anyway, much as I love a bit of banter, I've got a few questions for you about Saturday night."

"Yeah?"

"Who was working?"

"I was."

"Just you."

"Aye. Jill called in sick, and we couldn't get anyone else at short notice."

"That must have been fun, on your own on a Saturday night?"

"Hilarious. Anyway, it happens often enough. This about the poor wee lassie who got killed?"

"That's right."

He shook his head. "A tragedy."

"Did you serve her?"

"Look, if you're asking me were her and her friends intoxicated, they might have had a few, but there was no way they were so drunk I would have refused to serve them."

"Do you know they got kicked out of the Trumpeter's before they came here?"

"No, I didn't. They must have been rowdy or something. They were well behaved enough here. It was the end of the evening. Things were winding down. It wasn't them causing the trouble."

"But someone was?"

"Isn't someone always?"

"Tell me about it."

"Nothing much to tell, really." Murdoch picked up another glass from the dish rack and started drying it with the tea towel. "It was Saturday night, wasn't it? St. Patrick's Day, too. There always seems to be something, even on a normal Saturday. You get used to it. Didn't Elton John have a song about it? 'Saturday Night's Alright for Fighting'?"

"Don't know that one," said Templeton. "And this time?"

"Gang of yobs from Lyndgarth got into a barney with some students in the pool room. Eastvale's version of town and gown. It came to nothing. Lot of sound and fury signifying nothing."

"Where'd you get that line from?"

"It's Shakespeare. *Macbeth.*"

"Go to college, do you?"

"I've been."

"So, tell me, an educated lad like you, how does he end up working in a dive like this?"

"Just lucky, I suppose." Murdoch shrugged. "It's all right. There are worse places."

"So back to Saturday night. You're here behind the bar all alone, you've just calmed down a fracas. What happens next?"

"The Lyndgarth lot left and the girl and her friends came in. They knew some of the other students, so some of them started playing pool and the rest just sat around chatting."

"No incidents?"

"No incidents. That was earlier."

"The fracas?"

"And the vandalism."

"What vandalism?"

"The bastards smashed up the toilets, didn't they? Ladies and gents I think it was the Lyndgarth mob, but I can't prove it. Toilet rolls shoved down the bowl, light bulbs broken, glass all over the floor, piss –"

"I get the picture," said Templeton.

"Aye, well, I was here until nearly half past two in the morning cleaning it up."

"Half past two, you say?"

"That's right. Why?"

"We saw you leaving on the CCTV, that's all."

"You could have said."

Templeton grinned. "Look at it from my point of view. If you'd said you went home at half past twelve we'd have had a discrepancy, wouldn't we?"

"But I didn't. I left at half past two. Like you said, it's on candid camera."

"Anybody vouch for you?"

"I told you, I was here alone."

"So you could have nipped out into the Maze, raped and killed the girl, then got back to cleaning up the bog?"

"I suppose I could have, but I didn't. You already said you saw me leave on the CCTV."

"But you could have sneaked out earlier and come back."

"Look around you. There's only two ways out of this place on account of its location. There's not even a window opens on Taylor's Yard. We take all our brewery deliveries down the chute at the front. The only ways out of the place are the front, which leads to the market square, and the other side, the passageway between the toilets and the kitchen, which leads to Castle Road. I assume you've got CCTV there, too?"

"We have," said Templeton.

"There you go, then. You tell me how I'm supposed to get out, rape and murder a girl, and come back without being seen."

"Mind if I have a look around?"

"Not at all. I'll show you." Murdoch put the glass down, called to one of the regulars to keep his eye on the place and first took Templeton upstairs, where there was an office, a toilet, a storeroom full of cases of wine and spirits piled against the wall, and a sitting room with a TV set, fading wallpaper and a let-down sofa.

Next, Murdoch showed him the pool room and the toilets downstairs, which weren't in such bad shape, then the kitchen near the back, which was clean as it should be, and the side exit onto Castle Road. They went into the cellar next, a dank place with damp stone walls and barrels of beer in a row and crates of ale piled up. It stank of yeast and hops. The walls were solid everywhere, probably about three feet thick. Templeton couldn't see any possible way out, and he didn't particularly fancy staying down there a moment more than he needed, so he headed back up the worn stone steps.

"Seen enough?" asked Murdoch when they got back to the bar.

"For now," said Templeton. "This incident with the toilets. When did it happen?"

"Don't know for certain," said Murdoch. "The Lyndgarth yobs had been gone maybe about ten minutes or so when one of the students came and told me. Not that there was anything I could do about it right there and then, like, when I had drinks to serve. It was about that time the girl and her friends came in."

"Pretty near closing time, then?"

"Aye, not far off. I'd have shut up early except I had paying customers. I reckoned I'd see the punters off the premises at the usual time and get it cleaned up. Never imagined it would take so bloody long."

"This Lyndgarth lot, did they stick around the square?"

"I didn't see them again, but then I didn't get out till late."

"Any names?"

"Why? Are you going to prosecute them?"

"For what?"

"Vandalizing the pub."

"No, dickhead. They might be suspects in a murder investigation. Why, are you going to bring charges?"

"No way. I value my life."

"I'd still like to talk to them. Names?"

"You must be joking. Maybe one of them called his mate Steve, and there was another called Mick."

"Wonderful. Thanks a lot."

"I told you. Anyway, it shouldn't be too difficult for you to find them if you want. Just ask around. Lyndgarth's not a big place and the yobs are probably pretty well known there."

"And you'd recognize them again?"

"Aye, I'd recognize them."

"Had you seen the girl and her friends before?"

"They'd been in once or twice, yes."

"Regulars?"

"I wouldn't call them regulars, but I'd seen them occasionally in here on a Saturday night. Never caused any trouble."

"Did you hear anything from Taylor's Yard while you were cleaning up the toilets?"

"No."

"Did you see anyone go by the front?"

"No, but I wouldn't have, anyway. See, I was in the toilets, at the Castle Road side, as you've seen. Besides, I wasn't really paying attention. Cleaning up vandalized toilets sort of demands all your attention, if you know what I mean." Murdoch worked at a glass, then narrowed his eyes. "I can hardly believe it, you know."

"Believe what?"

He gestured over towards the toilets. "While I was busy cleaning up in there, what was happening in the Maze. That poor girl. I can hardly get my head around it."

"Don't even try," said Templeton, heading towards the door. "It'll only give you grief." And he left, rather pleased with himself for his piece of sage advice. He paused at the door and turned back. "And don't run away," he said, pointing his finger at Murdoch. "I might be back."

As befitting that of a senior partner, Julia Ford's office was both larger and better appointed than Constance Wells's. She had the same fine view of the square, but from higher up, and the room was fitted with a thick pile carpet and a solid teak desk. What looked to Annie like an original David Hockney Yorkshire landscape hung on one wall.

Julia Ford herself was elegance personified. Annie had no idea where her simple dark blue business suit and plain white blouse had come from, but it definitely wasn't Next or Primark. She bet there was a designer's name on it somewhere, and it probably came from Harvey Nicks. Her straight chestnut brown hair fell to her shoulders and was imbued with the kind of lustre Annie had seen only on television adverts. Julia Ford stood up, leaned across the table and shook hands with both Annie and Ginger, then bade them sit. Her chairs were padded and far more comfortable than Constance Wells's. She regarded them both with watchful brown eyes, then turned to Constance, who lingered in the doorway. "That's all right, Constance, thank you very much," she said. "You can go now." Constance shut the door behind her.

Julia Ford continued to regard Annie and Ginger with those serious hazel eyes and made a steeple of her hands on the table. No rings, Annie noticed. "I understand that Karen Drew has been murdered?" she said finally.

"That's right," said Annie. "We're trying –"

Julia Ford waved her hand dismissively. "I should imagine you are," she said, a definite smile now playing around the edges of her thin lips. "And I should also imagine you're not getting very far."

"It's like squeezing the proverbial blood out of the proverbial stone," Annie said. "We were wondering if Ms. Wells might be able to help, but she seemed to think we should talk to you."

"*I* thought you should talk to me. Constance has very specific instructions regarding Karen."

"And can you help?"

"Oh, I think you'll find I'll be able to help you a great deal," said Julia Ford.

"But *will* you?"

"Will I?" She spread her hands. "Of course I will. I've never hindered a police investigation."

Annie swallowed. Julia Ford had a reputation as a tough solicitor who would do anything she possibly could to discredit the police and get her client off.

"Can you tell us about her background, then?" Annie asked.

"I could, but I don't think that's really the main issue right now. You'll find out soon enough, anyway."

"Ms. Ford," said Annie, "with all due respect, aren't we supposed to be the ones who decide what questions we should ask?"

"Yes, yes, of course. I'm sorry. I wasn't meaning to be rude, and I'm not trying to do your job for you. What I'm trying to tell you is that there is something more important you need to know first."

"And what's that?"

"Karen Drew wasn't her real name."

"I see . . . May I ask what her real name was?"

"You may."

"And . . . ?"

Julia Ford paused and played with her Mont Blanc on the desk in front of her. Annie knew she was indulging in typical courtroom tactics for dramatic effect, but there was nothing she could do but wait out the theatrics. Finally, the solicitor tired of playing with her pen and leaned forward across the oak. "Her real name was Lucy Payne," she said.

"Jesus Christ," whispered Annie. "Lucy Payne. The Friend of the Devil. That changes everything."

"So what do you think of Jamie Murdoch?" Banks asked. He was sitting in his office comparing notes with Kevin Templeton and Winsome Jackman. Templeton, he noticed, kept sneaking a glance at Winsome's thighs under the tight black material of her trousers.

"He's got an attitude," Templeton said, "and he's a bit of a plonker. But that hardly qualifies him as a murderer. No more than being a Geordie does. I don't know. I'm sure we'll be able to verify his story about the vandalized bogs when we talk to Hayley's friends and the yobbos from Lyndgarth. We've got film of him leaving on his bike at half past two, and no sign of him before that. Like he says, there's no access to the Maze from the pub without using the front or side exits, and they were both covered by CCTV."

"Okay," said Banks. "Now, what do we make of this new angle Winsome's come up with?"

Winsome had been watching the rest of the CCTV footage and noticed someone coming out of the Maze from the narrow shopping arcade that led off Castle Road at 12:40, which was twenty minutes after Hayley had gone in. There was no CCTV record of the person's having entered. The images were indistinct, but Winsome thought he resembled one of the people Hayley Daniels had been talking to earlier in the square, just before she went off down Taylor's Yard by herself.

"Well," said Templeton, "he certainly hadn't been shopping at that time of night. Someone searching for her? A friend?"

"Could be," said Winsome. "Maybe he got worried when she didn't turn up at the Bar None. But why not use the Taylor's Yard entrance? It's nearer the club."

"Is there a back way from the Bar None to the Maze?" Banks asked.

"Yes, sir," said Templeton. "A fire exit."

"So he could have left that way," said Banks. "And I suppose it's possible that he knew about the market square CCTV, which is the set-up that gets all the publicity, but not about that on Castle Road. He didn't know he'd be seen coming out. Twenty minutes isn't very long, but it's probably long enough for what the killer did, and he seems in a bit of a hurry. This looks very promising. DC Wilson's at the college working on that list of names. It could take some time to get through them all. Do you think you can get technical support to come up with a still image from the video? Enhanced?"

"I can always try," said Winsome. "They're already working on that car number plate, but no luck so far."

"Ask them to do their best," said Banks. "It's another long shot, but it might save us time." Banks leaned back in his chair and ran his hand across his closely cropped hair. "Okay," he said, "let's review what we've got so far." He counted off on his fingers as he spoke. "Joseph Randall, who swears he was at home alone when Hayley was killed, but has no real alibi and also can't account for the eleven minutes between finding the body and reporting it. Oh, and he also eyed up the victim in the Duck and Drake earlier on the evening she was killed. After making a fuss, he volunteered a DNA sample and signed the waiver. The lab's working on it.

"Next we've got Jamie Murdoch, pub manager of the Fountain, who says he was fixing broken toilets during the time Hayley was raped and killed. He appears to have had no access to the murder scene, at least not without being spotted, and he doesn't show up on CCTV until he leaves on his bike at half past two. Finally, one of Hayley's friends is seen exiting the Maze by the Castle Road arcade at 12:40, but not seen going in. What had he been doing in there? How long had he been there? What was he hoping for? A quick grope in the ginnel?"

"Hayley's stepmother said she didn't have a steady boyfriend," Winsome said, "but she did think Hayley was sexually experienced."

Banks noticed Templeton give a little smile at Winsome's discomfort in talking about sex in front of them.

"We probably won't find out any more about that until we talk to the people she was with," said Banks.

"There's still the possibility that someone was lying in wait," Templeton said. He glanced at Banks. "A serial killer just starting out. Someone who knew how to come and go in the Maze without being seen, which probably means he's a local and knows the area."

"We won't forget that possibility, Kev," said Banks. "But so far we've had no luck with the local sex offenders." He turned back to Winsome. "What about the family? You talked to them."

"Yes, sir. I can't say I was very impressed by the father, but maybe it's hard to be impressed by a bloke you find tied naked to a bed in a hotel room."

"Oh, Winsome," said Templeton. "You disappoint me. Don't tell me it didn't turn you on."

"Shut up, Kev," said Banks.

Winsome glared at Templeton. "There's no way either of the parents could have done it," she went on. "Donna McCarthy was watching a DVD with Caroline Dexter, and Geoff Daniels and Martina Redfern have a watertight alibi. I found the taxi driver who drove them back from the nightclub to the hotel around half past two, and even he remembers them." She gave a nervous glance at Templeton, then looked back at Banks. "They were . . . you know . . . in the back of his taxi."

Even Banks had to smile at that. Templeton laughed out loud.

"Okay," said Banks. "So far our only suspects who don't seem to have an alibi are Randall and Hayley's friend on the Castle Road CCTV, and he should be easy enough to track down." Banks stood up. "Then there's the Lyndgarth yobs to sort out. They were angry at Jamie Murdoch. They could have hung around the Maze hoping to get a crack at him and found Hayley instead."

"The CCTV just shows them walking away," said Templeton.

"They still need looking into. Which is what we ought to be doing now instead of sitting around here. Thanks for bringing me up to date. Now let's get to work and see if we can close this one before the week's out."

A stunned silence followed Annie's response to the revelation of Karen Drew's real identity. Annie could hear other noises from the building – phone conversations, the clacking of a computer keyboard – mixed with the sounds of cars and birds from outside. She tried to digest what she'd just heard.

"You weren't involved in that case, were you?" Julia Ford asked.

"Peripherally," said Annie. "My boss was SIO."

Julia Ford smiled. "Ah, yes, Detective Superintendent Banks. I remember him well. How is he?"

"He's fine," said Annie. "Actually, he's a DCI. He was only acting super. I handled the Janet Taylor investigation." Janet Taylor was the policewoman who had killed Lucy Payne's husband, Terence, after he had murdered her partner with a machete and come at her with it. The law about reasonable force being what it was, she had been suspended and put under investigation, until she died in a drink-driving accident. The whole affair still left a bitter taste in Annie's mouth.

Julia Ford made a sympathetic grimace. "A tough one."

"Yes. Look, do you think you could –"

"Explain? Yes. Of course. I'll do my best." She glanced at Ginger. "Are you aware of who Lucy Payne was, DC –?"

"Baker," said Ginger. "And yes, I'm aware of who she was. She killed all those girls a few years ago. The newspapers called her the Friend of the Devil."

"So very melodramatic," said Julia Ford. "But what would you expect of the gutter press? As a matter of fact, Lucy Payne didn't murder anyone. Her husband was the killer, the devil in question."

"And how convenient that he was dead, so he couldn't tell his side of the story," said Annie.

"Well, you've only got Janet Taylor to blame for that, haven't you?"

"Janet did –"

"Look," Julia Ford interrupted, "as you know, I defended Lucy, so I'm hardly going to say she was guilty, am I? The Crown reviewed the evidence at the preliminary hearing, such as it was, and threw the case out of court. She never even went to trial."

"Wasn't that something to do with the fact that she was in a wheelchair?" said Annie.

"The state of her health may have been a mitigating factor. HM prisons have very limited facilities for dealing with quadriplegics. But the fact remains that there wasn't enough evidence against her to prove that she killed anyone."

"Weren't there some dodgy videos?" Ginger asked.

"Showing at the most sexual assault, at the least, consensual sex," said Julia Ford. "The Crown knew they were on shaky ground with the videos, so they weren't even admitted as evidence. As I said, the case collapsed before it went to trial. Not enough evidence. As is, sadly, so often the case."

Annie ignored the barb. "The fact that one of the star prosecution witnesses, Maggie Forrest, had a nervous breakdown and was unable to testify might have helped, too," she said.

"Possibly. But these things happen. Besides, even Maggie had no evidence to connect Lucy with any murders."

"All right," said Annie, raising her hand. "We'll get nowhere now debating Lucy Payne's role in the rape, torture and murder of those young girls."

"I agree," said Julia Ford. "I simply wanted to lay my cards on the table and let you know who you're really dealing with. The events took place six years ago, when Lucy was just twenty-two. When faced with arrest, Lucy jumped out of a window, Maggie Forrest's window. Lucy was in hospital after hospital for a long, long time, and the firm took care of her affairs. She had a number of serious operations, none of which was entirely successful, but they managed to keep her alive, after a fashion. In the end, we found her a place at Mapston Hall. Given the publicity surrounding the Payne case, once she had managed to disappear from the public view, and from the media, we thought it best that she assumed a new identity for the rest of her days. It was all perfectly legal. I have the papers."

"And what about the car accident they told us about at Mapston Hall? Drink driving?"

"Another necessary fiction."

"I'm sure it was," said Annie, "and I'm not really here to contest any of that. I thought I was looking for the killer of Karen Drew, but now I find out that I'm looking for who killed Lucy Payne. That changes things."

"I hope knowing that won't stop you from putting just as much effort into it."

Annie glared at her. "I won't even dignify that with a reply," she said.

"There were plenty at the time who said Lucy got exactly what she deserved when she ended up in a wheelchair. Perhaps you were one of them."

"No." Annie felt herself turn red. She had never said that, but she had thought it. Like Banks, she believed that Lucy Payne had been as guilty as her husband, and spending the rest of her days paralyzed was fitting enough punishment for what the two of them had done to those girls in their cellar, whether Lucy had actually delivered the killing blows or not. The videos showed that she knew all about what was going on and had been a willing participant in her husband's sick, elaborate sexual games with his victims. No, Lucy Payne's fate elicited no sympathy from Annie. And now someone had put her out of her misery. It could almost be viewed as an act of kindness. But she wouldn't let any of that cloud her judgment. She wouldn't give Julia Ford the satisfaction of being right. She would work this case as hard as any other, harder perhaps, until she had discovered who killed Lucy Payne and why.

"How does it change things?" Julia Ford asked.

"Well, it brings two important questions to mind," said Annie.

"Oh?"

"First, did the killer know she was killing Lucy Payne?"

"And the second?"

"Who knew that Karen Drew was Lucy Payne?"

"Well, Stuart," said Banks. "I think you've got some explaining to do, don't you?"

Stuart Kinsey sat opposite Banks in the interview room that evening pouting, picking at a fingernail, glancing at Winsome out of the corner of his eye. It had been a long two days; everyone was tired and wanted to go home. Kinsey wore the typical student uniform of denim and a T-shirt proclaiming The Who's triumphant return to Leeds University the previous June. His hair was shaggy, but not especially long, and Banks supposed he might be attractive to women in that surly, moody sort of way some of them liked. Whether he had been attractive to Hayley Daniels was another matter.

"Am I under arrest?" he asked.

Banks looked at Winsome. "Why does everyone ask us that?" he said.

"Don't know, sir," said Winsome. "Maybe they think it makes a difference."

"Doesn't it?" said Kinsey.

"Not really," said Banks. "See, we could arrest you. Nothing easier. A mere formality. I'd say 'Stuart Kinsey, you are under arrest on suspicion of the murder of Hayley Daniels. You don't have to say anything . . . blah blah blah.' The standard caution. Something along those lines. Then –"

"Wait a minute!" said Kinsey. "Murder? Now hold on. I had nothing to do with that."

"Then you'd ask for a solicitor, as is your right, and we'd have to bring one in for you. He or she would probably encourage you to answer most of our questions, so long as they didn't incriminate you. Which they wouldn't if you didn't do anything wrong. We could go that route. After the arrest comes the charge, which is a lot more serious. That's when we take you down to the custody suite, divest you of your belt, shoelaces and possessions and lock you in a cell for as long as we feel like." Banks tapped the side of his head. "Oh no, what was I thinking about? That was the good old days. Sorry. It's twenty-four hours, unless our boss authorizes further periods. And she's very upset about what happened to Hayley. Got kids of her own." Banks could sense Winsome rolling her eyes. But it worked. Kinsey had lost his cool and sullen demeanour, and he now appeared like a very frightened young man in a lot of trouble, which was exactly what Banks wanted.

"What do you want to know?" he asked.

Banks nodded to Winsome, who turned on the small television monitor they had set up. The first clip showed Hayley walking away from her friends, Kinsey included, and disappearing into Taylor's Yard. The time, 12:20, appeared along the bottom, along with the date and other technical details to prevent tampering. The second excerpt showed Stuart Kinsey dashing out of the arcade onto Castle Road. The time was 12:40. After the videos had finished, Banks paused to let the images sink in, then he said, "Whichever way you look at it, Stuart, you're in a lot of trouble. What were you doing running out of the Maze at twenty to one on Saturday night?"

"All right, I'd been looking for Hayley. But I didn't kill her."

"Tell me what happened."

"It was like you saw in the other tape. We all said goodbye outside the Fountain. Hayley was . . . well, she'd had a few, if you must know."

"I think we were aware of that," said Banks. "It looked as if you were arguing. Why was she going into the Maze alone?"

"You know."

"Tell me, Stuart."

"Look, she was going for a piss, all right? The bogs in the Fountain were out of order. She'd had a skinful and she was going for a piss. That's all. If it looks like we were arguing, it's because we were trying to persuade her not to be so daft. But you can't tell Hayley anything when she's made her mind up, especially if she's had a few."

"She never said anything about meeting anyone?"

"No."

"Wasn't she afraid?"

"What had she to be afraid of? She didn't know there was a murderer lurking there, did she?"

"Okay," said Banks. "Why didn't she wait until she got to the Bar None?"

"She just did things like that. She liked to be outrageous. She didn't care what people thought. Besides, she wasn't coming with us to the Bar None. Said she didn't like the music."

"Where was she going?"

"Dunno."

"Okay, Stuart. You went into the Maze through the back exit of the Bar None shortly after you got there. Why?"

"I went to see if Hayley was okay."

"You were worried about her? But you just told me you didn't think she was in any danger, or had any reason to be."

"Yeah, well, it just struck me that it's dark down there and, you know, she might get lost or something."

"And you wouldn't? You know your way around the Maze, do you?"

"I didn't really stop to think."

"No. You just dashed out back to go and watch Hayley Daniels have a piss. Are you a pervert or something, Stuart?"

"No! I told you, it wasn't like that at all. I wanted to . . . I wanted to see where she went."

"What do you mean?"

"It's pretty obvious, isn't it? After she'd finished . . . you know . . . I wanted to see where she went. I didn't do anything. Please. You have to believe me. I wouldn't have hurt Hayley. Not for anything."

"Were you in love with her?"

"I don't know about love," Kinsey said, "but I fancied her something rotten."

At least that sounded honest, Banks thought. "Did Hayley know that?"

"It was pretty obvious."

"What was her reaction?"

"Said we were friends. She blew hot and cold, did Hayley."

"What was your reaction?"

"What do you mean?"

"She rejected you. How did you react?"

"It wasn't like that!"

"Do you mean she accepted your advances? I'm confused."

"I didn't make any advances."

"So how did she know you were interested?"

"We talked, like, we got on, you know, had stuff in common, bands and things, went to the pictures a couple of times. And there's like an electricity between people, you know, you can feel it."

"Did Hayley feel it, too?" Banks asked.

"I don't suppose she did. At least she wouldn't admit it. Hayley could be very distant. You never really knew where you stood with her. Like I said, hot and cold. She liked to be a part of the crowd, the party girl."

"Centre of attention?"

"Well, it wasn't difficult for her. She was fit and she knew it. I mean, sometimes she got a bit rowdy, but it was just harmless fun. Sometimes I thought it was her way of, you know, keeping away any one particular person, being part of the group so you never really had to get close to someone, you could keep them at arm's length. You'd get into a conversation with her, and then she'd say something, and before you knew it everyone would be involved and she was laughing at someone else's joke. You couldn't have her to yourself for very long."

"That must have been very frustrating," Banks said.

"You're telling me."

"So where did it lead?"

"Well, it didn't lead anywhere, really. I didn't sleep with her or anything. Just snogging and stuff. Sometimes I got the impression recently that she . . . no, it doesn't matter."

"It might, Stuart," said Banks. "Let me be the judge."

Kinsey paused and chewed on his fingernail. "Can I have a cup of tea or something?" he asked. "I'm thirsty."

"Of course." Not wanting to interrupt the rhythm of the interview, Banks signalled to Winsome, who got up and asked the constable outside the door to rustle up some tea.

"Won't be long," Banks said to Kinsey. "Now, Stuart, you were going to tell me about that impression you had."

"Well, you know, it was just a sort of vague idea, like."

"Even so . . ."

"Sometimes I thought maybe she'd got a bloke."

"When did this start?"

"Couple of months ago. Around then."

"Any idea who this bloke was? One of the others in the group?"

"No. Someone she was keeping secret." He leaned forward on the table. "You see, that's what I meant when I said I was in the Maze because I wanted to see where she went. I was going to follow her, find out who the mystery bloke was."

"But you didn't see her?"

"No. I thought she must have already gone. I mean, it was a good five minutes or so after we left her that I went in. It doesn't take that long to . . . you know."

"Right," said Banks. Hayley had been sick, he remembered Dr. Burns telling him, which would have kept her there longer. "Did you see or hear anything while you were in there?"

"I . . . I thought I heard a door bang shut and a sort of . . . not a scream but a muffled sort of cry. You don't think it could have been her, do you? It creeped me out, I have to tell you."

"What time was this?"

"Just after I went in. I wasn't really aware of the time, but I suppose it was around twenty-five past, something like that."

Just five minutes after Hayley herself had entered the Maze, Banks thought. "Did you see anyone?"

"No, nothing."

"What did you do when you heard the noise? Is that why you were running?"

Kinsey nodded and studied the scratched table. "I got out of there pretty damn quickly," he said. "I figured she must have finished before I got there and left already. You don't really think it was her I heard, do you? Maybe I could have saved her, but I got scared. Oh, God." Kinsey put his head in his hands and started crying.

Banks was almost certain that it *was* Hayley whom Kinsey had heard, but he wasn't going to tell him that. His own imagination would torture him more than enough as it was. At least the time of the attack could be fixed more accurately now. Hayley's killer had grabbed her about five minutes after she had gone into the Maze, just after she had been sick and finished what she had gone there to do. Perhaps watching her had excited and inflamed him.

The timing made perfect sense, of course. Hayley would hardly have been hanging around there unless she had made an assignation. Again, what Kinsey had said about the mystery boyfriend came back to Banks. Maybe she had made a date with him? Maybe that was who had killed her? But why arrange to meet him in the Maze if she was going to spend the night with him? It would make far more sense to go to his flat or wherever he lived. And why would a boyfriend resort to rape, or murder? Such things did happen, Banks knew. Not long ago West Yorkshire police had arrested a man who regularly drugged and raped three girlfriends who would all have been perfectly happy to have consensual sex with him. Nothing much surprised Banks these days when it came to sexual deviance.

Hayley had carried condoms in her handbag, so she was obviously sexually active. Perhaps Stuart Kinsey *had* killed her, out of frustration, or out of jealousy. They were powerful emotions, as Banks knew from previous cases. Under the sway of jealousy, a man or a woman was capable of almost anything.

The tea arrived and Kinsey calmed down. "I'm sorry," he said. "I just couldn't bear the thought that I might have been able to do something, but I ran away."

"You didn't know what was happening," Banks said. It wasn't much consolation, but it was some. He leaned forward. "I'm very interested in this idea of yours about Hayley having a secret boyfriend," he went on. "Any ideas who it might be or why she might keep him a secret?"

6

"It's good to see you again, Alan," said Annie early on Tuesday afternoon in the Horse and Hounds, a quiet pub off the market square where you could get a decent salad and enjoy a pint without Detective Superintendent Catherine Gervaise finding out about it. There was a tiny, windowless, non-smoking bar, all dark gleaming wood and plush red velveteen, with old hunting prints on the wall – at least it was still legal to depict scenes of fox hunting – where it seemed that nobody ever sat. You had to go to the main bar to get drinks, but other than that, it was the ideal place for a private meeting.

Annie was drinking diet bitter lemon, having not touched a drop of alcohol since Saturday night. Banks was well into his pint of Tetley's Cask, and the obvious pleasure he was taking in it was making Annie feel envious. Well, she thought, it wasn't as if she had taken the pledge and was going to stop drinking forever. It was simply a small hiatus to get herself together, review the situation, and maybe lose a little weight. Tomorrow, perhaps, she'd have a pint. Or maybe a glass of wine after work tonight. Fortunately, the burger Banks also seemed to be enjoying held no appeal for her whatsoever.

"To what do I owe the pleasure?" Banks asked after a few minutes of small talk about mutual friends and acquaintances in Eastern Area.

"I know you're busy with the Maze case," Annie said. "I've heard about it. Poor girl. Any suspects yet?"

"A few. We're waiting on forensics and toxicology results," said Banks. "And there are some more people we need to talk to. Kev Templeton thinks we've got a serial killer on our hands already. He might have a point. Even though there's been only one definite victim so far, it has all the hallmarks of a violent sex crime, and people who do that don't usually stop at one."

"Kevin Templeton's an arsehole," said Annie.

"That may be, but he can be a good copper if he puts his mind to it."

Annie snorted in disbelief. "Anyway," she said, "I think you'll be interested in what's happened out Whitby way."

"Oh?" said Banks. "I'm intrigued. I did hear something about a woman in a wheelchair being killed out there."

"Yes," Annie said. "A woman by the name of Karen Drew."

"It doesn't ring any bells."

"It wouldn't," said Annie. "It's not her real name."

"Oh."

"No. Julia Ford told me what her real name was yesterday."

Banks paused with the burger halfway to his mouth and put it back down on the plate. "Julia Ford. Now there's a blast from the past."

"Starting to ring some bells?"

"Yes, but I don't like the sound they're making. Julia Ford. Woman in a wheelchair. Sounds very dissonant to me."

"It was Lucy Payne."

"Shit," said Banks. "I take it the media don't know yet?"

"No, but they'll find out soon enough. Detective Superintendent Brough's trying to head them off at the pass. He's called a press conference for this afternoon."

"I hope you don't expect me to feel any pity for her," Banks said.

"It always struck me that you had a very complicated relationship with her," said Annie. "That's partly why I've come to you."

"Complicated? With the Friend of the Devil? Ruined a perfectly good Grateful Dead song for me, that's all. Now, whenever I hear it, I see her face, see those bodies in the cellar."

"Alan, it's *me*, remember. Annie. I'm not Jim Hatchley. You don't have to play the yahoo with me."

Banks sipped some beer. Annie looked at him and tried to figure out what he was thinking. She never could. He thought he was transparent, but he was really as cloudy as an unfiltered pint.

"She was a complicated woman," Banks said. "But she was a killer."

"A young and beautiful killer," Annie added.

"That, too," Banks agreed. "Are you saying that affected my judgment?"

"Oh, come on. I've never known a time when a woman's beauty hasn't affected a man's judgment. You don't even need to go back as far as Helen of Troy to work that one out."

"I wasn't her champion, you'll remember," said Banks. "As far as I was concerned, she was as guilty as her husband, and I wanted her put away for it."

"Yes, I know, but you *understood* her, didn't you?"

"Not for a moment." Banks paused. "I'm not saying I might not have wanted to, or even tried to, but it wasn't anything to do with her beauty. She was in bandages most times I saw her, anyway. Look below the surface and there was a hell of a lot of darkness. Okay, I'll admit she was a complex and interesting killer. We've both come across those."

"Touché," said Annie, thinking of Phil Keane, who had wreaked so much havoc on her and Banks's lives not much more than a year ago, damage Annie had certainly not yet got over if her recent behaviour was anything to go by. A charming psychopath, Keane had used Annie to monitor the investigation of a crime he had committed, and when he came close to getting caught, he had almost killed Banks.

"But Lucy Payne had a most unusual and deeply troubled childhood," Banks went on. "I'm not saying that excuses anything she did, or even really explains it, but can you really get your head around being kept in a cage and sexually abused by your family day after day, year after year?"

"The abused becomes the abuser?"

"I know it sounds like a cliché, but isn't that often the case? Anyway, you didn't come to me for my theories on Lucy Payne. In a way, death was probably a blessing for her." He raised his glass for a moment, as if in a mock toast, then drank.

"True," said Annie. "What I was thinking was that I have to revisit that case if I want to have a hope in hell of catching her killer."

"And what makes you want to do that?"

"My nature," Annie said. "I can't even believe you'd ask me such a question."

"You thought she was as guilty as I did."

"I know," said Annie. "So what? If anything, that makes me want to solve her murder even more."

"To prove you can overcome your own prejudices?"

"What's so wrong with that? I might never have said it, but I was glad when she ended up paralyzed. Death would have been too easy for her. This way she suffered more, and a part of me thought that was just, given the way she'd made those poor girls suffer. Karma, if you like."

"And the other parts of you?"

"Told me what a load of self-justifying bollocks that was. Whatever she did, whatever she was, Lucy Payne was a human being. As a society, we don't tolerate executing people any more, but someone has taken the law into his or her own hands and slit Lucy Payne's throat as she sat there unable to defend herself. That goes against everything I believe in. No matter what she did, it was nobody's right to take Lucy Payne's life."

"What, they should have let her go on suffering a kind of living death? Someone did her a favour."

"It wasn't a mercy killing."

"How do you know?"

"Because I've never come across anyone who felt she deserved the tiniest drop of mercy, that's why. Except perhaps you."

"Well, I didn't kill her," said Banks.

"Now you're playing silly buggers."

Banks touched the scar beside his right eye. "I'm sorry. I didn't mean to be so sarcastic. All I'm saying is that you have to be sure you want to open that can of worms. You know who the main suspects will be."

"Of course I do," said Annie. "The parents and families and friends of the girls the Paynes raped, abused and killed, for a start. That neighbour, Maggie Forrest, who was taken in by Lucy and then betrayed. Maybe even one of the police officers on the case. A friend or relative of Janet Taylor, who was another victim of the whole business. When you get right down to it, lots of people would want her dead, including publicity seekers. Can you imagine the confessions we'll get?"

"So why do you want to go back there?"

"Because I have to. It's the only place to go, and only by going there can I get where I want to be."

"That sounds a bit too mystical to me, like the sound of one hand clapping."

"Well, you've listened to enough Pink Floyd. You ought to know what that sounds like. The thing is, Alan, why I'm here, what I wanted to ask, is can I count on you?"

Banks sighed, took another bite of his burger and washed it down with Tetley's. Then he stared Annie straight in the eye and gave her one of the most guileless looks she'd ever had from him. "Of course you can," he said softly. "You knew that from the start. I'll see if I can arrange a meeting for us with Phil Hartnell and Ken Blackstone in Leeds tomorrow morning."

Annie threw a chip at him. "Then why did you give me such a bloody hard time about it, then?"

Banks smiled. "You wouldn't have had it any other way. Anyway, now you're here, you can tell me about all the interesting things going on in your life these days."

"That's a laugh," said Annie, turning away and twirling her hair with her fingers.

Winsome had never liked working with Templeton. It wasn't because he beat her to sergeant, though that did rankle, but she didn't like his methods, his callous disregard of people's feelings, or the way he kept ogling her. If she was going to take a boyfriend, which she wasn't, Templeton would be the last on her list. But in the meantime they had to work together, so she tried to keep her feelings in check as he prattled on about clubs and DJs she'd never heard of, and hinted at a sexual prowess she wasn't interested in, as he sneaked glances at her thighs and breasts. She knew she could probably report him for sexual harassment, but that sort of thing had a way of coming back at you, especially if you were a woman. You didn't run to the boss and tell tales; you dealt with it yourself.

Winsome had told Banks that she thought he was taking a big risk in sending Templeton to talk to Hayley Daniels's parents. Banks said he knew that, but they were short-staffed, and it would help to have a different perspective. Sometimes, he added cryptically, Templeton's unsavoury and idiosyncratic methods could result in a breakthrough. Winsome remained unconvinced; she'd seen the bastard in action in ways that Banks hadn't. Annie Cabbot would understand, but she wasn't around.

Winsome pulled up outside the Daniels house in Swainshead, once again drawing curious stares from the old men on the bridge.

"What's up with them?" said Templeton. "They act like they've never seen a black woman before."

"They probably hadn't before I came along," Winsome said.

The reporters had gone and the house looked abandoned. It had been only two days since the news of Hayley's death, and already the place seemed shabbier somehow. When Winsome knocked, Geoff Daniels answered. He averted his eyes and appeared embarrassed to see her, as well he might, but he stood aside and let her and Templeton enter. Donna McCarthy was in the living room sitting on an armchair. She looked as if she hadn't slept since Sunday. There was a strained atmosphere, Winsome sensed, though she couldn't tell whether Templeton felt it. Even if he did, in her experience, he would simply ignore it and do what he wanted anyway.

"Any news?" asked Donna, as her husband slumped down in another armchair by the window. Winsome and Templeton took the sofa, and Winsome automatically pulled her skirt down over her knees. If she'd known she was going to be riding out with Templeton this morning, she would have worn trousers. As it was, she'd gone and put on a business-style pinstriped skirt and matching jacket. Already, she could see him eyeing up Donna McCarthy, assessing his chances there.

"Perhaps," said Templeton. "But we've got a few more questions to ask you."

"Oh?" said Donna.

"You told DC Jackman here that you didn't know of any particular boyfriends Hayley had, but that you thought she was sexually active. Am I right?"

Donna twisted her wedding ring. "Well . . . I . . ."

"Is that true, Donna?" Daniels butted in, face red with anger. "You told the police my daughter was some sort of slut?"

"I never said any such thing," said Donna.

"You've got some room to talk," said Templeton to Daniels, "tied to a bed while some young tart bounced up and down on your jollies."

"What's this?" Donna asked, looking at her husband. "What's he talking about?"

"You mean you don't know?" Templeton said, a smirk of disbelief on his face. "He didn't tell you?"

"I didn't think it was –" Winsome began.

"No," Templeton went on, waving her down. "I think she should know."

"Know what?" said Donna. "What are you talking about?"

"When we found your husband, he wasn't at a convention, unless it was a convention of perverts. He was tied to a hotel bed while a naked young lady had her way with him. Our Winsome here got a front-row seat, didn't you, love?"

"You bastard!" said Daniels. "I'll bloody have you for that."

"Is this true, Geoff? Who was she? That little bitch from the office, the one who can't keep her legs closed?"

Winsome rolled her eyes. "Calm down, everyone," she said. "I'm sorry, you'll just have to deal with this between yourselves later. We have more important things to talk about. And no one implied that your daughter was promiscuous, Mr. Daniels."

"She was innocent," Daniels said. "Innocent. A victim. Do you both get that?"

Winsome nodded, but she could see that Templeton was rallying for another attack. Not a good sign. "Of course," Templeton began. "And I'm sorry if I implied in any way that your late daughter was the town bicycle. That wasn't my intention. The point is that it has come to our attention that she might have had a secret boyfriend. We were wondering if you could shed any light on this."

"What boyfriend? Who said that?" said Daniels.

"It doesn't matter who said it," Templeton replied. "Is it true?"

"How would we know?" said Donna, still glaring at her husband. "If she kept it secret."

"What do you think?" Templeton asked. "Were there any signs, any unexplained absences, any occasions she wouldn't say where she was going, any nights she didn't come home?"

"She sometimes stayed with friends from college if she went into Eastvale for a night out."

"I know," said Templeton. "She didn't want to drive because she set out to get paralytic. Do you know that people can lose all sense of judgment when they're that pissed?"

"I don't think Hayley drank that much," said Donna. "She was just having fun with her mates."

"Come off it," said Templeton. "She was so bladdered on Saturday she went off into the Maze alone for a piss. You can't tell me that's using good judgment."

Donna started sobbing and Daniels lurched forward to make a grab for Templeton's jacket collar, shouting, "How can you talk about our daughter like that, you filthy heartless bastard?"

"Gerroff!" said Templeton, pushing him away and straightening his jacket.

Wonderful, thought Winsome, regretting that Daniels hadn't managed to land a good punch, another shambles of a Templeton interview. How on earth did such an insensitive pillock make sergeant in this day and age? She stepped into the breach. "Let's all calm down. DS Templeton might not always be diplomatic in his approach, but he has raised some serious questions, and any answers you give may help us catch Hayley's killer. Do either of you know anything about a boyfriend?"

They both shook their heads, Daniels glaring at Templeton the whole time and Donna looking as if she was ready to kill both of them.

"Well, somebody must know something," Templeton said. "Surely you didn't just let her run wild and do whatever she wanted?"

"She was nineteen, Mr. Templeton," said Donna. "You can't control a nineteen-year-old?"

"Did she never let anything slip?" Winsome asked. "Or didn't you notice any signs, woman to woman?"

"You're making me feel guilty now," Donna said, reaching for a tissue. "You're saying I should have paid more attention and it might not have happened."

"That's not true," Winsome said. "You shouldn't blame yourself. There's only one person responsible for what happened to Hayley, and that's the killer."

"But maybe if I'd just . . . I don't know . . . been there."

"Did you know she carried condoms in her handbag?" Templeton asked.

"No, I didn't," said Donna. "I never went through Hayley's handbag."

Daniels glanced over at Templeton in disgust.

"Does it surprise you?" Templeton asked.

"No," said Donna. "She knew if she was going to do anything she had to be careful. They all do these days."

"If she kept the boyfriend a secret," Winsome said, "we're wondering what the reason is. Perhaps he was an older man? Perhaps he was married?"

"I still can't tell you anything," said Donna.

Templeton turned to Daniels. "You've had some experience in that department, haven't you?" he said. "Shagging Martina Redfern while Hayley was getting herself killed? Like them young, do you? Maybe it's you we should be looking at a lot more closely."

If he expected to get a further rise out of Daniels, Winsome thought, he'd lost that one. Daniels sat there, spent and miserable. "I've made my mistakes," he said. "Plenty of them. And I only hope Donna can find it in her heart to forgive me. But my mistakes aren't going to help you catch my daughter's killer. Now, if you can't do anything except sit there and try to stir things up, why don't you just get up off your arse and start doing your job?"

"We are trying to do our jobs, sir," Winsome said, surprising herself that she was coming to Templeton's defence. But to defend the interview, she had to defend Templeton. She vowed she would never let anyone put her in this position again, no matter what they said. "Did she ever talk about any of her lecturers at college, for example?" she asked.

"Sometimes," said Donna. "But I didn't know them, so it never meant much to me."

"Was there any one in particular?"

"Austin," said Daniels suddenly. "Malcolm Austin. Remember, Donna, that bloke that led the class trip to Paris last April?"

"Yes," said Donna. "She mentioned him a few times. But that was her favourite class. I don't think there was . . . I mean . . ."

"Have you met him?" Winsome asked.

"No," said Donna. "We haven't met any of them. When she was at school we met her teachers, like, but when they're at college, I mean, you don't, do you?"

"So you don't know how old he is, whether he's married or anything?"

"Sorry," said Donna. "Can't help you there. You asked if she ever mentioned anyone and that was the only one."

"Romantic city, Paris," said Templeton, buffing his fingernails on his thigh the way a cricketer rubs the ball.

Winsome got to her feet. "Well, thanks," she said. "It's a start. We'll have a word with Mr. Austin."

Templeton remained seated, and his lack of movement was making Winsome nervous. She knew that he outranked her, so he should be the one to give the signal to leave, but she was so intent on damage control and getting out of there that she hadn't really thought about that. Finally, he stood up slowly, gave Daniels a long, lingering look and said, "We'll be talking to you again soon, mate." Then he took out his card and pointedly handed it to Donna, who was contemplating her husband as a matador contemplates a bull. "If you think of anything else, love," Templeton said, "don't hesitate to ring me, day or night."

When they got outside to the car, he grabbed Winsome's arm and leaned so close to her that she could smell the spearmint chewing gum on his breath and said, "Don't you *ever* do that to me again."

"There won't be any again," Winsome said, surprised at her own vehemence. Then she jerked her arm free and surprised herself even more by saying, "And take your fucking hands off me. Sir."

Banks was glad to get home at a reasonable hour on Tuesday, though he was still preoccupied with what Annie had told him about Lucy Payne's murder. He had watched Brough's Eastern Area press conference in the station that afternoon, and now Lucy Payne and the murders at 35 The Hill, or the House of Payne, as one newspaper had dubbed it at the time, were all over the news again.

Banks put Maria Muldaur's *Heart of Mine* on the CD player and peered out of his front window as he tried to decide whether to warm up the lamb korma or try another Marks and Spencer's chicken Kiev. Maria was singing Dylan's "Buckets of Rain," but the weather had improved considerably. The sun was going down and streaks of vermilion, magenta and crimson shot through the western sky, casting light on the fast-flowing Gratly Beck, so that at moments it seemed like a dark, swirling oil slick. Next weekend they would be putting the clocks ahead, and it would be light until late in the evening.

In the end, he made himself a ham-and-cheese sandwich and poured a glass of Peter Lehmann Shiraz. The main sound system was in the extension, along with the plasma TV, but he had set up speakers in the kitchen and in the front room, where he would sometimes sit and read or work on the computer. The couch was comfortable, the shaded lamps cozy, and the peat fire useful on cool winter evenings. He didn't need it tonight, but he decided to eat his dinner in there anyway and read the notes he had brought home with him from the office. He had got both Ken Blackstone and Phil Hartnell to agree to a meeting in Leeds the following morning. Annie was staying over at her cottage in Harkside that night, and he was due to pick her up there at half past nine in the morning. But before that, he needed to do his homework.

In a way, though, he already knew his subject. He didn't have to read the files to know their names: Kimberley Myers, aged fifteen, failed to return home from a school dance one Friday night; Kelly Diane Matthews, aged seventeen, went missing during a New Year's Eve party in Roundhay Park, Leeds; Samantha Jane Foster, eighteen years old, disappeared on her way home from a poetry reading at a pub near the University of Bradford; Leanne Wray, sixteen, vanished on a ten-minute walk between a pub and her parents' house in Eastvale; Melissa Horrocks, seventeen, failed to return home from a pop concert in Harrogate. Five young girls, all victims of Terence Payne (who came to be called the Chameleon) and, many people believed, also of his wife, Lucy Payne (who later became the notorious Friend of the Devil).

Two police officers on routine patrol had been called to the Payne house in west Leeds after a neighbour reported hearing sounds of an argument. There they found Lucy Payne unconscious in the hall, the apparent victim of an attack by her husband. In the cellar, Terence Payne had set upon the officers with a machete and killed PC Dennis Morrisey. Morrisey's partner, PC Janet Taylor, had managed to get in several blows with her nightstick, and she didn't stop hitting Terence Payne until he was no longer moving, no longer a threat. He subsequently died of his injuries.

Banks was called to the cellar, where the local police had found the body of Kimberley Myers bound naked and dead on a mattress surrounded by candles, her body slashed around the breasts and genitals. The other girls were found dismembered and buried in the next room, and post-mortems discovered them to have been similarly tortured. What Banks remembered most, apart from the smell, was the way their toes stuck up through the earth like tiny mushrooms. Sometimes he had nightmares about that time he had spent in the cellar at 35 The Hill.

He thought about his conversation with Annie that afternoon and decided that he had definitely been on the defensive. He remembered Lucy Payne best as she was the first time he had seen her in her hospital bed, when she hadn't been quite as beautiful as some of the photographs the newspapers printed. Half her face had been covered in bandages, her long hair had been spread out like a raven's wing on the pillow under her head, and the one good eye that stared at him with unnerving directness was as black as her hair.

Naturally, she had denied any involvement in or knowledge of her husband's crimes. When Banks had talked to her, he had sensed her striding always one step ahead, or aside, anticipating the questions, preparing her answers and the requisite emotions of regret and pain, but never of guilt. She had been, by turns, vulnerable or brazen, victim or willing sexual deviant. Her history, when it came out, recounted a childhood of unimaginable horrors in a remote coastal house, where the children of two families had been subjected to ritual sexual abuse by their parents until the social workers pounced one day amid rumours of Satanic rites.

Banks got up and poured another glass of wine. It was going down far too well. As he drank, he thought of the people he had encountered during the Chameleon investigation, from the parents of the victims to neighbours and schoolfriends of some of the girls. There was even a teacher who had come briefly under suspicion, a friend of Payne's called Geoffrey Brighouse. It was a large cast, but at least it would give Annie and her team somewhere to start.

Thinking of the Paynes' victims, Banks's mind drifted to Hayley Daniels. He couldn't let this new case of Annie's interfere with the investigation. He owed Hayley that much. With any luck, by the time he got back from Leeds tomorrow, some of the lab results would have started to trickle in, and between them, Wilson and Templeton would have talked to most of the friends Hayley was with on Saturday night and interviewed the possible boyfriend, Malcolm Austin.

Banks knew he had made a mistake in putting Winsome and Templeton together on the Daniels-McCarthy interview. He could tell from the atmosphere when the two returned to the station that it hadn't gone well. Neither would talk to him about it, he knew, though he sensed there was obviously more than Templeton's overactive libido behind it.

The problem was that Banks knew he had been right in what he told Annie: Templeton *could* be a good copper, and sometimes what made him one was his brusqueness and his disregard of the rules of common decency. But he also knew that when he had had to rethink whether there was room for someone like Templeton on the team, especially with Winsome progressing so well, he had decided that there wasn't. The transfer, then, was a good idea.

Banks tried to clear Lucy Payne and Hayley Daniels out of his mind. Maria Muldaur came to the end of "You Ain't Goin' Nowhere," so he went to put on a new CD. He decided on the Bill Evans *Half Moon Bay* concert, one he had always wished he had attended. After Evans introduced his bass player and drummer came the delightful "Waltz for Debby." It was still early, and Banks decided to spend the rest of the evening at home listening to the jazz collection that he was slowly rebuilding and reading *Postwar*. He was deeply into the Cold War and

"What Are You Doing the Rest of Your Life?" by the time he noticed that his glass was empty for the second time.

It seemed like ages since Annie had been to a restaurant in Eastvale, and she was glad that she had accepted Winsome's invitation, even though she knew it wouldn't be an entirely work-free evening. The Italian place they had picked above the shops built onto the back of the church in the market square was excellent: plenty of vegetarian choices and decent cheap plonk. She tucked into her pasta primavera and second glass of Chianti – feeling just a little guilty, but not too much, for not lasting longer on the wagon – while Winsome ate cannelloni and went full speed ahead in her verbal assault on Templeton.

"So you told him what you thought?" Annie said, the first opening she got.

"I told him."

"And what did he say?"

"Nothing. Not a word. I think he was so shocked that I swore at him. I mean, *I* was so shocked I swore at him. I *never* swear." She put her hand over her mouth and laughed. Annie laughed with her.

"Don't worry," Annie said. "Insults are like water off a duck's back with Templeton. He'll be back to normal tomorrow, or what passes for normal in his case."

"I'm not sure I want that," said Winsome. "Really. I mean it this time. One of us has to go. I can't work with him again, watch the way he tramples all over people's feelings. I don't know if I can wait for his transfer to come through."

"Look," said Annie, "nobody ever said being a copper was easy. Sometimes you have to play dirty, tough it out. Be patient and hang in there."

"I can't believe you're doing this," Winsome said. "You're *defending* him."

"I'm not bloody defending him," said Annie. "I'm just trying to tell you that if you want to survive in this job you have to toughen up, that's all."

"You don't think I'm strong enough?"

"You need to develop a thicker skin."

"You don't think black skin is thicker than white?"

"What?" said Annie.

"You heard me. How do you think I deal with all the innuendos and outright insults? People either look down on you, or they go out of their way to pretend they don't notice your colour, that you're really just like anybody else, but they end up talking to you like they talk to children. I don't know which is worse. Do you know what it's like to have someone stare at you or insult you like some sort of lesser being, an *animal*, just because of the colour of your skin? Like Hayley Daniels's father, or those old men on the bridge at Swainshead."

"I don't know about Hayley Daniels's father," said Annie, "but those old men don't know any better. I know it's no excuse, but they don't. And I might not know how it feels to have people look at me that way because of the colour of my skin, but I do know how it feels when they treat me like a lesser species because I'm a woman."

"Then double it!" said Winsome.

Annie looked at her, and they both started laughing so loudly an elderly couple sitting nearby frowned at them. "Oh, what the hell," said Annie, raising her glass. "Here's to kicking against the pricks."

They clinked glasses. Annie's mobile rang and she pulled it out of her handbag. "Yes?"

"Annie? It's Eric."

"Eric. What the hell do you want?"

"That's not very nice."

"I told you not to ring me on my mobile. I'm having dinner with a colleague."

"Male or female?"

"That's none of your bloody business."

"Okay. Okay. Sorry. Just asking. Look, I was thinking about you, and I thought, Why wait till Thursday? You're obviously busy tonight, but what about tomorrow? Wednesday. Lunch?"

"I have to go to Leeds tomorrow," Annie said, wondering why she was even bothering to tell Eric this. "And I told you I'm not coming on Thursday."

"Thursday it is, then," said Eric. "Sorry to bother you." And he ended the call.

Annie shoved her mobile back in her handbag.

"Something wrong?" asked Winsome.

Annie ground her teeth, then took a deep breath and a swallow of wine. She looked at Winsome, weighed up the pros and cons and said, "Yes, I think there is. With me. Let's order another bottle of wine and I'll tell you all the sordid details."

The waitress came with the Chianti. Winsome finished her cannelloni and rested her elbows on the table. Annie poured them both a generous glass.

"Come on, then," Winsome said. "Do tell."

"It's nothing, really," Annie said, feeling embarrassed and awkward now the time had come.

"You seemed annoyed enough on the phone. Who was it?"

"It's just . . . well, you know, the other night, Saturday night, I went out on the town with some friends." She touched her hair and laughed. "As much as you can go out on the town in a place like Whitby."

"What happened?"

"Well, I met this bloke and . . . one thing led to another. I had way too much to drink and we smoked a couple of joints and to cut a long story short, the next morning I woke up in his bed."

"You did what?"

"You heard me. I met this bloke and went back to his place."

"And you slept with him?"

"Well . . . yes."

"This was the first time you'd met him?"

"Yes. Winsome . . . what is it?"

"Nothing." Winsome shook her head. "Go on."

Annie took a long swig of wine. "He turned out to be a bit younger than I probably realized at first, and –"

"How young?"

Annie shrugged. "Dunno. Twenty-two, twenty-three, around there."

Winsome's eyes widened. "A boy! You picked up a *boy* in a bar and slept with him?"

"Don't be so naive. These things do happen, you know."

"Not to me, they don't."

"Well, you're obviously not going to the right bars."

"That's not what I mean and you know it. I'm serious. I would *never* go home with *anyone* I met in a bar, and I would certainly never go home with someone so young."

"But Winsome, you're only thirty!"

Winsome's eyes blazed. "And I would *still* never go to bed with a twenty-two-year-old. And you . . . how could you do that? It's sick. You must be old enough to be his mother."

"Winsome, lighten up. People are starting to look at us. Maybe if I'd had a baby when I was eighteen I could be his mother, okay? But I didn't, so cut the Oedipus shit."

"That's not what I'm talking about."

"I never knew you were such a prude."

"I am not a prude. You don't have to be a prude to have —"

"To have what? What's your point?"

"Moral standards. It's not right."

"Oh, moral standards is it, now? Not right?" Annie drank more wine. She was starting to feel dizzy and more than a touch angry. "Well, let me tell you what you can do with your moral standards, little miss high and mighty, you can shove them —"

"Don't say that!"

Annie stopped. There was something in Winsome's tone that caused her to back off. The two of them shuffled in their seats a while, eyeing one another. Annie poured herself some more wine. "I thought you were my friend," she said finally. "I didn't expect you to go all judgmental on me."

"I'm not being judgmental. I'm just shocked, that's all."

"What's the big deal? That's not the point of the story, anyway, his age or having a one-night stand or smoking a couple of joints, or whatever seems to have put that hair up your arse."

"Don't talk to me like that."

Annie held her hand up. "Fine, fine. I can see this isn't working. Another bad idea. Let's just pay the bill and go."

"You haven't finished your wine."

Annie picked up her glass and drained it. "You can have the rest of the bottle," she said, dropping a twenty-pound note on the table. "And you can keep the fucking change."

The sound of a car screeching to a halt in front of his cottage around half past nine startled Banks. He wasn't expecting anyone. The only person who usually dropped by on spec was his son, Brian, but he was supposed to be rehearsing in London with his new band. Well, it was the same band, really, the Blue Lamps, but they had replaced Brian's songwriting partner and fellow guitarist. Their sound had changed a little, but from the couple of demos Brian had played him, Banks thought the new guitarist was better than the one he replaced. The songwriting remained an issue, but Banks was certain Brian would come through, carry the burden.

By the time the knock at the door came, Banks was already there, and when he opened it, he was surprised to see Annie Cabbot standing there.

"Sorry it's so late," she said. "Can I come in?"

Banks stood back. "Of course. Anything wrong?"

"Wrong? No, why should there be anything wrong? Can't I drop in on an old friend when I feel like it?" As she walked in she stumbled against him slightly, and he took her arm. She looked at him and smiled lopsidedly. He let go.

"Of course you can," said Banks, puzzled by her manner and discomfited by being so jarringly dragged away from his evening alone with the book, wine and music. Bill Evans had given way to John Coltrane some time ago, and the tenor sax improvised away in the background, flinging out those famous sheets of sound. He knew it would take him a few moments to adjust to having company. "Drink?" he said.

"Lovely," said Annie, flinging off her jacket. It landed on the computer monitor. "I'll have what you're having."

Banks went into the kitchen and filled up a glass of wine for Annie and one more for himself, emptying the bottle. Annie leaned against the door jamb as he handed her the drink. "Is that all that's left?" she said.

"I've got another bottle."

"Good."

She was definitely unsteady on her feet, Banks thought, as he followed her back through to the living room and she flopped down on the armchair.

"So what brings you here?" he asked.

Annie drank some wine. "That's nice," she said. "What? Oh, nothing. Like I said, just a friendly visit. I was having dinner with Winsome in Eastvale and I just thought, you know, it's not far away."

"Eastvale's quite a drive from here."

"You're not insinuating I've had too much to drink, are you?"

"No. I –"

"Good, then." Annie held up her glass. "Cheers."

"Cheers," said Banks. "What did Winsome have to say?"

"Oh, just stuff. Boring stuff. That arsehole Templeton."

"I heard that the interview with Hayley's parents didn't go well."

"Well, it wouldn't, would it? What could you have been thinking of, putting those two together? What can you be thinking of even having him in the station?"

"Annie, I don't really want to discuss –"

Annie waved her hand in the air. "No. I know. Of course not. I don't, either. That's not why I came. Let's just forget about bloody Templeton and Winsome, shall we?"

"Fine with me."

"How about you, Alan? How are *you* doing? Julia Ford asked after you, you know. She's very attractive in a lawyerly sort of way. Don't you think?"

"I never really thought about her that way."

"Liar. What's the music?"

"John Coltrane?"

"It sounds weird."

Banks made to get up. "I'll put something else on if you like."

"No, no. Sit down. I didn't say I didn't like it, just that it sounded weird. I don't mind weird sometimes. In fact I quite like it." She gave him an odd smile and emptied her glass. "Oops, it looks as if we might need more wine, after all."

"That was quick," said Banks. He went into the kitchen to open another bottle, wondering what the hell he should do about Annie. He shouldn't really give her any more wine; she had clearly had enough already. But she wouldn't react well to being told that. There was always the spare room, if that was what it came to. That was what he decided upon.

Back in the living room, Annie had settled in the armchair with her legs tucked under her. It wasn't often she wore a skirt but she was wearing one today, and the material had creased up, exposing half her thighs. Banks handed her the glass. She smiled at him.

"Do you miss me?" she asked.

"We all miss you," Banks said. "When are you coming back?"

"No, I don't mean that, silly. I mean do *you* miss me?"

"Of course I do," said Banks.

"Of course I do," Annie echoed. "What do you think of toyboys?"

"Pardon?"

"You heard me."

"Yes, but I don't really know what you mean."

"Toyboys. You know what they are, don't you? Toyboys don't make good lovers, you know."

"No, I don't know." Banks tried to remember when he was a young boy. He had probably been a lousy lover. He probably was a lousy lover even now, if truth be told. If he wasn't, maybe he would have more luck finding and keeping a woman. Still, chance would be a fine thing; it would be nice to have the opportunity for more practice now and then.

"Oh, Alan," she said. "What shall I do with you?"

The next thing he knew, she was beside him on the sofa. He could feel her thighs warm against him and her breath in his ear. He could smell red wine and garlic. She rubbed her breasts against his arm and tried to kiss his lips, but he turned away.

"What's wrong?" she said.

"I don't know," said Banks. "It just doesn't feel right, that's all."

"Don't you want me?"

"You know I want you. I never didn't want you."

Annie started fumbling with the buttons of her blouse. "Then take me," she said, moving close again and breathing fast. "Men always want it, don't they, no matter what?"

Again, Banks backed off. "Not like this," he said.

"What do you mean?"

"You've been drinking."

"So?" She went back to the buttons. He could see the black lacy line of her bra and soft mounds of flesh beneath. "Not another bloody prude, are you?"

"Look," Banks said, "It's not –"

Annie put a finger to his lips. "Shhh."

He moved away. She gave him a puzzled glance. "What's wrong?"

"I've told you what's wrong," he said. "This just doesn't feel right, that's all. I don't believe you really want to do this, either. I don't know what's going on."

Annie moved away and quickly tried to fasten up the buttons. Her face was flushed and angry. "What do you mean, it doesn't feel right?" she said. "What's wrong with me? Am I too fat? Not pretty enough? Are my breasts not firm enough? Am I not attractive enough? Not good enough for you?"

"It's not any of those things," said Banks. "It's –"

"Or is it you? Because I have to wonder, you know," Annie went on, getting to her feet and reaching for her jacket and handbag, stumbling as she did so. "I really do have to wonder about a man like you. I mean, do you have so much going on in your miserable little life that you can afford to reject me? Do you, Alan? Do you have some pretty, young twenty-two-year-old girl hidden away somewhere? Is that it? Am I too old for you?"

"I told you. It's not any of those things. I –"

But it was too late. Banks just heard her say, "Oh, fuck you, Alan. Or not, as the case may be." Then she slammed the door behind her. When he got outside she was already starting the car. He knew he should try to stop her, that she was drunk, but he didn't know how, short of trying to drag her out of the driver's seat or throwing himself in front of the wheels. In her mood, she would probably run him over. Instead, he listened to the gears grate and watched her back out in a spray of gravel at an alarming speed. Then he heard the gears screech again, and she was off down the lane through Gratly.

Banks stood there, heart pounding, wondering what the hell was going on. When he went back inside Coltrane was just getting started on "My Favourite Things."

7

Malcolm Austin's office was tucked away in a corner of the travel and tourism department, located in a large old Victorian house on the fringes of the campus. Eastvale College had expanded over the past few years, and the squat 1960s brick-and-glass buildings were no longer big enough to house all the departments. Instead of putting up more faceless new blocks, the college authorities had bought up some of the surrounding land, including streets of old houses, and revitalized southeast Eastvale. Now it was a thriving area with popular pubs, coffee shops, cheap cafés and Indian restaurants, student flats and bedsits. The college even got decent bands to play in its new auditorium, and there was talk of the Blue Lamps making an appearance there to kick off their next tour.

Austin's office was on the first floor, and when Winsome knocked, he opened the door for her himself. It was a cozy room with a high, ornate ceiling and broad sash windows. In the bookcase were a lot of travel guides to various countries, some of them very old indeed, and on the wall was a poster of the Blue Mosque in Istanbul. Against one wall stood a battered old sofa with scuffed black-leather upholstery. The only window looked over a flagstone courtyard, where students sat at wooden tables between the trees eating sandwiches, talking and drinking coffee in the spring sunshine. It made Winsome yearn for her own student days.

Austin was about fifty, with his grey hair worn fashionably long and tied in a ponytail at the back. He also had a deep tan, probably one of the perks of the business, Winsome thought. He wore a loose blue cable-knit jumper and faded jeans torn at the knees. He kept himself in shape, and was attractive in a lanky, rangy sort of way, with a strong jaw, straight nose and large Adam's apple. Winsome noticed that he wasn't wearing a wedding ring. Austin pulled out a chair for her and sat behind his small, untidy desk.

Winsome first thanked Austin for agreeing to talk to her so early in the morning.

"That's all right," he said. "My first class is at ten o'clock, and I'm afraid my Wednesdays just get worse after that." His smile was engaging, and his teeth seemed well cared for. "It's about Hayley Daniels, isn't it?"

"Yes."

A frown creased his broad forehead. "It's a terrible tragedy. Such a bright girl."

"She was?" Winsome realized she knew nothing about Hayley's academic life.

"Oh, yes. Not just the written work, mind you. She had the personality for the job, too. You need personality in the travel business."

"I'm sure," said Winsome. "Do you know of any boyfriends or anyone on campus Hayley might have been involved with?"

Austin scratched his head. "I honestly can't say. She seemed a very gregarious type, always hanging out with a group rather than any particular individual. I think she enjoyed the attention."

"Do you know of anyone who disliked her?"

"Not enough to kill her."

"What do you mean?"

"Perhaps some of the other girls envied her her figure and her good looks, her easygoing manner, even her good marks. There is a school of thought that maintains you shouldn't have it all – brains *and* beauty. Perhaps some of the boys resented the fact that they couldn't have her."

"Stuart Kinsey?"

"He's one example that comes immediately to mind. He was always hanging around her, drooling. It was pretty obvious he was carrying a torch for her. But Stuart wouldn't harm a soul. He'd probably just go home and write sad love poems."

"What was *your* relationship with Hayley?"

Austin looked puzzled. "Relationship? I was her tutor. I marked her essays, she attended my lectures. I helped supervise her work experience, advised her on career paths, that sort of thing."

"Work experience?"

"Oh, yes. It's not just an academic course, you know. Students get the chance to work with travel agents and for airlines, sometimes even as overseas representatives and guides. I was trying to get Hayley a temporary position as a yellow shirt with Swan Hellenic, but I'm afraid they've lost their ship to Carnival, so things are a bit up in the air."

Winsome paused and crossed her legs. She was wearing jeans today – good ones – because she wasn't going to make the same mistake as yesterday, though the likelihood of her being paired with Templeton again was slim to nonexistent. "Hayley was a very attractive girl," she said.

"I suppose she was," said Austin. "There are a lot of attractive girls around the college, or hadn't you noticed?"

"But maybe Hayley was your type?"

"What on earth do you mean? Are you asking if we were having an affair?"

"Were you?"

"No, we were not. She was nineteen, for crying out loud."

Yes, Winsome thought, and Annie Cabbot's latest conquest was twenty-two. Only three years difference. *So what?* she almost said. "Are you married?"

Austin hesitated before saying, "I was. Twenty years. We separated four months ago. Irreconcilable differences."

"I'm sorry to hear that," said Winsome.

"These things happen. We'd been drifting apart for some time."

Marriage and a girl's age were the two things that never made much difference to most men, Winsome remembered from the number of passes she had evaded when she worked at the hotel. "Weren't you ever tempted?" she asked. "All those pretty young girls around, hanging on your every word. Surely they develop crushes on you sometimes? It's only natural, you being a teacher and all."

"You learn to deal with it."

Winsome paused, then asked, "Would you mind telling me where you were on Saturday night?"

"Am I a suspect?"

"If you wouldn't mind, sir."

"All right." Austin glared at her. "I was at home."

"Where's that?"

"Raglan Road."

"Near the town centre?"

"Yes. Not far."

"You didn't go out at all?"

"I went to the Mitre on York Road for a couple of pints between about nine and ten."

"Anyone see you?"

"The usual locals."

"Then what?"

"I went back home. There was nothing that interested me on TV, so I watched a DVD."

"What DVD?"

"*Chinatown*."

"An oldie."

"They're often the best. Film happens to be one of my passions. When it came to a career, it was a toss-up between that and the travel business. I suppose I chose the more practical course."

"But you didn't go into the market square?"

"On a Saturday night? Do you think I'm crazy?" Austin laughed. "I value my life more than that."

Winsome smiled. "We do have a bit of a problem, you see, sir. We know that Hayley wasn't expected home on Saturday, and she wasn't planning on going to the Bar None with her friends. She had somewhere mysterious to go, and nobody seems to know where it was."

"Well, I'm afraid I can't help you there."

"Are you sure she wasn't coming to see you?"

"Why would she do that? And why would I want a drunk and immature teenager in my house?"

Winsome could think of plenty of reasons, most of which would make her blush to say out loud, but she decided it was best to leave Austin to think of them himself. Instead, she ended the interview and walked out of the office, making a mental note of her reservations. She wasn't at all certain that she believed him about his relationship with Hayley, but without evidence there wasn't much she could do.

As she walked down the stairs, a skinny, long-haired male student she vaguely recognized was on his way up. He paused as they passed one another and glanced at her in an odd way. At first she thought it was because of her colour. She got that all the time, especially in a place like Eastvale that wasn't exactly high in its immigrant population. Only when she had reached the street did she realize it was something else. Recognition? Fear? Guilt? He had been one of the people with Hayley in the market square just before she disappeared down Taylor's Yard. Winsome was certain of it. One of the people DC Wilson hadn't traced and talked to yet, as far as she knew.

Banks was running late. He dressed hurriedly after his shower, went downstairs, grabbed his travel mug of coffee and jumped into the Porsche. Once he was on the unfenced road crossing the desolate moors, he plugged in his iPod. The shuffle started with Neko Case's "That Teenage Feeling." He checked the dashboard clock and realized he should make it to Annie's by half past nine, barring no unforeseen traffic problems when he hit the A roads.

He still felt stunned and puzzled by her behaviour of the previous evening. He had half expected a phone call of apology, and had stayed up late waiting, drinking more wine and listening to Miles Davis's *Bitches Brew*. But she didn't ring. When he called her number, the answering service kicked in; same with her mobile. He hoped she hadn't got into an accident or anything. He had even thought of calling the station when she drove away, but that was too much like telling tales on a friend. Annie could handle herself in a car, even after a few drinks. If she got done for drink driving, there'd be hell to pay in her career. He just hoped she had got home without incident, and that was the simple message he had left on her home phone.

When he got to Harkside and knocked on her door a couple of minutes early, he got no answer. He glanced up the street, where she usually parked her purple Astra, and saw it wasn't there. That worried him, but he assured himself that if anything had happened to her, an accident or something, it would have been on the local news that morning, and it hadn't been. Which meant that more than likely she had wanted to avoid travelling with him and had driven off by herself.

Feeling angry and resentful, Banks headed for the A1. Neil Young followed Neko Case – a blistering "Like a Hurricane" from *Live Rust*, which matched his mood. By the time he negotiated the traffic on the Inner Ringroad, parked and got to the office in "fortress" Millgarth, the Leeds city centre police station off Eastgate, he was six minutes late and Annie was sitting in Hartnell's office cool as anything with DI Ken Blackstone and Area Commander Phil Hartnell himself, who had been in overall charge of the Chameleon investigation six years ago.

"Sorry I'm late," Banks said, easing into a vacant chair. Annie avoided looking at him. Her eyes seemed swollen, he noticed, as if she had been crying or was allergic to something.

"That's all right, Alan," said Hartnell. "We hadn't really got down to business yet. Tea? Biscuits?" He gestured to the tray sitting on his desk.

"Thanks." Banks helped himself to tea and a couple of chocolate digestives.

Hartnell perched at the edge of his desk. "DI Cabbot was just bringing us up to speed on her investigation."

Banks glanced at Annie again. She still wouldn't meet his eyes. "Right," he said. "Well, it's DI Cabbot's case. I'm here merely to help out with the Chameleon angle."

"As are we all, Alan. As are we all," said Hartnell.

He had filled out over the past six years, as if he had stopped working out regularly, let himself go to seed. His hairline was receding, too. Age gets to us all eventually, Banks realized, and sooner than we expect, remembering when he had first noticed his own hair starting to grey at the temples. It'll be bloody liver spots next, he thought gloomily, and prostate cancer. That reminded him of the doctor's appointment he hadn't rescheduled. It was getting closer.

"You were saying about the pathologist's report?" Hartnell, still perching, said to Annie.

"Yes, sir," Annie said. "The post-mortem didn't really tell us anything we didn't know already. The pathologist repeated that it's often hard to tell handedness from slash injuries, but seemed to favour a left to right motion, considering pressure and depth of the wound. That gives us a right-handed killer, most likely. Again, he couldn't commit himself to the actual weapon used but stressed that it was extremely sharp, and an old-fashioned straight razor or some sort of scalpel were the most likely possibilities. Other than that, Lucy was, as we thought, a quadriplegic. In her case, that meant she couldn't move or speak. As for time of death, that was fixed at between half past eight and half past ten in the morning. As we know she left Mapston Hall at half past nine and was found at a quarter past ten, we can narrow that down quite a bit."

Hartnell went behind his desk and sat down. "So what exactly can we help you with?" he asked Annie.

"It's mostly a matter of names," Annie said. "The people at Mapston Hall said Karen – sorry, Lucy – had no visitors other than the mysterious 'Mary' who picked her up on Sunday morning at half past nine and, in all likelihood, killed her. It appears that nobody saw her car, and we can't get a decent description of her because they were busy and no one really noticed her apart from one staff member." Annie took an envelope from her briefcase and passed photocopied sheets of paper to everyone. When it came to Banks, he snatched his copy from her childishly. Annie ignored him. "This is the artist's impression worked out with Mel Danvers, Lucy's carer. As you can see, it's not a lot of use."

It certainly wasn't, Banks thought, studying the figure in the rain hat, glasses and a long baggy coat, face in shadow except for a vague sense of thin lips and an oval chin. "It seems as if she deliberately wanted to obscure her appearance," he said.

Annie said nothing.

"True enough," Hartnell agreed.

"Yes, sir," Annie said to him. "She didn't really need all that gear. It had been raining at the time, but it was clearing up by then. Mel also said she got the vague impression the woman was about forty."

"Are you working on the assumption that whoever killed Lucy Payne knew her real identity?" Hartnell asked, after examining the drawing and putting it aside.

"It seems a reasonable assumption to make at the moment, sir," Annie said. "Otherwise, what are we left with?"

"I see your point," said Hartnell. "Given that Karen Drew hadn't existed for very long, it would have been rather odd if someone wanted to kill her, unless the whole thing was random, someone who just wanted to kill a helpless victim in a wheelchair for the hell of it."

"Yes, sir," said Annie.

"Not entirely out of the question," said Blackstone, "but perhaps the most unlikely scenario."

"Exactly," Annie agreed. "Especially now we know who she really was."

Banks watched her as she spoke. She was focused on the job, but he knew it was costing her an effort, as was not looking at him. It was as if she were straining against powerful forces trying to turn her in another direction. Her jaw was set tight, and a tiny muscle twitched now and then under her left eye. He wished he could just put his arms around her and tell her everything would be okay, but whatever the problem was, he knew it went way beyond a simple hug.

"Which, I suppose," Hartnell went on, "brings us to the question of how many people knew that Karen Drew was really Lucy Payne."

"Yes, sir." Annie opened one of the folders she had brought with her. "Julia Ford gave us to believe that only she and a couple of other members of her law firm knew, including Constance Wells, of course, who handled Lucy's affairs."

"Well, she would say that, wouldn't she?" said Banks. "Julia Ford isn't going to take any responsibility for what happened to Lucy Payne."

"Certainly there were doctors and administrators at the hospital who knew," Annie went on as if Banks hadn't spoken. Ken Blackstone noticed and gave him a querying glance. Banks gave a small shake of his head in return. *Later.*

"What about Mapston Hall?" Hartnell asked.

"Julia Ford said not, and it was certainly in everyone's best interest to keep it quiet, but it's always possible someone there knew the truth."

"Could anyone simply have recognized her?" Blackstone asked.

"That's a difficult one, Ken," said Annie. "The short answer is, I don't think so. She was only twenty-eight, but she appeared to be well into her forties. Her hair was different, shorter, mostly grey, and it had lost its sheen. Her face was puffy and her figure . . . well, she'd become rather shapeless, lumpy. I doubt that anyone who had seen her six years ago would recognize her today. No, it's my guess they'd have to have known who she was by some other means."

"And we also have to contend with the fact that anyone who did know might have told someone else," Blackstone said.

"Yes, unfortunately," Annie agreed.

"Did any of the people at hospital or at Mapston have any connection with the Chameleon case?" Hartnell asked. "With the victims or their families?"

"A good question, sir, and that's what we're checking into right now," said Annie. "As yet, we haven't found anything, but it's early days."

Hartnell clapped his hands. "Right," he said. "I'm afraid you're going to have a long list from me, DI Cabbot."

"Better that than no ideas at all," said Annie.

Hartnell handed her a sheet of paper and passed copies to Banks and Blackstone. "I've made out a list of all the major players in the Chameleon case," he said. "As you can see, I've also included the families of the victims. In some cases, the husbands and wives have separated since then. In three cases, actually. It's not unusual that such a tragic event can tear apart an entire family. The Myers family, parents of the last victim, lived just down the hill from the Paynes, and they moved away down south very quickly. I believe they're in Devon now. Can't say I blame them. Anyway, there were certainly plenty of angry relatives when Lucy Payne got off. There's also Payne's friend, Maggie Forrest, though I believe she returned to Canada after her breakdown. She may be back. You can check on her, at any rate."

"I agree," said Banks. "I'd have a very close look at Maggie Forrest if she's around."

"Why's that, Alan?" Phil Hartnell asked.

"Because she was the closest to Lucy Payne in many ways, and she got seriously betrayed by her."

"She almost got killed, if it hadn't been for you, is what I heard," said Hartnell.

"Yes," said Banks. "Anyway, the point is that her feelings are bound to be deeply confused and conflicted on the issue. And let's not forget that she had a few problems of her own. She was seeing a psychiatrist."

"Okay," said Hartnell. "Looks as if your first priority, Annie, is finding out whether this Maggie Forrest is in the country, and if she is, could she have had access to Lucy Payne's identity and whereabouts?"

"Yes, sir," said Annie, clearly not pleased that Banks had come up with this.

"What about Janet Taylor's family?" Blackstone asked, looking up from the list. "If anyone was another Chameleon casualty, it was her."

Hartnell turned to Annie. "You carried out the investigation into the killing of Terence Payne by Janet Taylor, didn't you?"

"It wasn't my choice," said Annie, jaw tight.

"I understand that," Hartnell said. "It was a rotten and thankless task, but it had to be done." Banks happened to know that it was *because* of Hartnell that Annie had been given the "rotten and thankless task," to keep it close to home. He had tried to intercede on her behalf, but Annie had been working Complaints and Discipline at the time, just after her promotion to detective inspector, and the case had been pushed right into her lap. Annie didn't know that.

"Anyway," Annie went on, "Janet Taylor has an older brother, and the whole business turned him into a bitter drunk. He's been known to utter the occasional threat, though most of his vehemence is directed towards the police investigation into his sister's conduct. There's a chance that, if he knew where she was, he might have harboured a strong resentment against Lucy Payne, too. We'll check him out."

"Fine," said Hartnell. "Now is there anyone I've forgotten?"

"Well, I'm just thinking, it was six years ago," said Banks, "and that means a significant change in the ages of everyone involved. They've all been getting older, like the rest of us." Blackstone and Hartnell laughed. "But in some cases it means more."

"What are you getting at, Alan?" asked Hartnell.

"Well, sir," said Banks, "it's the ones who were kids at the time. I'm thinking specifically of Claire Toth. She was Kimberley Myers's best friend. That's the Chameleon's last victim, the one we found naked and dead on the mattress in the cellar at 35 The Hill. They went to the dance together, but when it was time for Kimberley to go home, Claire was dancing with a boy she fancied and didn't go with her. Kimberley went alone and Payne snatched her. Naturally, Claire felt guilty. What I'm saying is that there's a big difference between being fifteen and being twenty-one. And she's had six years to live with the guilt. I know Annie said Mel Danvers thought Mary was about forty, but she didn't get a good look. She could have been wrong. Quite frankly, the artist's impression she gave is useless. I'm just saying we don't rule out Claire or anyone else because they happen to be younger than forty, that's all."

"Then we'll add her to the list, by all means," said Hartnell. "And by the same token let's not overlook anyone else who was the victims' ages at the time. As Alan says, people change with age, and no one more quickly and unpredictably than the young. That includes boyfriends, girlfriends, siblings, whatever. I hope you've got a big team, DI Cabbot."

Annie managed a tight smile. "It'll be a stretch, sir, but we'll manage."

"Is there anything else we can do for you?" Hartnell asked.

"If you could have the Chameleon files put aside for me in a cubby-hole here somewhere . . . ? I might need to come in and check details from time to time."

"Consider it done," said Hartnell. "Ken, you'll see to it?"

"I will indeed," said Blackstone. "And you can use my office, Annie. We're a bit short on cubbyholes."

"Thanks, Ken," said Annie.

Hartnell stood up and looked at his watch, the mark of a busy man. "Well, I think that just about covers it," he said. "I know that none of us will be shedding any tears over the death of Lucy Payne, but at the same time I think we'd all like to see justice done."

"Yes, sir," they all muttered as they filed out of his office.

In the corridor, Banks tried to catch up with Annie, but she was hurrying away towards an open lift door. He managed to reach out and grasp her shoulder, but she pulled away with such force it stopped him in his tracks. He watched her get in the lift, and the doors closed behind her. A moment or so later, he felt a friendly hand between his shoulders. "Alan, old mate," Ken Blackstone said, "I think you need a drink, and they might just be serving lunch by now."

Winsome found a coffee shop across the street from Austin's department and decided to settle down and wait for the long-haired student to come out. She wasn't certain what she was going to do when he did emerge from Austin's building, but she knew she would think of something.

Winsome ordered her latte and sat on a stool by the window, where a long, orange moulded-plastic shelf ran at just the right height to rest her cup on. She was older than most of the patrons, but found it interesting that she didn't draw many curious glances. She was wearing black denims and a short zip-up jacket, which weren't completely out of place there, though perhaps a little upmarket for the student scene.

Most likely, she thought, nobody paid her much attention because there were two Chinese students in deep discussion at one table, a couple of Muslim girls wearing hijabs at another, and a young black woman with dreadlocks talking to a similarly coiffed white boy in a Bob Marley T-shirt. The rest were white, but this was the biggest racial mix Winsome had ever seen in Eastvale. She wondered where they all disappeared to on a Saturday afternoon, when she did her shopping, or on a Saturday evening when the market square turned into a youth disaster zone. She guessed that there were enough pubs, bars and cafés around campus to keep them entertained without their having to risk life and limb from a bunch of drunken squaddies or farm labourers. So why did Hayley and her friends head for the city centre? Living dangerously? Most likely, Winsome guessed, it was the students who actually *came* from Eastvale who haunted the market square scene, the locals, or the ones from outlying villages.

Winsome kept an eye on the door of Austin's building as she sipped the latte. While she waited, she couldn't help but return in her mind to Annie Cabbot's shocking confession of the previous evening. A twenty-two-year-old, for Lord's sake! What was she thinking? That was no more than a mere boy; DCI Banks's son, for example, must be about that age, or not much more. And she had regarded Annie as someone she could respect, look up to. She had also secretly thought that Annie and Banks would end up together. She had thought they made a good couple and would have been happy to serve as a bridesmaid at their wedding. How wrong she was. Poor Banks. If only he knew, he would surely be as disgusted as she was.

Winsome was surprised at her own prudish reaction, but she had had a strict religious and moral upbringing, and no amount of exposure

.to the loose ways of the modern world could completely undo that.

After Annie had stormed out, Winsome had gone home herself. She had been worried about Annie's driving, but when she got outside, the Astra was gone from the square. Too late. She also felt that she had let her friend down, hadn't said the right things, made the right noises, given her the sympathy and understanding she needed, but she had felt so shocked and at sea, so burdened by, rather than grateful for, the intimacy of the confession, that she hadn't been able to. She hadn't felt much sympathy. So much for sisterly solidarity. There had been something else, though, some trouble with this boy that Annie hadn't got the chance to tell her about, and that worried her, too.

Students ambled up and down the street carrying backpacks or shoulder bags, wearing T-shirts and jeans; nobody seemed in a hurry. That was the life, Winsome thought. They didn't have to deal with people like Templeton or face the dead bodies of young women first thing on a Sunday morning. And she bet they indulged in night after night of sweaty, guiltless sex. She felt as if she could sit there forever sipping coffee looking out on the sunshine, and a sense of childhood peace came over her, the kind she had felt back at home during the long, hot, still days when all she could hear were birds and the lazy clicking of banana leaves from the plantation.

But it didn't last. Before she had finished, the young man walked out of the door, glanced around as he went down the steps and turned up the street. Winsome picked up her briefcase and shoulder bag and set off in pursuit, leaving the rest of her latte. She had decided it would be best simply to approach him and have done with it. She was a police officer and he was a witness, at the very least.

"Excuse me," she called, as he was about to turn a corner.

He stopped, a puzzled expression on his face, and pointed his thumb to his chest. "Moi?"

"Yes, you. I want a word with you."

"What about?"

Winsome showed him her warrant card. "Hayley Daniels," she said.

"I know who you are, but I don't know —"

"Don't give me that. You were in the market square with her on Saturday night. We've got you on CCTV."

The boy turned pale. "I suppose I . . . well . . . let's go in here." He turned into a café. Winsome didn't want another coffee. Instead, she settled for a bottle of fizzy water while the boy, who said his name was Zack Lane, spooned sugar into his herbal tea. "Okay," he said. "I knew Hayley. So what?"

"Why didn't you come forward? You must have known we'd catch up with you eventually."

"And get involved in a murder investigation. Would you have come forward?"

"Of course I would," said Winsome. "What's the problem if you haven't done anything wrong?"

"Huh. Easy for you to say." He paused and examined her closely. "On the other hand, maybe it's not that easy. You ought to know better than most."

Winsome felt herself bristle. "What do you mean by that?"

"I can't even imagine why you'd want to be a cop. Someone like you. I'll bet your mates aren't too thrilled, are they? Always getting pulled over on sus because they're black. All you have to do is walk down the street and they —"

"Shut up. Stop right there," said Winsome, holding her palm up, and something in her tone stopped him in his tracks. "I'm not here to discuss racism or my career choices with you. I'm here to ask you questions about Hayley Daniels. Got that? You said you knew who I was when you saw me. How?"

Zack smiled. "There aren't any other black coppers in Eastvale," he said. "None except you, as far as I know, and you've had your photo in the paper. I can't say as I'm surprised, either. It didn't do you justice. Should have been page three."

"Knock it off," said Winsome. Shortly after she had been sent to Eastvale, the local paper had done a feature on her. She managed a smile. "You must have been very young back then."

"I'm older than I look. Grew up just down the road. I'm a local lad. My dad's an alderman, so he likes us all to keep in touch with the beating pulse of the metropolis." He laughed.

"You just went to see Malcolm Austin."

"So? He's my tutor."

"Any good, is he?"

"Why, thinking of enrolling as a mature student?"

"Stop being cheeky and answer my questions."

"Lighten up."

"Lighten up?" echoed Winsome in disbelief. Isn't that what Annie had said to her last night? She thought of making some sarcastic remark about it being difficult for someone of her colour, but instead she prodded him in the chest and said, "Lighten up? I was one of the first on the scene to see Hayley's body on Sunday morning, so don't tell me to lighten up. I saw her lying there dead. She'd been raped and strangled. So don't tell me to lighten up. And you're supposed to be a friend of hers."

Zack's face had gone pale now, and he was starting to appear contrite. "All right. I'm sorry," he said, sweeping back his hair. "I'm shaken up about Hayley, too, you know. I liked her, the silly cow."

"Why silly cow?"

"She was outrageous. She got us chucked out of the Trumpeter's and nearly did the same at the Fountain."

"I thought you were well behaved at the Fountain?"

"Been asking around, have you?"

"Doing our job."

"Just the facts, ma'am. Sure. Well, we were. Except Hayley wanted a p – She needed to go to the toilet badly, and some yobs had wrecked it. Happens all the time. Gave Jamie behind the bar a right mouthful, though it was hardly his fault."

"Jamie Murdoch?"

"Aye. You know him?"

"We've talked to him."

"I went to school with Jamie. He moved down from Tyneside with his parents when he was about twelve. He's all right. A bit quiet, lacking in ambition, maybe."

"In what way?"

"Jamie tried the college once, but he didn't take to it. He's actually quite bright, but not everyone can handle the academic life. He can do better than the pub, but I'm not sure he's got the balls to try."

"He was running it alone on Saturday night," said Winsome.

"Yeah, I know. He does that a lot. Can't seem to keep the staff. I think he's got Jill Sutherland working there at the moment, but I'll bet that won't last."

"Why not?"

"Too many airs and graces to last long in a dive like the Fountain, our Jill."

"What about the owner?"

"Terry Clarke? That wanker? He's never there. Got a time-share in Orlando or Fort Lauderdale or somewhere like that. It can't be easy for Jamie. He's not a natural authoritarian. He lets everyone just walk all over him. Anyway, Hayley got a bit mouthy when she saw the state of the bogs, called him a few names, told him to get in there and fix it or she'd do it on the floor. That was our Hayley. But we calmed her down before any real harm was done. We got to finish our drinks, at any rate."

Winsome made a note that someone should have another chat with Jamie Murdoch and also locate Jill Sutherland. "Is it true that Hayley went down Taylor's Yard to use the toilet?" she asked.

"Yes," said Zack. He cocked his head and studied Winsome. "Though that's an odd way of putting it. I mean, there isn't an actual toilet there. Like I said, Hayley could be pretty outrageous. As soon as we got outside the Fountain, she announced to all and sundry that she was off for a piss. Sorry. She needed to go to the toilet, and she was going in the Maze." He paused. "Maybe she should have done it on the floor, then she wouldn't have gone in there."

"Didn't any of you try to talk her out of it?"

"Yes, but you can't talk Hayley out of anything when she gets her mind set on it."

That was what Stuart Kinsey had said, Winsome remembered. "One of you could at least have gone with her . . ." Winsome realized what she had said too late and let the sentence trail off.

"I'm not saying she wouldn't have got plenty of volunteers," said Zack with a smirk. "Stuart, for one. Maybe even me, if I was drunk enough. But I can't say I'm into golden showers, and Hayley wasn't my type. Oh, we all joked about going down there and jumping out at her, giving her a fright, catching her with her knickers down, but it didn't happen. We ended up in the Bar None. And Hayley —"

"She wasn't planning on joining you later?"

"No, she was going to stay at a friend's."

"Who? A girlfriend?"

Zack laughed. "Whatever our Hayley was, she definitely wasn't a girl's girl. I'm not saying she didn't have a couple of mates – Susie and Kerry come to mind – but mostly she liked to hang around with the guys."

"Can you give me the names of everyone who was there on Saturday?"

"Let's see, there was me, Hayley, Susie Govindar, Kerry Vance, then there were Stuart Kinsey, Giles Faulkner and Keith Taft. That was about it. Will, that's Will Paisley, he was with us earlier but he went off to see some mates in Leeds early on. To be quite honest, I think he's got a boyfriend there, though he seems to be lingering overlong in the closet. Mind you, I can't say I blame him in a place like this."

"So most of the time, after this Will had gone off to Leeds, for what-ever reason, there were seven of you, right?"

"Give or take one or two we met on the way."

"You said that Hayley preferred the company of men. Why was that?"

"Why do you think? Because then she was the centre of attention. Because they'd do anything she wanted. Because she pretty much had all of them wrapped around her little finger."

"She sounds like a drunken lout to me."

Zack studied Winsome closely. "But you didn't know her," he said. "Actually, there was a lot more to her than that. Sure, she liked to cut loose on a Saturday night, go wild, get kalied and let her hair down. But she was a good student, she did her work on time, and she had a good future. She was bright, too. Sometimes you have to dig deeper than the flash clothes and the superficial bravado."

"And you did?"

"I went out with her a couple of times last year. But like I said, she wasn't really my type. And in case you were thinking of asking, no, I didn't sleep with her. Hayley wasn't a slag. Kept herself fastened up as tight as a Scotsman's wallet, in spite of the sexy clothes and all. It was strictly top only for me."

"So she was a tease?"

"I didn't say that."

"You implied it."

"No, not really. She could be. She liked playing games, flirting, winding you up. But she could be serious, too. I mean, you could have a good serious talk with Hayley. Politics. Music. History. Whatever. She had opinions and the knowledge to back them up. All I'm saying is that just because she dressed the way she did, it didn't mean she was giving it away to everyone. You should know that."

Winsome bristled. "What do you mean?"

Zack held his hand up. "Okay, don't get your kni – Don't take offence. I meant in your job you must hear that excuse about someone asking for it because of the way she dresses, and you know it shouldn't matter. A woman should be able to walk the streets of Eastvale stark naked if she wants, and no one has the right to touch her."

Winsome laughed. "I'm sure they'd have a good look, though."

"Well," said Zack, "that's one thing you lot haven't made illegal. Yet." He tapped the side of his head. "Along with what people think."

"We're trying to find out who Hayley had been seeing recently," Winsome went on. "If it wasn't you and it wasn't Stuart Kinsey, do you have any idea who it might have been?"

Zack paused. "Well, she didn't say anything, but . . ." He glanced out of the window back down the street they'd come. "I don't think you'd have to look much further than our Mr. Austin back there."

"Is that where she was going on Saturday night?"

"I think so."

"Austin denied that he had anything to do with her."

Zack laughed. "He would, wouldn't he? He'd stand to lose his job. They don't take kindly to that sort of thing around here."

"Do you know this for a fact?"

"About Mal and Hayley? Sure. I've seen them together, seen him with his hand creeping up her thigh, nibbling her neck."

"When was this?"

"About a month ago."

Winsome felt her pulse speed up. Zack Lane had been worth the wait, after all. "Where did you see them?"

"Pub outside Helmthorpe. The Green Man. They must have thought they were far enough out of the manor, but I was over there for a darts competition."

"Did they see you?"

"I don't think so. I cleared out pretty quickly when I saw them."

"Why?"

"It would have been awkward. Remember, Austin's my tutor, too."

"Yes," said Winsome. "Of course." She stood up. "Thanks, Mr. Lane. Thanks a lot." Now she had the corroboration she needed, Winsome had the feeling that things were starting to progress, and Malcolm Austin was going to have a lot of difficult questions to answer the next time he got a visit from the police.

8

"So what is it, Alan? What's going on? You could have cut the tension in there with a knife."

"Do you think Phil Hartnell noticed?"

"He didn't get where he is today by not noticing things like that. He probably thought you'd had a lovers' tiff."

"And you?"

"It seemed the logical assumption. But –"

"But what, Ken?"

"Well, you're not lovers, are you? At least I thought you two were no longer an item."

"We're not," said Banks. "At least I didn't think we were."

"What does that mean?"

They were sitting outside on a bench at the Packhorse, in a yard just off Briggate. The walls were higher, but it made Banks think of the Maze and Hayley Daniels. Banks tucked into his jumbo haddock and chips, a pint of Black Sheep beside him. There was already a group of students at one table discussing a Radiohead concert, and the lunchtime office crowd was starting to trickle in, men with their ties loosened and jackets slung over their shoulders, and the women in long print skirts and short-sleeved tops, open-toed shoes or sandals. The weather really had warmed up since Sunday, and it was looking good for the weekend.

"I wish I knew," said Banks. He didn't feel it was his place to tell Ken exactly what had happened the previous evening, so he gave the bare-bones version, leaving out any mention of the awkward pass Annie had made, or the way he had felt when her thighs and breasts brushed against him. Desire and danger. And he had chosen to protect himself from the danger rather than give in to the desire. But he couldn't explain that to Ken, either. There had been jealousy, too, when she talked about toyboys. He had read somewhere that jealousy cannot exist without desire.

"So what was all that about, then?" Blackstone asked.

Banks laughed. "Annie doesn't exactly confide in me these days. Besides, she's been over at Eastern Area for a couple of weeks. We've not been in touch. Something strange is going on in her life; that's all I can say for certain."

"She didn't look good this morning."

"I know."

"You say she was drunk when she came to see you?"

"That was definitely the impression I got."

"Maybe she's got a problem with the bottle? It happens often enough in our line of work."

Banks stared into his half-empty pint. Or was it half-full? Did he have a problem with the bottle? There were those who would say he did. He knew he drank too much, but he didn't drink enough to give him a hangover every morning or interfere with his job, so he tended not to worry about it too much. What harm was he doing sitting around by himself having a few glasses of wine listening to Thelonious Monk or the Grateful Dead? So, once in a while he got the blues and let himself wallow in a few late Billie Holiday torch songs, or Dylan's *Modern Times*, and perhaps poured an extra glass or two. So what? As Annie had said, what did he have in his miserable little life that was so wonderful he could afford to reject someone like her?

"I don't think it's that," Banks said. "Annie's always enjoyed a pint, and she can hold her booze. No, I think that's the symptom, not the cause."

"Man trouble?"

"Why do we always assume it's something along those lines?" Banks said. "Maybe it's job trouble?" But even as he spoke, he wasn't convinced. There were things that Annie had said last night, things he had only half understood, but if he read between the lines they pointed towards man trouble. He'd been involved in her love life before, and he didn't know if he wanted to be involved again. "Maybe it's dredging up that whole Lucy Payne and Janet Taylor business," he said, hoping at least to divert, if not completely change, the subject.

Blackstone sipped some beer. "She had a rough time of it," he said. "Definitely got the short end of the shitty stick on that one."

"We all had a rough time of it," said Banks. "But I know what you mean. Any ideas?"

"On who might have done it?"

"Yes."

"Like AC Hartnell said, it's a long list. One thing that brings me up short, though, is the . . . well, I suppose you could say the *precision* of it."

"What do you mean?"

"Well, first let's assume that one way or another it wasn't too hard for the killer to find out where Lucy Payne went when she left hospital. I know Julia Ford says her firm went to great lengths to disguise her identity and her whereabouts, but these things can all be circumvented if someone wanted to find out badly enough. A little inside help, a lot of public records, a few quid changing hands, whatever. So let's put that aside and assume finding her was no real challenge. What I'm thinking about is the method. If it had been an angry and disturbed member of a victim's family, say, then why not just take Lucy for a walk down the coast and push her over the cliff?"

"I see what you mean," said Banks. "To do it the way it was done, the killer had to go prepared. The razor, or whatever she used, for example."

"Yes. And even if we assume that someone set out to kill Lucy, that it was premeditated, it still makes more sense just to dump her over the side. It wasn't as if she could be forced to confess anything, or even show any fear or feel pain. She couldn't even talk."

"Are you suggesting that it wasn't someone involved in the Chameleon case?"

"I don't know what I'm suggesting," said Blackstone. "But it's a possibility worth considering. Could anyone who was that angry at Lucy Payne for what she'd done to a family member be that cold-blooded? Where was the anger?"

"If the killer had simply pushed Lucy off the edge of the cliff," Banks said, "there's always a chance that the body might never have been found."

"But they'd have recovered the wheelchair, surely, and that would have told them what happened."

"Perhaps."

"Maybe I'm wrong," said Blackstone. "I'm just thinking out loud. She might not have even died if she went over the cliff."

"No, Ken, I think you're heading in the right direction. This was a cold-blooded job, simple as that. A job that had to be done efficiently. Almost like a hit. The killer had to *know* that the victim had died at her hands – if it was a woman – perhaps even watch her die. She couldn't face the uncertainty. After all, if Lucy Payne was a quadriplegic already, there wasn't much more harm anyone could do to her other than extinguish her life completely, what little of it there was left."

"And all that was left was inside," said Blackstone.

"What?"

"I don't know. I'm just rambling. You're right, though. It was an efficient method. It got the job done, and it left the evidence in plain sight, for all to see. There has to be something in that."

"So whoever did it was making a statement?" said Banks.

"Yes. Draining her life's blood. And what was that statement? I think when we get the answer to that, we'll be a long way towards at least ruling out a lot of people."

"We?"

"I mean Annie's team."

"But it does feel like a continuation, doesn't it?" Banks said. "Like unfinished business."

"Yes," Blackstone agreed. "I was thinking of suggesting bringing in Jenny Fuller again, as a profiler. She worked the original case."

"I don't know where she is at the moment. I think she's left Eastvale for good. She could be in America or Australia as far as I know. I haven't seen her in ages."

"You sound as if you regret that. History?"

"Plenty," said Banks, "but not the kind you're thinking of. All my mistakes with Jenny are in what we *didn't* do, not in anything we did. Missed opportunities rather than anything hastily done and regretted."

"Hmm."

"We've known each other a long time, that's all," said Banks. "Ever since I've been up north, as a matter of fact. I met her on my very first case. Maybe things could have been different, but they're not, and it's too late now. It never happened."

They finished their drinks and headed out to Briggate. The fine weather had brought people out in the city centre, and the pedestrian precinct was packed, the shops doing brisk business: Marks and Spencer's, Harvey Nichols, Debenham's, Currys Digital. All the fourteen-year-old mothers were out showing off their solarium suntans, pushing the pram with one hand and holding a cigarette with the other. Or so it seemed. After saying goodbye to Blackstone at the Headrow and promising to get together soon for a curry and a few pints, Banks went into Muji and bought a handful of those little cardboard-bound notebooks he liked so much, then he wandered into Borders to see if they had *White Heat* on sale. He had enjoyed the first volume of Dominic Sandbrook's history of the 1950s in Britain, *Never Had It So Good*, and looked forward to reading the second – *his* period, the 1960s – after he'd finished *Postwar*. After that, he would check out the new CDs in HMV.

Annie didn't feel particularly proud of her performance at Millgarth as she drove into Whitby just over an hour and a half later. It was a beautiful day, and the sea lay spread out below her, all greens and blues, so much brighter and more vibrant than she had seen them before. The red pantile roofs of the houses straggled up the hillside, and the harbour walls stretched out into the water like pincers. The whole scene, flanked on either side by high cliffs, appeared more like an abstract landscape than a real place.

From the heights, she could easily see the town's two distinctive halves, split by the estuary: East Cliff, with its ruined abbey and St. Mary's Church, like an upturned boat; and West Cliff, with its rows of Victorian guest houses and hotels, the statue of Captain Cook and the massive jawbone of a whale. Though Annie took in the sight, and her painter's eye translated it to an abstract canvas, her mind was preoccupied with Banks, Eric and, most of all, her own erratic behaviour.

She's Lost Control. Didn't someone used to sing a song called that? Banks would know. Banks. *Damn him.* What *had* she been thinking? That one quick shag with him was going to make everything all right?

The more she thought about Saturday night, the more convinced she became that it wasn't the age difference that bothered her. After all, if it were the other way round, if she were a twenty-two year-old woman, it would seem perfectly normal for most men of forty and above to sleep with her – she bet there wasn't one of them would turn down a Keira Knightley or a Scarlett Johansson. There were also plenty of women in their forties who had bragged to Annie about making youthful conquests. She ought to be dead chuffed with herself for pulling Eric, rather than feeling so cheap and dirty. But she knew that she felt that way because that wasn't who she was.

Perhaps she felt so badly because she had always believed that she chose to sleep with men she could talk to in the morning, and the fact that they were often older than her, more mature, like Banks, never seemed to matter. They had more experience, more to talk about. The young were so self-obsessed, so image-conscious. Even when she was younger, she had felt the same way, had always preferred older men and thought boys her own age somewhat shallow and lacking in everything except sexual energy and frequency. Perhaps that was enough for some women. Perhaps it ought to be enough for her, but it wasn't; otherwise she wouldn't feel so badly.

What upset her most of all, and what refused to go away, was that she hadn't known what she was doing. She had lost control. For some reason, she had been drunk enough that being fancied by a fit, young lad when she'd just turned forty and was starting to feel ancient had appealed to her. Waking up with a blinding hangover and a stranger was never a good thing, in Annie's experience, but in this case the fact that he was young enough to be her son only made it worse.

And she couldn't even claim that she had been coerced or date-raped or anything. There had been no Rohypnol or GHB, only alcohol and a couple of joints, as far as she knew, and the worst thing about it was that, pissed as she had been, she knew she had been a willing participant in whatever had gone on. She couldn't remember the details of the sex, only hurried fumblings, graspings, rough grunts and a sense of everything being over very quickly, but she could remember her initial excitement and enthusiasm. In the end, she assumed that it had been as unsatisfactory for him as it had been for her.

Then there was the episode with Banks last night. Again, what on earth had she thought she was doing? Now things could never be the same; she'd never be able to face him with any self-respect again. And she had put both Banks and Winsome in an awkward position, driving in that state. She could have lost her licence, got suspended from her job. And that seemed the least of her problems.

The colours of the sea changed as she drove down the winding hill, and soon she was beside the houses, stopping at traffic lights in the streets of the town centre, busy with normal life. A herd of reporters had massed outside the station, waving microphones and tape recorders at anyone coming or going. Annie made her way through with the help of the uniformed officers on crowd control and went to the squad room, where she found the usual scene of controlled chaos. She had hardly got in when Ginger came up to her. "You all right, ma'am? You look a bit peaky."

"I'm fine," Annie growled. "Those bloody reporters are getting to me, that's all. Anything new?"

"Got a message for you from an ex-DI called Les Ferris," Ginger said.

"Who's he when he's at home?"

"Local. Used to work out of here, but he's down in Scarborough now. Put out to pasture, officially, but they give him a cubbyhole and employ him as a civilian researcher. Pretty good at it, apparently."

"And?"

"Just says he wants to see you, that's all."

"Aren't I the popular one?"

"He says it's about an old case, but he thinks it might be relevant to the Lucy Payne investigation."

"Okay," said Annie. "I'll try to sneak out and fit him in later. Anything else come up while I've been away?"

"Nothing, ma'am. We've talked to the people at Mapston Hall again. Nothing new there. If someone did know that Karen Drew was Lucy Payne, they're hiding it well."

"We're going to have to put a team on checking for leaks, dig a lot deeper," Annie said. "We need to look very closely at everyone in Julia Ford's practice, the Mapston Hall staff, the hospital, social services, the lot. See if you can get someone local to help down in Nottingham and divide the rest up among our best researchers. Tell them it'll mean overtime."

"Yes, guv," said Ginger.

"And I think we need to ask questions in other directions, too," said Annie, taking the folders out of her briefcase. "We're going to have to widen the base of our inquiry. Take this list of names and divide it up between yourself, DS Naylor and the rest of the team, will you? They're all people who suffered one way or another at Lucy Payne's hands six years ago, most of them in West Yorkshire. I've already liaised with the locals there, and they'll give us as much help as they can. We need statements, alibis, the lot. I'll pay a visit to Claire Toth myself tomorrow. She was close to the Paynes' last victim, blamed herself for what happened. Any questions?"

"No, ma'am," said Ginger, scanning the list. "But it certainly seems as if we've got our work cut out."

"I've got more, specially for you, Ginger."

"How nice, ma'am."

"There was a young Canadian woman living on The Hill opposite the Paynes. She became quite close friends with Lucy, even after the arrest. Appeared on TV as her champion, that sort of thing, thought Lucy was a poor victim."

"I see," said Ginger.

"She was also present when Lucy Payne had her 'accident.' Lucy was living in her house at the time. You can imagine the sense of betrayal she must have felt. Anyway, she has to be our chief suspect if she was anywhere near the scene. Her name's Maggie, or Margaret, Forrest. She worked as an illustrator of children's books, so the odds are that she's still in the same line of work. You can check publishers, professional associations, what have you. You know the drill." She passed a folder to Ginger. "The details are all in here."

"You said she's Canadian. What if she's gone home?"

"Then she's not our problem any more, is she?"

"And if I find her?"

"Come straight to me," said Annie. "That's another interview I'd like to do myself."

Jill Sutherland, part-time barmaid at the Fountain, was in the kitchen when Winsome called at her flat about a mile from the college. "I was just making a cup of tea," Jill said. "I only got home about five minutes ago. Can I offer you some?"

"That'd be great," said Winsome.

Jill carried the pot and two cups, along with milk and sugar, on a tray, then sat cross-legged on the small sofa in front of the coffee table. Her living room was light and airy, with a distinct whiff of air freshener. Innocuous pop music played on the radio, occasionally interrupted by a cheery voice turned so low that Winsome thankfully couldn't hear a word he said. She sat opposite Jill and took out her notebook.

Jill smiled. She was a pretty redhead with a button nose and a pale, freckled complexion, wearing jeans and a black T-shirt. All in all, she had an air of innocence that Winsome thought probably belied her experience. "What can I do for you?" she asked.

"I don't know, really," Winsome began. "It's about Saturday night in the Fountain. The girl who was killed, Hayley Daniels, had just been drinking there. We're trying to gather as much information as we can."

Jill's expression changed. "Yes, that was terrible. The poor girl. I read about her in the paper. And to think I could have been working just around the corner. Or even walking through there myself."

"You walk through the Maze alone?"

"Usually, if I've been working. It's a shortcut. I park in the Castle car park, and it's the fastest way. I never thought it was dangerous, really."

"You should be more careful."

Jill shrugged. "I never had any problems. There was never anyone else there."

"Even so . . . Did you know Hayley?"

"I'd seen her around."

"You're a student at the college, too?"

"Yes. Forensic science."

Winsome raised her eyebrows. "Forensic science? I didn't even know they had a course in that."

"It's quite new. After two years you can get into analytical chemistry at the University of Leeds."

"Is that where you met Hayley, at college?"

"Travel and tourism's just around the corner. We share a coffee shop. I'd seen her in town sometimes, too, shopping."

"And in the Fountain?"

"Once or twice."

"But you weren't friends."

"No, just acquaintances. I only knew her to say hello to."

"You called in poorly on Saturday, is that right?"

"Yes."

"What was wrong with you?"

"Just a cold."

Winsome guessed by the way Jill averted her eyes and flushed as she spoke, that she wasn't exactly telling the truth. As a further distraction, Jill chose that moment to lean forward and pour the tea. As she did so, she gave a small cough and put her hand to her mouth. "Milk and sugar?"

"Yes, please," said Winsome. She accepted the mug and went back to her question. "All better now?"

"Yes, thanks."

"Come on," said Winsome. "You can be honest with me. I've seen the Fountain. You didn't have a cold, did you? You just didn't want to go to work."

Jill's eyes filled with tears. "I need the money," she said. "My parents can't afford to support me."

"Surely there must be a better job?"

"I'm sure there is, and I'm looking. In the meantime, there's the Fountain."

"What's Jamie Murdoch like to work for?"

"Jamie's all right."

"Has he ever bothered you?"

"He asked me out a couple of times, but I said no." Jill wrinkled her nose. "He's not really my type. I mean, he's not exactly God's gift, is he?"

Winsome smiled. "How did he react to that?"

"He was disappointed, naturally, but he didn't push it. No, it's not working for Jamie that's the problem. It's just . . . I can't deal with all the drunks and the abuse. I mean, I know people aren't really themselves when they've had a lot to drink, but the mood can get very uncomfortable. There's rows and fights and all sorts, and it's not as if Jamie is the bouncer type."

"So what happens?"

"Oh, people usually calm down. I mean, no one ever got really hurt or anything. It's just the language flying around, and the rudeness. Not that I'm a prude or anything. And then there's the smoke. You wouldn't believe how bad it gets sometimes. First thing I have to do when I get home is put all my clothes in the basket and have a long soak in the bath."

"That should improve after the smoking ban in July," said Winsome. "Is there anything else about working there that bothers you?"

Jill paused and bit her lower lip. "I shouldn't be telling tales out of school," she said finally, "but in the summer, when me and Pauline drove across to France for a weekend, Jamie asked me to stop and fill the boot with cheap lager and cigarettes."

"It's not illegal," said Winsome.

"I know, but I think selling them in the pub is. I know lots of people do it, and like I said, I'm not a goody two-shoes, but I didn't want to do anything that might harm my future, especially if I'm going to be connected to law enforcement. That would be crazy."

"Quite right," said Winsome. Illegal booze and cigarettes was not exactly the kind of breakthrough she was looking for, but it was another snippet to add to the file. As far as telling Customs and Excise was concerned, though, a pub like the Fountain was so low down the pecking order when it came to smuggling that it would hardly be worth their while. "Jamie says he was there until half past two cleaning up after someone wrecked the toilets," she said.

"I know. He told me. I can't say I'm surprised."

"Has it happened before?"

"Not that bad, but someone broke some glasses once. And they often stuff toilet paper down the bowl. That's what I mean about working there. You dread going to work on a weekend, and the rest of the time it's dead, except for lunch sometimes. I'm sorry I left Jamie in the lurch like that. I feel really bad now I know he was there all by himself when, you know, it happened."

Winsome stood up. "He'll survive. Thanks a lot, Jill, you've been a great help."

"I have?"

Winsome smiled. "Like I said, every little bit helps."

Detective Superintendent Catherine Gervaise had called the progress review meeting in the boardroom of Western Area Headquarters for five o'clock that Wednesday afternoon, by which time some of the forensic reports had started trickling in. DS Stefan Nowak, the crime scene coordinator, was there as liaison with the lab, along with Dr. Elizabeth Wallace, Banks, Templeton, Wilson, Hatchley and Winsome, just back from talking to Jill Sutherland.

"Okay," said Gervaise, when everyone had settled with coffee, pads and pens in front of them. "Let's add up what we've got so far. First off, DS Nowak is here on behalf of forensic services. I know it's probably too early yet, but do you have anything for us, Stefan?"

"Not a lot, I'm afraid, ma'am," said Nowak. "And most of it's negative. Technical support did manage to enhance the number plate of the car that passed by around the same time Hayley Daniels went into Taylor's Yard, but it turns out it was just a couple on their way home from celebrating their twenty-fifth wedding anniversary at that posh restaurant down Market Street."

"What about Hayley herself?" Gervaise asked. "Anything more on what happened there?"

"The rapist wore a condom, so we don't –"

"Hang on a minute," said Banks. "What about the semen on the victim's thigh?"

"I was getting to that," said Nowak. "All I can suggest is that he was in a hurry and it spilled out when he removed the condom, or it belongs to someone else. We're still waiting on DNA results."

"There were *two* of them?" said Gervaise.

"Not necessarily two attackers," said Nowak. "Someone could have had consensual sex with her, in accordance with the theory that she went into the Maze to meet someone."

"Then someone else killed her?" said Templeton.

"Possibly."

"She went into the Maze to relieve herself," said Winsome. "And she wasn't a slut."

"I'm not suggesting that she was," said Nowak, looking taken aback. "Just that the results are inconsistent. We know that someone had sex with Hayley using a condom because we found traces of a lubricant used on a common brand, but we also found traces of semen on her thigh and on two of the adjacent leather remnants. Those are the facts. It's not up to me to speculate, but I'd ask why a killer clever enough to clean up the body to some extent would miss the semen, unless it happened at a different time, or perhaps was left by someone else. There was one slight inconsistency."

"Yes?" said Gervaise.

"The seminal fluid wasn't quite as dry as it should have been given the time of death."

"As I've explained many times," said Dr. Wallace with a definite hint of defensiveness in her tone, "time of death is always, at best, a rough estimate."

"That's what I thought," said Nowak.

"What time then?" asked Banks.

Nowak looked at Dr. Wallace before answering. "I don't see any reason to argue with the original estimate, between midnight and two in the morning," he said. "There could be other reasons for the inconsistency. I'll work on it."

"Very well," said Gervaise.

"I noted in my post-mortem that Hayley might have tried to fight off her attacker," said Dr. Wallace. "Did you find any tissue in the samples we scraped from under her fingernails?"

"Alas, no," said Nowak. "As you mentioned in your report, the nails were too short to actually scratch anyone. All we got were a few common cotton fibres."

"Any luck identifying them?" Gervaise asked.

Nowak shook his head. "We're still working with them, but they could come from any number of brands. Not only that," Nowak went on, "but she could have picked them up at any time during the evening. Remember, she was with a large group of people, and the odds were that some or all of them touched or brushed against the others at some point."

"Hair?" Banks asked.

"Only hers and Joseph Randall's."

"So our killer wore a balaclava, or he's bald," said Hatchley.

Nobody laughed.

"There's evidence the killer cleaned her up," said Dr. Wallace. "Washed her pubic area."

"Except he missed that semen," Banks said.

"It looks that way," said Nowak. "Or that happened *after* he'd cleaned her up."

"Possible," Dr. Wallace agreed.

"Fingerprints?" asked Banks.

"None. Sorry."

"I thought you lot could perform miracles these days," said Banks, seeing everything slipping away.

Nowak looked at Dr. Wallace. "Sometimes it seems that way, but we're only as good as the evidence we collect."

"Any luck with the known offenders?" Gervaise asked.

"Nothing," said Banks. "They've all been interviewed, and they all have alibis. We're still working on it."

Gervaise turned to Nowak again. "Have we missed something?"

"I don't think so," said Nowak. "The SOCOs went over that place as thoroughly as any scene they've ever handled. One other thing we found was traces of the girl's urine on the ground outside the storage room, which is consistent with her friend's statement that she went down Taylor's Yard to relieve herself. We also found traces of vomit, which we matched to her stomach contents, so it looks very much as if she was sick, too. The team also went through the neighbouring buildings. Most of them are empty or used for storage of some kind. Nothing there."

"So are we dealing with a particularly clever killer?" Templeton asked.

"Not necessarily," said Nowak. "You've got to wonder how smart a killer is when he cleans up a body but misses a drop of semen. Maybe he's just lucky. But let's be honest, anyone who sets out to commit a crime today has seen *The Bill*, probably *Silent Witness* and *CSI*, too. The general public knows way too much about forensics, no matter how much of it on the telly is fabricated. People know to be careful, and what to be careful about. In some cases, they even know how to go about it."

"What I'm getting at, ma'am," Templeton said to Gervaise, "is that we might be dealing with the first in a series. The more well prepared our killer went out, the more he cleaned up after himself, the more it suggests forward planning, surely?"

"It doesn't mean that he had any victim in mind beyond Hayley Daniels," argued Banks, "or that it wasn't someone who knew her. If Stefan is right and there are two distinct people involved, perhaps her killer wasn't her rapist. Has anyone traced Hayley's biological mother, by the way?"

"She went off to South Africa with her boyfriend," said Winsome. "Hasn't been back."

Banks turned to Templeton. "I think we all take your point, Kev," he said. "Jim, did your search turn up any similar crimes anywhere in the country over the past eighteen months?"

"There are plenty of teenaged girls gone missing," said Hatchley, "but most of them have turned up, and the ones who haven't didn't disappear in circumstances like Hayley Daniels."

"Thanks, Jim. Keep searching." Banks turned back to Templeton. "What I'm saying, Kev, is that we'll only know for sure we're dealing with a serial killer if there's a second and a third. It could have been a spontaneous crime, a rape gone wrong, not necessarily a serial killer in the making."

"But we can at least put some men in the Maze on weekends, can't we?"

Banks looked to Catherine Gervaise. "I'm not sure we can justify that expense, DS Templeton," she said. "We just don't have the manpower. We're already over budget on the forensics."

"It *had to be* a spontaneous attack to some extent," added Winsome. "Nobody knew Hayley was going to go into the Maze until she left the Fountain with her friends at twelve seventeen."

"But they all knew?" Gervaise asked.

"Yes. She told them outside the pub. It's on CCTV."

"Who else knew?"

"Nobody, as far as we know."

"Then it's one of her friends," said Gervaise. "Or the Lyndgarth yobs, the ones who gave the bartender in the Fountain such a hard time."

"No, ma'am," said Templeton. "I've just finished checking on them. Seems that after they were kicked out of the pub they nicked a car and went for a joyride. They crashed it outside York. Nothing serious, just cuts and bruises, but they were tied up at the hospital and with the York police most of the night."

"Well that's one we can cross off our list," said Gervaise.

"There is one small point," Winsome said. "Just now, when I spoke to Jill Sutherland, she told me that she often walks through the Maze when she's been working at the Fountain. It's a shortcut to the car park."

"So you think the killer was waiting for Jill and got Hayley instead?" Gervaise said.

"No, not necessarily, ma'am," Winsome answered. "Just that he might have known he had a good chance of finding a victim there if he knew about that."

"What I was saying," Templeton went on, "is that the killer was already waiting in there, *inside* the Maze. Winsome's right. It's the *location* that counts, not the specific victim. Maybe he'd been there on previous occasions, staking the place out, but nothing happened, and he was waiting. He knew it would happen sometime, that some unfortunate girl would walk in there alone – Jill Sutherland, for example – and he could strike. These people have infinite amounts of patience. This time he got lucky."

"I think DS Templeton has a point," said Dr. Wallace. She was in her casual civilian clothes today and Banks had hardly recognized her at first, a slight figure, with her hair drawn back from her forehead and pinned up tight, black turtleneck top and jeans, Nike trainers. He got the impression that she could be quite attractive if she wanted to be, but that it didn't interest her. "In my experience," she went on, "times before I've seen such cases, or even read case histories involving such injuries as I found on Hayley Daniels's body, they were almost always part of a series. I've looked at the crime scene photos," she went on, "and there was a definite 'posed' quality about the body. She wouldn't have been left in that position naturally after he'd finished with her. She would have been exposed, open, abandoned like a used doll. But she wasn't. He carefully turned her on her side, hid the damage he'd done, the trauma he had caused, so she just looked as if she were sleeping. He even cleaned her body. One-off killers don't usually go to such trouble."

"I understand what you're saying," said Banks, "but I've seen examples where someone has killed someone close to them and covered up the injuries in that way out of shame, or even covered the body with a jacket or a sheet. No killer except the habitual one knows what he's going to feel like after he's finished, and that sort of reaction, horror at the results of the crime, is common enough."

"Well," said Dr. Wallace, "I bow to your expert knowledge, of course, but I repeat: This could be only the beginning. There are indications the killer will strike again. And the Maze is a perfect location."

"All right," said Gervaise. "Point taken, DS Templeton and Dr. Wallace. But as I said before, at this stage we can hardly afford the manpower to saturate the Maze with police officers on Fridays and Saturdays. Besides," she went on, "don't you think that if you're right, and this is a potential serial killer, then he'll have the good sense to choose another location next time?"

"Not necessarily," said Dr. Wallace. "I'm not a psychologist, but I do know something about criminal behaviour, and people do become attached to certain places. The Maze is certainly big and complicated enough to be attractive to that sort of personality. He might find that it mirrors his inner state, for example, his inner turmoil. Lots of shadows and nooks and crannies to disappear into and appear from."

"And lots of ways in and out without being caught on camera," said Templeton. "The doc's right," he went on, getting a frown from Dr. Wallace, which he didn't notice. "He's lurking in an area at times when there are likely to be a lot of drunken young girls nearby not exercising a great degree of common sense. There are probably other similar dark and isolated areas close to the town centre, like the Castle Gardens and the Green, and they should be covered, too, but they're all more open. The Maze is perfect for him. Remember, Jack the Ripper only operated in Whitechapel."

"Even so, that was a much larger area," said Gervaise. "Anyway, I'm sorry but the best we can do at this point is increase the number of regular patrols in the area and put up warnings in the pubs advising people to avoid the Maze if they're alone, especially females," said Gervaise. "Also to stay in groups, not to wander off alone. That ought to be enough for now. Besides, the place is still a crime scene and will be for a while yet. It's taped off."

"Only the part of it near Taylor's Yard," argued Templeton, "and if you're bent on murder you're hardly likely to worry about a small infringement like –"

"That's enough, DS Templeton," said Gervaise. "The subject's closed."

"Yes, ma'am," said Templeton, tight-lipped.

Everyone was silent for a few moments, then Gervaise asked Banks what was next.

"We have a list of possibles," said Banks. "Joseph Randall, Stuart Kinsey, Zack Lane, Jamie Murdoch and Malcolm Austin. And the serial killer angle," he added, looking at Templeton. "I think the next thing we need to do is have another go at all our suspects a bit harder than we have before and see if we can't find a chink in someone's armour."

Someone knocked at the door, and one of Stefan Nowak's colleagues delivered an envelope to him. There was silence while he opened it. When he had finished, he glanced over at Banks. "That might not be necessary," he said. "Remember I said our killer might not be as smart as you think? Well, according to the lab, the DNA found in the semen sample on Hayley Daniels's thigh is the same as the saliva sample freely given by Joseph Randall. It looks very much as if we've got a positive match."

9

───────

"Thanks for taking the trouble to come down and see me," said Les Ferris, the researcher who said he had information, when Annie appeared in his office late that afternoon. "It's almost knocking-off time, and I don't get out much," he went on, picking up his rumpled tweed jacket from the back of his chair, "so why not let me treat you to a pint? Or a cup of tea, if that's your poison?"

Annie thought for a moment. She'd fallen off the wagon last night with disastrous consequences, but she was feeling better now, and one pint wouldn't do her any harm. Besides, the office was a mess and smelled of overripe banana skins. "Okay," she said, "you're on. A pint it is."

Les Ferris smiled, showing stained and crooked teeth. He was a bald, roly-poly sort of man with a red face, white whiskers and sad eyes.

It was a beautiful evening in Scarborough, the sort you didn't often get before the holiday season – or even during it, for that matter – and the locals were taking full advantage. Couples walked hand in hand on the prom, and families with young children, or pushing prams, lingered at the edge of the sea, kids throwing pebbles at the waves. One brave man even rolled up his trouser legs and tested the water, but he didn't last more than a few seconds. Annie could smell salt and seaweed and hear the gulls screeching overhead. For a second, they made her think of Lucy Payne's body, and she shivered.

"Cold?" asked Ferris.

Annie smiled. "No," she said. "Someone just walked over my grave."

Ahead, where the high promontory of Scarborough Castle bulged out and brooded over the bay, Annie could see the waves smashing against the sea wall, the salt-spray flying high. Ferris picked a cozy pub on a corner near Marine Drive. It looked over the harbour. The tide was out and a few white, red or green fishing boats rested on the wet sand. One man in a blue jersey was painting his hull. The pub was a Jennings house with guest beers, and Annie chose a pint of Cock-a-Hoop. Ferris reached for his cigarettes after he set the drinks down on the scratched table. "Do you mind?" he asked.

"Not at all," said Annie. The place already reeked of smoke and several people at nearby tables were smoking. "Make the best of it while you can."

"I've tried to stop about twenty times," said Ferris, "but somehow I just can't seem to manage it. I'm about to turn sixty-five next month, so at this point I think I'd better just resign myself to my fate, don't you?"

That wasn't what Annie had meant. She had been referring to the smoking ban coming into effect in July. But it didn't matter. "Sixty-five isn't old," she said. "You might just as easily live to be ninety. If you stop." She raised her glass. "Cheers. To ninety."

"Cheers. I'll drink to that." After he drank, Ferris inhaled deeply on his cigarette.

"You said you had something to tell me," Annie said.

"Yes. I'm not really sure if any of it's relevant, but when I heard about the identity of your victim it rang a bell."

"I'm hardly surprised," said Annie. "Lucy Payne was quite notorious in her day."

"No, it's not that. Not Lucy Payne."

"Perhaps you'd better start at the beginning?"

"Yes," said Ferris. "Yes, perhaps I had. I haven't always been a humble researcher, you know," he went on. "I've put in my time on East Yorkshire CID, as it was then. I might be past it now, but I was quite the dashing young detective at one time." His eyes twinkled as he spoke.

"I'll bet you were," said Annie, hoping a bit of flattery might help him get a move on. She had no particular plans for the evening, but she was looking forward to a quiet night in her room watching TV.

"Not that we ever got many murders along this stretch of coast," he went on, "which is probably why I thought of it. People say I've got a bee in my bonnet. For some reason, though, it's always haunted me. Perhaps because it all ended up as mysterious as it began."

"What?" said Annie. "You've got me intrigued."

"A case I worked on back in 1989. A mere callow youth of forty-seven, I was then. I'd just made DS. None of your accelerated promotion rubbish in those days. Back then, you earned your stripes."

"So I've heard," Annie said.

"Aye, well, not that there aren't plenty of good men around these days. A few women, too," he added hastily.

"This 1989 case," Annie said, lest he put his foot even further in his mouth. "What exactly brought it to your mind when you heard about Lucy Payne?"

"I was just getting to that." Ferris drained his pint. "Another?"

"Not for me. I'm driving," said Annie. "But let me get you one."

"Aye, all right," Ferris said. "Women's lib and all that. I'll have another pint of Sneck Lifter, please."

"Sneck Lifter?"

"Aye. I know it's strong, but I don't have far to go. Not driving, like you."

Annie went to the bar and asked for a pint of Sneck Lifter. The barmaid smiled and pulled it for her. She jerked her head over at Ferris. "It'll take more than this to lift his sneck," she said.

Annie laughed. "Luckily," she said, "I won't be around to find out."

The barmaid laughed with her, handed Annie her change and said, "Cheers, love."

Back at the table, Ferris thanked her for the pint and stared out of the window towards the sea. "Aye," he said. "September 1989. Nasty business it was. I was working out of Whitby then, way you are now. Mostly quiet apart from a few pickpockets in high season, the occasional pub brawl, break-in or domestic incident."

"What happened?" Annie asked him.

"Well, that's just it," Ferris said, scratching his chin. "We never rightly did find out. It was all nobbut speculation and conjecture. Based on what few facts we had, of course. We did our best. Anyroad, it's stayed with me all these years."

Annie sipped some beer. Might as well relax and let him tell it in his own time, she thought as she noticed the shadows lengthening outside. "I'm sure you did," she said. "But what makes you think it's linked to Lucy Payne's murder?"

"I never said that it was. It's just a funny coincidence, that's all, and if you're as good a copper as you're supposed to be, you won't trust coincidence any more than I do."

"I don't," said Annie. "Go on."

"First off, as I said, we don't get many murders in these parts, and you tend to remember all of them. We got even fewer back then. It started when a local bloke, a cabinetmaker called Jack Grimley, disappeared one night after leaving a pub called the Lucky Fisherman. A couple of days later his body washed up on the beach over Sandsend way."

"Murdered?"

"Hard to say for certain," said Ferris. "Could have been a head wound, the doc said, a smooth, rounded object, but he'd been in the water a couple of days, been bashed about on the rocks." He paused. "And the fish had been at him."

"Water in the lungs?"

"No. That's the thing."

That meant he hadn't drowned. "So he hit the rocks first as he fell in?"

"That was one theory."

"What was the coroner's verdict?"

"Death by misadventure. But DI Cromer, that's Paddy Cromer, who was in charge of the investigation, were never satisfied. He's dead now, or I'd suggest you have a word with him yourself. He had as much of a bee in his bonnet about it as I did, right up to the end. I was his DS."

Annie had no idea why Ferris was telling her this, or how it was relevant to the Lucy Payne murder, but she had some beer left in her glass and was content enough to spin it out for another few minutes while the sun went down. Pity they were facing east, she thought, or it would be a spectacular view. As it was, the delicate shade of blue reminded her of the blue in a piece of sculpted glass she had seen on the Venetian island of Murano once, many years ago, when she was a student. "Why wasn't DI Cromer convinced?" she asked.

Ferris touched the side of his red veined nose. "Instinct," he said. "Like women's intuition, only more reliable. Copper's instinct."

"So he had a hunch," Annie said. "I still don't get it."

Ferris gave her a dirty look, and for a moment she thought she'd ruined whatever rapport she had with him, but then he grinned. "No flies on you, are there? Anyway, whatever it was, Paddy wasn't happy. Me, neither. I mean, Jack Grimley could have fallen off the cliff. It's happened before. But according to his mates he hadn't had much to drink, and he lived in the other direction. There was no reason for him to be walking on the cliff edge. Besides, there's a beach at the bottom, not rocks. And that was when we first heard of the mysterious woman."

Annie pricked up her ears. "What mysterious woman?"

"Patience, lass, patience. A witness thought he saw Jack talking to a woman up near the Cook statue. It was dark, though, and he admitted he could have been mistaken. Still, it was all we had at the time, the only piece of information that placed him near the cliffs. And he was with someone."

"Had he said anything earlier about meeting a woman?" Annie asked.

Ferris shook his head. "Not to his mates he hadn't."

"Not like a man," said Annie. "Still, I suppose there could be any number of reasons for that. If it was a woman he was meeting, maybe she was married? Maybe even to one of his mates?"

"We thought of that. Thing is, no one ever came forward. We dug around, too, turned up nothing. Anyway," he hurried on, "if that was all that had happened, I wouldn't have dragged you all the way down here. Not that it isn't always a pleasure to have a drink with a pretty young girl."

Annie rolled her eyes and laughed. "How very gallant of you."

"I meant it," said Ferris. "You *are* a pretty lass."

"It was the 'young' bit I was referring to."

"Well, it's all relative, isn't it?"

"Indeed it is," said Annie, an image of the naked Eric flashing across her mind's eye. "So there's more?"

"There certainly is. I told you that Jack Grimley was just the first in a series of odd incidents that September. Odd enough to stick in my mind all these years as if they were yesterday. The second occurred a few days later when a young Australian lad called Keith McLaren was found with a serious head wound in some woods near Dalehouse, up the coast a ways, inland from Staithes."

"I know it," said Annie. "Isolated spot."

"Very. Anyway, the head wound showed remarkable similarities to Jack Grimley's. A smooth, rounded object. It was touch-and-go with young McLaren for a while, but he pulled through. Problem was, he'd no memory of what happened to him. The doctors said it might come back in time, in bits and pieces – it wasn't due to any physical brain damage – but that was no use to us. Now, the interesting thing is that a couple of people said they saw him down by the harbour in Staithes, probably the day it happened, walking with a young woman with short brown hair, wearing jeans, a grey windcheater and a checked shirt. It was better than the description we got from the witness who saw Jack Grimley with a woman by the Cook statue because it was dark then, but we'd no way of proving it was even the same person, let alone of knowing who she was."

"Anyone get a good look at her?"

"No, that's the problem. We couldn't even come up with a decent identikit from what we got."

"Any idea of her age?"

"Young, they said. As in twentyish."

"And you worked on the assumption it was the same woman in both cases?"

"Wouldn't you?"

"Probably, given the pathologist's assessment of the wounds. What happened to McLaren?"

"He recovered and went back to Australia."

"Do you have an address?"

"God knows where he is now. He was from Sydney. I seem to remember he was set on becoming a lawyer, if that's any help."

"Okay," said Annie, making a note. "So this mystery woman shows up in two separate accounts involving two serious attacks in the area, linked by the similarity in head wounds, possibly made by a smooth, rounded object, one resulting in death. And this is an area where you get very few violent incidents. Am I to take it that you're making a connection here between this woman and the one who showed up at Mapston Hall to take Karen Drew – or Lucy Payne – for a walk on Sunday morning?"

"That's right."

"But that was eighteen years ago, Les," said Annie. "What could it possibly have to do with what happened the other day?"

Ferris grinned and shook his empty glass. "But there's more. Buy us another Sneck Lifter and I'll tell you the whole story."

"Hello, Mr. Randall," said Banks, when the officers brought Joseph Randall into the interview room. "Nice to see you again."

"You can spare me the pleasantries," said Randall. "What do you mean by sending a police car to drag me out of my home? You couldn't possibly have sent a more obvious signal to my neighbours if you'd tried."

"Signal of what?" Banks asked.

"You know damn well what I'm talking about."

"Well, we wouldn't want you to have to walk all this way, would we?"

"Stop playing silly buggers. They wouldn't even give me any reason why they were bringing me here."

"They probably didn't know, themselves," said Banks. "You know how it is. Lowly PCs. Need-to-know basis. We don't tell them everything."

Randall folded his arms. "This time I've called my solicitor. He'll be meeting me here momentarily."

"Good idea," said Banks. "We like to make sure everything's above board when we get to this stage of an investigation."

Randall paused in his display of indignation and gave Banks a worried glance. "What do you mean, 'this stage'?"

"Endgame," said Banks, casually shuffling the papers in front of him. "We find it works best for us in court if everyone knows his or her rights, so there are no possibilities of infringement. So, if you like, we'll just wait here quietly until your solicitor arrives. It's not the most salubrious of places." Banks glanced around at the flaking institutional green paint, the high, barred window and the bare light bulb covered by a flyblown grille. "Still . . . Cup of tea while we wait?"

Randall grunted. "No, I don't want a bloody cup of tea. I want this over with so I can get out of here and go home."

"Mind if I have one?"

"I don't care what you do."

Banks asked the constable on guard to send for tea, and before it arrived, Randall's solicitor popped his head around the door, appearing lost. As Banks had expected, he wasn't used to having criminal clients. Most Eastvale solicitors weren't. This one looked as if it was his first time inside a police interview room.

"Come in," said Banks. He didn't recognize the young man in the ill-fitting suit, untidy hair and large spectacles. "You are?"

The solicitor shook Randall's hand and sat down in the spare chair. "Crawford. Sebastian Crawford. Solicitor."

"Sebastian takes care of all my affairs," said Randall.

"Good," said Banks. "I'll just call my colleague and we'll be ready to start." If Sebastian Crawford took care of all Randall's interests, Banks thought, then he wasn't likely to be very much of a criminal lawyer. With any luck, he would soon be way out of his depth.

The tea arrived, along with DS Stefan Nowak, and they settled down in the interview room. When he was ready, Banks turned on the video and tape machines and stated the details of date, time, place and those present. He could see how this made Randall nervous, while Crawford just sat there, fascinated by the whole routine.

"Now then, Mr. Randall," Banks began. "There've been a few interesting developments since we last talked, but before we get to them, I'd just like to recap briefly what you told us on the previous two times we talked to you, make sure it's accurate."

Randall glanced towards Crawford, who nodded. "I can see no harm in that, Joseph," he advised. "Do as they say."

"As I remember it," Banks said, "you were surprised to find that you'd spent eleven minutes in the storeroom with Hayley Daniels's body before reporting it to the police station. Is that correct?"

"It was you who said I spent eleven minutes there. I didn't think it was that long. You say someone saw me, but I thought I entered the building at quarter past eight, not ten past eight, as your witness said."

"It was ten past eight," said Banks. "Don't forget, Joseph, the CCTV cameras run in the daytime as well, and they are accurately timed. Eleven minutes is a long time to spend with a corpse. Unless there were matters to attend to, of course."

"Mr. Banks!" said Crawford. "What are you suggesting?"

"Nothing, yet," said Banks, keeping his eyes on Randall. "You also admitted that you were in the Duck and Drake earlier on Saturday evening, when Hayley and her friends were there, and that you were ogling her while she stood at the bar."

Randall looked at Crawford. "That was *his* word, not mine. I admitted to no such thing, Sebastian. You see? This is what they do. They twist what you say, put words into your mouth."

"But you *did* see her there," Banks went on. "And you *did* try to gloss over that fact in our first interview, didn't you?"

"I told you I didn't remember seeing her."

"Well, she certainly hadn't changed her clothes," said Banks. "And the only thing different about her appearance the following morning was that she was dead. But if you expect me to believe you saw an attractive young girl in a very revealing outfit at seven o'clock one evening and then again just after eight o'clock the next morning and didn't know it was the same girl, I suppose I have to believe you."

"It was the shock," said Randall. "For Christ's sake, man, she was dead. It might be par for the course as far as you're concerned, but I'm not used to seeing dead bodies on my property."

"Let's move on to what you did on Saturday night," said Banks. "You told me that you were at home between the hours of twelve and two, that you put the cat out and went to bed about a quarter to one. Do you stand by that?"

"Of course I do. It's what happened."

"It's not very far from where you live to Taylor's Yard, is it?" Banks said. "Though it might make more sense to drive to the car park at the back of the Maze and slip in through one of the passages not covered by CCTV."

"What on earth are you talking about?"

"Yes, Mr. Banks, what are you talking about?" Crawford chipped in. "My client has told you what he did on Saturday night."

"I'm presenting an alternative version," said Banks.

"But how could I have known the girl would go into the Maze at whatever time she did?" said Randall.

It was a good question, Banks had to admit, and he didn't have a ready answer. The whole element of spontaneity, of Hayley's deciding at the last minute to head into the Maze to relieve herself, bothered him. It was a stumbling block. But, he had to keep telling himself, it didn't preclude the possibility that there was somebody *already in there* just waiting for an opportunity, as Templeton believed. "You know the layout back there," he said. "What was to stop you from hiding out and waiting for a victim? It was simply a matter of time, after all, before some poor young drunken lass wandered in and got lost in there. Perhaps you'd been in the Fountain on previous occasions and knew that the barmaid there used it as a shortcut to the car park. Maybe you didn't know she was off work that night. No matter. Everything turned out well in the end, didn't it? I'll bet you couldn't believe your luck when you saw it was the girl you'd had your eye on in the Duck and Drake earlier that evening."

"Now, Mr. Banks," said Crawford with a nervous laugh. "Surely this is stretching our credulity a bit far, isn't it? Do you really expect us to believe this . . . er . . . coincidence?"

"Until Mr. Randall tells us how it really happened," said Banks, "I'm afraid it's the best we can do."

"I've told you how it happened," said Randall. "After the Duck and Drake I went home and spent the rest of the evening watching television. At about a quarter to one, I put the cat out and went to bed. End of story."

"I'd like to believe you," said Banks, "but I'm afraid what you're saying goes against the evidence."

"What evidence?" asked Crawford. "Are you saying you can produce evidence to corroborate what you're accusing my client of?"

Banks turned to Stefan Nowak. "We have evidence that goes a long way towards proving it," he said. "Stefan?"

Nowak opened a folder in front of him. "According to our independent analysis, the DNA from the sample you freely gave us matches the DNA taken from traces of semen found on Hayley Daniels's body and on two leather remnants close to the body."

"What are you saying?" said Randall, mouth gaping.

"That the chances it was someone else who left those semen traces on Hayley Daniels's body are about five billion to one," said Banks. "Am I right, DS Nowak?"

"About that, yes," said Nowak.

"And that's good enough for any court in the country," said Banks. "Joseph Randall, I'm charging you with the murder of Hayley Daniels. You do not have to say anything. But it may harm your defence if you do not mention when questioned something that you later rely on in court. Anything you do say may be given in evidence." Banks stood up and opened the door. Two burly constables walked in. "Take him down to the custody suite," said Banks.

"You can't do this to me!" said Randall. "Sebastian, help me! Stop them. That sample was taken under duress."

"You gave your consent," Banks said. "We have the waiver."

"Under duress. Sebastian! Stop them! Please don't let them do this to me."

Crawford wouldn't look his client in the eye. "There's nothing I can do right now, Joseph," he said. "They're quite within their rights. But believe me, I'll do everything in my power to help you."

"Get me out of this!" yelled Randall, red-faced, twisting his head back towards Crawford as the constables dragged him out of the interview room. "Sebastian! Get me out of this now!"

Crawford was pale and hunched. He managed to summon up only the grimmest of smiles as he edged past Banks into the corridor and followed his client down the stairs.

"Now this is where it gets really interesting," said Ferris after a long swig of Sneck Lifter. He could certainly put it away, Annie thought, checking her watch. She could write off *Coronation Street* tonight, and maybe *The Bill*, too, the way things were going. Still, if Ferris's story was as interesting as he obviously thought it was, maybe it would be worthwhile.

"A week or so after we found Jack Grimley's body and the Australian lad got hurt, another local chap by the name of Greg Eastcote was reported missing by a workmate. Apparently, he hadn't turned up at his job for several days. He was a delivery man for a fish wholesaler. We never found him, nor any trace of him."

"Why do I get the feeling there's always more?" said Annie. "This case is starting to resemble a hall of mirrors." There was perhaps a quarter of an inch of beer left in her glass, but she wasn't going to have another one, not this time. Control. Getting it back.

"It is, rather, isn't it?" said Ferris. "Anyway, we went into Eastcote's house to see if we could find any clues to his disappearance. He lived alone. I was there, along with Paddy Cromer. We had no evidence at all that there was any connection with what happened to Grimley and McLaren, but such mysterious disappearances and violent assaults were pretty rare around these parts, as I said. As far as his workmates were concerned, Eastcote was happy with his job and seemed generally uncomplicated and worry-free, if perhaps rather quiet and antisocial. A bit of an 'odd duck,' as one of them put it. To be honest, we didn't know what we'd stumbled into at the time."

"And now?"

Ferris laughed. "I'm not much the wiser." He drank some more beer and resumed his tale. The lights dimmed and the pub started to fill up with evening drinkers. Annie felt somehow cut off from the laughter and gaiety of the crowd, as if she and Ferris were adrift on their own island of reality, or unreality, depending on how you saw it. She couldn't explain why she felt that way, but somehow she knew that what Ferris was telling her was important, and that it had something to do with Lucy Payne's murder, though Lucy would have been only ten in 1989. "It was what we found there, in his home, that puzzled us," Ferris said. "In almost every respect it was a perfectly normal house. Neat and tidy, clean, the usual books, TV and videos. Normal."

"But?"

"This never made the media," Ferris said, "but in one of the sideboard drawers, we found seven locks of hair tied up in pink ribbons."

Annie felt her chest constrict. Ferris must have noticed some change in her because he went on quickly, "No, there's nothing normal about that, is there?"

"Did you? I mean . . ."

"Everyone knew there had been a serial killer operating in the north, and the general feeling was that now we'd found him, or at least found out who he was. We never did find Eastcote himself. As far as our tally was concerned, he had claimed six victims, but there were other young women missing, other unexplained disappearances, and one who survived."

Annie raised an eyebrow.

"Kirsten Farrow. Someone interrupted him before he could finish her off," Ferris went on. "She was in a pretty bad way for a long time, but she recovered."

"Did you talk to her?"

"Yes. She'd been staying in Leeds at the time with a friend called Sarah Bingham. She was vague, Kirsten, but you can expect that when someone suffered the way she did, poor lass. She really couldn't remember much about what happened to her at all. We also consulted with the investigators on the case, Detective Superintendent Elswick and his DS, Dicky Heywood. Greg Eastcote's delivery routes coincided with the disappearances and murders of all six girls and with Kirsten's assault. We also managed to match Kirsten's hair sample with one of the locks, so we know that he took a sample from her, even though she survived, and another lock matched that of his most recent victim. The others were . . . well, they'd been buried for a while, but we did our best. And you know what hair's like at the best of times; it's hardy and durable enough, but practically damned impossible to make a match that'll stand up in court, and these were early days for DNA. Too early. None of us had really heard much about it, and I doubt you could have got DNA from a hair follicle, even if there'd been one. But the hair had been shorn with sharp scissors, so that was pretty unlikely, anyway. And court was never an issue."

"No?"

"Like I said, we never found Eastcote. A local woman said she thought she'd seen two people struggling on the cliff path just up past the abbey on the way to Robin Hood's Bay, but she was a long way off, and she couldn't tell us any more than that. We searched the area and found one of the fence posts had come out of the ground. It seemed as if someone had gone over the edge. We also found blood and fibres on the barbed wire, but we'd no way of knowing whose they were. We got Eastcote's blood group from medical records, of course, and it matched, but so did 44 per cent of the country's."

"Were there any more killings?"

"Not after that. Not around here."

"You think he went over?"

"We didn't know for certain, but it was a reasonable assumption that his body had been carried out to sea on the tide."

"So what did you do?"

"What could we do? We followed a few minor leads, queried some of the local B and Bs. One woman remembered Keith McLaren staying at her guest house, and that he struck up a conversation with a young woman there. Seems only natural, I suppose, when you're young."

"Did you question him about it?"

"When he came out of his coma, yes. He did remember something about a girl. Apparently they had a drink together, but that's all."

"Name?"

"Didn't remember. Who knows, maybe he remembers more now. It's been eighteen years."

"Was there any follow-up?"

Ferris shook his head. "Years passed and nothing new came up. You know what it's like." He laughed. "Not like books or TV where the detective won't give up until he gets his man."

"Or woman."

"Aye. Anyway, officially there was no murder, remember. Jack Grimley was killed by a fall, and Greg Eastcote disappeared. The only actual crime was the one against Keith McLaren, and he couldn't remember anything, then he buggered off back to Australia. Pardon my French." Ferris paused. "Besides, the feeling was that if Greg Eastcote was a serial killer, as he appeared to be, then someone had done us a bloody big favour."

"I think you'd have been hard-pushed telling that to Jack Grimley's family, or to Keith McLaren."

"Aye, well, I never said it sat well with me over the years, did I, but that's the way things go, sometimes."

"So you did nothing?"

"My hands were tied."

"And that's where it stands today?"

Ferris sighed. "Until now," he said.

Annie frowned. The noise of laughter and conversation ebbed and flowed around them. Behind the bar, a glass smashed. "I still don't get it," she said. "It's a fascinating story, but you must realize there's nothing to connect those events directly with what happened to Lucy Payne the other day except the bee in your bonnet. It's been eighteen years. The whole idea's ludicrous."

"Yes, of course. I know that. But if *Eastcote* was the serial killer, and a woman sent him over that cliff..."

"And Kirsten Farrow was the surviving victim –"

"The mysterious woman seen with Grimley and McLaren. Exactly."

"But how could she be?" Annie said. "You told me yourself that she couldn't have known who her attacker was, and she was in Leeds with her friend at the time of the crimes."

Ferris shrugged. "That's what she told us. And her friend corroborated it. But alibis can be fabricated. What if she *had* found out?"

"Have you talked to anyone else about this?"

Ferris gave her a hurt look. "What do you think I am?"

Annie rubbed her forehead. "Sorry," she said. "The media's already in a feeding frenzy since they found out it was Lucy Payne on the edge of that cliff."

Ferris chuckled. "I'll bet they are. Anyroad, they'll get nothing from me."

Annie took out her notebook. "Okay, I'll make a few preliminary inquiries," she said. "You'd better start by giving me some names and last-known addresses. The Australian, Kirsten's friend. We're really pushed for manpower as it is, but maybe it'd be worth a bit of digging." Then she stopped, struck by an idea that might be as crazy as it sounded.

"What is it?" Ferris said.

"You know those locks of hair you told me about?"

"Yes."

"Did you keep them?"

"They'd be with the rest of the case material somewhere, yes," said Ferris.

"Do you think you could dig them out?"

Ferris's face lit up as if he had been given a new purpose in life. "Is the Pope Catholic?" he said, beaming. "I don't see why not. I am a researcher, after all."

The beer was flowing in the Queen's Arms, where the landlord had put two long tables together, and even Detective Superintendent Catherine Gervaise was joining in the celebrations with a smile on her face. Only Banks stood apart, leaning against the windowsill pensively sipping his pint, occasionally glancing out through the diamond-shaped panes at the passersby on Market Street as the shadows lengthened, feeling that something wasn't quite right, that they were perhaps being premature. But a DNA match was solid, an arrest was an arrest, and it demanded celebration. The Arctic Monkeys were on the jukebox and all was well with the world.

"What is it, sir?" asked Winsome, suddenly standing by his side, a purple drink topped with a maraschino cherry in her hand. Banks didn't even want to know what it was. She was a little wobbly, but her voice and her eyes were clear.

"Nothing," said Banks. "Having fun?"

"I suppose so."

"Something wrong?"

"No," said Winsome. "You just seemed far away. I wondered –"

"What?"

"Nothing, sir."

"Out with it."

"It's none of my business."

"What isn't?"

Someone bumped into Winsome, but she managed to hold on to her drink without spilling any. The man apologized and moved on.

Hatchley was telling a joke over the music and everyone at the table was waiting for the punchline. Banks had heard it before. "Busy in here tonight, isn't it?" Winsome said.

"You can't just start to say something, then cut it off in midstream," said Banks. "What's on your mind?"

"DI Cabbot, sir."

"Annie?"

"I told you, it's none of my business. I don't want to speak out of turn, but I know you two are friends."

"I used to think so, too," said Banks. Through the window, a couple of schoolgirls in dishevelled uniforms walked home from a late band practice, one carrying a violin case, the other a flute.

Hatchley reached his punchline and the table started laughing. "Sir?"

"Nothing. What about DI Cabbot?"

"I think something's bothering her."

"Bothering her? In what way?"

"I don't know, sir." Winsome lowered her voice. "I think it's a boyfriend. Stalking? Threatening?"

"I'll have a word," Banks said, wondering just how on earth he would manage to do that given their last encounter and the present climate of their relationship.

"You won't tell her I said anything?"

"Don't worry," said Banks. He saw the desk sergeant enter the pub, glance around and walk straight towards him. He groaned. "Shit, Ernie, what do you want?" he said.

"Always nice to find a warm welcome, sir," said Ernie.

"I'm sure it happens a lot when you're always the bearer of good news."

"You're not going to like it."

"I never do, but that's not stopped you yet."

"Bloke just came in, neighbour of Joseph Randall, the one you charged."

"And?"

"Says Randall can't possibly have done it, sir. Wants to talk to the man in charge."

"*Man* in charge?" Banks glanced over at Superintendent Gervaise, who seemed to be enjoying a private chat with DC Wilson, and wondered if feminism might actually work *for* him, just this once, then he decided just as quickly that it wouldn't. Why rain on their parade? If there was anything in it, they'd find out soon enough. "All right," he said, getting to his feet. "Lead on."

Annie mulled over her conversation with Les Ferris as she drove the A171, along the edge of the North York Moors, quiet at that time of evening, just after dark. She put some foot-tapping pop music on the radio to keep her going, but the chatter between songs irritated her so much that she turned it off. On the face of it, what Ferris had come up with sounded absurd: one murder, one serious assault and one unsolved disappearance of eighteen years ago, a mysterious woman seen in proximity to two of the three scenes. As he had said, there was only ever officially one crime: Keith McLaren's assault.

What could any of this possibly have to do with what happened on Sunday? Curiously enough, Annie thought there were quite a few connections. First was location. There had been no other murders around the cliffs in the past eighteen years, so why again now? Second came the strong possibility of a female killer. Women murderers are much rarer than men. Third, two of the victims were serial killers, or perceived by many to be serial killers: Greg Eastcote and Lucy Payne. Four, the murderer of eighteen years ago had not been caught. And that led to the fifth and final point of similarity: if the killer had been around eighteen years ago, that put her at almost forty now, and that was about the only thing they knew about the elusive Mary. Mel Danvers thought she had been about that age. It was still very tenuous, but the more Annie thought about it, the more she became convinced that it at least merited some investigation.

What about Keith McLaren, the Australian? Perhaps he had recovered more of his memory now. It was all moot until Les Ferris came up with the hair samples, anyway, and then a lot depended on whether they could match Kirsten's to any of the hairs found on Lucy Payne's blanket. If not, it was a washout, but if they did, they were in business.

It was a beautiful, clear evening, Annie thought, as she passed the road to Robin Hood's Bay. She could see the afterglow of the sunset, dark strata of red and purple silhouetting the western hills. To the east, over the North Sea, spread that magical shade of luminescent dark blue you saw only at the time of night opposite a sunset. A silver moon hung low to the north.

Soon Annie was amidst the traffic lights and streetlights, and the pleasures of the open road were lost. She found a parking spot only yards from her temporary accommodation and let herself in. The place seemed cool and dark, as if it had been abandoned far longer than it actually had. Perhaps the nicest thing about it, Annie thought, was that she could just see a wedge of sea between the rooftops. She turned the lights on, hung up her jacket and headed for the kitchenette. She hadn't eaten dinner, had only sipped that one pint to Ferris's three, and she could do with a glass of wine and a plate of cheese and crackers.

Tomorrow would be a busy day, she reflected, as she put the plate and glass beside her on the desk and turned on her laptop. There were people connected with the Paynes' victims to be interviewed, and now another line of inquiry coming out of Les Ferris's story.

Only one thing was certain: given the workload they had already, if they were to follow Ferris's leads, they were going to be seriously overstretched. Which meant Annie had to approach Superintendent Brough for both overtime, as she had already promised Ginger, and for extra personnel. These were the two things no budget-conscious administrator liked to authorize these days. It would be hard to sell it to Brough, but she'd worry about that later. Besides, he was bound to have his hands full with the press.

The one good thing about Brough, Annie had learned in the short time she had been working at Eastern, was that he didn't really listen. He was easily distracted and tended to focus on matters of public opinion and image; he was also the kind of person who was well on to his response to the next press question before you'd finished speaking. Consequently, a lot passed by him, which you could legitimately claim to have told him, and he tended to nod abruptly, agree and say okay simply to facilitate being able to move on, to say something he thought more interesting.

The Internet connection was slow. The guest house didn't have broadband, and Annie had to rely on the phone line and the computer's internal modem. But it was good enough for e-mail, which was all she really wanted. Tonight it seemed to take an unusually long time to download. She cursed whoever it was had decided to send her a large attachment, probably some silly joke or holiday snap, then she saw Eric's name appear next to a paper clip and her heart constricted.

How had he got hold of her e-mail address? Then it dawned on her: the BlackBerry. Eric had showed her how to attach photos and send them. She had sent one to him in the club. That was how he had got her e-mail address. How could she be so careless?

The other messages were all junk – Viagra, breast enlargement and genuine Rolex offers, along with various sales newsletters.

She opened Eric's message. It was short, in blue italic script, and to the point:

> *Dear Annie,*
> *I hope you enjoyed Saturday as much as I did. You were fantas-*
> *tic!! I can't wait to do it again (and more ☺). In the meantime*
> *I'm really looking forward to our lunch tomorrow and getting*
> *to know you a bit more. I don't even know where you come from*
> *or what you do for a living! Don't forget 12 noon at the Black*
> *Horse, I'll be waiting.*
> *Love,*
> *Eric.*

Annie's heart sank when she opened the attached JPEG. She definitely didn't remember posing for this one. It was a slightly blurred picture of her and Eric, no doubt using the self-timer. This time she had her head resting on his shoulder, his arm encircling her. Her hair was dishevelled, and her eyes unfocused. All of which would have been perfectly inno-cent, albeit a little embarrassing, except that it was clear, even from the head and shoulders, that both she and Eric were stark naked, and that she was holding a joint between her thumb and forefinger. And bugger it if she wasn't smiling.

"Well, Joseph," said Banks, back in the same interview room with the tape recorder running and Sebastian Crawford hovering nervously in the background again. "It looks as if we're not at the bottom of this yet, doesn't it?"

"I don't know what you're talking about," said Randall.

"I think you do," said Banks. He leaned forward. "And I think it would be in your best interests to admit that you do."

Randall licked his lips and looked to Crawford for guidance. Crawford said nothing.

"Right," said Banks, leaning back in his chair. "Let me lay it out for you, then. We've just had a visit from your neighbour, Roger Colegate, who tells us that he saw you putting the cat out at half past twelve on Saturday night. Though we don't as yet know the exact time Hayley Daniels was murdered, we do have evidence pointing towards the fact that she entered the Maze at twenty past twelve and was most likely accosted by her attacker by twenty-five past twelve or thereabouts."

"Well, there you are then," said Randall with a triumphant glance towards Sebastian Crawford. "I couldn't have done it, could I?"

"It would probably have taken you at least fifteen minutes to walk up to the market square from where you live," Banks went on, "even if you had been capable of walking in a straight line at the time."

"What do you mean?" Randall said.

"According to your neighbour, you were pissed," said Banks. "In fact, according to Mr. Colegate you were usually pissed by that time most nights."

"That's a lie," said Randall. "I might have had a drink or two, but there's no law against that, is there?"

"Not at all," said Banks. "No law against getting pissed, either, providing you don't cause any bother."

"Well . . . ?"

"Mr. Colegate says you were unsteady on your feet and that when he called out good evening, you replied in a slurred voice. You don't even remember that, do you?"

"No," said Randall, "but it doesn't matter, does it? *He* remembers it. That's what counts. Like you say, there's no law against getting a little drunk in one's own home once in a while, is there? I'm off the hook. I *can't* have done this terrible thing. You have to let me go."

Banks paused. "You did find the body, however."

"You already knew that. I was the one who reported it to you. And I had a legitimate reason for being there."

"Yes, we've checked with the customer you told us about. You did have a rush order for a handbag. But that's hardly relevant."

"What do you mean?"

"You spent eleven minutes alone with Hayley Daniels's body."

"So? She was dead when I found her."

"I know that," said Banks.

"Look, I think you should just apologize, cut your losses, let me go and have done with it. Sebastian?"

Crawford cleared his throat. "Er . . . My client does have a point, Chief Inspector. After all, you've already agreed that he couldn't possibly have been responsible for the murder of Hayley Daniels, which is what you've been holding him for."

"That could change," Banks said.

"What do you mean?" Randall asked.

"The problem remains," Banks went on. "Our forensic experts definitely found your DNA in semen samples taken from the victim. In fact, our crime scene coordinator had been puzzled that the semen hadn't dried as much as he would have predicted, had it been there overnight."

Randall folded his arms. "I told you, I'm sorry, but I can't help you there."

"Oh, I think you can," said Banks. He leaned forward and rested his palms on the desk, face only a couple of feet from Randall's. "Would you like me to tell you what I think *really* happened in that storeroom, Joseph?"

Randall licked his lips. "What's the point? You'll tell me anyway. More fantasy."

"Perhaps it started as a fantasy," said Banks, "but it wasn't mine. I think you're telling the truth, and so is Mr. Colegate. I think you saw Hayley Daniels in the Duck and Drake after you closed up shop on Saturday night and you liked what you saw. Perhaps you'd seen her there before? After all, she frequently spent Saturday nights on the town with her college friends. Or perhaps it didn't really matter who you saw as long as she was young and scantily dressed. I believe you went home, as you said you did, watched television, or perhaps some porn on DVD, and drank yourself into a stupor, fuelling your fantasies, until you could hardly stand up at half past twelve, when you put the cat out and, in all likelihood, went to bed."

"So what if any of this is true?" said Randall. "None of it's illegal."

"I'd like to believe that you dashed back to the shop, saw Hayley Daniels conveniently walking into the Maze and hurried after her," Banks went on, "but in all fairness, I don't think that's very realistic. The timing doesn't work, and it would be far too much of a coincidence."

"Well, thank heaven for that! Can I go now?"

"But you did find the body the following morning," Banks said.

"And reported it."

"Something happened in those eleven minutes, didn't it, Joseph? Something came over you, some urge you couldn't resist."

"I don't know what you're talking about."

"I think you do."

"Chief Inspector –"

"Please be quiet, Mr. Crawford. I'm not infringing your client's rights in any way." Banks turned back to Randall. "That's what happened, isn't it, Joseph? You walked into your storeroom as usual to pick out some suitable remnants, turned on the light, and you saw her there, lying on her side on the soft pile of scraps as if she were asleep, some poor lost babe in the woods taking shelter from the storm. She looked so innocent and beautiful lying there, didn't she? And you couldn't help yourself. I'll bet you touched her, didn't you, Joseph? Fondled those small firm breasts, small *cold* breasts? Did it really turn you on, her being dead like that, unable to respond, to say or do anything, to stop you? You were in complete control, weren't you, probably for the first time in your life? There wasn't a thing she could do, was there? So you touched her skin, and you ran your hands over her thighs. Did you kiss her, Joseph? Did you kiss those dead lips? I think you probably did. How could you resist? She was all yours."

Randall hung his head in hands. Crawford moved over to him. "You don't have to say anything, Joseph," he said. "This is sick."

"Indeed it is," said Banks. "And he's right. You don't have to say anything. I already know, Joseph. I know everything. I know how you felt as you knelt beside her and unzipped. You were hard, weren't you, harder than you'd ever been? And with one hand you touched her between her legs and with the other you touched yourself, and it happened, didn't it? Perhaps sooner than you expected. Then you had to clean up. You didn't do a very good job. That's why we found what we did, isn't it? You thought you'd got it all, but you were in a hurry and you missed some. Eleven minutes, Joseph."

Randall sobbed into his hands. Crawford had one arm draped awkwardly over his shoulders. "I didn't kill her," Randall cried. "I didn't hurt her. I would never have hurt her." He looked up at Banks with a tear-streaked face. "You must believe me. I'm sorry. I'm so sorry."

Banks felt sick. He edged his chair back, stood up and went to open the door. "Take him back down to the custody suite," he said to the constable on guard. "And ask the sergeant to charge him with committing an indignity on a dead body, or whatever the bloody hell they call it these days. Go with him, please, Mr. Crawford. Go quick. Just get him out of my sight. Now!"

Crawford helped Randall to his feet and they shuffled out into the grasp of the waiting constable. Alone in the small interview room with only the hum of the recording machines breaking the silence, Banks let out a loud expletive and kicked the only chair that wasn't bolted to the floor so hard that it sailed across the room and smashed into the tape recorder. Then all was silent.

10

It was almost twenty past twelve when Annie made her way along Church Street to the Black Horse, having escaped the station and the media. She half hoped that Eric would have left by now; it would save her the trouble of dumping him in person. It would have been easier simply not to turn up, of course, but she already had the impression that Eric wasn't the type to let go easily; he would need a bit of coaxing.

Annie had deliberately dressed down for the occasion in a pair of old trainers, a shapeless, knee-length skirt and a black turtleneck jumper under her denim jacket. She had also resisted putting on any makeup. It had been difficult, more so than she would have expected. She wasn't vain, but in some ways she would like to have made a stunning entry, turned all the heads in the pub, and then given him his marching orders. But she also wanted to do nothing to encourage him.

As it turned out, such was her natural appeal – or perhaps it was because everyone in the pub was male – that heads turned anyway when she entered the small, busy bar. Including Eric's. Annie's heart sank as she dredged up a weak smile and sat opposite him. "Sorry I'm late," she said, pushing her hair back. "Something came up at the office." It was partly true. Her meeting with Superintendent Brough had gone on longer than expected, mostly because it was hard to convince him that Les Ferris's information amounted to anything at all. Finally, she had got Brough to agree to let her initiate a limited search for the Australian and for Sarah Bingham, while Les Ferris tried to find the hair samples for comparison.

"That's all right," Eric said, smiling. "I'm just glad you came at all. Drink?"

"Slimline tonic, please." Annie was determined to do this in a civilized way, over lunch, but with a clear head.

"Are you sure?" Eric had a pint of Guinness in front of him, almost finished.

"Yes, thanks," Annie said. "Tough afternoon ahead. I'll need all my wits about me."

"You must have a really demanding job. I'll be back in a minute, and you can tell me all about it."

Eric headed for the bar and Annie studied the menu. She was starving. Given the lack of choice, the veggie panini would have to do. Either that or a cheese-and-onion sandwich. When she looked up, Eric was on his way back with the drinks, smiling at her. His teeth were straight and white, his black hair flopped over one eye, and he hadn't shaved since she had last seen him, by the looks of it. He handed her the drink and clinked glasses.

"Decided?" he asked.

"What?"

"Food."

"Oh, yes," said Annie. "I think I'll have a panini with mushrooms, mozzarella and roasted red peppers. Tell me what you want, and I'll go order."

Eric put his hand on her arm and stood up. "No. I insist. I invited you. As it happens, I'm a vegetarian, so I'll have the same." He smiled. "Is that something else we have in common?"

Annie said nothing. She watched him walk away again and found herself thinking that he had a nice bum and wondering what he thought they had in common other than being vegetarians. She chastised herself for the impure thought and steeled herself for what she had to do, faltering for just a moment as to why she had to do it. But she had no place in her life and career for a young, marijuana-smoking musician, no matter how nice his bum or his smile.

"It'll only be a few minutes," Eric said as he sat down again and lit a cigarette. He offered Annie one, but she said no.

Annie sipped some Slimline tonic. "That e-mail you sent me last night wasn't too cool, you know," she said.

"What? I'm sorry. I just thought it was a laugh, that's all."

"Yeah, well. That's the difference between you and me. I didn't. If anyone else saw it –"

"Who else is likely to see it? I only sent it to you. Why would you show it to anyone else?"

"That's not the point. You know what I mean. E-mails are hardly private."

"I'm sorry. I didn't realize you worked for MI5. Sworn the Official Secrets Act, have you?"

"I don't, and I haven't."

"What exactly *do* you do?"

"That's none of your bloody business."

"Sorry. Don't you have a sense of humour?"

"That's neither here nor there."

"Are we on again?"

"What do you mean?"

"You and me. We've had our first fight, and we're over it, so why don't we make a few plans for some more lovely evenings like the other night?"

"I don't think so, Eric," said Annie.

His face dropped. "Why not?"

"It's what I wanted to talk to you about. Why I'm here." She paused again but not for dramatic effect. Her throat was suddenly dry, and she sipped some more tonic. Why did it come in such small bottles? The serving girl came over with their paninis. Eric tucked in and eyed her expectantly. "I really don't know how to say this," Annie went on, not touching her food. "I mean, you seem like a nice guy, and I had a lovely time the other night and all, but I don't think . . . I mean, I just don't think it has to lead anywhere. What I'm saying is that I don't want it to lead anywhere."

"A one-night stand?"

"If you like."

Eric put his panini down and shook his head. A slimy sliver of red pepper with a charred edge hung out of the bread. "I don't like. I *definitely* don't like. I don't go in for one-night stands."

What was Annie supposed to say to that? she wondered. That she did? "Look," she went on, "it's not something I make a habit of, either. We had a few drinks and a good time and we ended up, well, you know, but that's it. It was fun. It doesn't have to go any further. I hope we can still be friends." Christ, Annie, she thought, that sounded pathetic.

"Friends? Why would we be friends?"

"Fine," said Annie, feeling herself redden. "We won't. I was just trying to be nice."

"Well, don't bother on my account. What's wrong with you?" He had raised his voice so much that some of the other customers were glancing their way.

"What do you mean?" Annie scanned the pub, feeling her panic rise. "And keep your voice down."

"Why are you saying this? Keep my voice down? I mean, look at you, you're old enough to be my mother. You should be bloody grateful I picked you up in that pub and gave you a good shag, and here you are trying to work it out so that *you're* dumping *me*. Just how do you get to that, I wonder?"

Annie couldn't believe what she was hearing. Her ears buzzed and her breath caught in her throat. She could only sit there with her mouth open and her skin burning, aware of the silence all around them and everyone's eyes on her.

"Maybe you don't remember," Eric went on, "but I do. Christ, you couldn't get enough of it the other night. You were *screaming* for it. You should be flattered. I mean, isn't that just what you older women want, a young stud to give you –"

"You *bastard*!" Annie stood up and tossed the rest of her Slimline tonic in his face. Unfortunately for her, there wasn't much left in the bottom of her glass, which undermined the dramatic effect somewhat, but as she shot to her feet, her thighs caught the underside of the table and tipped it over, spilling Eric's full pint of Guinness and his panini with the slimy red peppers all over his lap. Then, as fast as she could, she dashed out into Church Street and made her way, tears in her eyes, towards the 199 steps up St. Mary's Church. Only when she had got to the top and stood in the almost deserted graveyard leaning on a windworn tombstone did she stop for breath and start sobbing as the seagulls screeched around her, the wind howled and waves crashed on the rocks below.

"It must mean business if someone of your rank is paying house calls," said Malcolm Austin as he let Banks and Winsome into his office Thursday late afternoon. Winsome had argued for bringing the professor into the station, but Banks thought it would be a better idea to go at him harder once more on his own territory, where he was surrounded by everything he had to lose.

Banks glanced around at the overflowing bookcases. Sometimes he thought he wouldn't have minded being an academic, spending his life surrounded by books and eager young minds. But he knew he'd miss the thrill of the chase, and that the young minds were not necessarily as eager or as exciting as he might think. The window was open a few inches, and Banks could smell coffee and fresh bread from the courtyard café below and hear the hum of distant conversations. All morning his mind had been full of Lucy Payne and her crimes, and of Annie's mysterious behaviour, Winsome's aside in the Queen's Arms, how he could approach Annie about it, but now he needed to concentrate on the job at hand: finding Hayley Daniels's killer.

Austin bade them sit and arranged his lanky body, legs crossed, in the swivel chair behind his messy desk. He wore track pants and a red sweatshirt emblazoned with an American basketball team logo. An open laptop sat on the desk in front of him, and as he sat down he closed it. "How can I help you?" he asked.

"Do you remember the last time I talked to you?"

"Who could forget such —"

"Never mind the bollocks, Mr. Austin," said Banks. "You told DC Jackman that you weren't having an affair with Hayley Daniels. Information has come to light that indicates you were lying. What do you have to say about that?"

"What information? I resent the implication."

"Is it true or not that you were having an affair with Hayley Daniels?"

Austin looked at Winsome, then back at Banks. Finally he com-
pressed his lips, bellowed up his cheeks and let the air out slowly. "All
right," he said. "Hayley and I had been seeing one another for two
months. We started about a month or so after my wife left. Which means,
strictly speaking, that whatever Hayley and I had, it wasn't an affair."

"Semantics," said Banks. "Teacher shagging student. What do you
call it?"

"It wasn't like that," said Austin. "You make it sound so sordid. We
were in love."

"Excuse me while I reach for a bucket."

"Inspector! The woman I love has just been murdered. The least you
can do is show some respect."

"How old are you, Malcolm?"

"Fifty-one."

"And Hayley Daniels was nineteen."

"Yes, but she was —"

"That's an age difference of thirty-two years, according to my calculations. It makes you technically old enough to be her grandfather."

"I told you, we were in love. Do you think love recognizes such
mundane barriers as age?"

"Christ, you're starting to sound like a bloody pedophile," said
Banks. "If I had a quid for every time I've heard that argument."

Austin flushed with anger. "I resent that remark. Where do you
draw the line, Inspector? Nineteen? Twenty? Twenty-one? You know
you don't have a leg to stand on as far as the law is concerned." He
paused. "Besides, as I was about to tell you, Hayley was much older than
her years, very mature for her age."

"Emotionally?"

"Well, yes."

"Tell me what emotionally mature young woman goes out drinking
with a group of friends on a Saturday night, wearing practically
nothing, and drinks so much she gets legless and totters down a dark
alley for a piss?" Banks could sense Winsome staring at him, and he
knew she was thinking he was acting almost as badly as Templeton. But
self-righteous pricks like Austin, who abused their positions of power to
indulge their desires for young girls, or boys, always made him angry,

and he still felt plenty of residual anger from his interview with Randall the previous evening. He knew he needed to tone it down, though, or Austin would clam up completely, so he indicated subtly to Winsome that he had got her message, knew what he was doing and was easing his foot off the accelerator.

"I think what Mr. Banks means," said Winsome, "is what sort of shape would Hayley have been in on Saturday night when she got to your house? If you remember, you did indicate last time I talked to you that you didn't want a drunk and immature teenager in your house. Now you're saying that Hayley was mature for her years. Maybe you can see our problem? We're getting a few conflicting remarks here."

"That's it exactly," Banks said. "You see, Malcolm, according to all accounts, Hayley was pretty far gone. I find myself wondering what use she could have possibly been to you in that state."

Austin glared. "You might not understand this, Mr. Banks," he said, "but love isn't always a matter of 'using,' of what you can get from someone. If Hayley had come to me on Saturday night and she'd been drinking, I wouldn't have taken advantage of her. I didn't need for her to be drunk to make love. I would have made her some coffee, left her to sleep it off, made her as comfortable as possible."

Banks remembered Annie's drunken visit of the other night. Is that what he should have done? Settled her down, made her comfortable? "Admirable," he said. "But were you expecting her?"

Austin paused to examine something on his desk, then he said, "She told me she might come by. Saturday was always a casual arrangement. It was her night."

"Then why did you lie to DC Jackman the last time she spoke to you?"

Austin looked guiltily at Winsome. "I'm sorry," he said. "It was just that I was afraid of exactly the kind of reaction I got from you just now. Our relationship is not easy to explain. People don't always understand." He glared at Banks again.

"Look," said Banks, in his best we're-men-of-the-world manner, "no man would deny the attractiveness of a lissome nineteen-year-old beauty like Hayley Daniels, and no one could fail to understand why you wanted to bed her. The love bit's a touch harder to fathom, I will admit, but granted, it happens. People are strange that way. The problem isn't so much the age difference, but that you're a teacher and she was your student. What do the college authorities think of this sort of thing?"

Austin looked away. "They don't know, of course. I doubt that they'd be sympathetic. They frown on teacher-student relationships."

"So you didn't want them to know? It could mean your career?"

"That's one reason I wasn't completely truthful, yes. I've worked very hard for many years to get where I am now."

"Only one reason?"

"Well, no one wants to be dragged into a murder investigation, do they?"

"But you're in it now. Up to your neck. Did you really think you could get away with lying about something like that?" Banks shook his head. "It just boggles my mind that people must think we're so stupid as to overlook the obvious." A hint of marijuana smoke drifted up from the courtyard.

"I don't think you're stupid," said Austin. "I just didn't think it was that obvious. We tried to be discreet. We were going to go public when she finished her diploma. Now it's all out in the open, what is it you want to know? I had nothing to do with Hayley's death. As I told you, I love her. Loved her."

"Had she dropped by after going out drinking on a Saturday night before?" Banks asked.

"Yes. I can't honestly say I was too thrilled. I mean, she was usually, as you said, a bit the worse for alcohol. But it was her night out with her friends, and if, well, quite frankly . . ."

"What?" said Banks.

"Well, if she had to spend the night somewhere, I'd rather she spent it with me."

"You didn't trust her?"

"I didn't say that. But she's young. Vulnerable."

"So you were jealous," said Banks. "Stands to reason. I'd be jealous too if I had a beautiful young girlfriend. A few drinks in her, and she might start shagging someone her own age." Banks felt Winsome bristle again. Templeton-phobia or no, she had to loosen up, he thought. You sometimes had to shake the tree pretty hard to get the coconut to fall.

Austin was an educated type, not without a touch of arrogance, and you weren't going to get to him by logical argument and civilized banter.

"If, as I am," Austin said, "you are fortunate enough to have the love of a young woman, you soon learn that you can't afford to be clinging in the relationship."

"What did you think when she didn't turn up?" Winsome asked.

"I didn't think anything, really. I mean, it was by no means definite that she would."

"You weren't worried about her?"

"No."

"But she wasn't expected at home," Banks cut in, "so where did you think she was staying?"

"With friends, I suppose."

"With someone else? And you were jealous. Did you go out searching for her?"

"I told you, it doesn't pay to be clinging. Besides, I trusted Hayley. Yes, as I said, I would rather her stop with me, but if she stopped at a friend's flat, it didn't mean she would be sleeping with him." His eyes misted over. "In a way," he said, "I suppose I hoped she wouldn't come. I always found it hard to deal with her in that state, and I was tired on Saturday."

"Hard to handle when she was drunk, was she?" said Banks.

"She could be."

"What was she like?"

"Irrational, unpredictable, overtalkative."

"Would Hayley have arrived by one o'clock if she was coming?"

"Usually, yes. Anyway, she had a key."

"Very trusting of you."

"It's called love, Inspector. You really ought to try it."

"Chance would be a fine thing. Why should we believe you?"

"I don't follow."

Banks scratched the scar beside his right eye. "You've lied to us once or twice, so why should we believe anything you tell us now?"

"Because it's the truth."

"Easy for you to say. But look at it from my point of view. Hayley makes her way to your house the worse for wear. You're fed up with her drunken antics and you tell her so, in no uncertain terms. Maybe she teases you, makes fun of your age or something, and you see red. She doesn't want it, but she's drunk and you don't care what she wants. You know what you want. So you do it anyway. She struggles, but that just makes it all the more exciting. Afterwards she's making such a fuss, maybe even threatening to tell the college what you've done. You can't have that, so you strangle her. Then you're stuck with a body. Best thing you can think of at short notice is to shove it in the boot of your car and dump it in the Maze." A few of the facts didn't quite match the story Banks was telling, such as the violence of the rape, the timing, and the CCTV tapes, but Austin wasn't to know that. "How am I doing?"

"You should write detective fiction," Austin said. "With an imagination like that, I'm surprised you waste it on being a policeman."

"You'd be surprised how useful imagination is in my job," said Banks. "Am I at least close?"

"Miles away." Austin leaned back in his chair. "Inspector, it would save us all a lot of trouble if you would just believe that I didn't kill Hayley. Whatever you might think of me, I really did love her, and if I could help you, I would." He glanced at Winsome. "I'm sorry I lied, but I really didn't want to lose my job over this and have my name dragged through the mud. Those are the only reasons I said what I did."

"How well did you know Hayley?" Banks asked.

"Well enough, I suppose. As I said, we'd been together for about two months, but I'd known her for about a year in all. And before you ask, there was nothing between us in that time." He paused. "I don't want you to get the wrong impression. Whatever you might have heard about Hayley's behaviour on Saturday night, it was . . . youthful high spirits. Just that. She sometimes needed to let off steam. Most of the time, as anyone will tell you, Hayley was an intelligent, sober, quiet-spoken, hard-working and ambitious young woman. That's what I meant when I referred to her maturity. Mostly she found boys of her own age trivial and obsessed with only one thing."

"And you weren't?"

"I'll admit that knowing Hayley gave me a new lease on life in that direction, but you mustn't make the mistake of assuming that was what it was all about."

"What was it all about?"

"Sharing a nice meal. Just being together. Talking. Going for walks. Holding hands. Breakfast in bed. Going to a concert. Listening to classical music. Cuddling. Discussing a book we'd both read. Simple things. I could hardly wait until we were able to come out in the open with it. The secrecy was such agony. I'll miss her more than you could ever imagine."

Banks felt jealous. He hadn't done any of those things with anyone for years, if ever, or felt that way about anyone. He and his ex-wife, Sandra, had had such different tastes and interests that their lives had been parallel rather than joined. And when the parallel lines started to diverge slightly, the end had come quickly. Even with Annie there had been more differences than things in common. Still, he wasn't going to let sentimentality and sympathy for Austin cloud his vision. "You say you want to help," he went on. "If you didn't kill her, have you any idea who did?"

"I don't know. Some maniac by the sound of it."

"The truth could be closer to home," said Winsome. "What about enemies? Is there anyone in her immediate circle she had problems with?"

"There's Stuart Kinsey, I suppose. He was always chasing after her."

"But you told me he wouldn't harm anyone," said Winsome.

"I still don't think he would," said Austin, "but you asked me, and I can't think of anyone else. Hayley just wasn't the sort of person to make enemies."

"Well, she made one," said Banks, standing up. "Thanks for your time, Malcolm. And stick around. We might need to talk to you again."

Intense and rejected in love. That was a very bad combination, Banks knew. A very bad combination indeed. And Stuart Kinsey had admitted to going into the Maze, ostensibly to spy on Hayley, to find out who she was seeing. That gave him motive and opportunity. Could means be far behind? Time for another word with Mr. Kinsey.

It was a good hour and a half or more from Whitby to Leeds, depending on the traffic, and this was the second time Annie had done it in two days. Her feelings were still smarting from the lunch with Eric. It hadn't taken him long to show his true colours. Now she worried about what other photos he might still have on his mobile or his computer. What would he do with them? Post them on the Internet? How could she have been so bloody foolish, drunk or not? Her hands gripped the steering wheel tightly and her teeth gritted as she thought about it and remembered what he said. He had been lashing out just to be cruel, of course, but was there any truth in it? Had she seemed too desperate, too eager, too *grateful*?

She drove along Stanningley Road, turned off before Bramley and found her way to The Hill. The Paynes had lived close to the top, just before the railway bridge, on the right as you drove down, and Claire Toth and her family lived practically over the street, where a row of old, detached houses with overgrown gardens stood at the top of a steep rise. It was six years since Annie had last driven by, and then there had been police barriers and crime scene tape all over the place. Now all that was gone, of course, but so was number 35, and in its place stood two new red-brick semis. Well, she supposed no one would want to live in the House of Payne, as the newspapers had called it, or next door, for that matter.

As she slowed down, Annie shivered at a sudden memory of the time she went down into the cellar: the obscene poster of the woman with her legs spread; the dank, claustrophobic atmosphere with its smell of blood and urine; the occult symbols on the walls. Fortunately for Annie, the body of Kimberley Myers had been removed by the time she got there, along with the bloody mattress.

Annie could imagine the ground haunted by the ghosts of the poor girls who had been raped, tortured and buried down there. And Lucy Payne, the woman in the wheelchair with her throat cut, had definitely been involved in that. Banks had spent a lot of time interviewing Lucy, first as a victim and later as a possible suspect, and she had certainly had an effect on him, no matter what he claimed, but it was clear that even now he hadn't any more understanding of what really went on in that cellar, or why, than anyone else.

Annie parked at the bottom of the steps in front of Claire's house and pulled herself together. She knew that she had to get over what happened the other night and talk to Banks. Sober this time. So she had made a fool of herself. So what? It wasn't the first time, and it wouldn't be the last. Explain. He'd understand. God knew, he was understanding enough; he wasn't going to toss her out on her ear. Was she so afraid of a little embarrassment? That didn't sound like the woman she thought she was. But was she who she thought she was?

She climbed the steps, noting as she went that the garden that straggled down to the pavement seemed even more overgrown than ever, especially for the time of year, and a high fence about halfway up blocked the view of the house from below. Annie opened the gate and carried on climbing the last flight of steps.

The front door needed a coat of paint, and a dog or cat had clearly been scratching at the wood. The small lawn was patchy and overgrown with weeds. Annie wasn't quite sure how she was going to approach Claire. Was the girl a serious suspect? If not, was she likely to know anything that would help? It seemed that all she was doing was going in there to reopen old wounds. Taking a deep breath, she made a fist and knocked on the frosted glass.

After a few moments a woman answered the door in a blue cardigan and grey slacks.

"Mrs. Toth?" Annie said.

"That's right, love. You must be DI Cabbot. Please come in. Claire's not back yet, but she'll be here any minute."

Annie went in. The front room had high ceilings and a bay window looking west, over the tops of the houses opposite. A television set stood in the corner. *Daily Cooks* had just started, with that dishy French chef Jean-Christophe Novelli. Annie bet the French never made a fuss about a one-night stand. Mrs. Toth didn't make a move to turn the TV off, but when Annie asked her, she turned the volume down a notch or two. While they made small talk, Mrs. Toth was watching from the corner of her eye. Finally, she offered a cup of tea, and Annie accepted gratefully. Left to herself in the cavernous living room for a moment, Annie stood at the window and watched the fluffy clouds drifting across the blue sky on the horizon. Another beautiful spring day. She fancied she could even see as far as the bulky shapes of the Pennines in the distance.

Around the same time Mrs. Toth returned with the tray, the front door opened and shut and a young woman walked in wearing a supermarket shift, which she immediately took off and threw over a chair. "Claire!" said her mother. "If I've told you once, I've told you a thousand times. Hang up your coat."

Claire gave Annie a long-suffering look and did as she was told. Annie had never seen her before, so she hadn't really known what to expect. Claire took a packet of Dunhills out of her handbag and lit one with a Bic lighter. Her dirty blonde hair was tied back and she was wearing jeans and a white men's-style shirt. It wasn't hard to see that she was overweight, the jeans tight on her, flesh bulging at the hips and waist, and her makeup-free complexion was bad – pasty and spotty chipmunk cheeks, teeth stained yellow from nicotine. She certainly didn't resemble the slight figure of Mary whom Mel Danvers had seen at Mapston Hall. She was also too young, but as Banks had pointed out, Mel Danvers could have been wrong about the age. Claire certainly seemed old before her time in some of her mannerisms.

As soon as Claire had got the cigarette going, she poured herself a glass of wine without offering any to Annie. Not that she wanted any. Tea was fine.

Mrs. Toth placed herself in an armchair in the corner, and her cup clinked on her saucer every now and then as she took a sip. *Daily Cooks* continued quietly in the background.

"What do you want?" Claire asked. "Mum told me you're from the police."

"Have you been following the news?" Annie asked.

"I don't really bother."

"Only Lucy Payne was killed the other day."

Claire paused, the glass inches from her lips. "She . . . ? But I thought she was in a wheelchair?"

"She was."

Claire sipped some wine, took a drag on her cigarette and shrugged. "Well, what do you expect me to say? That I'm sorry?"

"Are you?"

"No way. Do you know what that woman did?"

"I know," said Annie.

"And you lot just let her go."

"We didn't just let her go, Claire," Annie tried to explain.

"You did. They said there wasn't enough evidence. After what she did. Not enough evidence. Can you believe that?"

"There was no way she could ever harm anyone else, wherever she was," Annie said. "She couldn't move a muscle."

"That's not the point."

"What is the point, then?"

"An eye for an eye. She shouldn't have been allowed to live."

"But we don't have the death penalty in England any more."

"*He's* dead, isn't he?"

"Terence Payne?"

A shadow flitted in the back of Claire's eyes. "Yes, him."

"Yes, he's dead."

"Well, then?" Claire stubbed out her half-smoked cigarette and drank some more wine. "I'm sorry," she said. "It's been a long day."

"What do you do?"

"Claire's on the checkout at the local supermarket," said her mother. "Aren't you, dear?"

"Yes, Mother." Claire stared defiantly at Annie.

There was no easy response to that. You could hardly say, "Oh, that's interesting." It was a job, and an honest one at that, but Annie felt sad for her. According to all accounts, Claire had been a bright, pretty young girl of fifteen with a good future: GCSEs, A levels, university, a professional career, but something had happened to put paid to all that. Terence and Lucy Payne. Now she had grossly underachieved and she hated her body. Annie had seen the signs before. It wouldn't have surprised her to find the scars of self-administered burns and cuts under the long sleeves of Claire's shirt. She wondered if she had been getting psychiatric help, but realized it was none of her business. She wasn't here as a social worker; she was here for information about a murder.

"Did you know Lucy Payne at all?"

"I'd seen her around, at the shops, like. Everyone knew who she was. The teacher's wife."

"But you never talked to her?"

"No. Except to say hello."

"Do you know where she was living?" she asked.

"The last I heard was that there wasn't enough of a case against her and she was unfit to stand trial anyway, so you were letting her go."

"As I told you," Annie repeated. "She couldn't harm anyone ever again. She was in an institution, a place where they take care of people like her."

"Murderers?"

"Quadriplegics."

"I suppose they fed her and bathed her and let her watch whatever she wanted on television, didn't they?"

"They took care of her," Annie said. "She couldn't do anything for herself. Claire, I understand your anger. I know it seems –"

"Do you? Do you really?" Claire said. She reached for another cigarette and lit it. "I don't think you do. Look at me. Do you think I don't know how ugly and unattractive I am? I've seen a shrink. I went for years and it didn't do me a scrap of good at all. I still can't bear the thought of a boy touching me." She laughed harshly. "That's a joke, isn't it? As if any boy would *want* to touch me, the way I look. And all that's down to Lucy and Terence Payne." She glared at Annie. "Well, go on, then!"

"What?"

"Tell me I don't look so bad. Tell me with just a dab of makeup and the right clothes I'll be all right. Like they all do. Like all I need is Trinny and fucking Susannah."

As far as Annie was concerned, nobody needed Trinny and Susannah, but that was another matter. Wave after wave of aggression rolled off of Claire, and Annie just didn't feel equipped to cope with it. Truth be told, she had enough hangups of her own eating away at her.

"Even my dad couldn't stand it," Claire said disgustedly, glancing at her mother. "It didn't take him long to desert the sinking ship. And Kim's parents moved away right after you let Lucy Payne go. Couldn't sell their house for years, though. In the end, they got practically nothing for it."

Mrs. Toth reached for a tissue and dabbed her eyes but said nothing. Annie was beginning to feel oppressed by the weight of sadness and loss in the room. Irrationally, she found herself picturing Eric in her mind's eye for a split second and felt like throttling him. It was all too much for her; her chest felt tight and she was having difficulty breathing. It was too hot in there. Get a grip, Annie, she told herself. Get a bloody grip. Control.

"So you didn't know where Lucy was?" Annie asked Claire.

"Obviously not, or I'd have probably strangled her myself."

"What makes you think she was strangled?"

"Nothing. I don't know. Why? Does it matter?"

"No, not really."

"Where was she?"

"As I told you, she was in a home. It was near Whitby."

"A home at the seaside. How nice. I haven't been to the seaside since I was a kid. I suppose she had a nice view?"

"Have you ever been to Whitby?"

"No. We always used to go to Blackpool. Or Llandudno."

"Do you drive a car?"

"Never learned, did I? No point."

"Why not?"

"I can walk to work and back. Where else would I go?"

"Oh, I don't know," said Annie. "Out with friends, maybe?"

"I don't have any friends."

"Surely there must be someone?"

"I used to go and see Maggie up the road, but she went away, too."

"Where did she go?"

"Back to Canada, I suppose. I don't know. She wasn't going to stay around here after what happened, was she?"

"Did you ever write to one another?"

"No."

"But she was your friend, wasn't she?"

"She was *her* friend."

There didn't seem much that Annie could say to that. "Do you know where she went in Canada?"

"Ask the Everetts. Ruth and Charles. It's their house she was living in, and they're her friends."

"Thanks," said Annie, "I will."

"I never went back to school, you know," Claire said.

"What?"

"After, you know, Kim. I just couldn't face going back. I suppose I could have done my exams, maybe gone to university, but none of it seemed to matter somehow."

"And now?"

"Well, I've got a job. Me and Mum are all right, aren't we?"

Mrs. Toth smiled.

Annie could think of nothing else to ask, and she couldn't stand being in the room for a moment longer. "Look," she said to Claire as she stood up and reached for her briefcase. "If you think of anything that might help . . ." She handed her a card.

"Help with *what* exactly?"

"I'm investigating Lucy Payne's murder."

Claire's brow furrowed. She ripped the card in pieces and scattered them on the floor. "When hell freezes over," she said, folding her arms.

The open-air café below Malcolm Austin's window seemed a reasonable place for a second interview with Stuart Kinsey, Banks thought, as he and Winsome settled down at the flimsy fold-up chairs and rickety table under the shade of a budding plane tree. And as they had found him in the department library working on an essay, it was a short trip for everyone. It was still a bit chilly to sit outside for long, and Banks was glad of his leather jacket. Every now and then, a breeze rattled the branches of the tree and ruffled the surface of Banks's coffee.

"What is it you want now?" Kinsey asked. "I've already told you what I know."

"That wasn't very much, was it?" Winsome said.

"I can't help it, can I? I feel awful enough as it is, knowing I was there, so close –"

"What could you have done?" Banks asked.

"I . . . I don't –"

"Nothing," said Banks. It probably wasn't strictly true. If Kinsey had arrived in Taylor's Yard at the same time the killer was assaulting Hayley, he might have interrupted things, and the killer might have fled, leaving her alive. But what was the point in letting *him* believe that? "You had no idea what was going on," he said, "and besides, it was all over by then. Stop whipping yourself."

Kinsey said nothing for a few moments, just stared down into his coffee.

"How fond of Hayley were you?" Banks asked.

Kinsey looked at him. He had an angry red spot beside his mouth. "Why are you asking me that? Do you still believe I'd hurt her?"

"Calm down," Banks said. "Nobody's saying that. You told us the last time we talked to you that you fancied Hayley, but that she didn't reciprocate."

"That's right."

"I'm just wondering how that made you feel."

"How it made me *feel*? How do you think it made me feel? How does it make *you* feel when someone you want so much you can't even sleep doesn't so much as acknowledge your existence?"

"Surely it wasn't as bad as that?" Banks said. "You hung out with Hayley, you saw plenty of her, went to the pictures and so on."

"Yeah, but mostly the whole crew was around. It was rare we were together, just me and her."

"You had conversations. You admitted you even kissed her once."

Kinsey gave Banks a withering glance. Banks felt he probably deserved it. Conversation and a couple of friendly kisses weren't much compensation when you were walking around with a hard-on that took up so much skin you couldn't close your eyes.

"Stuart, you're the only person we can place at the scene of the crime at the right time," said Winsome in as matter-of-fact and reasonable a voice as she could manage. "And you've got the motive, too: your unrequited infatuation with Hayley. We need some answers."

"Means, motive and opportunity. How bloody convenient for you. How many more times do I have to tell you that I didn't do it? For all the frustrations, I cared about Hayley, and I don't think I could ever kill anyone. I'm a fucking pacifist, for crying out loud. A poet."

"No need to swear," said Winsome.

He looked at her, contrite. "I'm sorry. That was rude of me. It's just so unfair, that's all. I lose a friend and all you do is try to make me into a criminal."

"What happened in the Maze that night?" Banks asked.

"I've already told you."

"Tell us again. More coffee?"

"No. No, thanks. I'm wired enough already."

"I wouldn't mind a cup," said Banks. Winsome rolled her eyes and went over to the stand.

"Just between you and me," Banks said, leaning forward, "did you ever get anywhere with Hayley beyond a couple of kisses in the back row at the movies? Come on, you can tell me the truth."

Kinsey licked his lips. He seemed on the verge of tears. Finally, he nodded. "Just once," he said. "That's what hurts so much."

"You slept with her?"

"No. Good Lord, no. Not that. We just, you know, kissed and messed about. And then it was like she didn't want to know me."

"That would make any man angry," said Banks, seeing Winsome on her way back with the coffee. "Having her right there, tasting her, then having her taken away forever. Thinking of other people having her."

"I wasn't angry. Disappointed, I suppose. It wasn't as if she made any promises or anything. We'd had a couple of drinks. It just felt so . . . right and then it was like it never happened. For her. Now, no matter what, it'll never happen again."

Winsome put one coffee down in front of Banks and took one for herself. "Let's get back to Saturday night in the Maze," Banks said. "There might be something you've forgotten. I know it's difficult, but try to reimagine it."

"I'll try," said Kinsey.

Banks sipped some hot, weak coffee and blew on the surface. "You all went into the Bar None around twenty past twelve, is that right?"

"That's right," said Kinsey. "The music was bloody awful, some sort of industrial hip-hop sub-electronic disco . . . I don't know what. It was loud too. I felt, you know, we'd all been drinking, and it was hot in there. I was thinking about Hayley, just wishing she'd come with us and feeling jealous that, you know, she was off to see some other lucky bloke."

"So you were upset?" Winsome asked.

"I suppose so. Not really. I mean, I wasn't in a rage or anything, just more disappointed. I needed a p – I needed to go to the toilet, too, so I went to the back of the club, where the toilets are, and I saw the door. I knew where it went. I'd been out that way before when I –"

"When you what?" Banks asked.

Kinsey managed a rare smile. "When I was under eighteen and the police came."

Banks smiled back. "I know what you mean." He'd been drinking in pubs since the age of sixteen. "Go on."

"I didn't think she'd have gone far. I know it's confusing back there, so I figured she'd stick close to the square, just out of sight, maybe round the first corner. I don't know what I was thinking. Honest. I suppose it was my plan to follow her and see where she went afterwards, try to find out who she was seeing. I certainly wasn't going to hurt her or anything."

"What happened next?"

"You know what happened next. I didn't find her. I was quite deep in the Maze before I knew it, and I thought I heard something from back towards the square. I walked closer, but I didn't hear it again."

"Can you describe the sound again?"

"It was like a muffled sort of thump, as if you hit a door or something with a pillow round your fist. And there was like a scream – no, not a scream – that would have really made me think there was something wrong, but like a gasp, a cry. I mean, to be honest –"

"What?" Banks asked.

Kinsey shot a sheepish glance at Winsome, then looked back at Banks. "I thought it was, you know, maybe someone having a quick one."

"Okay, Stuart," Banks said. "You're doing fine. Carry on."

"That's it, really. I was scared. I scarpered. I didn't want to interrupt anyone on the job. It can make a bloke pretty violent, that, being interrupted, you know, on the job."

"Did you hear anything else?"

"There was the music."

"What music? You didn't mention that before."

Kinsey frowned. "I don't know. I'd forgotten. It was familiar, just a snatch of some sort of rap-type thing, but I just can't place it, you know, the way it drives you crazy sometimes when you know what something is, it's like on the tip of your tongue. Anyway, it just came and went, like . . . just a short burst, as if a door opencd and closed, or a car shot by . . . I don't know."

"Like what?" said Banks. "Try to remember. It could be important."

"Well, it just started and stopped, really short, you know, passing by, like a car going by."

"Can you remember anything else about it?"

"No," said Kinsey.

"What did you do next?"

"I went back to the Bar None. I walked down that arcade that leads into Castle Road – I'd gone that far into the Maze and it was the closest exit. Then I had to go back in the club the front way because the back door only stays open if you wedge it, and I hadn't. It's got one of those bars you push down, but only on the inside. I had a stamp on my hand so I could get back in no problem."

"And that's it?"

"That's it. I'm sorry. Can I go? I really have to finish that essay."

There was no point keeping him, Banks thought. "Try to remember that music you heard," he said. "It might help. Here's my card."

Kinsey took the card and left.

"Do you really think the music's important, sir?" Winsome asked.

"I honestly don't know," said Banks. "There was a car passing by on the CCTV tape, and Stuart said he thought the music might have been coming from a passing car. But the timing isn't quite right, and we're pretty sure the people in the car were going home from an anniversary dinner. They were in their fifties, too, so I doubt they'd have been listening to rap. Still, it's a new piece of information. Who knows what might come of it?"

"What do you think, sir?" said Winsome. "I mean, in general. Where are we?"

"I think we're running out of suspects pretty damn quickly," Banks said. "First Joseph Randall, then Malcolm Austin and now Stuart Kinsey."

"You don't think he did it?"

"I doubt it. Oh, I suppose he could be lying. They all could. Hayley Daniels certainly had a knack for turning young men into pale and panting admirers. Talk about *la belle dame sans merci*. We should certainly check Austin's alibi, see if anyone saw him the way the neighbour saw Joseph Randall. But I believe Kinsey. I don't think he's the sort of person who could rape and murder someone he cared about and then return to a night out with his mates as if nothing had happened. He's the kind of person who's affected by things, even little things. Give him a kiss and he'll be trembling and putting his fingers to his lips all night."

"No, thank you, sir!"

Banks grinned. "I was speaking metaphorically, Winsome. Stuart Kinsey is a sensitive kid, a romantic. A poet, like he said. He's not a dissembler, probably not a very good actor, either. Pretty much what you see is what you get. And if something important happened to him, or he did something important, people would know. If he'd killed Hayley, he'd probably have staggered into the station and admitted it."

"I suppose so," said Winsome. "Which leaves?"

"Your guess is as good as mine," said Banks. "Come on, let's call it a day."

"What about DI Cabbot, sir?"

"Don't worry," Banks said with that sinking feeling. "I'll have a word with DI Cabbot."

Annie was glad she had decided to come home to Harkside after her visit with Claire Toth, rather than go all the way back to Whitby. It would mean an early start in the morning, but she could handle that, especially if she didn't drink too much. She was feeling as if she had been put through the wringer after her disastrous lunchtime meeting with Eric and her afternoon chat with Claire. A few home comforts might help. Glass of wine, book, bath, lots of bubbles. *Heat* magazine.

At least Les Ferris had phoned her mobile on her way home and told her he had a line on the hair samples and should be able to get his hands on them before the weekend, so that was one piece of good news.

As darkness fell, Annie closed the curtains and turned on a couple of small shaded table lamps that gave a nice warm glow to the room. She wasn't very hungry, but she ate some cold leftover pasta and poured herself a healthy glass of Tesco's Soave from the three-litre box. Banks might have turned into a wine snob since he had inherited his brother's cellar, but Annie hadn't. She couldn't tell a forward leathery nose from a hole in the ground. All she knew was whether she liked it, or if it was off, and usually if it came from a box it wasn't off.

She picked up the second volume of Hilary Spurling's Matisse biography, but she couldn't concentrate on the words for thinking about Claire and the events that had stunted her life so early. She could get beyond it, of course; there was still time, with the right help, but could she ever recover from that much damage? When Annie remembered the look Claire gave her when she said she was seeking Lucy's killer, she felt like giving up. What was the point? Did anyone want the killer of the notorious Friend of the Devil brought to justice? Could anyone ever forgive Lucy Payne? Had Maggie Forrest forgiven her? And had she moved on?

Annie remembered a TV film she'd seen a few months ago about Lord Longford's campaign to free Myra Hindley. It had been hard viewing. The Moors Murders were well before her time, but like every other copper, she had heard all about them and about the tape recording Brady and Hindley had made. On the one hand, the church asked you to forgive, told you that nobody was beyond forgiveness, held the possibility of redemption sacred, but Lord Longford aside, you'd be hard-pushed to find anyone Christian enough to forgive Myra Hindley her crimes, even though, as a woman, she had been judged less responsible for the murders than Brady had. It was the same with Lucy Payne, though circumstances had conspired both to deliver her from justice and imprison her in her own body at the same time.

Tommy Naylor and the other members of the team had been out all day in West Yorkshire questioning the Paynes' victims' families, while Ginger had been busy trying to come up with leads in the Kirsten Farrow business. Annie had talked to Naylor on her mobile and got the impression that they all felt as depressed as Annie did tonight, if not more so. When you expose yourself to so much accumulated grief and outraged sense of injustice, how can you keep a clear focus on the job you're supposed to be doing?

Annie was just about to take a bath when she heard a knock at the door. Her heart leaped into her mouth. Her first thought was that Eric had found out where she lived, and she didn't want to see him now. For a moment, she thought of ignoring it, pretending she wasn't home. Then whoever was there knocked again. Annie risked tiptoeing over to the window and peeking through the curtain. She couldn't see very well from that angle in the poor light, but she could tell it wasn't Eric. Then she saw the Porsche parked just along the street. Banks. Shit, she didn't really want to see him right now, either, not after the embarrassment of the other night. He wouldn't give up easily, though. He stood his ground and knocked again. She had the TV on with the sound turned off, and he could probably see the light flickering.

Finally, Annie answered the door, stood aside and let him enter. He was carrying a bottle of wine in a gift bag. Peace offering? Why would he need that? If anyone needed to offer the olive branch it was Annie. Ever the bloody tactician, Banks, disarming the enemy before a word was spoken. Or perhaps that was unfair of her.

"How did you know I was here?" she asked.

"Lucky guess, I suppose," said Banks. "Phil Hartnell said you'd been in Leeds talking to Claire Toth today, and I thought you might decide to come home rather than go all the way back to Whitby."

"I suppose that's why you're a DCI and I'm a mere DI."

"Elementary, my dear Watson."

"You could have rung."

"You only would have told me not to bother coming."

Annie fidgeted with a strand of hair. He was right. "Well, you might as well sit down, seeing as you're here."

Banks handed her the bottle and sat on the sofa. "I assume you want to drink some of this?" she asked.

"I'll have a glass, please, sure."

Annie went into the kitchen for the corkscrew. The wine was a Vacqueyras she had drunk with Banks before and enjoyed. Nothing special, but nice. An understated gesture, then. She poured him a glass, filled her own with the cheap Soave and went back and sat in the arm-chair. Her living room suddenly seemed too small for the two of them. "Music?" she asked, more for a distraction than that she really wanted to listen to anything in particular.

"If you like."

"You choose."

Banks got on his knees by her small CD collection and picked Alice Coltrane's *Journey in Satchidananda*. Annie had to applaud his choice. It suited her mood and the swirling harp figures over the slow, melodic bass line always soothed her when she was troubled. She remembered that John Coltrane had been playing when she visited Banks the other night, but she found him a lot harder to listen to than his wife, except on the one CD she owned, *The Gentle Side*.

"How was your interview with Claire Toth?" Banks asked when he had sat down again.

"Bloody awful and not very useful," said Annie. "I mean, I didn't think she had anything to do with it, but she, well, she's angry, but I'm not even sure she's got enough left in her to go after revenge. What happened to her friend had an appalling effect on her, too."

"She still blames herself?"

"To the point of deliberately making herself unattractive and underselling her brains and ability. The father did a bunk. That probably didn't help. Mum seems in a bit of a Prozac haze."

"What about the victims' families?"

"Nothing yet. The general consensus seems to be that the justice system let them down but God didn't, and they're glad she's dead. It gives them 'closure.' "

"Covers a multitude of sins, that word," said Banks, "the way it's bandied about by everyone these days."

"Well, I don't suppose you can blame them," said Annie.

"So you're no closer?"

"I wouldn't say that. I had a quick chat with Charles Everett before I came back here, too. He says he doesn't know what happened to Maggie Forrest, but if she's in the country, I'd say we'll certainly be viewing her as a prime suspect. Lucy Payne befriended her and used her, then betrayed her, and Maggie might have come to see revenge as a way of putting her life back together, of redeeming the past."

"Maybe," said Banks. "Any idea where she is?"

"Not yet. Ginger's going to check with the publishers tomorrow. There's something else come up, too." Annie explained briefly about Les Ferris's theory, and Banks seemed to allow it far more credence than she would have expected. Still, Banks had solved his share of crimes spanning different eras, so he was less cynical about these connections than most. "And Ginger tracked down Keith McLaren, the Australian," Annie added. "He's back in Sydney working for a firm of solicitors. Seems he made a full recovery, so maybe he's even got bits of his memory back. He's not a suspect, of course, but he might be able to help fill in a few blanks."

"Going over there?"

"You must be joking! He's supposed to ring sometime this weekend."

"What about the girl, Kirsten Farrow?"

"Ginger's been trying to trace her, too. Nothing so far. It's odd, but she seems to have disappeared off the face of the earth. We've checked just about every source we can think of, and beyond about 1992 there's no Kirsten Farrow. Her father's been dead for ten years, and her mother's in a home – Alzheimer's – so she's not a lot of use. We're trying to find the old university friend she was staying with in Leeds when she disappeared: Sarah Bingham. Ginger's discovered that she went on to study law, so we do have a line to follow, but it's just all so bloody slow and painstaking."

"The toughest part of the job," Banks agreed. "Waiting, digging, checking, rechecking. Have you thought that Kirsten may be living abroad?"

"Well, if she is, she's not the one we want, is she? Les Ferris also says he can come up with the hair samples in the 1988 murders, so we can compare Kirsten's with the hairs found on Lucy Payne. That should tell us one way or another whether this outlandish theory has any basis in reality at all."

"Hair matches are often far from perfect," said Banks, "but in this case I'd say it's good enough for rock and roll. So what's your plan?"

"Just keep on searching. For Kirsten and for Maggie. And Sarah Bingham. For a while longer, at any rate, until we can either count them in or rule them out. It's not as if we've got a lot of other lines of inquiry screaming us in the face. Still," Annie said after a sip of wine and a harp arpeggio that sent a shiver up her spine, "that's not what you came all this way to talk about, is it?"

"Not exactly," said Banks.

"Before you say anything," Annie began, glancing away, "I'd like to apologize for the other night. I don't know what . . . I'd had a couple of drinks with Winsome and then some more at your place, and it just all went to my head for some reason. Maybe because I was tired. I shouldn't even have been driving. I'd had way too much. It was unforgivable of me to put you in a position like that. I'm sorry."

For a while, Banks said nothing, and Annie could sense her heart pounding under the music. "That's not really why I came, either," he said eventually, "though I daresay it has something to do with it."

"I don't understand. What, then?"

"You and I have been finished for a long time," Banks said, "so I won't deny it came as a shock when you . . . anyway . . . that's always difficult, that side of whatever we have. I never stopped wanting you, you know, and when you act like that, well, you were right, I mean, there's not a lot going on in my life that I can afford to turn down an offer as good as that. But it didn't feel right. It wouldn't have been right. At least I thought we were friends, however difficult it seems sometimes. That you'd tell me if anything was bothering you."

"Like what?"

"Well, it's not every night you come around drunk and practically jump on me. There must be something wrong."

"Why must there be something wrong?" Annie said. "I've told you I was drunk and overtired. Pressure of work. I'm sorry. There's no point making a mountain out of a molehill."

"You said some very odd things."

"What things?" Annie pushed her hair back. "I'm sorry, I don't remember." She remembered perfectly well what she had said to Banks – she hadn't been as drunk as on that woeful night with Eric – but she was damned if she was going to let him know that.

"About toyboys."

Annie put her hand to her mouth. "I didn't, did I?"

"You did."

"But that's terrible of me. I shouldn't tell tales out of school."

"What do you mean?"

"Another drink?"

"I'd better not. I'm driving."

"I think I will."

"It's your house."

Annie hurried into the kitchen and refilled her glass. It also gave her a moment to think and let her heart calm down. The last thing she wanted was Banks messing around in her personal life again like some knight in shining armour. She could handle the Eric situation herself, thank you very much. She didn't need anyone to go and beat him up for her, or warn him off.

She sat down again and said, "What I said the other night. It was just . . . Look, if you must know, I'd had an argument with my boy-friend and I –"

"I thought you'd been out for dinner with Winsome?"

"Before that. I was angry and upset, that's all. I said some things I should never have said. I regret them now."

Banks sipped some wine and Annie could see that he was thinking, the frown line etched in his forehead. "Is that this toyboy you were talking about?" Banks asked. "Your boyfriend?"

"Yes. He's young. Twenty-two."

"I see."

"We had a row, that's all."

"I didn't know you were seeing someone."

"It's quite recent."

"And you're fighting already?"

"Well . . ."

"Maybe it's the age difference?"

Annie jerked upright in the armchair. "What age difference are you talking about, Alan? The one between me and Eric, or the one between me and you? Don't be a hypocrite. It doesn't suit you."

"Touché," said Banks, gently putting his wine down on the glass table. There was a good mouthful left, and smooth legs down the side of the glass, Annie noticed. "So you're not in any trouble?" he went on.

"No. Of course not. What makes you think that?"

"Everything's okay? Nobody's bothering you? Stalking you? Threatening you?"

"No, of course not. Don't be silly. I'm fine. Everything's fine. Just because I made one bloody silly mistake before, it doesn't mean I need a big brother or someone looking out for me. I can manage my own life, thank you very much. Boyfriends and all."

"Right, then." Banks stood up. "I suppose I'd better go. Busy day tomorrow."

Annie got up and walked with him to the door. She felt in a daze. Why had she lied to him, misled him so? Why had she spoken so harshly? "Are you sure you won't stay a while?" she asked. "Another half-glass won't do you any harm."

"Better not," said Banks, opening the door. "Besides, I think we've said all there is to say, don't you? You take care of yourself, Annie. I'll see you soon." Then he leaned forward, pecked her on the cheek and was gone.

As she listened to his car drive away, Annie wondered why she felt so sad, so much like crying. He hadn't stayed long. Alice Coltrane was still on the CD player, only now she didn't sound so calming after all. Annie slammed the door shut and said fuck over and over to herself until she did cry.

11

The market square had a different character at lunchtime, Banks thought as he walked towards the Fountain with Winsome, especially on a Friday when the weather was fine. All the pretty young girls from the banks and estate agents offices were out window shopping, ID tags hanging from their blouses, having coffee and a sandwich with their boyfriends or a pub lunch in groups of three or four, laughing and talking about their weekend plans. The schoolkids descended en masse, shirts hanging out, ties askew, laughing, pushing and shoving, eating pies and pasties outside Greggs.

They found Jamie Murdoch behind the bar of the Fountain, and the pub was doing nice business. The menu was interesting, adding curries and Thai dishes to the usual burgers, fish and chips and giant Yorkshires stuffed with mince or sausages. Banks was hungry, but decided it would be best to eat elsewhere afterwards, maybe the Queen's Arms. Jamie had help both at the bar and in the kitchen, so he was able to take a quick break when Banks called him over to a corner table. The jukebox, or digital radio set-up, was playing "Sultans of Swing." The air smelled of curry sauce, smoke and hops.

"What is it this time?" Jamie asked, pushing his glasses up to the bridge of his nose with his thumb. "Can't you see we're busy?"

"Just a few more questions," Banks said.

"Questions, questions. I told your Mr. Templeton everything the other day. Besides, it says in the paper this morning that some ex-boyfriend probably did it."

Banks had seen the article. Irresponsible journalism, he thought. Someone in the station had no doubt let it slip that they'd questioned a couple of Hayley's ex-boyfriends and the story had grown legs and started running.

"I wouldn't believe everything I read in the papers if I were you," Banks said. "The way you told it to DS Templeton, Hayley Daniels came in late with a group of rowdy friends –"

"They weren't that rowdy."

"Let's say high-spirited, then. You'd already had some trouble with a gang from Lyndgarth who had wrecked the pub toilets."

"That's right."

"So far so good. Hayley and her friends were the last to leave, right?" Jamie nodded.

"And that would have been about a quarter past twelve?"

"That's right."

"What did you do next?"

"I locked up."

"As soon as they left?"

"Of course. I've heard about robbers busting in just as you're closing up."

"Very sensible," said Banks. "Did you know where they were going?"

"Who?"

"Hayley and her friends."

"Someone had mentioned the Bar None. It's the only place left open at that time, anyway, except the Taj."

"Right," said Banks. "Did Hayley say anything about not going with them?"

"Not that I heard."

"I understand she got stroppy with you."

"Not really."

"But she did mouth off when she found out the toilets were closed?"

"Well, she was upset, I suppose," said Jamie, shifting awkwardly in his chair. "Why? I mean, it's not important, is it?"

"It might be," said Banks. "What did she say?"

"I don't remember."

"Gave you quite a mouthful, I heard."

"Well, she wasn't pleased. She might have said something about pissing on the floor."

"The way I hear it is that you're not exactly God's gift to women, and here comes this snooty bitch telling you to get down there in the toilet on your hands and knees and clean it up or she'll piss on your floor. How did it make you feel?"

"It wasn't like that," Jamie said.

"But you didn't get angry and follow her out to give her what for?"

Jamie edged back in the chair. "What do you mean? You know I didn't. You've seen me on the cameras. It was as I said. I locked up, and then I spent the next couple of hours cleaning the toilets and replacing the bulbs, sweeping up the glass."

"I understand your help didn't turn up on Saturday," Banks said.

"Jill. That's right. Said she had a cold."

"Did you believe her?"

"Not much choice, had I?"

"Does she do that often, call in poorly?"

"Once in a while."

A group of office workers sat at the next table and started talking loudly. "Do you mind if we have a quick word with you in the back?" Banks asked.

Jamie seemed nervous. "Why? What do you want?"

"It's all right," Winsome assured him, "we're not going to beat you up." She glanced around at the busy pub. "It's just more quiet and private, that's all. We wouldn't want the whole place to know your business."

Reluctantly, Jamie told one of his bar staff to take charge and led them upstairs, to the room with the TV and the sofa. It was small and stuffy, but at least it was private. Banks could hear Fleetwood Mac's "Shake Your Moneymaker" playing downstairs. "The thing is, Jamie," he began, "we've been asking around, and we think you've been getting your friends and employees to bring back contraband booze and cigarettes from France."

"It's not illegal any more," he said. "You can bring back as much as you want. We're in Europe, you know."

"It is illegal to sell them on licensed premises, though," Banks said. "Is that what's been going on? Has it got anything to do with Hayley's murder?"

Jamie's jaw dropped. "What are you saying? You can't –"

"Did Hayley know? Jill did. You even asked her to make a run for you. That's why she doesn't like working here, among other reasons."

"But it's, I mean, okay, so what if we were selling the odd bottle of lager or packet of fags? That's no reason to go and murder someone, is it? Especially like, you know, the way –"

"You mean the rape?"

"Yeah."

"Maybe that wasn't the real motive, though. Could have been done to make it look that way. On the other hand, there's not many a man isn't going to try the goods before he gets rid of it, is there?"

"This is sick," Jamie said. "You're sick." He looked at Winsome as if he had been betrayed. "Both of you."

"Come on, Jamie," said Banks. "We know what's what. Is that what happened? Hayley was going to blow the whistle on you. You had to get rid of her, so you thought you might as well have her first."

"It's ridiculous as well as sick," Jamie said.

"Where are they?" Banks asked.

"What?"

"The booze and fags."

"What booze and fags? I don't have anything other than the legitimate stock you've already seen."

"Where are you hiding it?"

"I'm telling the truth. I don't have any."

It made sense, Banks thought. With the police sniffing around in the wake of Hayley's murder, and no doubt guessing that Jill might not be as discreet as he would have liked, Murdoch was bound to have got rid of any contraband goods he had. It wasn't much of a theory, anyway, Banks thought. No one was going to murder anyone over small-time fiddling. He had just wanted to push the buttons and see what happened.

Nothing much, as it turned out. He gave the signal to Winsome and they stood up to leave. Just before they went downstairs, he asked Jamie, "Did you hear any music shortly after you locked up on Saturday?"

"Music? I don't really remember. What music?"

"I'm not sure what it was."

"I heard a car go by, but the rest of the time I was over the far side, cleaning up the toilets."

"Did you have the radio or the jukebox on?"

"No. I turned everything off when I locked up. Force of habit."

"Right," said Banks, thinking at least he'd like to listen to some music if he had to spend a couple of hours pulling soggy bog roll out of the toilets. He headed for the stairs. "Nice talking to you. If you think of anything else, we're just across the square."

The traffic on the A1 slowed to a crawl just past the Angel of the North, standing there on its hilltop ahead like a rusty spitfire on its tail. More fool me, Annie thought, for driving up to Newcastle on a Friday afternoon when everyone was knocking off work early and heading to the Team Valley Retail World or the MetroCentre. The day had started out with sunshine and distant cloud, but just north of Scotch Corner, the sky had quickly turned murky grey, brooding over Weardale to her left, and it had been raining on and off ever since. They say if you don't like the weather up north, wait ten minutes, but what they don't add is that if you still don't like it, drive ten miles in any direction.

Annie had spent the morning with the team, going over the interviews with the families of the Paynes' victims to no avail. Nobody expressed an ounce of sympathy for Lucy, and some were more hostile than others, but nobody even stood out remotely as a possible suspect. There were still alibis to be checked, but it was a depressing result. DS Brough had appeared near the end of the meeting, and even his words of encouragement had sounded hollow. If they could at least get a break on the leak of Lucy Payne's identity and previous whereabouts, Annie kept thinking, they would be a hell of a lot closer. Ginger was grumbling about trying to find anyone who could tell her anything in a publisher's office on a Friday, but she was waiting for a call back from

Maggie Forrest's previous art director and keeping her fingers crossed.

Before that, Ginger had been busy tracking down Sarah Bingham, Kirsten Farrow's old friend, after she had finished her law degree, and in that she had succeeded. Better yet, Sarah was working at home that afternoon. She had said on the phone that she could spare Annie half an hour or so. She lived in one of the chic apartment complexes by the river, which had been completely redeveloped into an upmarket area since Annie had last been that far north, all expensive restaurants and boutique hotels lining Tyneside in shiny new buildings, angular modern designs in steel, concrete and glass, jutting out over the water. As Annie was looking for the visitor parking, her mobile rang. It was Les Ferris, and he sounded excited. She pulled over to the side of the road and stopped.

"Annie, I've found those hair samples."

"That's great," Annie said. "When can Liam get started?"

"There's a small problem," Les admitted. "Liam's all set to go at the drop of a hat, but they're at West Yorkshire Headquarters along with the rest of the evidence in the 1988 serial killings, which makes sense. That's not a problem in itself, but right now it's Friday afternoon, the shift's changed, the weekend's coming up, and there's nobody to sign them out. There's a right bastard guarding exhibits, and we need someone with authority. DS Brough is –"

"Probably playing golf," said Annie. "What's the bottom line, Les? I'm sorry, but I'm in a bit of a hurry myself."

"Right. Got it. The bottom line is Monday. We should be able to get them to the lab and have Liam and his expert do a comparison check sometime Monday morning. All being well."

"That's great," Annie said. "We've waited this long. We can wait till Monday. And if it's necessary, and if my authority will do, don't hesitate to give me a ring later. Good work, Les. Thanks a lot."

"My pleasure," said Ferris and rang off.

In the meantime, Annie thought, she would just carry on as she had been doing. If the hair proved that Kirsten Farrow *wasn't* involved in the Lucy Payne murder, then she could scratch that line of inquiry. It had been a long shot, anyway. She would have wasted a bit of time on a wild goose chase, but sometimes things like that happened. Then she would have to redirect all her resources into other lines of inquiry.

Maggie Forrest, for example. Janet Taylor's brother had been a possible, too, but Tommy Naylor had tracked him down at a detox centre in Kent, where he'd been drying out for the past month, so that was another dead end.

Annie found the visitors area and parked, checked in with the security desk and found herself buzzed up to a fourth-floor apartment. At the end of the thickly carpeted corridor, Sarah Bingham opened the door to her and led her through to the living room. It wasn't large, but the floor-to-ceiling window with balcony created more than enough sense of space. The view south to Gateshead wasn't an idyllic one, more dockside than docklands, but it was probably an expensive one. Annie felt suspended above the water and was glad she didn't suffer from vertigo.

The furnishings were all red leather modular designs, and what appeared to be a couple of original pieces of contemporary art hung on the walls, which were painted a subtle shade somewhere between cream and pink that Annie couldn't quite name. It was probably a combination of some exotic place and a wildflower, like Tuscan primrose or Peloponnesian carnation.

Annie expressed her admiration for the paintings, especially the one made up of different coloured dots, and Sarah seemed pleased at her appreciation. Maybe most of her guests didn't like abstract art. A large flat-screen TV hung on one wall, and an expensive Bang & Olufsen stereo system took up the other side. There were small speakers on stands in all corners from which orchestral music issued very softly. Annie couldn't tell what it was, but she couldn't really pick out a tune, so she guessed it was probably twentieth century. It was the very contemporary habitat of a very contemporary young woman. A quick calculation told Annie that Sarah must be about forty, the same age as her.

Sarah Bingham herself was chic, from ash-blonde hair so perfectly coiffed, layered and tinted that it looked natural, to the white silk shirt and black designer cargo pants. Perhaps the only dissonant note was a pair of pink fluffy slippers. But she *was* at home. She made Annie feel quite dowdy in her Levi's and black turtleneck jumper. She also had the kind of lithe body you only get from an hour at the gym each day. Annie didn't have time for that, even if she had had the inclination. A white MacBook surrounded by papers and file folders sat on the chrome-and-glass work table by the window. So much for the paperless office, Annie thought. A Hermés handbag lay on the next chair, as if tossed there casually.

"I don't know what I can do for you," said Sarah as she sat in a sculpted armchair, "but you've certainly got me intrigued." Her accent was posh but not forced. Like everything else about her, it seemed natural.

"It's about Kirsten Farrow."

"Yes, you said on the phone." Sarah made a vague hand gesture. "But that was all so many years ago."

"What do you remember about that time?"

"Ooh, let me see. Well, Kirsty and I became friends at university. We were both reading English lit. I was seriously into feminist criticism and all that stuff, but Kirsty was more traditional. F.R. Leavis, I.A. Richards and so on. Very unfashionable in the heady days of deconstructionism and what have you."

"What about the attack?" asked Annie, anxious not to waste too much of her allotted time on literary criticism.

"That was awful," said Sarah. "I visited her in hospital and she was . . . I mean, it took her months to put herself back together. If she ever did."

"What do you mean?"

"Perhaps you never really get over something like that. I don't know. Do you?"

"No," said Annie, "but some people learn to function in spite of it. Did you spend a lot of time with her in that period?"

"Yes," said Sarah. "It seemed important to stick by her while everyone else was busy getting on with their lives."

"And what about your life?"

"On hold. I planned to do graduate work, a Ph.D. in Victorian fiction. I wanted to become a professor of English." She laughed.

"Wanted to?"

"Yes. I got bored by it all in my first year. I dropped out and bummed around Europe for a while, as one does, and when I got back I went in for law, at my parents' suggestion."

Annie looked around. "You seem to be doing all right."

"Not bad, I suppose. I wasted a few years on the way, but I soon made up for it. Now I'm one of the youngest partners in one of the biggest law firms in the Northeast. Would you like something to drink? You've come such a long way. How rude of me not to ask sooner."

"That's okay," said Annie. "I'll have something cold and fizzy, if you've got it, thanks." She'd had a couple more glasses of wine than she had planned after Banks had gone the previous evening, and it had left her with a dry mouth. She regretted lying to him about Eric, but sometimes it was the only way to keep someone out of your business. Banks's, and Winsome's, intentions might be good, but the last thing she needed right now was someone meddling in her life.

Sarah stood up. "Something cold and fizzy it is," she said and went to the cocktail cabinet. She came back with a chilled Perrier and ice for Annie and a gin and tonic for herself, then she settled in the chair again, curling her legs under her.

"Married?" Annie asked. She had noticed that Sarah wasn't wearing a ring, but that didn't necessarily mean anything.

Sarah shook her head. "Once," she said, "but it didn't take." She laughed. "He said he couldn't handle my working all hours, our never seeing each other, but the truth is that he was a layabout and a sponger. You?"

"Never found the right man," said Annie, smiling. "Back to Kirsten. I hope it's not too painful for you?"

Sarah waved her hand. "No. As I said, it was all so long ago. It seems like another lifetime. Kirsten was attacked in June 1988. We'd just finished finals and we'd been out celebrating. We all got turfed out of some pub or other and ended up at a party at one of the university residences, about six of us. We were pretty drunk already, if truth be told, except maybe Kirsten. She had to head home early the next morning so she was pacing herself. The party was still going when she left. Nobody really thought anything of it. I mean, people were coming and going all the time, at all times of the day and night. But that was when it happened, you know, on her way home across the park."

"And someone interrupted?"

"Yes. A man walking his dog. Thank God for that, at least."

"But her attacker got away?"

"Yes. The police thought it was the same man who'd raped and murdered five other girls, a serial killer, I suppose you'd call him.

But poor Kirsty couldn't remember a thing about the attack, which was perhaps a mercy. Can you imagine having to relive something like that?"

Annie sipped some more Perrier. "Did she talk about it much?"

"A bit. I saw her a few times in hospital, and I went to stay with her and her parents that first Christmas after she came out of hospital. They lived in a big house near Bath. I think Kirsty had been undergoing hypnosis at the time. I do remember that it really frustrated her that she couldn't remember anything after leaving the party. She said she wanted to remember it all, find out who did it and go after him."

"She said that?"

"Yes, but she was very upset at the time. She didn't really mean it. I mean, the hypnosis was only frustrating her. I think it might have been the police's idea."

"Did you tell the police what she said to you?"

"Well, no. I mean, why would I? It was just angry talk. She'd no idea who it was."

"Do you remember the name of the hypnotist, by any chance?"

"I'm sorry, no. I don't recall that Kirsty ever even mentioned it."

"But this was in Bath in 1988?"

"Yes. Winter."

"Go on."

"Kirsty's parents went out on New Year's Eve, some party or other. Anyway, Kirsty and I got drunk on her father's cognac and she told me everything."

Annie edged forward in her seat. "What do you mean?"

"About what he'd done to her. The bastard." For the first time, Sarah seemed shaken by what she was remembering.

"What had he done?" Annie knew she could dig out the medical report, which had to be in the archives somewhere, but she wanted to hear Sarah's version.

"He used a sharp knife on her. Here." She moved her hands over her breasts. "And between her legs. She didn't show me, of course, but she said she had a lot of scarring and stitching. But that wasn't the worst of it. She also told me the damage to her vagina and uterus had been so extensive that she couldn't enjoy sex, and she couldn't have children."

Sarah wiped a tear from her eyes with the back of her hand. "I'm sorry. I didn't think I'd be like this just talking about it. I thought I would be okay, that it was long enough ago."

"Are you all right?"

Sarah sniffed and went to get a tissue. She blew her nose. "I'm fine," she said. "It was just the power of the memory took me by surprise. I could see her sitting there, with that forlorn expression on her face. I mean, can you imagine how that must screw you up? Being sentenced to celibacy and childlessness for the rest of your life? And she was only twenty-one, for crying out loud. I think at that moment I'd gladly have killed him myself if I'd known who it was."

"Was there ever any suggestion that it was someone close to her?" Annie asked. "Perhaps someone who'd left the party early?"

"The police certainly never told me what they were thinking, but they grilled everyone who'd been there, and all her uni friends."

As Annie guessed, it would have been standard procedure. Still, there was always a chance that they had missed something. "Did you see her after that New Year's Eve?"

"Oh, yes. A few times. But she never really talked about it in that sort of detail again. I do remember one night in particular," Sarah went on. "Odd, isn't it, how some things stick in your memory? It was the first time Kirsty had come back up north after . . . since the attack. Over a year later. She'd been in hospital for quite a while, then she'd been at home with her parents recuperating for a long time. Anyway, I had a poky little bedsit then – it used to be Kirsten's – and she came to stay for a while. September 1989, I think it was, not long before term started. We had a lot to drink that first night, and she said some very odd things. Her behaviour quite frightened me, in fact."

"What odd things?"

"I can't remember the details, just that it was creepy, you know? She was talking about an eye for an eye and saying she felt like a victim of AIDS or vampirism."

"AIDS?"

"She didn't mean it literally. I told you she was talking crazy. She didn't have AIDS, at least not as far as I knew. No, she meant like some sort of contagion she'd caught from her attacker. I told her it was crazy talk and she stopped. That's all I remember. But it gave me a chill at the time. Still, I thought, better out than bottled up inside."

"She spoke about revenge?"

"An eye for an eye, yes. She said again that if she knew who it was she'd kill him."

"Did she give any indication that she did know?"

"No. How could she?"

"Sorry, go on."

Sarah gave a nervous laugh. "It was just the wine talking, really. We were into our second bottle by then. Anyway, things went on pretty much as normal for the next while, then term started."

"So Kirsten was staying with you all the time she was up north that September?"

"Yes. Until the middle of October, I think."

"You don't sound so certain. Are you sure?"

Sarah turned away. "That's what I told the police."

"But is it true?"

She studied her fingernails. "Well, you know, she sort of came and went."

"Came and went?"

"Yes. She spent a few days walking in the Dales, okay?"

"Were you with her?"

"No. She wanted some time by herself."

"When was this exactly?"

"I can't remember. It was so long ago. September, though, I think. Soon after she came to stay."

"Did you tell the police about this?"

"I . . . no. She asked me not to."

"Any idea why?"

"No. I mean, look, I'm sorry, but I didn't have a very good opinion of the police back then. The last thing Kirsten needed was any hassle from them. She'd suffered enough."

"Any particular reason you didn't like the police?"

Sarah shrugged. "I was just a radical, that's all, and a feminist. They seemed to be only interested in upholding archaic laws made by men and in supporting the status quo."

"I used to think that, too," said Annie. "Of course, it might have been more true back then than now, but there are a few dinosaurs left."

"I still can't say they're my favourites," said Sarah, "but I've developed a lot more respect over the years, and I don't generalize as much as I used to. I don't practise criminal law, but I've come across a few good police officers in my line of work. It's as you say, there are dinosaurs. Bad apples, too, I suppose."

"Oh, yes," said Annie, thinking of Kev Templeton. He might not be a bad apple in the sense of being crooked, but he was certainly a shit of the first degree.

"But back then you lied to them?"

"I suppose so. Honestly, I'd forgotten all about it. Am I in trouble?"

"I don't think anyone really cares about an eighteen-year-old lie, except that it might be relevant today."

"I don't see how."

"What did happen?"

"I told you. She went to the Dales for a while, then she came back. She was in and out a lot over the next couple of weeks, then she took the room on the upper floor. She started her post-graduate work, same as me, but she got bored even sooner."

"So she dropped out?"

"Yes. Went back home, I think. At least for a while."

"And then?"

Sarah looked down at her fingernails again, beautifully manicured and painted a tasteful shade of pink. "We sort of drifted apart, you know, the way people do. As I told you, after I got out of the graduate program I went travelling for a while, then I got immersed in my law studies."

"So you didn't see Kirsten again?"

"Only once or twice over the next couple of years. We'd have a drink for old times' sake."

"What did you talk about?"

"The past, mostly. The time before the attack."

"Did she ever mention Whitby?"

"Whitby? No. Why should she?"

"Did she ever talk about someone called Eastcote, Greg Eastcote?"

"No."

"Jack Grimley?"

"Never heard of him."

"Keith McLaren, an Australian?"

"No, never. I haven't heard of any of these people. Who are they?"

"Was she in touch with any of the others you used to know back then, the old uni crowd?"

"No, I don't think so. Her boyfriend had gone off to Canada or America or somewhere, and the rest had scattered all over the country. She seemed very much a loner, as if she had cut herself off. I thought maybe it was because of what had happened to her. She couldn't adjust, pretend to be normal. I don't know. It wasn't that we didn't have a nice chat and a drink and all, but there was always something remote about her, as if she'd sort of set herself apart from the rest. I don't know how else to describe it. She even looked different, let herself go, cut her hair and stuff. She used to be quite lovely, but, you know, she just stopped bothering."

"Do you know what she was doing with her life?"

"I don't think she was doing anything, really. I think she was kind of lost. She talked of travelling, China, America, the Far East, but I don't know if it was a real goal or just wishful thinking." Sarah checked her watch for the first time. "I don't mean to be rude but" – she glanced over at the MacBook – "I do have to finish this job before I meet with the client this evening."

"That's all right," said Annie. "I think I've just about got to the end of my questions, anyway."

"I'm sorry you came all this way for nothing."

"It's not for nothing," said Annie. "You've finally told the truth at last. Have you seen or heard anything of Kirsten in the last few years?"

"No," said Sarah. "The last time I saw her must have been 1991 or early 1992, and after that it was just as if she had disappeared."

"Ever heard of Lucy Payne?"

"Isn't she the one who killed all those girls with her husband, the one who just got murdered? Is that what this is about? I don't understand."

"Maggie Forrest?"

"No, never."

"Right," said Annie, standing up to leave and handing Sarah her card. "If you remember anything else, please give me a call."

"What is it all about, anyway?" Sarah asked at the door. "You haven't told me anything. Why were you asking me about all these people and what happened years ago? Can't you at least give me a hint?"

"If there's anything in it," Annie said, "you'll find out soon enough."

"Typical police," said Sarah, folding her arms. "Some things never change, do they?"

Annie's mobile rang as she arrived at her car. It was Ginger.

"It's me, guv. I've got a line on that Maggie Forrest. The publisher rang me back."

"Great," said Annie, fiddling for her keys, phone wedged under her chin.

"We're in luck. She's back in the country. Living in Leeds again. Down by the canal."

"Okay," said Annie. "Maybe I should drive down there now."

"Won't do you any good. She's in London at the moment – meetings with said publisher. She's heading back Saturday evening, though."

"Fine," said Annie. "I'd got nothing else planned for Sunday, anyway. I might as well go talk to her then. Thanks, Ginger. Great work."

"No problem."

Annie turned off her phone and headed for the A1.

Annie remembered where Eric lived, and it was after dark when she turned up at his flat, having taken a while to pluck up the courage and stopped to fortify herself with a stiff double brandy at a pub on the way. She was on foot, so it didn't matter whether she had a couple of drinks. Even though she had convinced herself that this would be easy, she still felt on edge. Confrontations at work were one thing, but in her private life they were another matter entirely. She knew that she had walked away from more than one relationship in the past rather than confront what was wrong with it. The problem with Banks was that she couldn't quite walk away entirely; neither her job nor the remnants of her feelings for him, so easily stirred up by working so closely together, would let her. That was partly why she had accepted the temporary posting to Eastern Area so eagerly, to put some distance between them for a while. It didn't seem to be working very well.

Eric answered her ring with a curt "Oh, it's you," then he turned his back and walked inside, leaving the door open. "I was just getting ready to go out," he said when she followed him into the living room. There was no evidence of this. A cigarette burned in the ashtray and a can of lager sat by a half-full glass on the low table. The TV was on, tuned to *EastEnders*. Eric sprawled on the sofa, legs splayed and arms stretched out. He was wearing jeans and a torn black T-shirt. His hair was greasy, as if it needed a good wash, and a stray lock hung over one eye, as usual. "What do you want?" he asked.

Annie held her hand out. "Give me your mobile."

"What?"

"You heard. Give me your mobile."

"Why?"

"You know why."

Eric grinned. "Those photos? You want to delete them, don't you? You don't trust me."

"That's right. We'll start with your mobile, then we'll move on to your computer."

"What do you think I'll do? Post them on the Internet?" He rubbed his chin in mock conjecture. "I suppose I could, couldn't I? Do you think they'll accept nudes?"

"I don't think you're going to do anything with them," Annie said. "You're going to give me your mobile, then we're going to check your computer, and I'm going to delete them."

"Look, why don't you sit down and have a drink? I'm not in a great hurry. We can talk about it."

"I don't want a drink, and I'm not staying long enough to sit down," Annie said, holding her hand out. "There's nothing to talk about. Give."

"If I didn't know better, I'd think you were making an obscene suggestion."

"But you do, and I'm not. Come on."

Eric folded his arms and stared at her defiantly. "No," he said.

Annie sighed. She had thought he might want to play games. So be it. She sat down.

"So you will have that drink?" Eric said.

"I'll sit down because this is clearly going to take longer than I expected," Annie said, "but I still don't want a drink. You know what I want."

"I know what you wanted the other night," said Eric. "But now I'm not so sure. There are some other pictures, you know. Ones you haven't seen yet. Better ones."

"I don't care," said Annie. "Just delete them, then we'll forget all about it, forget it ever happened."

"But I don't want to forget it ever happened. Can't you at least leave me something to remember you by?"

"I'll leave you more than enough to remember me by if you *don't* do as I say."

"Is that a threat?"

"Take it as you will, Eric. I've had a long day. I'm running out of patience. Are you going to give me that mobile?"

"Or what?"

"All right," said Annie. "We'll do it your way. You were right the first time when you guessed what I do for a living. I'm a policewoman. A detective inspector, as a matter of fact."

"Am I supposed to be impressed?"

"You're supposed to do as I say."

"What will you do if I don't?"

"Do I have to spell it out?"

"Get some of your Neanderthal cronies to beat me up?"

Annie smiled and shook her head slowly. "I really don't think I'd have to bring in any help, but no, that's not the plan."

"Pretty confident, aren't you?"

"Look," said Annie, "let's stop playing games, shall we? What happened happened. Maybe it was good. I don't know. I don't remember, and it doesn't do me any credit to say that. But no matter what, it was a mistake. If —"

"How do you know?"

"What?"

Eric sat up. "How do you know it was a mistake? You haven't given me a chance to —"

"It was a mistake for me. Just accept that. And your recent behaviour hasn't helped matters at all."

"But why?"

"I really don't want to go into it. I didn't come here to cause trouble. I just came to ask you — nicely — to let me delete those photos. They're embarrassing and, quite frankly, I wouldn't even want to consider a relationship with anyone who would take them."

"You didn't object at the time. And don't forget, you took some, too. Can't you lighten up a bit, cut me a bit of slack? It was just harmless fun."

"Give me the fucking mobile!" Annie was shocked at her own vehemence, but Eric was pushing her patience way beyond its limits. She couldn't be bothered explaining the difference between her taking a few innocent photos for fun in a club and his taking more intimate ones, that she couldn't even remember, in the privacy of the bedroom. If he couldn't understand that himself, he didn't deserve any slack.

He seemed shocked, too. He said nothing for a moment, then reached into his hip pocket, pulled out his BlackBerry and tossed it to her. She caught it. "Thank you," she said. When she found the media library, she scrolled through all the photos he had taken that night. In addition to the ones she had seen, in which she had at least been awake, there were others of her sleeping, hair tousled, a breast exposed. Nothing really dirty, but crude and invasive. She deleted them all. "Now the computer."

He waved her to the desk in the corner. "Be my guest."

The same pictures were on his computer, so she deleted all those, too. Just as a precaution, she also emptied his recycle bin. She knew there were ways of getting back erased data, but she doubted that Eric was up to the task, or even that he cared, for that matter. Maybe he'd stored them on a CD or a smart drive, too, but short of ransacking his entire flat she couldn't do much about that. "Is that all?" she asked.

"Yeah, that's all. You've got what you came for. Now just fuck off." He turned away, picked up his drink and pretended to watch television.

"Before I go," Annie said, "let me just tell you what will happen if you do have copies and if any of them turn up on the Internet. You were wrong about me enlisting people I know to beat you up. That's way too crude. But I do have friends, and, believe me, we can make your life very uncomfortable indeed."

"Oh, yeah," said Eric, keeping his eyes on the television. "And just how will you do that?"

"If any of those photos turn up anywhere, I'll not only claim I was drunk at the time they were taken, which is true, and which anyone can see, but that I think I was given a date-rape drug."

Eric turned to face her slowly, an uncomprehending expression on his face. "You'd actually do that?" he said.

"Yes. And if it became necessary, the police officers who searched your flat would find Rohypnol or GHB or some such thing. You'd be surprised how much we have lying around the station spare." Annie felt her heart beating in her chest, and she was sure that Eric must be able to hear it, or even see the twitching. She wasn't used to lying, or threatening, like this.

Eric lit another cigarette. He had turned pale and Annie could see that his hands were shaking. "You know," he said, "I really believe that you would. When I met you, I thought you were a nice person."

"Don't give me that crap. When you met me, you thought here's a not-too-bad-looking drunk old bitch I can get into bed without too much trouble."

Eric's jaw hung open.

"What's wrong?" Annie went on. "Home truths not palatable to you?"

"I . . . just . . ." He shook his head in wonder. "You're really something else, a real piece of work."

"Believe it," said Annie. "I take it I don't need to say any more?"

Eric swallowed. "No."

"On that note, then, I'll say goodbye."

Annie was careful not to slam the door behind her. As angry and upset as she was, she needed to demonstrate to Eric that she was in control, even if she wasn't. When she walked into the cool night air, she paused at the corner of the street and took a few deep breaths. She'd done it, she told herself. Problem over. Sorted. So much for Annie

Cabbot, *Angel of Mercy*. Why was it, though, she thought as she walked down the street and looked out at the dark, glittering sea beyond, that as obnoxious as Eric was, she felt as if she had just broken a butterfly on a wheel? But then, she reminded herself, he wasn't a butterfly at all, more like a snake, and she smiled.

12

Clutching his bottle of wine in one hand, Banks took a deep breath and rang the doorbell. It felt strange being back on the street where he had lived with Sandra and the kids for so many years. Now Sandra had remarried and become a mother again, Tracy had finished university, and Brian was in a successful rock band. But when Banks looked at the drawn curtains of his old home, an unremarkable semi with bay window, new door and pebble-dashed facade, the memories flooded back: sharing a late-night cup of hot chocolate with Tracy when she was twelve, having come home late and depressed from investigating the murder of a girl about her age, Strauss's "Four Last Songs" on the stereo; Brian's first stumbling musical attempts at playing "Sunshine of Your Love" on the acoustic guitar Banks had bought him for his sixteenth birthday; making love to Sandra as quietly as possible downstairs on the sofa after the kids had gone to bed, trying not to burst out laughing when they fell on the floor. He also remembered his last few weeks alone there, passing out on the sofa with the bottle of Laphroaig on the floor beside him, *Blood on the Tracks* on repeat on the CD player.

Before he could travel any further down the perilous path of memory, the door opened and Harriet Weaver stood there, looking hardly a day older than when she had first welcomed Banks and his family to the neighbourhood twenty years ago. Banks leaned forward and kissed her on both cheeks.

"Hello, Alan," she said. "I'm so glad you could come." Banks handed her the wine. "You shouldn't have. Come in."

Banks followed her into the hall, where he hung up his coat, then they went through to the living room. Most of the guests had already arrived and were sitting in the convivial glow of orange-shaded table lamps, chatting and drinking. There were twelve people in all, and Banks knew two couples from his years next door: Colin and Stella Hutchinson, from number twenty-four, and Ray and Max, the gay couple from across the street. The others were either Harriet's friends from the library, or her husband David's colleagues from the arcane and, to Banks, deadly dull, world of computers. Some of them he had met before briefly.

He had driven straight from the station, about five minutes away, stopping only to pick up the bottle of wine from Oddbins, having spent most of the day in his office going over the statements and forensic reports on the Hayley Daniels case. He had also been occasionally distracted by the thought of Annie's case: Lucy Payne in a wheelchair with her throat slit. He remembered Lucy lying in her hospital bed, in some ways a pitiful, fragile figure with her pale, beautiful, half-bandaged face, in other ways enigmatic, scheming, manipulative, and perhaps truly evil. Banks had never made up his mind on that score, though he was one of the few who had seen the videos, which convinced him that Lucy had been as involved as her husband, Terry, in the abduction and sexual torture of the girls. Whether she had actually killed anyone was another matter entirely, and one the courts never had to decide upon. Everyone *believed* she did, no matter what. Her eyes had given nothing away and her instinct for self-preservation had been strong.

It was always difficult to make the transition from the macabre to the mundane, Banks found, but sometimes inconsequential small talk about England's chances of scoring against Andorra after their pathetic 0–0 draw with Israel, or the Tories' chances in the next election, were a welcome antidote to the day's preoccupations.

Dinner parties always made him nervous for some reason, and he couldn't even drink too much to take the edge off because he had to drive home. He wasn't going to take the kind of risk that Annie had the other night. She had been lucky. Thinking about Annie, he realized that he would probably have invited her as his "date" if they had been on better terms. Even though they were no longer romantically involved, they gave one another moral support in social situations like this from time to time, strength in numbers. But after her odd behaviour on the last two occasions they had met, he didn't know how things stood between them, or how they would develop.

Greetings over, Banks took the glass of wine David offered and sat next to Colin and Stella. Colin was a paramedic, so he was hardly likely to start going on about RAM and gigs. Dead or dying bodies Banks could handle. Stella ran an antiques shop on Castle Road, and she always had an interesting tale or two to tell.

As he made small talk, Banks glanced around at the others. There were a couple of supercilious prats he recognized from a previous party and didn't particularly like, the kind who got a few drinks in them and became convinced that they could do a better job than anyone else of putting the world to rights. But the rest were okay. Most were around his age, mid-fifties, or a little younger. Harriet had put on some soft classical music in the background, Bach by the sound of it, and the smell of lamb roasting with garlic and rosemary drifted in from the kitchen. A couple of plates of hors d'oeuvres were doing the rounds, and Banks helped himself to a small sausage roll when it came his way.

Fortunately, he wasn't the only stray of the group. Most of the guests were couples, but Banks knew that Graham Kirk, from the next street over, had recently split up with his wife, and Gemma Bradley, already three sheets to the wind, had driven her third husband out two years ago and hadn't found a fourth yet. Harriet worked with Gemma, though, and clearly felt sorry for her. The other odd man out was Trevor Willis, a rather surly widower who kept nipping outside for a smoke with Daphne Venables, wife of one of David's colleagues. Banks knew from previous occasions that Trevor was the kind who got quieter and more morose the more he drank, until he ended up nodding off – once, with dramatic effect, right into his trifle.

It was at times like this when Banks dearly wished he still smoked, especially on a mild March evening. Sometimes it was good to have an excuse to escape outside for a few minutes when the conversation got too loud or too dull.

Colin was in the middle of a story about an old woman who regularly called an ambulance just to get a lift to her hospital appointments, and how, just to scare her, one of the paramedics had remarked upon noticing a problem with her leg and said it would have to come off, when Harriet called them through to dinner.

It took her a few minutes to get everyone seated according to the plan, and Banks found himself between Daphne and Ray, opposite Max and Stella. It could have been worse, he reflected, accepting a refill of wine from David as Harriet dished out plates of goat's cheese and caramelized onion tart. The only ones already drunk were Gemma and Trevor, though Daphne seemed well on her way, judging by how she kept squeezing Banks's arm whenever she spoke to him. The tart was delicious, and there was enough free-flowing conversation for Banks to sit quietly and enjoy it without being drawn in.

He had just finished his tart, and Daphne was holding his arm telling him a funny story about a runaway mobile library, when the doorbell rang. Everyone carried on with their conversations while Harriet got up and rushed out to answer it. Daphne was demanding all Banks's attention, breathing Sancerre and stale tobacco his way, while exuding wafts of whatever strong perfume she was wearing.

The next thing he knew, Harriet was pulling up another chair at the end of the table. Thirteen for dinner, Banks thought, remembering the Poirot story. It was supposed to be unlucky. Conversations paused, men gawped and women stiffened. Banks still couldn't escape Daphne's grip on his left arm. He felt as if he'd been cornered by the Ancient Mariner. Over to his right, he heard an unfamiliar female voice say, "I'm sorry I'm so late."

Finally, Daphne let go of him, and, without being rude, he was able to glance over and see Harriet fussing about how being late was no problem, setting an extra place for the new guest, who looked over at him and smiled. Then he remembered: Sophia had arrived at last.

Chelsea was running late. She put her mascara on too thickly but didn't really have time to apply it all over again. It would have to do. She tugged at her bra under the skimpy top and squirmed until it felt comfortable, then dashed downstairs and put her heels on.

"Bloody hell," said her father, turning away from the television for a rare moment as Chelsea teetered on one leg in the hallway. "Do you have any idea what you look like, girl?"

"Shut up, Duane," her mother said. "Leave the poor lass alone. Didn't you ever go out and have a good time when you were a young lad?"

"Maybe, but I didn't dress like a fucking –"

Chelsea didn't wait to hear what he said. She'd heard it all before anyway. It would be tart, trollop, whore, tom or some such variation on the theme. She snatched up her handbag, where she kept her cigarettes, a touch of makeup and some extra money in case she needed to buy a round of drinks or pay for a taxi home, blew a kiss to her mother, who called after her to be careful and to remember what happened to that poor girl, and dashed out, hearing raised voices as the door closed behind her. They would be at it for a while, she knew, then her mother would give up and go to bingo, as usual. When Chelsea got home late, her mother would be in bed and her father would be in front of the TV snoring through some naff old thriller or horror movie on Freeview, a full ashtray and a few empty beer cans on the ringed and stained table beside him. They were just that bloody predictable.

How she wished she lived in Leeds or Manchester or Newcastle, then she'd be able to stay out later, all night if she wanted, but Eastvale had pretty much closed down by half past twelve or one o'clock on a Saturday night, except for the Bar None, where they had a naff DJ and lousy music, and the Taj Mahal, which was full of sad, drunken squaddies drinking lager by the gallon and shovelling down vindaloo before they got shipped off to Iraq. Tomorrow she was going to see the Long Blondes at the Sage, in Gateshead, with Shane, in his car, their first real date without anyone else around. That would be excellent. Then on Monday it was back to work in the shop. Such was her life.

They were all meeting in the market square. Chelsea couldn't see a bus anywhere, they were so few and far between after six o'clock on the East Side Estate, so she'd have a fifteen-minute walk to get there, across the river, then up the hill past the gardens and the castle. It was already dark and her high heels made it tough going. They would be starting out at the Red Lion, she knew, and if she missed them there, they would most likely drop by the Trumpeter's for a couple of games of pool before moving on to the Horse and Hounds, where there was usually a band playing covers of famous old songs like "Satisfaction" and "Hey Jude." They weren't bad sometimes. Better than the decrepit traditional jazz they had on Sunday lunchtimes, at any rate.

Chelsea picked up her pace after she had climbed the hill and walked around Castle Road, down into the market square, already jumping with young people well on their way. She said hello to a few people she knew as she crossed the square. The cobbles were really difficult to manage in the shoes she was wearing, and she almost tipped over on a couple of occasions before she got to the pub, opened the door, and saw them all there. Shane grinned at her through the smoke and she smiled back. It was going to be all right, then. Saturday night had started, and it was going to be all right.

To say that Sophia's arrival changed the tenor of dinner-table conversation would be an understatement. The men almost visibly puffed themselves up and set about impressing her. Colin started commenting on the wine, findings hints of chocolate, vanilla and tobacco that he had clearly memorized from a book, and Graham Kirk began a lecture on the future of computing, ostensibly to Max, but with the occasional sideways, approval-seeking glance at Sophia, who wasn't listening. Sophia appeared, to Banks, quite oblivious to it all. She couldn't help it that men fell all over her, her confident demeanour seemed to say. And if she found the phenomenon amusing, she didn't give that away, either.

Banks found himself enjoying the show tremendously. He felt invisible, lighter than air, a fly on the wall, noting facial expressions, body language of all kinds, as if no one were aware of his presence. Disappearing was a skill he had possessed since childhood, and it often came in useful in his job. It used to drive Sandra crazy, he remembered. She thought it was rude, not joining in. But then Sandra was very social and was very much always there all the time.

Since Sophia's arrival, even Daphne had stopped hanging on to his arm and talking to him, and had taken instead to sulking and sipping her wine rather faster than she had before. Someone at the far end spilled a glass of red all over the white tablecloth and everyone oohed and fussed over that for a while with cloths and sponges while Harriet tried to calm them down and told them to ignore it, it would all come out in the wash.

In the confusion, Banks stole a glance at Sophia. That she was beautiful had been obvious enough even before he had clapped eyes on her. The mere effect of her entry into the room had been enough to tell him that. But the more he looked, the more he understood. Her dark hair was tied loosely behind, at the nape of her long neck, her olive skin smooth and flawless. She wore a jade top, scooped just low enough to show the promise of cleavage without showing anything, and an antique locket on a thin silver chain around her neck, which she touched with her thumb and forefinger every now and then. Her lips were full, and her eyes were the darkest and most beguiling that Banks had ever seen. A man could drown himself in those eyes. She caught him staring at her and smiled again. He felt himself blush. He was no longer invisible.

Conversation moved around, as it inevitably did, to the crime statistics, to binge drinking, gangs, robbery, the unsafe streets, general murder and mayhem, and the apparent inability of the plods to solve even the simplest and most obvious of crimes, or keep the tax-paying citizens safe from muggers and burglars and rapists. Though none of this was specifically directed at Banks, there were nonetheless certain pointed challenges and expectations, and when he didn't rise to the bait, Quentin, Daphne's husband and one of the supercilious prats, started to zoom in on specifics, like the Hayley Daniels case.

"Look at that poor girl who got herself murdered right here in town just last week," he said, lips a little too wet and red from the wine, a shine in his eyes and a sheen of sweat on his upper lip and brow. Daphne sat stiffly next to Banks, arms crossed, looking as if she'd just sucked on a lemon. "According to all the papers," Quentin went on, "it was someone close to her, an ex-boyfriend or something. It always is, isn't it? But has there been an arrest? No. I mean, what's stopping them? Are they dim or something? You'd think they'd know by now."

Someone started laying the blame on the lenient judges, the Crown Prosecution Service and the slick defence barristers, and still Banks didn't say anything. One or two people laughed nervously and Max said, "Oh, they probably just misplaced the evidence. They're always doing that, aren't they? Or faking it." He glanced at Banks.

Then Sophia's voice cut through the rest. "For crying out loud, you should hear yourselves talk. Are you all such sheep that you believe everything you read in the papers or see on the news? If you ask me, you've all been watching too many police programs. Too much Frost and Morse and Rebus. How do you think it happens? Do you really believe the policeman wakes up in the middle of the night with a brilliant idea and says to himself, 'Ah-ha, eureka, I've got it! I have the solution!?' Grow up. It's hard slog."

That silenced them. After a short pause, Banks glanced over at Sophia and said, "Well, I do occasionally wake up in the middle of the night with a brilliant idea, but most of the time it turns out to be indigestion."

There was another pause, and then everyone laughed. Sophia held Banks's gaze and seemed to be searching him with those dark eyes of hers. Then she smiled again, and this time there was something different about it, something more intimate about their contact.

The conversation split into smaller groups and moved on. Banks found himself talking to Sophia about how much she enjoyed walking around London at night, and he told her about some of his favourite Dales walks, then Harriet joined in with a few funny stories about when she used to drive a mobile library. Dessert came, an apple-and-rhubarb crumble with custard, then they returned to the living room for coffee and after-dinner drinks, which Banks declined.

The evening was winding down. The drunks had subsided into silence, punctuated only by the occasional snore from Trevor and twitch from Gemma. Those left talked quietly as the steam rose from their coffee cups, everyone feeling full and sleepy from all the food and wine. Even the lamplight in the living room seemed dimmer and warmer. Bach had been replaced by Paul Simon's *Graceland*, quiet and in the background. Banks felt warm and comfortable enough to fall asleep in his chair, but that wouldn't do. People started to get up and head for the hall. It was time to go, time for the long drive back to Gratly, perhaps with something loud on the iPod to keep him awake.

"Time, ladies and gentlemen, please," the landlord of the Horse and Hounds called out close to half past eleven. "Come on, let's be having you. Haven't you got no homes to go to?"

Chelsea still had half a Bacardi Breezer in front of her. Her fifth, or was it her sixth, of the evening? She couldn't remember. Most of the others had varying degrees of alcohol left, too, mostly lager for the blokes and white wine for the girls. The band had stopped half an hour ago, but the place was still full and noisy. They hadn't been too bad tonight, she thought, but if she had to hear one more cover version of "Satisfaction" she would scream. She had never liked the song anyway, never even liked the Rolling Stones. They were wrinklies when she was born.

Chelsea lit a cigarette. She knew they could probably hang on another ten minutes or so if they behaved. If she got home after midnight, things were bound to be quiet by then. She could put her headphones on and listen to the new Killers CD in bed. It had been a good night, and she was feeling a bit woozy and tired. Shane had kissed her on the couple of occasions they had passed one another in the corridor on the way to the loo, and they were still on for the Sage tomorrow. She would have to spend some time thinking about what to wear, going through her wardrobe.

For the moment, though, everyone seemed to be finishing up their drinks and moving on. Outside, the market square was busy, and there were already a couple of female slanging matches and a fight, Chelsea noticed. A police van stood on the other side, but no one paid much attention. The police would only get involved if a full fledged gang fight broke out.

In front of the police station, one girl was hitting a skinny young man with her handbag, and everyone was laughing except the young man. Another girl, apparently on her own, seemed to be staggering across the cobbles with a broken heel, crying, her mascara running. Occasionally, a whoop went up from some group or other over towards York Road, on their way to the Taj Mahal. Down the alley beside the pub, two boys were sharing a joint. Chelsea could smell it as she passed. She turned away. She didn't want them fixing their stoned and screwed-up attention on her. She linked arms with Katrina and Paula and they swayed from side to side, singing an old Robbie Williams song as they headed across the square towards Castle Road. Chelsea hated Robbie Williams almost as much as the Rolling Stones, but you couldn't get away from him. He was sort of a national institution, like Manchester United, and she loathed them, too. The weather was still mild, and the waxing moon shone down from the clear night sky. The boys walked in front, smoking and shoving one another playfully.

"We could go to the Three Kings," said Shane. "They'll probably be open for another half-hour or more. Have another drink?"

"The Three Kings is really crap," said Katrina. "Full of old geezers. Makes my fucking skin crawl when I walk in there, the way they look at you."

"Not at this time of night," said Shane, walking backwards as he spoke to them. "All the old geezers will be home and tucked up in bed by now. What about the Fountain? They're usually open till midnight."

"No," said Chelsea. "That was where the girl was. Hayley Daniels. The one who got killed." Chelsea didn't know Hayley, but she had seen her now and then in one pub or another on a Saturday night. She used to play in the Maze when she was a child, and the thought of someone being killed there was really creepy to her.

"Spoilsport," said Shane, turning and accepting a cigarette from Mickey.

"What's up?" Mickey said to Chelsea in that mocking, challenging tone she hated. "Scared of being too close to the Maze, are you? Scared of the dark? Of the ghosties? Hannibal the Cannibal?"

"Oh, shut up," said Chelsea. "I'm not scared. It's all taped off, anyway. Look at it."

"That's only the Taylor's Yard entrance," Mickey shot back. "You can get in easily from Castle Road or the car park at the back. I bet you daren't. I bet you're well scared."

"What do you mean?" said Chelsea, feeling the ground under her wobble. She wasn't sure whether it was because she was drunk or afraid.

"You heard me," said Mickey with a wink at his mates. "I bet you daren't go in there, in the Maze. By yourself."

"Of course I dare," said Chelsea.

"Go on, then."

"What?"

They had all stopped now, and Mickey turned to face the girls. "I dare you. I dare you to go in there for just five minutes. Alone."

"What do you bet?" Chelsea asked, hoping she sounded braver than she felt.

"If you do it, I'll take you back to my flat and give you a good tonguing."

"Hang on a minute, Mickey," Shane said. "That's out of order."

"Sorry, mate," said Mickey, laughing. "But they just can't say no." He eyed Chelsea again. "What do you say, love?"

"You can keep your tongue for the slappers you usually go down on," Chelsea said, "but I'll take ten quid off you for five minutes alone in the Maze."

"You don't have to do it, Chel," Shane pleaded. "He's well pissed. He's being an arsehole, as usual, that's all. Just ignore him."

"So what's new?" Chelsea stood her ground, hands on her hips. "What about it, then, big boy?" she said. "Or can't you afford to lose a tenner?"

"You don't know what you're missing out on," said Mickey, sticking out his tongue and running it over his rubbery lips. "But all right. Seeing as it's you. And if you come running out screaming before your five minutes are up, *you* owe *me* a tenner. All right?"

"You're on."

They shook hands and the group headed towards Castle Road, past the Fountain, which Chelsea noticed was already closed. Maybe what had happened last week had affected their business, she thought.

Chelsea was beginning to wish she hadn't been so impulsive as to accept Mickey's dare. But what had she to fear, really? Everyone was saying that Hayley Daniels's ex-boyfriend, or someone else she knew, had killed her, and he'd hardly be likely to do it to Chelsea as well, would

he? Besides, she knew her way around the Maze, knew shortcuts and
ways out most people had no idea existed. And a tenner. That would be
a bit extra to spend at the Sage tomorrow. Why not? She'd do it, she
decided. She'd take stupid Mickey's dare and win the tenner.

Why it always seemed to take forever for people to say goodbye at the
end of a dinner party was beyond Banks. Urgent new conversations
began, it seemed, at the eleventh hour, and people finally got around to
saying what they had been wanting to say all evening. Eventually, maybe
twenty minutes or so after they had made their first moves towards the
front door, they all drifted away in the directions they had come from.
Trevor and Gemma needed help, which their neighbours kindly gave
them. Helen seemed to be able to walk without Quentin's assistance,
and insisted on doing so with a wobble in her step. Banks thanked
Harriet and David, promised not to be such a stranger in future, and
wandered down the path in the mild night air, looking up at the clear
sky. The lightest of breezes blew, hardly even ruffling the new leaves. It
felt cool on his skin after the warmth of the dining room.

Somehow or other, he found himself leaving at the same time as
Sophia, and they both ended up at the bottom of the path under the
glow of a street lamp. Sophia was waiting for Harriet, who had dashed
upstairs to fetch an old family photo album she had promised to lend
her. It was the first time they had been alone, and Banks didn't quite
know what to say. He was also seeing her for the first time away from the
table, and he noticed that she was wearing skin-hugging jeans, which
suited her long legs, and that she was taller than he had first imagined.

Finally, they both spoke at once. It was one of those embarrassing
moments you can laugh at, and it broke the ice.

"I was going to say," Sophia went on, "that I met you once before,
years ago."

"I don't remember that."

She made a mock pout. "I'm hurt." Then she smiled. "It was twenty
years ago. I was at uni, visiting Harriet. I think you'd just moved in and
she introduced me to you."

"Twenty years," said Banks. "A lot's changed since then."

"For you and me both. Look, I was thinking. Even a big hotshot detective like you must get a few hours off once in a while. I just wondered if you'd fancy going on one of those long walks you were telling me about? Maybe tomorrow afternoon?"

"I'd love to," said Banks.

"Great. I'll give you my mobile number. Got some paper? And I don't mean your policeman's little black book. I don't want to end up in there with all the usual suspects and perverts."

"Don't worry." Banks pulled a Somerfield's receipt from his trouser pocket and a pen from his jacket. "Go on."

She told him the number. He hurried to scribble it down on the back, for some reason feeling as if they were doing something furtive, something they didn't want Harriet to see.

"I'll give you a ring tomorrow when I see how things are going," he said, "but I don't think it'll be a problem."

"Excellent."

They both stood in the pool of light from the street lamp. For a moment, Banks had the strangest feeling that the world outside of it no longer existed. "Right, then," he said. "I'd better be off. Can I give you a lift anywhere?"

"No. Really. It's not far. I like to walk."

"Are you sure?"

"Absolutely. Here's Harriet." She turned away. "I'll see you tomorrow," she whispered over her shoulder.

"Yes," said Banks. Then he walked out of the strange light back into the real world of shadows, where he immediately heard shouting and a bottle smash in the distance. Saturday night in Eastvale. He got in the Porsche, turned on the iPod and cranked up the volume on the Jesus & Mary Chain's "Just Like Honey" as he sped off towards Gratly.

Despite her show of bravado, Chelsea was feeling decidedly nervous as she walked down the arcade off Castle Road, past the closed shops – Past Times, Whittard's, Castle Books – and entered the dark Maze. Five minutes could be a long time, and a lot could happen.

Her footsteps echoed from the high walls, and the occasional dim, overhanging bulb over a warehouse door cast her long shadow on the cobbles. She almost tripped over a cat, which screeched loudly and ran off, causing her heartbeat to speed up and get louder. Maybe she shouldn't have taken Mickey's bet. Ten quid didn't buy you much these days. But it wasn't the money – she knew that – it was her pride.

An ex-boyfriend had killed Hayley Daniels, Chelsea repeated to herself. Remember that. Then she wondered if any of her ex-boyfriends might want to kill her. She had been cruel enough in her short time, she realized. She had two-timed Derek Orton, for a start, and he hadn't been too happy when he found out. And she hadn't replied to any of Paul Jarvis's letters or e-mails for months after he went off to Strathclyde University until he'd finally given up on her. Maybe he had started stalking her? He had said many times that he loved her. Then she had slept with Ian McRae's best friend just to hurt him, and made sure he knew about it. That had been about the worst. But Ian was still in jail for mugging that old woman, surely?

Chelsea turned a corner and ventured farther into the Maze. She knew where she was going. It would take her about five minutes to get through from the Castle Road arcade to the car park exit. But the deeper in she got, the more anxious she became, the more she jumped at each little noise and shadow and cursed Mickey for goading her into it in the first place.

As she was crossing a small, ill-lit square, she thought she heard a swishing noise behind her, like the sound someone's clothes make when they walk. She turned, and when she saw a man all in black, his face in shadows, she froze. In her mind she was making the calculations. If she ran now, she could probably get to the exit before he could catch her. But those damn high heels she was wearing would be a hindrance. She would have to lose them.

As she started to kick her shoes off, he came towards her, and she saw him open his mouth as if to say something, but before she knew what was happening, another figure appeared behind him, this one also wearing dark clothing, impossible to make out clearly. The figure moved quickly, drawing a hand across the man's throat from behind. They were only about three feet away now, and a warm and faintly sweet, metallic spray hit Chelsea on her face and chest. The man seemed confused and put his fingers to his neck. The other figure disappeared back into the shadows.

Chelsea staggered back a few paces. She was left alone with the man now, but he seemed fixed to the spot. He took his hand away from his throat and looked at it, then he opened his mouth as if he was trying to say something to her, but no sound came out. Then he dropped to his knees. Chelsea heard them crack as they hit the flagstones. As she stood there, hand to her mouth, the man toppled forward and fell on his face. She heard another crack as his nose hit the ground. Only then did she start screaming and running for the exit.

Josh Ritter was singing "Girl in the War" as Banks drove the dark, winding road on the daleside just above the river. He was finally beginning to like the Porsche, he realized. It was starting to fit him better. It was a bit shabbier now, more lived-in, less ostentatious, and it handled beautifully on winding, hilly roads like this. Maybe he would hang on to it after all. The daleside rose steeply to his left, fields giving way to outcrops of limestone and moors of gorse and heather, just looming shapes in the night, and the river gleamed in the moonlight as it meandered over the wide, lush valley bottom through the Leas. He passed the drumlin with the four trees permanently bent by the wind and knew he would soon be on the home stretch.

As he drove and half listened to the music, he thought of Sophia and what a breath of fresh air she had breathed into Harriet's dinner party. He wondered if she was married. An attractive woman like her probably had a serious boyfriend, at the very least, perhaps even lived with him. He knew there was no point, not even for a moment, in allowing himself to think that her invitation to go for a walk together meant anything more than it seemed, and he remembered his earlier advice to himself not to fall in love with her. Not much chance of that. He hoped he would at least have time to see her again on Sunday, though. As she had said, even a hotshot detective needed a few hours off now and then. And he was the boss, or close enough.

The so-called random shuffle seemed to go into folk mode, as it did from time to time. Eliza Carthy's "Worcester City" followed Kate Rusby's "No Names." Then came Isobel Campbell's "O Love Is Teasin.'" Sometimes Banks didn't believe it was random at all but had a devious mind of its own. Once it had followed the Small Faces' "Here Come the Nice" with the Nice's "America." Nobody could convince Banks that was random.

A mile or so past the drumlin, Banks's mobile rang. He fumbled with it and managed to get it to his ear without losing the rhythm of his driving. He was in a very dodgy area for coverage, and what came over the line was crackly and faint, fading in and out. He got the impression that it was Winsome talking, and he thought he heard the words *murder* and *the Maze* before reception broke down completely. With a growing sense of anxiety, he switched off his mobile and at the next farm gate turned around and headed back towards Eastvale.

13

It was with a terrible sense of déjà vu that Banks pulled into the market square around one o'clock in the morning and saw the crowds held back by police barriers. Many of the onlookers were drunk, having just staggered from the pubs at closing time and seen all the activity by the entrance to the Maze. One or two of them had become aggressive, and the uniforms were having a hard time keeping them back. When Banks saw the sergeant from the station, he asked him to call for reinforcements. They might not need any – drunks often lost interest as quickly as they found it – but it was better to be safe than sorry. Still feeling a sense of deep anxiety, Banks told the officers to block off the entire Maze this time, all exits.

"But, sir," one of the constables argued. "There are four terraced cottages near the back. People live there."

"We'll worry about them later," said Banks. "Someone has to interview them as soon as possible anyway. For the moment, I want the entire area sealed. No one goes in or out without me knowing about it. Got that?"

"Yes, sir." The constable scuttled off.

Banks rapped on the door of the Fountain.

"He's gone home, sir," said Winsome, emerging from Taylor's Yard and slipping under the police tape. "The place is all shut up."

Banks grunted. "I wish the rest of them would do the same." He noticed the occasional camera flash – press, most likely – and one or two people were holding their mobiles in the air and taking photographs, or even video-recording the scene, the way they did at rock concerts. In some ways it was a sick trend, but it sometimes got results; occasionally, someone captured something none of the CCTV cameras or police photographers did, a suspect in the crowd, for example, and it could help bring about an early solution.

"What the hell's going on, anyway?" Banks asked. "I couldn't hear a word you said over the phone. Who's the victim? Is she dead?"

"No, sir," said Winsome. "This one survived. If she was meant to be the victim. But someone's dead. I haven't had a look at the body yet. It's dark and I didn't want to disturb anything before you got here. We're waiting on SOCO, but Dr. Burns has just arrived."

"Okay. I'm sure Dr. Burns will be more than adequate. Ready?"

"As I'll ever be," said Winsome.

Banks followed her under the tape and into the Maze, deeper than the previous week, past the end of Taylor's Yard, around corners and across small cobbled squares, down ginnels so narrow they almost had to walk sideways. And all the while he could see beams of light sweeping the darkness, hear the crackle of police radios in the distance. It was a labyrinth in here, and Banks wished they'd brought a ball of twine. He remembered he had said the same thing about Annie's cottage in Harkside the first time he had dinner with her there – the first time they had made love – that it was hidden at the centre of a labyrinth and he could never find his way out alone. It had been a good way of suggesting he stay the night, at any rate.

There was little light in the Maze, so it was sometimes hard to see exactly where they were going, but Banks trusted to Winsome. She seemed to know her way without the twine.

"Where's Kev Templeton?" he asked from behind her.

"Don't know, sir. Couldn't raise him. Maybe he's at some club or other."

They came to a ginnel that led into a square, and Banks could see lights at the end, hear conversation and radios. When they approached, he noticed that someone had already put up arc lights, so the place was lit up like Christmas. Everyone seemed pale and pink around the gills. Banks recognized Jim Hatchley and Doug Wilson lingering by one wall,

and a couple of the uniformed officers were making notes. Peter Darby
was taking photographs and videotaping the entire scene, though Banks
supposed it could hardly be videotape if it was digital, the way they were
these days. Everyone glanced Banks's way as he entered the square, then
turned nervously away and a hush fell over them. His heart was in his
throat. There was something going on, something he needed to be prepared for.

Dr. Burns bent over the body, which lay face down on the ground,
an enormous pool of dark blood spread from the head area towards the
wall. Dr. Burns, almost as pale and shaken as the rest, stood up to greet
Banks and Winsome. "I don't want to touch or move the body until the
SOCOs get here," he said. Even Banks could see from where he was
standing that it wasn't the body of a woman.

"Can we have a look now?" he asked.

"Of course," said Dr. Burns. "Just be careful."

Banks and Winsome knelt. The stone flags were hard and cold.
Banks took a torch one of the uniformed officers offered him, knelt and
shone it on the face as best he could. When he saw the young, bloodless
profile, he fell back on his tailbone and slumped against the wall as if he
had been pushed.

Winsome squatted at his side. "Bloody hell, sir," she said. "It's Kev.
It's Kev Templeton. What the hell was he doing here?"

All Banks could think was that he had never heard Winsome swear
before.

One of the uniformed officers had been dispatched to fetch a pot of
fresh, hot coffee, even if he had to wake up one of the coffee-shop
owners in the market square, and the rest of the weary troupe filed into
the boardroom of Western Area Headquarters, no more than about a
quarter of a mile from where the body of their colleague lay, undergoing
the ministrations of Stefan Nowak and his SOCOs.

When DS Nowak and his team had arrived in the Maze, they had
made it clear they wanted the scene to themselves, and that the little
square was far too crowded. It was a relief for most of the officers
attending there to leave, and a signal to get the investigation in motion.

Everyone was stunned by Templeton's murder, and no one seemed able to take it in, but all that confusion had to be translated into action as quickly as possible.

Dr. Burns and Peter Darby stuck with the SOCOs, and the rest, about ten of them in all, including Banks, Hatchley and Winsome, returned to the station. Superintendent Gervaise had arrived straight from bed, hurriedly dressed in black denims and a fur-collared jacket, and she was busy setting up the whiteboard while the others arranged themselves around the long polished table, pads and pens in front of them. They wouldn't need a mobile van near the scene because the station itself was so close, but they would need to set up a special incident room, with extra phone lines, computers and civilian staff. For the moment, they would work out of the Hayley Daniels incident room, given space limitations and the shared location of the crimes.

They would also have to assign the usual roles – office manager, receiver, statement readers, action allocators and so on. Banks was already designated SIO and Gervaise would "interface with the media," as she put it. But she also made it clear that she wanted to be hands on and to be kept informed every step of the way. This was one of their own, and it went without saying that there would be no concessions, no quarter. But first they needed to know what had happened to Templeton, and why.

When the coffee arrived, everyone took a Styrofoam cup. They passed milk and sugar around, along with a packet of stale custard cream biscuits someone had found in a desk drawer. Banks joined Gervaise at the head of the table, and the first thing they asked for was a summary from the officer on the scene, a PC Kerrigan, who had just happened to be on duty in the public order detail that night. "What happened?" Banks asked. "Take it slowly, lad, step by step."

The young PC looked as if he'd been sick, which he probably had. At least he had had the presence of mind to do it away from the immediate scene. He took a deep breath, then began. "I was standing outside my van trying to decide whether to . . ." He glanced at Gervaise.

"It's all right, man," she said. "At the moment I don't care whether you were having a smoke or a blow job. Get on with it."

The constable blushed, and everyone else was taken aback, even Banks. He hadn't heard Gervaise talk like that before, any more than he had heard Winsome swear, but he ought to know by now that she was full of surprises. This was turning out to be a night of firsts.

"Y-yes, ma'am," Kerrigan said. "Well, you see, there was a minor fracas going on over by the Trumpeter's, and we were wondering whether we should just let it run its natural course, you know, like, or jump in there and risk exacerbating matters. The long and the short of it is that we decided to let it run its course. Just at that moment – and I checked my watch, ma'am, it was three minutes to twelve – a young woman came running out of the Maze covered in blood and screaming her head off."

"What did you do then?" Gervaise asked.

"Well, ma'am, I couldn't help but think that she'd been attacked, like, especially after last week, so I ran over to her. She seemed all right physically, but, as I said, there was quite a lot of blood on her, and she was pale as a ghost and shaking like a leaf."

"Spare us the clichés, constable, and get on with the story," said Gervaise.

"Sorry, ma'am. I asked her what was wrong, and she just pointed back where she'd come from. I asked her to take me there, and she froze. She was terrified, shaking her head. Said she was never going back in there. I asked her what she'd seen, but she couldn't tell me that either, or where it was. In the end, I persuaded her that she would be safe with me. She stuck to me like . . . like a . . ." He glanced at Gervaise. "She stuck close to me and led me to, well, you know what to."

"In your own words," said Banks. "Be calm, Kerrigan. Take it easy."

"Yes, sir." Constable Kerrigan took a deep breath. "We reached the area where the body was lying. I didn't know who it was, of course. You just couldn't tell, the way the face was squashed down on the flagstone like that. There was such a lot of blood."

"Did you or the girl go anywhere near the body?" Banks asked.

"No, sir. Except right at first, to get a closer look to see if he was still alive."

"Did either of you touch anything?"

"No, sir. I knew to stay well back, and there was no way she was going anywhere near it. She cowered back by the wall."

"Very good," said Banks. "Go on."

"Well, that's about it, sir. My mates from the van weren't far behind me, and when I heard them all piling into the square behind me, I told them to stop, turn back and go to station and call everyone they could think of. Maybe I shouldn't have panicked like that, but —"

"You did the right thing," said Gervaise. "You stayed with the body while they went?"

"Yes, ma'am."

"And the girl?"

"She stayed, too. She sort of slid down the wall and held her head in her hands. I did get her name and address. Chelsea Pilton. Funny name, I thought. Sounds like an underground stop, doesn't it? Daft thing naming a kid after a bun or a flower show, anyway, if you ask me," he added. "But that seems to be the way of the world these days, doesn't it?"

"Thank you for those words of wisdom," muttered Gervaise with her eyes closed and the knuckle of her right middle finger against her forehead.

"Maybe she was named after the football team," Banks offered.

Gervaise gave him a withering glance.

"She lives on the East Side Estate," Constable Kerrigan added.

"Where is she now?" Gervaise asked.

"I sent her to the hospital with Constable Carruthers, ma'am. She was in a proper state, the girl. I didn't see any sense in keeping her there, next to, well, you know."

"You did right," said Banks. "They'll know what to do. I assume Carruthers has instructions to stay with her until someone gets there?"

"Yes, sir. Of course, sir."

"Excellent. The parents?"

"Carruthers informed them, sir. I think they're at the hospital now."

"How old is she?"

"Nineteen, sir."

"Good work." Banks called down the corridor for a constable. "Get down to the hospital," he said, "and make sure that Chelsea Pilton is taken straight to the Sexual Assault Referral Centre. Got that? Chelsea Pilton. They'll know what to do with her there. Ask for Shirley Wong, if she's in tonight. That's Dr. Shirley Wong." The new referral centre, the only one in the Western Area, was attached to the hospital, and was seen by many as a rather sad sign of the times. "And see if they can get the parents out of the way. The girl's nineteen, so they don't have to be present during any interview or examination, and I'd rather they weren't. Their presence might cause her to clam up. I'll talk to them separately later."

"Yes, sir." The constable set off.

"She's not a suspect, is she, sir?" Kerrigan asked.

"At the moment," Banks said, "even you're a suspect." Then he smiled. "We have to follow certain procedures. You ought to know that, constable."

Kerrigan swallowed. "Yes, sir."

"You mentioned that she had blood on her," Banks said.

"Yes. It looked like it had sprayed onto her face and chest. Funny, it seemed like freckles in the dim light." Kerrigan glanced nervously at Gervaise, who rolled her eyes and muttered, "God help us, a poetic PC."

"Did she say where it had come from?" Banks asked.

"No, sir. I just assumed, well, that she'd been close when it happened."

"Did you ask her?"

"Yes, sir, but she wouldn't answer."

"Did you see or hear anything or anyone else in the Maze while you were there?" Banks went on.

"Not a dicky bird, sir."

"Any music or anything?"

"No, sir. Just a bit of argy-bargy from the market square. Drunks singing, cars revving up, glass breaking, the usual sort of thing."

More coffee arrived, a large urn this time, indicating that it was going to be a long night for everyone, and two constables set it up at the far end of the table. Someone had obviously gained access to the station canteen. They had also brought a bigger stack of Styrofoam cups, fresh milk, a bag of sugar and a packet of Fig Newtons. Everyone helped themselves. It was definitely canteen coffee, weak and bitter, but it did the trick. Banks noticed his hand trembling slightly as he raised the cup to his mouth. Delayed shock. He still found it impossible to accept that Kevin Templeton was dead, despite what he had seen with his own eyes. It just didn't make sense. He ate a fig biscuit. Maybe the sugar would help.

"Did Chelsea tell you anything about what she witnessed?" Banks asked.

"No, sir," said Kerrigan. "She was too stunned. Near mute with terror, she was. It'll be a long time before she has an easy night's sleep again, I can tell you."

Me, too, thought Banks, but he didn't say anything about that. "Right," he said. "You did a good job, Constable Kerrigan. You can go now. Stick around the station for now. We might need to talk to you again."

"Of course, sir. Thank you, sir."

Kerrigan left and no one said anything for a while. Finally, Gervaise said, "Anyone met Templeton's parents? I understand they live in Salford."

"That's right," said Banks. "I met them once, a few years back, when they came to Eastvale to visit him. Nice couple. I got the impression he didn't get along very well with them, though. He never said much about them. They'll have to be told."

"I'll see to it," said Gervaise. "I know DS Templeton wasn't exactly the most popular detective in the station," she went on, "but I know that won't stop anyone from doing their jobs." She stared pointedly at Winsome, who said nothing. "Right, then," Gervaise said. "As long as that's understood, we can get down to work. Any theories?"

"Well," said Banks, "first of all we have to ask ourselves what Kev was doing in the Maze close to midnight."

"You're implying that he was about to rape and kill Chelsea Pilton?" Gervaise said.

"Not at all," Banks answered, "though we'd be remiss in our duties if we failed to acknowledge that possibility."

"Pushing that unpleasant thought aside for moment," Gervaise said, "do you have any other theories for us to consider?"

"Assuming that Kev wasn't the Maze killer," Banks said, "I think it's a pretty good guess that he was there because he hoped he might catch him. Remember at the last meeting how he was convinced it was a serial killer who'd strike again soon in the same area?"

"And I ridiculed him," said Gervaise. "Yes, I don't need reminding."

"I don't mean to do that, ma'am," said Banks. "You were right. We had no evidence to justify the expense of a full-saturation operation. But it does appear rather as if Templeton took matters upon himself."

"Our Dr. Wallace agreed with him, too, as I remember," said Gervaise.

"I'm not arguing right and wrong here," Banks said. "I'm just trying to ascertain why Templeton was where he was."

Gervaise nodded brusquely. "Go on."

"I think he might have been there late on Friday, too," Banks added. "I remember he was a bit peaky and tired yesterday, dragging his feet. I thought he'd been clubbing, woke up with a hangover, and I gave him a bollocking. He didn't disabuse me of the notion." Banks knew that his last words to Templeton had been harsh – something about growing up and behaving like a professional – and he also now knew that they had been unjustified, though how professional was it to wander a possible murder site alone and unarmed? Still, it didn't make Banks feel any better.

He knew how Templeton rubbed most people the wrong way – accomplished women like Winsome and Annie in particular, and parents of difficult teenagers. No doubt there were some personal issues there. He could also be a racist, sexist bastard, and he had a personality that would steamroller over a person's finer feelings if he thought it would get him what he wanted. Sometimes you had to do that to a certain extent, Banks knew – he had even done it himself with Malcolm Austin – but Templeton didn't only do it out of necessity; he also seemed to relish it. Even Banks had seen him reduce witnesses to tears or rage on occasion, and Winsome and Annie had seen it happen far more often.

He was also bright, hard-working and ambitious, and whether he would have matured with age, Banks didn't know. He wouldn't have the option now. He was gone, snuffed out, and that wasn't bloody right. Even Winsome looked upset, Banks noticed, when he cast quick glances in her direction. He needed to talk to her. She could be carrying around a lot of guilt about the way she felt about Templeton, and it wouldn't help the investigation. He remembered that one of the subjects she and Annie had discussed at dinner was the way Templeton had behaved with Hayley Daniels's parents. Winsome hadn't told Banks exactly what had gone on between them, but he knew that a line had been crossed, a bridge burned. It could be eating away at her now, when they all needed to start focusing and thinking clearly.

"I also find myself wondering if he was just hanging out there on spec," Banks said, "or if he knew something."

"What do you mean?" Gervaise asked.

"Maybe he had a theory, or some special knowledge, something he was working on that he didn't share with the team."

"That sounds like Templeton," said Gervaise. "You mean he might have had inside knowledge, knew who was doing it, that it would happen again tonight, and he was after the glory?"

"Something like that," said Banks. "We'd better have a very close look at his movements since the Hayley Daniels case began."

"We're overstretched as it is," said Gervaise. "First Hayley Daniels and now this. I'll see about bringing in extra personnel."

"Are you sure it's not the same investigation?" Banks asked.

"At this moment," said Gervaise, "we don't know enough to say one way or another. Let's wait at least until we get some forensics and talk to the girl, then we'll have another session."

"I'll talk to her now," said Banks. "And there's another thing."

"What?"

"Kev's throat was cut. You can see it clearly. That's the same way Lucy Payne was killed out Whitby way."

"Oh, bloody hell," said Gervaise. "Another complication we could do without. Right, I think you'd better start trying to find some answers." She eyed the team grimly. "I want everybody out there on the streets, all night if necessary. Knocking on doors, checking CCTV footage. Wake the whole bloody town up if you have to. I don't care. There has to be something. Kevin Templeton may have been an arsehole, but let's not forget he was *our* arsehole and he deserves our best efforts." She clapped her hands. "Now go to it!"

Banks paid another visit to the crime scene before heading for the hospital to see Chelsea Pilton. It was about half past two in the morning, and the market square was deserted except for the police cars, the SOCO van and the constable guarding the entrance who jotted Banks's name down and let him through. Some bright spark had chalked yellow markings on the pavements and flagstones to guide the way. Not exactly a ball of twine, but the next best thing, and it did make the Maze a lot easier to negotiate.

The SOCOs had erected a canvas covering over the square in which Templeton's body had been found, and it was brightly lit from all directions. Officers were walking the ginnels and connecting passages with bright torches, searching for clues of any kind. The area immediately around the body had already been thoroughly searched, and Crime Scene Coordinator Stefan Nowak gestured for Banks to come forward into the covered area.

"Alan," he said. "I'm sorry."

"Me, too," said Banks. "Me, too. Anything?"

"Early days yet. From what we've been able to gather from the blood spatter analysis so far, he was attacked from behind. He wouldn't have known what hit him. Or cut him."

"He would have known he was dying, though?"

"For a few seconds, yes, but there are no messages scrawled in blood, if that's what you're thinking."

"One lives in hope. Pocket contents?"

Stefan fetched a plastic bag. Inside it, Banks found Templeton's wallet, some chewing gum, keys, a Swiss Army knife, warrant card, ballpoint pen and a slim notebook. "May I?" he asked, indicating the notebook. Stefan gave him a pair of plastic gloves and handed it to him. The handwriting was hard to read, perhaps because it had been written quickly, but it seemed as if Templeton liked to make brief notes, like an artist's sketches. He hadn't written the murderer's name in there, either. There was nothing since the previous evening, when it appeared that he had also been haunting the Maze, to no avail, as Banks had suspected. He would examine the notebook in more detail later to see if there was anything in the theory that Templeton was following leads of his own, but for now he handed it back. "Thank you. Dr. Burns finished yet?"

"He's over there."

Banks hadn't noticed the doctor in another corner of the square, dressed in navy or black, jotting in his notebook. He went over.

"DCI Banks. What can I do for you?"

"I'm hoping you can tell me a few things."

"I can't really tell you much at all," said a tired Burns. "You'll have to wait until Dr. Wallace gets him on the table."

"Can we start with the basics? His throat was cut, wasn't it?"

Burns sighed. "That's the way it looks to me."

"From behind?"

"The type of wound certainly supports DS Nowak's blood spatter analysis."

"Left- or right-handed?"

"Impossible to say at this point. You'll have to wait for the post-mortem, and even that might not tell you."

Banks grunted. "Weapon?"

"A very sharp blade of some sort. Razor or scalpel, something like that. Not an ordinary knife, at any rate. From what I can see on even a cursory examination, it's a clean, deep cut. The way it looks is that he simply bled to death. The blade cut through both the carotid and the jugular and severed his windpipe. The poor devil didn't have a hope in hell."

"How do you think it happened?"

"Your guess is as good as mine. I understand there was a witness?"

"Yes," said Banks. "A girl. She saw it happen. I'm on my way to talk to her."

"Then she might be able to tell you more. Perhaps he was following her?"

"Why? To warn her, protect her?"

"Or attack her."

Kev Templeton, the Maze killer? Banks didn't want to believe it, even though he had been the first to voice the possibility. "I don't think so," he said.

"I'm just trying to keep an open mind," said Dr. Burns.

"I know," said Banks. "We all are. I wonder what the *killer* thought Kev was doing, though?"

"What do you mean?"

"Nothing. I was just thinking of something else." Annie's case had come into his mind again. Lucy Payne sitting in her wheelchair, her throat cut with a sharp blade, a razor or a scalpel, a similar weapon to the one that had killed Templeton.

"I'm sure that Dr. Wallace will attend to the post-mortem as soon as she can on this one," Dr. Burns said. "She should be able to give you more answers."

"Right," said Banks. "And thanks. I'd better get to the hospital now and talk to the witness." As he walked away, he was still thinking about Lucy Payne, and he knew that as soon as it reached a reasonable hour in the morning he would have to ring Annie in Whitby and see if they could get together to compare notes.

It wasn't as if Annie was sleeping well, or even sleeping at all. Banks could have rung her right then, and she would have been awake enough to hold a conversation. A sound had woken her from a bad dream, and she had lain there not moving, listening hard, until she was sure it was just a creak from the old house and nothing else. Who did she think it was, anyway? Eric come to get her? Phil Keane returned? The men who had raped her? She couldn't let her life be ruled by fear. Try as she might, by then she couldn't remember the dream.

Unable to sleep, she got out of bed and put on the kettle. Her mouth was dry, and she realized she had polished off the best part of a bottle of Sauvignon Blanc by herself last night. It was getting to be a habit, a bad one.

She peered through the curtains across the pantile rooftops down to the harbour, where the moon frosted the water's surface. She wondered if she should have gone home to Harkside for the night, but she liked being close to the sea. It reminded her of her childhood in St. Ives, the long walks along the cliffs with her father, who kept stopping to sketch a rusty farm implement or a particularly arresting rock formation while she was left to amuse herself. It was then that she had learned to create her own world, a place she could go to and exist in when the real world was too tough to handle, like when her mother died. She only remembered one walk with her mother, who had died when she was six, and all the way along the rough clifftop path her mother had held her hand as they struggled against the wind and rain and told her stories about the places they would visit one day: San Francisco, Marrakesh, Angkor Wat. Like many other things in her life, that wasn't going to happen.

The kettle boiled and Annie poured water on the jasmine tea bag in her mug. When the tea was ready, she lifted the bag out with a spoon, added sugar and sat cradling her fragrant drink, inhaling the perfume as she stared out to sea, noting the way the moonlight shimmered on the water's ripples and brought out the texture and silvery-grey colour of the clouds against the blue-black sky.

As she sat there watching the night, Annie felt a strange connection with the young woman who had come to Whitby eighteen years ago. Was it Kirsten Farrow? Had she looked out on the same view as this, all those years ago, planning murder? Annie certainly didn't condone what she had done, but she felt some empathy with the damaged psyche. She didn't know what the young woman had felt, but if she had done the things Annie thought she had, and if she had been Kirsten Farrow, it had been because that was her only way of striking back at the man who had condemned her to a kind of living death. There are some kinds of damage that take you far beyond normal rules and systems of ethics and morality – beyond this point be monsters, as the ancients used to say. The young woman had gone there; Annie had only stood at the edge of the world and stared into the abyss. But it was enough.

Annie had the overwhelming sensation that she was at an important crossroads in her life, but she didn't know what the directions were; the signposts were either blurred or blank. The only thing she knew was that she had been behaving and feeling so strangely of late. She couldn't trust herself to get close to a man. Consequently, she had abandoned her control to alcohol and gone home with a boy. Whatever demons were driving her, she needed to get sorted, get a grip, develop a new perspective and perhaps even a plan. Maybe she even needed outside help, though the thought caused her to curl up inside and tremble with panic. Then she might be able to read the signposts. Whatever she did, she had to break the circle of folly and self-delusion she had let herself get trapped in.

And there was Banks, of course; it seemed that there was always Banks. Why had she kept him at arm's length for so long? Why had she abused their friendship so much this past week, thrown herself at him in some sort of drunken rage, then lied to his face about having a row with her boyfriend when he tried to help? Because he was there? Because she . . . ? It was no use. No matter how hard she tried, Annie couldn't even remember what it was that had split them apart. Had it been so insurmountable? Was it just the job? Or was that an excuse? She knew that she had been afraid of the sudden intensity of her feelings for him, their intimacy, and that had been one thing that had caused her to start backing away, that and the attachment he inevitably felt for his ex-wife and family. It had been raw back then. She sipped some hot jasmine tea and stared out to the horizon. She thought of Lucy Payne's body, sitting there at the cliff edge. Her last sight had probably been that same horizon.

She needed to get things back on a professional footing, talk to Banks again about the Kirsten Farrow case and its history, especially since her conversation with Sarah Bingham. If Kirsten had disappeared, there was a good chance she had turned up in Whitby to kill Eastcote, the man who had stolen her future. Sarah Bingham had certainly lied about Kirsten's movements, and the truth left her with no alibi at all.

Annie finished her tea and noticed it had started to rain lightly. Perhaps the sound of the raindrops tapping against her window would help her get back to sleep, the way they had when she was a child, after her mother's death, but she doubted it.

The Sexual Assault Referral Centre, new pride and joy of Eastvale General Infirmary, was designed in its every aspect to make its patients feel at ease. The lighting was muted – no overhead fluorescent tubes or bare bulbs – and the colours were calming, shades of green and blue with a dash of orange for warmth. A large vase of tulips stood on the low glass table, and seascapes and landscapes hung on the walls. The armchairs were comfortable, and Banks knew that even the couches used for examinations in the adjoining room were also as relaxing as such things could be, and the colours there were muted too. Everything was designed to make the victim's second ordeal of the night as painless as possible.

Banks and Winsome stood just outside the door with Dr. Shirley Wong, whom Banks had met there on a number of previous occasions and had even had drinks with once or twice, though only as a colleague. Dr. Wong was a dedicated and gentle woman, perfect for the job. She also made a point of keeping in touch with everyone who passed through her doors and had a memory for detail Banks envied. She was a petite, short-haired woman in her late forties and wore silver-rimmed glasses. Banks was always surprised by her Geordie accent, but she had been born and bred in Durham. He introduced her to Winsome and they shook hands.

"I'm sorry to hear about your friend," Dr. Wong said. "Detective Sergeant Templeton, wasn't it? I don't think I knew him."

"He wasn't really a friend," Banks said. "More of a colleague. But thank you." He gestured towards the room. "How is she?"

Dr. Wong raised her eyebrows. "Physically? She's fine. From what I've seen there are no signs of injury, or of sexual assault, or even sexual activity. But I suspect you already knew that. Which sort of brings me to the question . . ."

"Why is she here?"

"Yes."

Banks explained the chaotic situation in the Maze, and the less than satisfactory option of taking Chelsea to the station and offering her a set of paper overalls while they bagged her clothes, no doubt with her parents fussing around, all under bright fluorescent light.

"You did right, then," said Dr. Wong. "The parents are in the family room, by the way, if you need to talk to them."

"So you're not going to report us to the board for wasting hospital resources?"

"I don't think so. Not this time. Given a suitable donation to the victims' fund, of course, and a single malt of my choice. Seriously, though, she's all right physically, but she's had a terrible shock. Sobered her up pretty quickly, I'd say. I gave her a mild sedative – nothing that will knock her out or interact badly with the alcohol she had clearly been drinking – so she should be lucid enough if you want to talk to her."

"I would, yes."

Dr. Wong pushed the door open with her shoulder. "Follow me."

She introduced Banks and Winsome to Chelsea, and Banks sat opposite the girl in a matching deep armchair. Winsome sat off to the side and took out her notebook unobtrusively. Soft music played in the background. It was nothing Banks recognized but was no doubt calculated to induce maximum relaxation and a sense of calm. They could at least have used Brian Eno's ambient music, he thought, say, *Ambient 1: Music for Airports* or *Thursday Afternoon*. Either of those would have worked as well.

Chelsea wore a blue hospital gown, and her long hair was tied back in a ponytail, making her appear more like a lost little girl than a young woman. Her eyes were red-rimmed, but clear and focused. She had a nice bone structure, Banks noticed, high cheekbones, a strong jaw and pale, freckled skin. She sat with her legs curled under her and her hands resting on the arms of the chair.

"Coffee?" asked Dr. Wong.

Chelsea declined the offer, but Banks and Winsome said yes. "I'm not fetching it for you, myself, you understand," Dr. Wong said. "I wouldn't stoop that low."

"I don't care who gets it," said Banks, "as long as it's black and strong."

Dr. Wong smiled. "I just wanted you to know." Then she left the room.

Banks smiled at Chelsea, who seemed wary of him. "Doctors," he said with a shrug.

She nodded, and a hint of a smile flitted across the corners of her lips.

"I know this is tough for you," Banks went on, "but I'd like you to tell me in your own words, and in your own time, exactly what happened in the Maze tonight, and my friend Winsome over there will write it all down. You can start with why you were there."

Chelsea glanced at Winsome, then at the floor. "It was so stupid of me," she said. "A dare. Mickey Johnston dared me. Just five minutes. I didn't think, you know, the papers said it was her ex-boyfriend or someone. My mum told me to be careful, but I really couldn't believe I would be in any danger."

Banks made a mental note of the name. Mr. Mickey Johnston could expect a whole lot of grief to come in his direction soon. "Okay," he said, "but it must have been a little bit scary, wasn't it?" A nurse walked in quietly with the two coffees on a tray, which she placed on the table beside the tulips. It was from the machine down the hall. Banks could tell by the plastic cups before he even took a sip. It had both milk and sugar. He let his sit there, but Winsome took hers over to her corner.

"I jumped at my own shadow and every noise I heard," said Chelsea. "I couldn't wait to get out of there."

"You knew your way around?"

"Yes. I used to play there when I was little."

"Tell me what happened."

Chelsea paused. "I was near the end of the five minutes, and I heard . . ." She paused. "Well, I don't think I really heard anything at first. It was more like a feeling, you know, like something itchy crawling in your scalp. Once there was an outbreak of nits at school, and the nit nurse came around. I didn't get them, but my best friend Siobhan did, and she told me what it was like."

"I know what you mean," said Banks. The nit nurse had visited his school on more than one occasion, too, and he hadn't always been as lucky as Chelsea. "Go on."

"Well, that's what I felt at first, then I thought I heard a noise."

"What sort of noise?"

She shrugged. "I don't know. Behind me. Just like there was somebody there. A jacket brushing against the wall, perhaps. Something like that."

"Did you hear any music?"

"No."

"What about footsteps?"

"No, more of a swishing sound like your jeans or your tights make sometimes when you walk."

"All right," said Banks. "What did you do next?"

"I wanted to run, but something told me to slow down and turn around, so that's what I was doing when . . . when . . ." She put her fist to her mouth.

"It's all right, Chelsea," said Banks. "Take a few deep breaths. That's right. No hurry. Take your time."

"That was when I saw him."

"How close was he?"

"I don't know. A few feet, maybe five or six. But I know I felt that if I turned and ran right then I'd be able to get away from him."

"Why didn't you run?"

"I had to get my shoes off first, and by then . . . He wasn't the only one there. And we were sort of frozen. I couldn't move. It's hard to explain. He stopped when he knew I'd seen him, and he looked, I don't know, I mean, he wasn't wearing a mask or anything. It was dark but my eyes had adjusted. I know this sounds well stupid and all, but he was really good-looking, and his face, you know, his expression, it was *concerned*, like he cared, not like he wanted to . . . you know . . ."

"Did he say anything?"

"No. He . . . he was just going to open his mouth to say something when . . ."

"Go on," said Banks. "What happened?"

She hugged her knees tighter. "It was all so fast and like slow motion at the same time. All such a blur. I saw a movement behind him, another figure."

"Did you see a face?"

"No."

"Was it wearing a mask?"

"No. Maybe a scarf or something, covering the mouth, like when you come back from the dentist's in the cold. I got the impression that most of the face was covered anyway. It's funny, I remember thinking even then, you know, it was like some superhero out of a comic book."

"Was this figure taller or shorter than the man?"

"Shorter."

"How much?"

"Maybe five or six inches."

Templeton was five-foot-ten, which made his attacker around five-four or five-five, Banks calculated. "And what happened?"

"Like I said, it was all just a blur. This second figure reached in front, like you'd put your arm around someone's neck if you were playing or messing about, and just sort of brushed its hand across the other's neck, like . . ." She demonstrated on her own neck. "Really gently, like it was tickling."

"Did you see a blade of any kind?"

"Something flashed, but I didn't really see what it was."

"You're doing really well, Chelsea," said Banks. "Almost there."

"Can I go home soon?"

"Yes," said Banks. "Your parents are waiting for you down the hall."
Chelsea pulled a face.

"Is that a problem?"

"No-o-o. Not really. I mean, my mum's okay, but my dad . . ."

"What about your dad?"

"Oh, he's just always on at me, the way I dress, the way I talk, chew
gum, the music I listen to."

Banks smiled. "Mine was the same. Still is."

"Really?"

"Really."

"It's funny," she went on. "I tell myself I don't really like them, like
they're really naff and all, but at times like this . . ." A tear rolled down
her cheek.

"I know," said Banks. "Don't worry. You'll soon be with them. Soon
be tucked up safe and warm in your own bed."

Chelsea wiped her cheek with the back of her hand. "I was just,
like, rooted to the spot. I didn't know what was happening. The one
who was following me just stopped and seemed surprised. I don't think
he knew what had happened to him. *I* didn't know. I felt something
warm spray on my face, and I think I might have screamed. It was all so
fast and so ordinary."

"What did he do next?"

"He went down on his knees. I could hear the cracking sound. I
remember thinking it must have hurt, but he didn't cry out or anything;
he just looked surprised. Then he put his hand to his throat, like, and
took it away and stared at it, then he fell forward right on his face on the
flags. It was terrible. I just stood there. I didn't know what to do. I could
feel all this . . . *stuff* on me, warm and sticky stuff, like from a spray, and I
didn't know at first it was blood. It's silly, but I thought he'd sneezed or
something, and I thought, great, now I'll get a cold and I won't be able to
go to work. I don't get paid if I'm not there, you see."

"Did you get a look at his attacker at all?"

"No. Like I said, she was smaller than him, so most of the time he
was in the way, in front, blocking her from view, and then afterwards,
when he fell, she just sort of melted back into the shadows and I couldn't
see her any more."

"You said she."

"Did I?"

"Yes."

Chelsea frowned. "Well, I don't know. That must have been the impression I got. Maybe because she was so small and slight. I can't be certain, though."

"Could it have been a man?"

"I suppose so. But I did get the impression that it was a woman. I don't really know why, and I couldn't swear to it, of course."

"Did you see any of her features?"

"No. She was wearing a hat. I remember that, too. Like a beret or something. It must have been the way she moved that made me think she was a woman. I couldn't be certain, though. Maybe I was mistaken."

"Maybe," said Banks with a glance towards Winsome, who indicated that she was getting it all down. "But it *could* have been a woman?"

Chelsea thought for a moment and said, "Yes. Yes, I think it could have been."

"What was she wearing?"

"Dark clothing. Jeans and a black jacket. Maybe leather."

"Could you have a guess at the age?"

"I never got a good look at her. Sorry. Not really old, though, I mean, you know, she moved fast enough."

"What happened next?" Banks asked.

"I think I screamed again, then I ran for the market square, by the Fountain. I knew that was where I had the best chance of finding a policeman, and even if there wasn't one standing around watching all the fun, the station's just across the square. Well, you know that."

"Good thinking," said Banks.

Chelsea shivered. "I still can't believe it. What was going on, Mr. Banks? What did I see?"

"I don't know," said Banks. "All I know is that you're safe now." He glanced towards Winsome, who took Chelsea's hand.

"Come on, love," she said. "Let me take you back to your parents. They'll take you home."

"What about my clothes?"

"We're going to have to keep them for the moment to do some tests," Banks said. "The blood. It helps our forensic scientists. We'll see if Dr. Wong can rustle up something temporary for you."

On her way out, Chelsea looked at Banks. "The man," she said. "Was he going to kill me?"

"No," said Banks. "I think he was there to protect you."

After Chelsea and Winsome had gone, Banks sat for a long time in the calm room mulling over what he'd just heard. Now, even more than before, he knew that he had to contact Annie Cabbot about this. Possibly a female killer. A sharp blade. A slit throat. Banks didn't believe in coincidences like that, and he knew Annie didn't, either.

14

When her telephone rang at half past seven on Sunday morning, Annie had hardly managed to get back to sleep since the noise and the bad dream had woken her at three. She had lain awake thinking about Banks and Eric and Lucy Payne and Kirsten Farrow and Maggie Forrest until they all became a tangled mess in her mind, and then she had dozed fitfully for a while. Now the telephone.

Annie fumbled with the receiver and muttered her name.

"Sorry, did I wake you?" said the voice on the other end. She noticed something odd about it. At least it wasn't Eric.

"That's all right," she said. "Time to get up, anyway."

"I did wait until a reasonable hour. I called the police station first and they told me you'd be at this number. It's half seven over there, right, and you police get up early, don't you?"

"About that," said Annie. Now she could place the accent. Australian. "You must be Keith McLaren," she said.

"That's right. I'm calling from Sydney. It's half past six in the evening here."

"I wish it was that here. Then my working day would be over."

McLaren laughed. He sounded as if he were in the room with her. "But it's Sunday."

"Ha!" said Annie. "As if that makes any difference to Superintendent Brough. Anyway, it's good to hear from you so promptly. Thanks for calling."

"I don't know if I can tell you anything new, but the officer who rang me did say it was important."

Ginger had got in touch with McLaren through the Sydney police. It wasn't that he had a criminal record, but they had been informed about what happened to him in Yorkshire eighteen years ago, and he was in their files. "It could be," Annie said, tucking the cordless phone under her chin as she went to get some water and put the kettle on. She was naked, which felt like a disadvantage, but no one could see her, she told herself, and it would be hard to get dressed and talk at the same time. She sipped some water and opened the pad on the table before her. Already she could hear the kettle building to a boil. "I hope these aren't painful memories for you," she went on, "but I want to talk about what happened to you in England eighteen years ago."

"Why? Have you finally found out who did it?"

"We don't know yet, but there may be a connection with a case I'm working on. It came up, anyway. Have you been able to remember anything more about what happened over the years?"

"A few things, yes. Little details. They weren't there, and suddenly they are. I've been writing things down as they come back. My doctor told me it would be good therapy and it really does help. As I'm writing one detail I sometimes remember another. It's odd. On the whole, I can remember quite a bit until Staithes, then it all becomes a blur. Isn't it funny? I remember so little about my holiday of a lifetime. Waste of money, when you come to think of it. Maybe I should have asked for a refund."

Annie laughed. "I suppose so. What about that day at Staithes? Someone thought they saw you walking near the harbour there with a young woman."

"I know. Like I said, it's a blur. All I have is a vague sense of talking to someone down by the harbour, and I *thought* it was someone I knew. But I don't even know if it was a man or a woman."

"It was a woman," Annie said. "Where do you think you knew her from?"

"That I don't know. It's just a feeling, without foundation. The police told me I met a girl at a B & B in Whitby, and I do remember her now. They seemed to think it was the same girl, but I don't know. I've had recurring dreams, nightmares, I suppose, but I don't know how truthfully they reflect the reality."

"What nightmares?"

"It's a bit, you know, awkward."

"I'm a police officer," Annie said. "Just think of me as a doctor."

"You're still a woman."

"I'm afraid I can't do anything about that."

McLaren laughed. "I'll do my best. It's a bit sexual, you see. The dream. We're in the woods, you know, on the ground, making out, kissing and stuff."

"Got you so far," Annie said. "And just for the record, I haven't blushed once." The kettle was boiling, and she put the phone under her chin as she poured the water on the tea bag in her cup, careful not to splash any on her exposed skin.

"Well, it turns into a horror story after that," McLaren went on. "All of a sudden she's not a lovely young girl any more, but a monster, with like a dog's head, or a wolf's, sort of like a werewolf, I suppose, but her chest is more like raw human skin, only there's just one nipple, bleeding, and the rest is all criss-crossed with red lines where her breasts and other nipple should be. Then my head splits open. I told you it was pretty weird."

"That's the nature of dreams," Annie said. "Don't worry, I'm not going to psychoanalyze you."

"That's no worry. I've been there. Anyway, that's about it. I wake up in a sweat."

Annie knew from her conversation with Sarah Bingham that Kirsten Farrow had had surgery on her breasts after the attack, and on her vagina and pubic region. "What do you think it's about?"

"That's what my shrink asked me. Beats me."

"What were you doing in Whitby?"

"I'd just finished uni and wanted to see something of the world before settling down back home. I had some money saved up, so I came over to Europe, like so many Aussies do. We're such a long way from anywhere, and it's such a huge country, so we feel we have to do the big trip once before settling down back here. I have an ancestor who came from Whitby. A transport. Stole a loaf of bread or something.

So it was a place I'd heard a lot about while I was growing up, and I wanted to visit."

"Tell me about the girl you met."

"Can you just hang on a minute? I'll get my notebook. Everything I remember is in there."

"Great," said Annie. She waited about thirty seconds and McLaren came on the line again.

"Got it," he said. "I met her at breakfast one day. She said her name was Mary, or Martha, or something like that. I never have been able to remember exactly which."

Annie felt a pulse of excitement. The woman who took Lucy from Mapston Hall had called herself Mary. "Not Kirsten?" she asked.

"That doesn't ring any bells."

"What sort of impression did she make on you?" Annie asked, sketching the view from her window on the writing pad, the mist like feathers over the corrugated red roof tiles, the sea a vague haze under its shroud, grey on grey, and a sun so pale and weak you could stare at it forever and not go blind.

"I remember thinking she was an interesting girl," McLaren said. "I can't remember what she looked like now, but she was easy on the eyes, at any rate. I didn't know anybody in the place. I was just being friendly, really, I wasn't on the make. Well, not much. She was very defensive, I remember. Evasive. Like she just wanted to be left alone. Maybe I did come on a bit too strong. Us Aussies sometimes strike people that way. Direct. Anyway, I suggested she might show me around town, but she said she was busy. Something to do with some research project. So I asked her out for a drink that evening."

"You don't give up easily, do you?"

McLaren laughed. "It was like pulling teeth. Anyway, she agreed to meet me for a drink in a pub. Just a sec . . . yes, it's here . . . the Lucky Fisherman. Seemed to know her way around."

"The Lucky Fisherman?" Annie's ears pricked up. That was Jack Grimley's local, the one he had just left the evening he disappeared. "Did you tell the police this?" she asked.

"No. It's just something I remembered years later, and they never got back to me. I didn't think it was important."

"It doesn't matter," said Annie, thinking there were more holes in this case than in a lump of Swiss cheese. But Ferris was right: they didn't have the luxury of pursuing every mystery to its solution the way TV cops did. Things fell through the cracks. "Did she turn up?"

"Yeah. It wasn't easy having a conversation with her. It was like she was very distracted, thinking of something else. And she'd never heard of Crocodile Dundee. That's something I remembered years later. He was big at the time."

"Even I've heard of Crocodile Dundee," said Annie.

"Well, there you go. Anyway, I was quickly getting the impression she'd rather be elsewhere. Except . . ."

"What?"

"Well, she wanted to know about fishing. You know, the boats, when and where they landed the catch and all that. I mean, I didn't know, but I just thought it was another weird thing about her. To be quite honest, I was beginning to think I'd made a big mistake. Anyway, I went to the loo, and when I came back I got the distinct impression she was staring at some other bloke."

"Who?" Annie asked.

"Dunno. Local. Wearing one of those fisherman's jerseys. Good-looking enough in a rough sort of way, I suppose, but really . . ."

Jack Grimley, Annie was willing to bet, though he wasn't actually a fisherman, and she doubted that Kirsten, if that was who it was, was studying him because she thought he was a nice bit of rough.

"Then what?"

"We left. Walked around town. Ended up sitting on a bench talking, but again I got the impression she was somewhere else."

"Did anything happen?"

"No. Oh, I made my tentative move, you know, put my arm around her, gave her a kiss. But it obviously wasn't going anywhere, so I gave up and we went back to the B and B."

"To your own rooms?"

"Of course."

"Did you see her again?"

"Not that I know of, though, as I said, the police think I might have."

"You don't remember anything else about that day in Staithes?"

"No. Sorry."

"I understand it was touch-and-go for a while?"

"I'm lucky to be here. Everyone said so. I'm even more lucky to have been able to pick up my life and carry on, become a lawyer, get a good job, the lot. Everything except marriage and kids. And that just never seemed to happen. But there was some talk at the time of possible permanent brain damage. My guess is they don't understand the Aussie brain over here. It's much tougher than you pommies think."

Annie laughed. "I'm glad." She liked Keith McLaren, at least what she could gather of him over the telephone. He sounded as if he would be fun to go out with. He'd also be about the right age for her. Single, too. She wondered if he was good-looking. But Sydney was a long, long way away. It was nice to have the fantasy, though. "You must have wondered why it happened," she asked. "Why you?"

"Hardly a day goes by."

"Any answers?"

McLaren paused before speaking. "Nobody ever came right out and said it at the time," he said, "perhaps because I was either in a coma or recovering from one, but I got the distinct impression that the police didn't discount the theory that I'd tried it on a bit too aggressively and she defended herself."

That didn't surprise Annie. She was almost loath to admit it, especially after talking to McLaren and liking him, but it was one of the first things that would have occurred to her, too. Whether that was because she was a woman or a police officer, or both, she didn't know. Maybe it was because she'd been raped herself. "They suggested you'd assaulted her, tried to rape her?"

"Not in so many words, but I got the message loud and clear. It was only the fact that there were two unexplained bodies around and she seemed to have done a runner that kept me out of jail."

"Did you ever see her naked?"

"What a question!"

"It could be important."

"Well, the answer's no. Not that I remember. Like I said, I don't know what happened that day in the woods, but I think my memory up to that point is as clear as it's going to get. I mean, she just didn't want to know. I kissed her that once, on the bench near the Cook statue, but that's all."

So, Annie thought, he couldn't have known about Kirsten's chest injuries – if, indeed, it was Kirsten – until they were in the woods together, which he couldn't remember, and he had somehow got her top off. But the dream indicated that he had some subconscious knowledge of her injuries. He must have tried something with her, then, or perhaps it was mutual up to a point, then she began to struggle, to panic. Kirsten knew by that point that she couldn't have sex, so what was going on?

If McLaren had cottoned on to who she was, as he may well have done even if she had modified her appearance, seen through her disguise and posed a threat to her agenda of vengeance, then wasn't there a chance that she had cold-bloodedly lured him into the woods and set out to get rid of him? That she had led him on and, when he was sufficiently distracted, attempted to kill him? What kind of creature was Annie dealing with? The moment she thought she had some kind of connection with Kirsten, the damn woman slipped beyond her understanding and sympathy again.

"What do you think about the police's theory?" Annie asked.

"I don't see it," McLaren said. "I mean, it might sound weird to you, but I'm just not like that. I don't think I have it in me. You might think every man does, I don't know. I suppose you've seen it all in your line of work, and you're a woman, but I don't. I honestly don't believe that I would ever attack or attempt to rape a woman."

Even though Annie had also experienced rape, she didn't happen to believe that every man was a potential rapist. "Thanks for your time, Keith," she said. "You've been really helpful. And if it's any consolation, I don't believe you're that sort of person, either."

"You're welcome," said Keith. "And if you're ever in Sydney, look me up. I'll treat you to the best seafood you've ever had."

Annie laughed. "I will," she said. "Take care."

When she hung up, she held her lukewarm tea to her skin and stared out to sea. Sydney. Now that would be fun. Images of the Harbour Bridge and the opera house that she had seen on television came into her mind. The mist was burning off the sea now and rising in thin wisps to vanish in the air, the sun was brighter, harder to look at, and a green fishing trawler was making its way to shore. A few minutes later, her phone rang again.

Kevin Templeton had lived in a one-bedroom flat in a converted school near the Green, just across the river, not far from where profiler Jenny Fuller lived when she was in town. From his third-floor window, a door led out to a small balcony that gave a magnificent west-facing view of the terraced gardens, up to the majestic ruined castle towering over the scene, high on its hill. Across the Green to the east was the East Side Estate, a blight on the face of Eastvale, but a source of continuing employment for Banks and the rest at Western Area Headquarters. It was mostly obscured by trees, but you could see the rows of identical red-brick boxes between the bare branches.

The flat was an empty shell, Banks thought, as he stood in the living room, and one that didn't give away a great deal about its occupant. The furniture was all modern, probably from Ikea or some similar flat-box merchant, no doubt pieced together in a flurry of activity one weekend with an Allen key, a six-pack of cheap lager and a great deal of swearing.

There was a DAB radio, but no stereo system or CDs. A widescreen TV dominated one wall, and beside it stood a bookcase crammed with DVDs. A lot of sports, Banks noticed, some blockbuster movies and a few American TV series, such as *The Simpsons*, *24* and *CSI*. There were a few books, too, mostly tattered paperbacks by Ken Follett, Jack Higgins, Chris Ryan or Andy McNab, along with some texts on criminal law and American tomes on investigative procedure. There were no framed family photographs on the mantelpiece, and the only wall decoration was a cheaply framed poster for *Vertigo* that Banks remembered had been given away free in a newspaper just last year.

The toilet and bathroom combination revealed the usual things – shampoo, toothpaste, paracetamol, hair gel, razor, shaving cream and so on. No prescription drugs. The towel that hung over the side of the bath was still damp, and beads of moisture dotted the sides and bottom of the tub and wall tiles.

In the kitchen, Templeton's freezer was empty apart from a tray of ice cubes, and in the fridge Banks found milk, eggs, cheese, HP sauce,

tomato sauce, the remains of an Indian take-away and a Tupperware
container of leftover spaghetti Bolognese. There was also a wine rack
full of Tesco's and Sainsbury's wines – pretty good ones, too, Banks
noticed – and a fairly expensive espresso-making machine.

Which left the small bedroom, with its double bed and night table
with shaded lamp, and one large wardrobe full of clothes and shoes. The
suits were good quality. Not exactly Armani or Paul Smith, but Banks
would have been very suspicious if Templeton had owned such expensive clothing on a detective sergeant's salary. The only photograph in the
flat stood on his dressing table under the window. It showed a young
girl, perhaps eighteen or nineteen, her long hair blowing in the wind,
hand held up to hold it out of her eyes, smiling at the camera, squinting
slightly in the sun, autumn leaves swirling around her. Banks had no
idea who it was or why Templeton kept it in his bedroom. A girlfriend
perhaps? He had never talked about his private life.

There was nothing but loose change, condoms and pen and paper
in the night-table drawer. A digital alarm clock set for 6 a.m. stood
on top.

Banks went back into the living room and sat at Templeton's desk.
The laptop computer was password-protected and would have to go
down to technical support for analysis. Banks rifled through the drawers
and found a stack of ledger-sized notebooks filled with Templeton's neat
but crabbed hand. Entries were dated, like a diary, but all Templeton
wrote about was the cases he worked on. Banks checked the most recent
ledger and found that Templeton had written up what he had done on
Friday night:

> ooooh. Entered Maze via car park entrance. Light poor.
> Buildings high, many overhanging. Impossible to keep an
> eye on the whole place. Distant sounds from square as the
> pubs close. Nobody comes here. No footsteps.
> 0023h. Hear snatch of the Streets "Fit But You Know It" from
> a car whizzing by, or a door opening and closing, then it's
> gone. Muffled dance music from inside the Bar None. More
> waiting. More nothing. Still sure I'm right. Killer will strike

again, and what a good way of having a laugh at us it would
be if he did it the following week, in the same place!

Summary: Hung around until two o'clock and nothing happened. When the town had been silent for half an hour and it
was clear that neither killer nor victim was going to come here
tonight, I decided to end the surveillance for this evening.

So Banks's theory about Templeton privately policing the Maze had
been right. Not that it was any great consolation in the face of the young
lad's murder. Banks took one more glance around the flat, then he
locked up and headed back to the station, taking the ledger with him.

It was a long drive to Eastvale and Annie wasn't entirely sure that it was
justified, but what Banks had said over the phone had intrigued and disturbed her enough. There had been no way she was going back to bed
after Keith McLaren's phone call anyway, no matter how tired she felt.
And so she meandered over the moors that Sunday morning, with hardly
any traffic to slow her down. The sun had burned off the morning mist
completely by then, and it was a freshly scrubbed spring day.

When Annie walked into the Western Area Headquarters at about
half past ten, she could sense the strained and melancholy atmosphere.
Even if Banks hadn't told her, she would have known immediately that a
policeman had been killed. There was no other atmosphere like it.
People bent over their tasks with gritted teeth, tempers were short and
over it all lay a pall of shock and outrage.

Banks was in his office with Winsome standing beside him as he
shuffled through a pile of papers on his desk. He stood up to greet
Annie, and she could detect none of the hostility from him that she
might have expected after their last meeting. That only made her feel
worse. He ought to hate her. Of the two, only Winsome seemed frosty.
She left almost immediately after a brusque hello. Banks gestured for
Annie to sit down and called for coffee.

"Sorry I rang so early," he said. "I hope you didn't have a wild night
on the town last night."

"Why would you think that?" Annie said.

"No reason. It was Saturday night, that's all. People do tend to go out. Or maybe you stayed in with your boyfriend?"

"What boyfriend?"

"The one you told me about the other night. The young lad."

Annie reddened. "Oh, him. Yeah, well, have you ever had a wild night out in Whitby?"

"Many times," said Banks with a smile.

"Then you know more about the hidden charms of the place than I do. Anyway, I was already up and working when you rang." She paused. "I really am sorry to hear about Kev. I wasn't a fan, as you know, but no matter what I thought of him as a man or as a detective, I'm sorry about what happened to him."

"He wasn't a man, really," said Banks. "The poor sod was just a boy. A lot of us seemed to forget that."

"What do you mean?"

"He was headstrong, impetuous, immature."

Annie managed a weak grin. "Those qualities are the prerogative of youth all of a sudden, are they?"

"Touché," said Banks. "Anyway, that's what I want to talk to you about, really. What happened to Kev." Banks gave her a quick rundown of what he knew so far, most of which he had pieced together from Chelsea Pilton's eyewitness account and scraps of information from PC Kerrigan, Stefan Nowak and Dr. Burns. "You'll agree there are similarities with the Lucy Payne murder?"

"My God, yes." Annie ran her hand through her tousled hair. "I had no idea." She told Banks about her conversations with Sarah Bingham and Keith McLaren, and how the mysterious Kirsten Farrow's name kept coming up. "What the hell is going on, Alan?" she asked.

"I wish I knew," said Banks. "But whatever it is, I don't like it."

"You and me, neither. Any ideas on who this mystery woman is?"

"I suppose it could be this Kirsten. Anything on Maggie Forrest yet?"

"Yes. Ginger tracked her down through her publishers. She's back in Leeds. I was thinking of paying her a visit this afternoon. But what makes you think of her? I mean, she might have had a good motive for

Lucy Payne's murder, but she had none at all for Templeton's, as far as we know."

"True," said Banks. "It could be two different killers. We'll try to keep an open mind, but my guess, like yours, is that if it's not Maggie, it could be Kirsten Farrow somehow, and for some reason, returned, remodelled. But how or why, or who or where she is, I have no idea. I don't even know how we can get a lead on that. She dropped out of sight years ago. It's a pity the Australian's memory isn't any better."

"The only thing I can think of," said Annie, "is to go back to the source of the leak again."

"Leak?"

"Yes. It was one of the first things we started thinking about when we discovered that Karen Drew was really Lucy Payne. Who knew? And how?"

"And?"

"We still don't know. Our people have been questioning the staff at Mapston Hall, and the Nottingham police have been helping us out down there at the hospital and social services. I mean, it's a tricky one. Anyone could be lying, and we'd be hard-pushed to prove it."

"What we need," said Banks, "is a connection between one of the people who knew that Karen was Lucy, and someone who might possibly be Kirsten Farrow or Maggie Forrest, or *know* one of them."

"Yes," said Annie, "but how do we unearth that? And how would we know if we'd found it? We don't even know where to start looking for Kirsten. For Christ's sake, we don't even know that it *was* her who killed those men eighteen years ago."

"But you've got a pretty strong feeling that it was, haven't you?"

"Yes."

"What do *you* think happened to her?"

Annie thought for a moment. Her brain felt sluggish, but she recalled Les Ferris's tale and what she had since heard from Keith McLaren and Sarah Bingham, and she tried to string her thoughts into something resembling a logical sequence. "From what I can piece together," she said, "Kirsten must have figured out somehow the identity of her attacker, only she didn't pass this information on to the police;

she went after revenge herself. She finally tracked him down to Whitby – how, I don't know – and after a false start – Jack Grimley, the unlucky sod – she killed him."

"And the Australian?"

"I don't know. We talked about that. It's possible he came too close to working out what was going on. If he knew she was the same person who was in Whitby when Grimley died, and he could link her to him . . . ? Keith McLaren did tell me that he'd noticed Kirsten staring at someone in the Lucky Fisherman – and this is something he only remembered fairly recently – so she might have figured he was a danger to her. Or . . ."

"Yes?"

"Well, we know he was found in some woods outside Staithes, and that he was seen with a young woman. Say they went for a walk in the woods, things went too far for Kirsten – remember, she was totally traumatized by her experiences as well as mutilated – and she killed him, or thought she had."

"Self-defence?"

"In her eyes. Maybe overkill in ours. I really don't believe that Keith McLaren is a rapist."

"Okay," said Banks. "And next?"

"I can't imagine how she must have felt when she had done what she set out to do and finally killed Eastcote, but she couldn't go back to her old life. She hung around the fringes of it for a while, saw Sarah a few more times, her parents, perhaps played at being normal, then she finally dropped out of sight a couple of years later. She wasn't a serious suspect at the time, remember. She had an alibi, and as far as anyone knew she had no way of knowing that Greg Eastcote was her attacker. That only came out later, when the police searched his house. It's only now that she seems to have become a suspect in four murders, two of them eighteen years after the others. Anything could have happened since then. She could have gone anywhere, become anyone, done anything."

"So what do we know about her?" Banks said. "She'd be, what, forty by now?"

"About that, if she'd just finished uni in 1988."

"And she could be anyone, in any walk of life?"

"Yes. But let's not forget that she had a university degree. Only English lit, but even so . . . By all accounts she was a bright girl with a great future ahead of her. I mean, the odds are that we might be dealing with a professional woman."

"Unless her experiences completely undermined her ambitions," Banks argued. "But it's a good point. If she really has done what we think she's done, she's incredibly focused, determined and resourceful. Anyway, it narrows things down. We can certainly check university records. We're looking for a professional woman, most likely, who could have known that Karen Drew was Lucy Payne."

"Julia Ford, Lucy's lawyer, for a start. Ginger went to talk to her again on Friday afternoon and she wasn't convinced she was telling us everything she knows."

"Lawyers are naturally tight when it comes to giving information."

"I know," said Annie. "But Ginger thinks it was more than that with Julia Ford. I trust her instincts."

"Maybe I should go and have a word with Ms. Ford," Banks said. "It's been a while since we crossed swords."

"Sarah Bingham's a lawyer, too, though she says she hasn't seen Kirsten in years."

"Believe her?"

"I think so," Annie said.

"Okay. Who else?"

"A doctor?" Annie suggested. "Perhaps from the hospital she was in near Nottingham. Or Mapston Hall. There are doctors and nurses there."

"Good point," said Banks.

"One thing still gets me, though," said Annie. "If we're on the right track, why would she kill Templeton?"

"Another mistake?" Banks suggested. "She thought he was the killer stalking the girl, when in fact he was protecting her, like she must have thought Grimley was her attacker eighteen years ago? But you're right. We need much more corroboration than we've got so far that the murders are linked. Who's your crime scene coordinator?"

"Liam McCullough."

"He's a good bloke," said Banks. "Have him consult with Stefan on this. There has to be trace evidence in common: hairs, fibres, blood, the dimensions of the wound, something to link Lucy Payne and Kev. Let's see if we can get the pathologists talking to one another, too, when Dr. Wallace has finished with Kev."

"Okay," said Annie. "Les Ferris has tracked down the hair samples from the Greg Eastcote case to compare Kirsten's with the ones Liam and his team collected from Lucy Payne. He says he should be able to get a comparison fixed up for tomorrow morning. That could at least tell us once and for all whether it's her we are dealing with. We also need to know why, if it is Kirsten, she started again after all this time."

"If we're right about her motivation," said Banks, "then I'd guess it's because she hasn't been close to any other sex murderers over the past eighteen years. I'm going down to Leeds again sometime this week. While I'm there, I'll talk to Julia Ford, see if I can push her in the right direction, and I'll have a read through the old Chameleon post-mortem reports Phil Hartnell got out. I have to check, but I seem to remember that the wounds the Paynes inflicted on their victims were similar to those that Kirsten's attacker inflicted on her, from what you tell me. I know it can't have been the same killer – Terence Payne is dead, and this Greg Eastcote seemed pretty definite for the killings eighteen years back – but maybe the similarity set her off."

"But how could Kirsten know that the Paynes inflicted similar wounds on their victims?" Annie asked.

"There were plenty of media reports at the time, and later, after Lucy Payne was kicked loose. The press didn't waste a moment in reminding people exactly what had been set free amongst them by our legal system, whether she could walk or not. Kirsten Farrow is also scarred physically, remember, and that could help us, too."

"I don't see how," said Annie. "We can hardly ask every woman connected with the case to strip to the waist."

"Pity," said Banks. "But you're right."

Annie rolled her eyes.

"Anyway," Banks went on, "we've got more than enough to be going on with. Let's compare notes again when you've talked to Maggie Forrest."

Annie stood up. "Right you are." She paused at the door. "Alan?"
"Yes?"
"It's good to be working together again."

The rest of Banks's Sunday went by in a whirl of meetings and interviews, none of which threw any more light on either the Hayley Daniels
or the Kevin Templeton murders – both, apparently, killed by different
people, for different reasons, in the same place.

Templeton's parents arrived from Salford to identify their son's body,
and Banks had a brief meeting with them in the mortuary. It was the least
courtesy he could offer under the circumstances. He thought it would
also be a good idea to let them believe their son had been killed in the line
of duty rather than acting on his own initiative. Templeton's mother
broke down in tears and talked about how they'd failed him, and how it
all went back to when his sister ran away from home at seventeen, though
she swore it wasn't really their fault, that they couldn't keep a girl who
was sleeping with men the way she was in a God-fearing house. They'd
tried to find her afterwards, the father explained, even reported her
missing to the police, but to no avail. And now they'd lost their son, too.

Banks now thought he knew who was in the photograph on
Templeton's bedside table, and why Kev had sometimes been so hard on
families he interviewed. Christ, he thought, the secrets and burdens
people carry around with them.

He needed to talk to Stuart Kinsey again about the snatch of music
he had heard in the Maze the night Hayley was killed. Templeton said he
had heard something similar in his notes, and Banks had a theory
he wanted to put to the test.

As a result of all that, it was past six o'clock before he realized that he
hadn't rung Sophia about their proposed walk. It wasn't that he hadn't
thought of her often during the day – in fact, she was powerfully and
frequently present in his thoughts for someone he had only just met –
but time and events had conspired to push making the call out of his
consciousness. It was too late for the walk now, he realized, reaching for
the telephone, but at least he could apologize. He dialled the number
she had given him. Her voice answered on the fourth ring.

"Sophia? It's Alan. Alan Banks."

"Oh, Alan. Thanks for calling. I heard about what happened last night on the news. I thought it would keep you busy."

"I'm sorry about the walk," said Banks.

"Well, maybe some other time."

"You go back home on Tuesday?"

"Yes. But I'll be back again."

"Look," Banks said, "even under the circumstances, I was thinking I've got to eat. I haven't had anything except Fig Newtons all day. There's a nice bistro on Castle Hill. Café de Provence. Would you consider having dinner with me instead?"

There was the briefest of pauses, then she said, "Yes. Yes, that would be nice. I'd like that. If you're sure you can make it."

Banks felt a knot of excitement in his chest. "I'm sure. I might not be able to stay long, but it's better than nothing." He checked his watch. "How about seven? Is that too early?"

"No, seven's fine."

"Shall I pick you up?"

"I'll walk. It's not far."

"Okay. See you there, then. Seven."

"Right."

When he put the receiver down, Banks's palm was sweaty and his heart was beating fast. Grow up, he told himself, and he reached for his jacket.

Maggie Forrest was not only still living and working as a children's book illustrator in the U.K., she was still living in Leeds. She had spent three years in Toronto before returning and subletting a flat on the waterfront, down by the canal, and going back to her old line of work.

Granary Wharf had been developed in an area of decrepit old warehouses by the River Aire and the Leeds and Liverpool Canal at the back of City Station in the late 1980s and was now a thriving area with its own shops, market, flats, restaurants, entertainment and a cobbled canal walk. On Sunday afternoon, when Annie arrived at the car park near the canal basin, it was quiet. She found Maggie Forrest in a third-floor flat. They had met briefly during the Chameleon business, but Maggie didn't appear to remember her. Annie showed her warrant card, and Maggie let her in.

The flat was spacious, done in bright warm shades of orange and yellow. There was also plenty of light coming in through a large skylight, which Maggie would need for her artwork, Annie guessed.

"What's it about?" asked Maggie as Annie sat on a beige modular couch. Maggie sat cross-legged in a large, winged armchair opposite. The window looked out on the building site at the back of the Yorkshire Post Building, where yet more flats were going up. On examination, Annie thought, Maggie Forrest certainly had that slight, waiflike look about her that Chelsea Pilton had noticed in the killer, and that Mel Danvers at Mapston Hall had spotted about Mary. Her nose was a bit long, and her chin rather pointed, but other than that she was an attractive woman. Her hair was cut short and peppered with grey. Her eyes looked haunted, nervous. Annie wondered if anyone – Mel, Chelsea – might recognize her from an identification parade?

"It's a nice flat," said Annie. "How long have you been here?"

"Eighteen months," Maggie answered.

"Never visit your friends down on The Hill? Ruth and Charles. It's not far away. They don't even know you're in town."

Maggie looked away. "I'm sorry. I've neglected Ruth and Charles," she said. "They were good to me."

"What about Claire Toth? She misses you."

"She hates me. I let her down."

"She needs help, Maggie. She's grown up now and what happened to her friend has left her with a lot of problems. You might be able to do some good there."

"I'm not a psychiatrist, damn it. Don't you think I've done enough damage? That part of my life is over. I can't go back there."

"Why not move farther away, then, make a clean break?"

"Because I'm from here. I need to be close to my roots. And it's far enough." She gestured towards the window. "Could be any modern development in any city."

That was true, Annie thought. "Married?" she asked.

"No. Not that it's any of your business," Maggie answered. "And I don't have a boyfriend, either. There's no man in my life. I'm quite happy."

"Fine," said Annie. Maybe she could be happy without a man in her life, too. She'd hardly been all that happy *with* one. Or then again, maybe she was doomed to repeat the patterns of her old mistakes.

Maggie didn't offer tea or coffee, and Annie was parched. She'd treat herself to something later in one of the city centre cafés. "Do you own a car?" she asked.

"Yes. A red Megane. What have I done now?"

"That's what I'm trying to find out," said Annie. "Where were you last Sunday morning, the eighteenth of March? Mother's Day."

"Here, of course. Where else would I be?"

"How about the Whitby area? Ever been there?"

"A few times, yes, but not last Sunday morning."

"Know a place called Mapston Hall?"

"Only from the news," said Maggie. "This is about Lucy Payne, isn't it? I should have known."

"I would have thought you did," said Annie. "Anyway, yes. It's about Lucy Payne."

"You think I killed her?"

"I never said that."

"But you do, don't you?"

"Did you?"

"No. I was here. I told you."

"Alone?"

"Yes. Alone. I'm always alone. I like it best that way. When you're alone, you can't hurt anyone, and no one can hurt you."

"Except yourself."

"That doesn't count."

A diesel train blew its horn as it entered Leeds City Station. "So there's no way you can *prove* you were here?" Annie asked.

"I never thought I'd have to."

"What did you do?"

"I don't remember."

"It's only a week ago," said Annie. "Try. Didn't you visit your mother?"

"My mother's dead. I was probably reading the Sunday papers. That's what I do on Sunday mornings. Sometimes, if it's nice, I take them down to that café with the tables outside, but I think that morning was windy and cold."

"Remember that, do you?" said Annie.

"It's why I stayed inside to read the papers."

"Ever heard of Karen Drew?"

Maggie seemed surprised by the question. "No," she said. "I can't say that I have."

"Funny," said Annie. "It was in the papers when they got hold of the story about Lucy Payne. It was the name she was going under."

"I didn't know that. I must have missed it."

"How do you feel about Lucy?"

"The woman tried to kill me. When it came time to go to court, you told me the Crown Prosecutor Service wasn't even going to bother prosecuting her. How do you think I feel?"

"Resentful?"

"You could start there. Lucy Payne took my trust, took my help when she needed it the most, then she turned around and not only betrayed me, but she would have killed me, I know, if the police hadn't arrived. So how do you think I feel?"

"Angry enough to have killed her?"

"Yes. But I didn't. I didn't know where she was, for a start."

"Do you know Julia Ford?"

"I've met her. She was Lucy's lawyer."

"Stay in touch?"

"I use her firm whenever I need legal work done, which isn't often. But do we play golf or go to the pub together? No. Anyway, I don't need a criminal lawyer. Mostly I deal with Constance. Constance Wells. We're quite friendly, I suppose. She helped me find this place."

Of course, Annie thought, remembering the framed illustration on Constance Wells's wall. One of Maggie's, no doubt. "You gave her that *Hansel and Gretel* illustration."

Maggie looked surprised. "Yes. You've seen it?"

"I was in her office last week. It's very good."

"You don't have to patronize me."

"I wasn't. I mean it."

Maggie gave a little dismissive gesture with her shoulders.

"Where were you at about midnight last night?"

"I'd just got home from London. I had a meeting with my publishers on Friday afternoon, so I decided to stay down until Saturday, do some shopping. That's about as much of London as I can take these days."

"Where did you stay?"

"Hazlitt's. Frith Street. My publisher always puts me up there. It's very convenient."

"And they would verify this?"

"Of course."

Well, Annie thought, getting ready to leave, it had been a long shot, but subject to corroboration of her alibi, it didn't look as if Maggie Forrest could have killed Kevin Templeton. When it came to Lucy Payne, though, Maggie was still high on the list. And she didn't have an alibi for that.

Banks arrived first at the bistro, and it wasn't so busy that Marcel, the genuine French maître d' couldn't give him an effusive welcome and a quiet, secluded table, complete with white linen tablecloth and a long-stemmed rose in a glass vase. He hoped it wasn't over the top, that Sophia wouldn't think he was trying to impress her or something. He had no expectations of anything, but it felt good to be having dinner with a beautiful and intelligent woman. He couldn't remember how long it had been.

Sophia arrived on time, and Banks was able to watch her as she handed her coat to Marcel and walked towards the table, fixing his eyes with hers and smiling. She was wearing designer jeans and some sort of wraparound top that tied at the small of her back. Women have to be pretty good at using their hands behind their backs, Banks had noticed over the years; they spent so much time fastening things like ponytails, bras, wraparound clothes and difficult necklace clasps.

Sophia moved elegantly towards him, with unhurried grace, and seemed to flow naturally into a comfortable position once she sat. Her hair was tied loosely at the nape of her long neck again, and a few dark, stray tresses curled over her cheeks and forehead. Her eyes were every bit as dark as he remembered, shining and obsidian in the candlelight. She wore no lipstick, but her full lips had natural colour, well set off by her flawless olive skin.

"I'm glad you could make it," said Banks.

"Me, too. I knew our walk was out of the question when I heard the news. Look at you. I'll bet you didn't get much sleep."

"None," said Banks. He realized as he spoke that not only hadn't he slept or eaten since he had seen Sophia last night, but he hadn't even been home, and he was wearing the same clothes he had worn to Harriet's dinner party. He had to remember to keep a change of clothing at the station. It was embarrassing, but Sophia was clearly too much of a lady to say anything about it. They studied the menu and discussed a few items – Sophia, it turned out, was a keen gourmet cook and a food nut – and Banks ordered a bottle of decent claret.

"So it's Sophia, is it?" Banks asked when they had ordered – steak and frites for him, and sea bass for Sophia, with Stilton, pear and walnut salad to start.

"Sophia Katerina Morton."

"Not Sophie?"

"No."

"Kate?"

"Never."

"Sophia it is, then."

"Just don't call me 'sugar.'"

"What?"

She smiled. "It's a song. Thea Gilmore. It's a bit cheeky, actually."

"I know her," Banks said. "She did an old Beatles song on one of those *MOJO* freebies. I liked it enough to buy a CD of other covers she'd recorded."

"*Loft Music*," said Sophia. "That's good, but you should try her own songs."

"I will. Do you work in the music business?"

"No. No, I'm a producer with the BBC. Arts radio, so I do occasionally get involved in music specials. I did a series about John Peel not too long ago, and I've done a few programs with Bob Harris."

"*The Old Grey Whistle Test* Bob Harris?"

"One and the same. He introduced me to Thea at his birthday party."

"I'm impressed."

"You would have been. Robert Plant was there, too. I've never met your son, though."

"Ah, I see. You're wooing me just to get to my son. They all try it. It won't work, you know."

Sophia laughed, and it lit up her features. "I'd hardly call this wooing."

"You know what I mean." Banks felt himself blushing.

"I do. He is a remarkable success, though, your Brian. Cute, too. You must be very proud."

"I am. It took a while to get used to, mind you. I don't know about the cute bit – you should have seen him when he was a surly, spotty teenager – but it's not the easiest thing to deal with when your son decides to leave poly and join a rock band."

"I suppose not," said Sophia.

"If you don't mind my asking," Banks said, "what were you doing at Harriet's dinner party last night? I mean, I must admit, it didn't really seem like your scene at all."

"It wasn't. And I wasn't going to go."

"So why did you?"

"I wouldn't have wanted to pass over a chance to meet Eastvale's top cop."

"Seriously."

"Seriously! I'd heard so much about you over the years. It might sound silly, but I've felt I've known you ever since that first meeting. When Harriet told me she was inviting you to the dinner, I said I'd do my best to get there. Really, I wasn't going to go. That's why I was late. I only decided after it had started that I'd kick myself if I didn't take the chance. It could have been a dreadful bore, of course, but . . ."

"But?"

"It wasn't." She smiled. "Anyway, you clearly enjoyed it so much you didn't even want to change your clothes. I must say, it's the first time I've been out with a man who wore the same clothes two nights in a row."

So not too much of a lady, then. Banks liked that. He smiled back, and they laughed.

Their starters arrived, and they toasted with the wine and tucked in. Banks felt he would probably be better wolfing down a burger and chips rather than the delicate and beautifully presented salad, but he tried not to let his hunger show. At least the steak and frites would fill him up. Sophia took tiny bites and seemed to savour each one. As they ate they talked about music, London, country walks – anything but murder – and Banks found out that Sophia lived in a small house in Chelsea, that she had once been married to a successful record producer, but was now divorced, and had no children, that she loved her job and enjoyed the luxury of her father's Eastvale flat to visit whenever she wanted.

She was half-Greek and half-English. Banks remembered Harriet saying something about having a brother in the diplomatic service, and that was Sophia's father. He had met her mother while posted in Athens, where her mother had worked in her father's taverna, and against all advice they had married and had just celebrated their ruby wedding anniversary. They were away in Greece at the moment.

Sophia had spent a great deal of her childhood moving from place to place, never settling long enough in a school or a city to make friends, so now she valued those she had more than ever. Through her job, she met a lot of interesting people in the various arts – literature, music, painting and sculpture – and she went out to a lot of events – such as concerts, exhibitions, festivals.

It sounded like an exhausting life to Banks, a real social whirl, and he realized he simply didn't have time for that sort of thing. His job took pretty much all he had, and what little time he had left over he used to relax with music or a DVD and a glass of wine. He went to Opera North when he could get there, took long walks in the hills when the weather was good, dropped by the local Helmthorpe pub for folk night once in a while, though less often now that Penny Cartwright, the local femme fatale, had turned him down.

As the evening continued and they topped up their wineglasses, it felt to Banks as it had under the street lamp at the bottom of Harriet's path, as if their illuminated circle of the universe were the only real place, and everything outside it was as insubstantial as shadows. That illusion was pierced when Marcel brought the bill. Banks paid, despite Sophia's objections, and once again they found themselves out in the street saying goodnight. Banks had to go back to the station to see if there had been any progress. He felt extremely lucky that neither his pager nor his mobile had gone off during dinner.

Sophia thanked him for the meal, then they leaned towards one another to do the awkward cheek-kissing thing that had become so popular, but before Banks knew how it happened, their lips were touching in a real kiss, long and sweet. When it was over, they walked off in opposite directions. Banks set off down the hill back to the station, realizing that he had made no specific arrangements to see Sophia again, and after about ten paces, he turned around. At about the same moment, Sophia looked back, too, and they smiled at one another. How odd, Banks thought. He *never* looked back, and he was willing to bet that Sophia never did, either.

15

Annie was in the station bright and early on Monday morning after a good night's sleep and nothing stronger than a cup of hot chocolate over the course of the evening. She was just kicking the coffee machine the way you had to to get a cup out of it when Superintendent Brough walked by and said, "My office, DI Cabbot. Now."

Annie felt a chill. Was Brough a defender of the coffee machine or had Eric set out to harm her career? Had he got more photos that she hadn't seen and sent them to Brough, or the chief constable? Or had he reported her behaviour the other night? It didn't bear thinking about.

Brough's office was spacious and well appointed, as befit a senior officer. He sat behind his desk and gruffly bade Annie sit opposite him in the hard chair. Her heart was thudding. She could argue that she had been drunk, but that reflected no better on her than sleeping with a snake like Eric in the first place.

"What have you got to say for yourself?" Brough asked, which didn't help a great deal.

"About what?" Annie said.

"You know damn well what. The Lucy Payne murder. I've got the press so far up my arse I can taste their pencil lead, and absolutely bugger all to tell them. It's been a week now, and as far as I can see you've just been marking time."

In an odd way, Annie felt relieved that it was about the case and not about Eric. He hadn't been in touch since Annie had paid him her visit on Friday, and that, she thought, was a good sign. Maybe he'd got the hint, which had been about as subtle as a blow to the head with a blunt object.

This was professional. This she could deal with. "With all due respect, sir," she said, "we've done everything we can to trace this mystery woman, but she seems to have disappeared into thin air. We've questioned every-one at Mapston Hall twice – staff and patients alike, wherever possible – but no one there seems able to provide us with any kind of a lead or infor-mation whatsoever. No one knew anything about Karen Drew. It's not as if most of the people there lead active social lives."

Brough grunted. "Is someone lying?"

"Could be, sir. But all the staff members are accounted for during the time of the murder. If anyone there *was* involved, it was in passing over the information that Karen Drew was Lucy Payne and not in com-mitting the actual murder itself. Believe me, sir, we're working on it."

"Why is it all taking so long?"

"These things do take a long time, sir. Background checks. Ferreting out information. Ginger and DS Naylor are as good as it gets, but it takes time, follow-ups and more follow-ups."

"I hear you've been going off on a tangent over some old case, gal-livanting off to Leeds and Eastvale to talk to your old boyfriend. I'm not running a dating service here, DI Cabbot. You'd do well to remem-ber that."

"I resent that implication," Annie said. She could only take so much from authority, and then her father's streak of anarchy and rebellion broke through, and to the devil with the consequences. "And you've no right to speak to me like that."

Brough seemed taken aback by her outburst, but it sobered him. He straightened his tie and the red drained from his features. "You don't know how much pressure I'm under to get a result here," he said, by way of a lame explanation.

"Then I suggest you do it by encouraging your team and supporting them, rather than by resorting to personal insults. Sir."

Brough looked like a slapped arse. He flustered and blathered and then got around to asking Annie exactly where she thought she was going with the Kirsten Farrow angle.

"I don't know for certain that I'm going anywhere yet," said Annie, "but it's starting to appear very much as if the same killer – whoever it is – has now killed again."

"That Eastvale detective, yes. Templeton. Bad business."

"It is, sir. I knew Kev Templeton." Annie stopped short of saying he was a friend of hers, but she wanted Brough to dig into whatever reserves of police solidarity and sympathy he might have. "And in my opinion he was killed by the same person who killed Lucy Payne. We don't have that many murders around here, for a start, the distance isn't that great, and how many do we have that, according to witnesses, were committed by a mysterious woman using a straight razor or some such similar sharp blade, to slit the throat of the victim?"

"But Templeton's not our case, damn it."

"He is if it's the same killer, sir. Do you really believe there are two women going around slitting people's throats – people they *believe* to be dangerous killers?"

"Put like that, it does sound –"

"And do you find it so hard to believe that these might be related to an unsolved case in which a woman also may have killed two men, one of whom was a serial killer and one of whom she may have mistaken for him?"

"May have. You said, 'May have.' I've looked over the files, DI Cabbot. There's absolutely no evidence whatsoever that Greg Eastcote was murdered, either by a woman or by anyone else. He could have faked his disappearance because he thought the police were getting too close. In fact, that's the most logical explanation."

"He could have," Annie agreed. "But the police *weren't* getting close. And a woman was seen with Jack Grimley and with the Australian boy, Keith McLaren, and she conveniently disappeared, too."

"But this was *eighteen* years ago, for God's sake. You can't even prove that this Kirsten, or whoever she was, knew that Eastcote had attacked her. It's absurd."

"No more than most cases when you don't have all the pieces, sir. I'm also trying to locate Kirsten's psychiatrist. She had a course of hypnosis in Bath in 1988, and it might have helped her recover some of her memory of the attack."

Brough grunted. Not impressed by the idea of hypnotherapy, Annie guessed. "The MO is completely different," he went on. "The attacker used a rock on Keith McLaren and some short of sharp blade on Lucy Payne."

"MOs can change. And perhaps if she only kills killers, or people she mistakes for them, she hasn't come across any in the last eighteen years? Perhaps she's been abroad?"

"It's all speculation."

"If you don't speculate, sir, you don't get anywhere."

"But I need something I can tell the press. Something real. Something substantial."

"Since when have the press cared about reality or substance?"

"DI Cabbot!"

"Sorry, sir. Why don't you tell them we've got a new lead we're following, but you can't say any more about it right now. They'll understand."

"What new lead?"

"Kirsten Farrow. We're going to interview everyone we know who was connected with Karen/Lucy until we get a connection to the killer."

"Whom you believe to be Kirsten Farrow?"

"Yes," said Annie. "But you don't have to tell them that. Even if I'm wrong, we're heading in the right direction. I'm not wearing blinkers, sir. *Someone* knew that Karen was Lucy, and that someone is either the killer herself or the person who told the killer. And I'm trying to get some evidence to prove that Kirsten killed Lucy Payne. With any luck I should have it before the end of the day."

"Okay," said Brough. "That's the kind of thing I want to hear. And I do take your point. It makes sense when you get rid of all that 1989 gobbledygook. Just be careful whose feet you're treading on. Remember, these are professional people, you know, doctors and the like."

"Oh, don't worry, sir, I won't eat any of them," Annie said. "May I go?"

He jerked his head. "Go on. Get to work. And hurry up. And this evidence? Don't forget, I expect to see some positive results before the end of the day."

"Yes, sir," Annie said as she left the office, fingers crossed.

Despite being dog-tired, Banks hadn't slept at all well when he got home from the station well after midnight on Monday. They were no closer to finding Templeton's killer, or Hayley Daniels's, for that matter, and part of the program for the day was to start a complete review of both cases so far.

Everything about the Hayley Daniels murder pointed towards a scared rapist, someone the victim knew, who had strangled Hayley to avoid being named and caught, someone who was also possibly ashamed of what he'd done and had arranged the body in a pose more suggestive of sleep than rape and murder. Under further questioning, Joseph Randall had finally admitted that he had touched Hayley and masturbated at the scene, but he insisted that he hadn't changed the position of the body, and Banks believed him. At that point, he had no reason to lie.

The Templeton murder, efficient and practical as it had been, seemed very much as if it had been a mistake on the part of the killer, who in the darkness of the Maze had thought she had been protecting Chelsea Pilton and ridding the world of a budding serial killer.

When Banks asked himself who might think that and why, he came back to Kirsten Farrow. And nobody knew what had become of her. The only thing that gave rise to any doubts at all in Banks's mind about Kirsten's being responsible was that the first murders, the 1989 ones, involved someone who had directly harmed Kirsten, mutilated her, and she had *not* been a victim of Lucy and Terence Payne. That meant that, if it was her, she had extended her parameters.

Or, Banks thought, with a quiver of excitement, perhaps she did have *some* connection with the Paynes. What it could be, he had no idea, but it was a direction worth pursuing, and something he needed to tell Annie about, if she hadn't thought of it herself. Annie had been right yesterday when she said it was good to be working together again. It was. Personal problems aside, he hadn't realized how much he had missed her since she had gone to Eastern Area.

First thing on the agenda was another look at all the CCTV footage they had on both cases. Hayley Daniels first. As soon as the team was gathered – Banks, Winsome, Hatchley, Wilson, the gaping absence of Templeton and the off-the-wall comments everyone had come to expect from him – they started watching the footage.

There it was again, the familiar scene of the market square at closing time, young men and women being sick, squabbling, singing with their arms around one another. Then the group from the Fountain standing together briefly while Hayley explained that she was going down Taylor's Yard for a piss and then . . . ? Well, she hadn't told them where after that. To Malcolm Austin's, perhaps?

But why would she want to go there? She was nineteen, pissed as a newt, out with her mates for a night on the town. Why would she want to go and visit a sober, older lover, who was probably lounging around in his carpet slippers sipping sherry and watching films that were made long before she was born? Well, love is blind, they say, but sometimes Banks thought it must be drunk as well. It didn't matter, anyway. Wherever Hayley had intended to go, she didn't get there. Someone intercepted her, and unless it was someone who had been lying in wait for *any* young girl to come by, as Templeton had believed, then it had to be someone who knew she would be there, a decision she had made only in the last minute or so, as they watched.

Banks glanced again at the people around her. He recognized Stuart Kinsey, Zack Lane and a couple of others. Their names were all on file. Their alibis had been checked and rechecked, their statements taken. They could all be re-interviewed. Someone had to know something. Maybe someone was covering for a friend he *thought* had done it?

The car went by, the couple on their way back from celebrating their wedding anniversary. And there was that annoying, flickering strip of light, like on restored copies of old black-and-white films. Banks made a note to ask technical services if they could get rid of it, though doing so probably wouldn't reveal anything new. Then Hayley staggered off down Taylor's Yard, and the rest headed for the Bar None.

Banks knew that Stuart Kinsey had sneaked out of the back exit almost immediately to spy on Hayley, but what about the others? They said they stayed at the Bar None until about two o'clock, and various staff, customers and doormen said they had seen them during that period. But it didn't take long to sneak out, and if you were clever enough, you could wedge the back door open and hope no one noticed before the time you got back. But why would Hayley linger in the Maze once she had done what she went there to do? She had no reason to do so, unless she was meeting someone there, and why would she do that when she had Malcolm Austin waiting for her? Unless there was someone else.

It didn't make sense. The killer had to be someone who knew that Hayley was going into the Maze, which meant that whoever it was had to act fast. How long does it take a woman to go down an alley and relieve herself in the dark? She was drunk, which would definitely slow her progress. And she'd been sick too. On the other hand, she had little in the way of clothing to inhibit her. He could always ask a female constable to go in and do it, and time her. That would go down about as well as asking every woman connected with the Lucy Payne murder to take her top off. Sometimes the easiest and most obvious route was the only way you *couldn't* go.

Banks estimated about five minutes, in and out, and felt that was fairly generous. That gave the killer about three or four minutes to follow Hayley and grab her before she finished. Stuart Kinsey had gone in there about three or four minutes after her, which made it unlikely that anyone else in the Bar None could have gone out the same way at the same time. They would have bumped into one another. And Stuart Kinsey had at least heard part of the assault against Hayley, and he said he had seen no one else in the Maze.

The tapes went on and on, Jamie Murdoch leaving with his bicycle at two-thirty, a few stragglers from the Bar None getting into a shoving match, then nothing. DC Doug Wilson switched off the player, put on the lights, and they all stretched. Over three hours had gone by, and nothing. It was time to send the team out on the streets to start talking to people again, and Banks had an appointment he wished he didn't have to keep.

Banks leaned on the wall outside Eastvale General Infirmary, feeling queasy, and took a few slow, deep breaths. Dr. Wallace had performed her post-mortem on Kevin Templeton with her usual brisk speed and efficiency, but it had been difficult to watch. There had been no banter, no black humour – hardly a word spoken, in fact – and she had seemed to work with the utmost concentration and detachment.

And nothing new had come of her efforts.

Cause of death was the cut throat, time was fixed by the eyewitness Chelsea Pilton, and other than the fact that he was dead, Templeton had been in good health. The post-mortem also hadn't told Dr. Wallace anything more about the weapon, though she leaned towards the theory that a straight-blade razor had been used, pulled most likely from left to right across Templeton's throat, cutting the carotid, the jugular and the windpipe. It had been quick, as Dr. Burns had noted at the scene, but long enough for Templeton to have known what was happening to him as he struggled for breath and felt himself weaken through loss of blood and oxygen. The consolation was that he would have been in no great pain, but when it came down to it, Banks thought, only Templeton himself could have known that for certain.

Banks stood on the steps of the infirmary, leaning beside the door, with a chill March wind blowing around him, and when he had regained his composure, he decided to drive over to Eastvale College to talk to Stuart Kinsey again. On his way, he plucked up the courage to ring Sophia and ask her if she fancied a drink later. She did.

He tracked Kinsey down in the coffee lounge, and they found a dim, quiet corner. Banks bought two lattes and a couple of KitKats at the counter and sat down.

"What is it now?" Stuart asked. "I thought you believed me?"

"I do believe you," said Banks. "At least I believe that you didn't murder Hayley Daniels."

"What, then?"

"Just a few more questions, that's all."

"I've got a lecture at three."

"That's okay. I'll be done long before then if we can make a start."

"All right," said Stuart, reaching for a cigarette. "What do you want to know?"

"It's about the night you followed Hayley into the Maze."

"I didn't follow her."

"But you went to spy on her. You knew she was there." The smoke drifted towards Banks, and for the first time in ages it didn't bother him. In fact, it made him crave a smoke himself. Must have been the stress of seeing Templeton opened up on the table. He fought the urge and it waned.

"I wasn't spying!" Stuart said, glancing around to make sure no one could hear them. "I'm not a pervert. I told you, I wanted to see where she went."

"Did you think she was meeting someone?"

"Not there, no. Whatever I thought of Hayley, I didn't think she was the type for a quick drunken fumble in a dark alley. No, she went there for a piss, that's all. I thought she was going to meet someone later, somewhere else."

Banks removed the silver paper from his KitKat. "Did Hayley give any indications, either that night or at any other time that there was something or someone bothering her?"

"No. Not that I can think of. Why?"

"She wasn't worried about anything?"

"You've asked me this before. Or the other officer did."

"Well, I'm asking you again."

"No. Nothing. Hayley was pretty happy-go-lucky. I mean, I never saw her really down about anything."

"Angry?"

"She had a bit of a temper. Had quite a mouth on her. But it took a lot to get her riled."

"She was upset in the Fountain, right? And she took it out on Jamie Murdoch."

"Yeah, a bit. I mean, he was the only one there apart from us. She called him a few names. Limp dick, dickhead, stuff like that. She was way out of line."

"How did he take it?"

"How would *you* take it? He wasn't happy."

"He told me it wasn't a big deal."

"Well, he would, wouldn't he? He wouldn't want you to think he had a motive for hurting Hayley."

"Did he? Was he really that angry?"

"I don't know. More like embarrassed. He rushed us out pretty quickly after that."

"Were they ever close at all, Hayley and Jamie?"

"No way! Jamie was a loser. He dropped out of college. I mean, look at him, stuck in the grotty pub night after night, half the time by himself while the landlord suns himself in Florida."

"Was there anyone in any of the pubs that night – especially the Fountain – who paid undue attention to Hayley, apart from the leather shop owner?"

"Men looked at her, yes, but nothing weird, not that I can remember. Nothing different from usual, anyway. And like I said, we were the last to leave the Fountain. Nobody followed us."

"Okay, Stuart, let's get back to the Maze now."

Stuart squirmed in his chair. "Must we?"

"It's important." Banks gestured to the second KitKat on the table. "Do you want that?" Stuart shook his head. Banks picked it up and began to eat it. He had forgotten how hungry he was.

"I don't feel good about it," Stuart said. "I've thought and thought since we last talked, and I *know* I must have heard it happening. I know I could have stopped it if I'd just done something. Made a lot of noise, banged a dustbin lid on the wall. I don't know. But I bottled out. I got scared and ran away, and because of that Hayley died."

"You don't know that," said Banks. "Stop beating yourself up over it. I'm interested in what you heard."

"I've already told you."

"Yes, but you also said you heard some music, a snatch of a song, as if from a passing car. Rap, you said it was. And familiar. You couldn't remember what it was when I last talked to you. Do you have any idea now?"

"Oh, yeah, that. I think I do . . . you know, since we talked I've been playing it over and over in my mind, the whole thing, and I think it was the Streets, 'Fit But You Know It.'"

"I know that one," said Banks. "Are you sure?"

If Stuart was surprised that Banks knew the song, he didn't show it. "Yeah," he said. "I've got the CD. Just haven't played it in a while."

"And you're certain you heard it around the same time you heard the other sounds?"

"Yes. Why? Is it important?"

"Maybe," said Banks. He checked his watch. "You'll be late for your lecture," he said, standing up. "Thanks for your time."

"That's all?"

"That's all." Banks finished his latte, screwed up the KitKat wrappers, dropped them in the ashtray and left, thinking he had a pretty good idea why both Stuart Kinsey and Kevin Templeton heard the same music on different nights.

Just after dark that evening, Annie found herself wandering down St. Ann's Staith by the estuary, past the blackboard with the tide tables on the short bridge that linked east and west. The strings of red and yellow harbour lights had just come on and made a hazy glow in the slight evening mist. They reflected, swaying slightly, in the narrow channels of the ebbing tide. Fishing boats leaned at odd angles in the silt, their masts tilting towards the fading light and rattling in the light breeze. A ghostly moon was just visible out to sea above the wraiths of mist. The air smelled of salt and dead fish. It was chilly, and Annie was glad she was wearing her wool coat and a pashmina wrapped around her neck.

She walked along beside the railings, the shops opposite closed for the evening, a glow coming from the pubs and one or two cafés still serving fish and chips. Vinegar and deep-frying fat mingled with the harbour smells. A group of goths dressed in black, faces white, hung out smoking and talking by the sheds, near the Dracula Experience, and even so, long before the holiday season, a few tourist couples walked hand in hand and families tried to control their unruly children. The large amusement arcade was doing plenty of business, Annie noticed. She was almost tempted to go in and lose a few coins on the one-armed bandits. But she resisted.

She was feeling excited because Les Ferris had phoned late in the afternoon and told her the hair and fibres expert, Famke Larsen, had matched Kirsten Farrow's sample of eighteen years ago with a hair taken from Lucy Payne's blanket last week. So it *was* her. Back and in action again. Annie's long shot had paid off and she could trust her copper's instincts again. It gave her the focus she needed, and it appeased DS Brough for a while.

According to Famke, the similarities in colour, diameter, medulla pattern and the intensity of pigment granules were enough to go on, but it wasn't a match that would stand up in court. Annie didn't care about that; she'd half expected it, anyway. Les Ferris had reminded her that hair was *class* evidence – that it was not possible to match a human hair to any single head – but for her purposes, the identification was enough. Both samples were fine, Caucasian, with evenly distributed pigment and a slightly oval cross-section.

An unexpected bonus was that the hair found on Lucy Payne's blanket hadn't been sheared off; it came complete with its root. The only drawback, Famke had explained to Liam and Les, was that it was in what she called the telogen stage. In other words, it hadn't been pulled out, it had fallen out, and that meant there were no healthy root cells and attached matter. The best they could hope for, Les summed up, was mitochondrial DNA, which is material that comes from outside the nucleus of the cells, and from the mother. Even so, it could help them come up with a DNA profile of Kirsten Farrow, Lucy Payne's killer.

The tide was out, so Annie went down the steps and onto the beach. There was no one else around now, perhaps because of the late March chill. As she walked, she wondered about Jack Grimley. Would a fall to the beach from the top of the cliffs have killed him? The beach wasn't particularly rocky. She looked behind at the looming mass towering above her. It might have. But if he'd been lying on the sand for a while, wasn't it likely that someone would have seen him? What if Kirsten had lured him down there, believing him to be her attacker, and killed him? There were some small caves in the bottom of the cliff face. Annie walked inside one. It was pitch-black and smelled of seaweed and stagnant rock pools. It wasn't very deep, as far as she could tell, but you could hide a body there, behind a rock, at night especially, until the tide came and took it out to sea.

She left the beach and walked up the steps from Pier Road to the Cook statue. For a moment, she sat on the bench there and thought, This is where Keith and Kirsten sat, where he kissed her and got no response.

Was she so preoccupied with her revenge that she had gone beyond the merely human? It was also near here that a woman had been seen with Jack Grimley, and though she hadn't been identified as Kirsten, Annie was certain that was who it was. What had they talked about? Had she lured him to the beach with promises of sex and killed him? Was that also how she had got Keith McLaren into the woods?

Not too far away, Annie noticed lights and a pub sign. When she peered closer, she saw that it was the Lucky Fisherman. Curious, she walked over and went inside. The door to her left opened into a small, smoky public bar, where about five or six men stood around chatting, a couple of them smoking pipes. A football game played on a small television over the door, but nobody paid it much attention. When Annie walked in, they all stared at her, fell silent for a moment, then went back to their conversations. There were only a few tables, one of them occupied by an old woman and her dog, so Annie went out again and through the door on the right. This was the lounge, quite a bit bigger, but barely populated. A couple of kids were feeding coins into the machines, and four people were playing darts. It was warm, so Annie took her coat off and ordered a pint, taking it over to a table in the corner. Nobody paid her any attention.

So this was where Keith had met Kirsten that evening, and where she had seen Jack Grimley, who, Annie guessed, she had believed for some reason to be the man who had hurt her. She hadn't approached him, as far as Keith remembered, so she must have come back another night and perhaps waited for him outside. It wasn't hard to lead a man where you wanted him to go if you were young and pretty. He wanted to go there, too.

Annie sat sipping her beer and thinking about the past while she flipped through the pages of the latest *Hello!* magazine she had bought earlier and carried in her shoulder bag. After a few moments, she became aware of someone standing over her. Slowly, she looked up to see a broad-shouldered man with a shaved head and a handlebar moustache, probably in his early fifties.

"Can I help you?" she asked.

"Are you that there new policewoman?"

"I'm DI Cabbot, yes. Why?"

"Thought I saw your picture in the paper this morning. You'll be after the person who killed that woman in the wheelchair, then, won't you?"

"That would be one of my jobs, yes." Annie put her magazine down. "Why? Do you know anything that could help?"

He gave her a questioning glance, and she realized that he was asking if it was okay to join her for a moment. She nodded.

"No," he said. "I don't know owt. And the way I've heard it, I reckon she only got what she deserved. Still, it's a terrible way to go, in a wheelchair and all, can't defend yourself. I'd say it's a coward's work."

"Perhaps," said Annie, taking a swig of beer.

"But it was summat else I wanted to ask you about. I heard a rumour the police was asking questions about an old crime, something involving an old friend of mine."

"Oh?" said Annie. "Who would that be?"

"Jack Grimley."

"You knew Jack Grimley?"

"Best mates. Well, am I right?"

"I don't know where you got your information from," Annie said, "but we've taken an interest in the case, yes."

"More than anyone could say at the time."

"I wasn't here, then."

He eyed her scornfully. "Aye, I can see that for myself."

Annie laughed. "Mr. . . . ?"

"Kilbride."

"Mr. Kilbride, much as I'd love to sit and chat with you, I have to get back to work. Is there anything you want to tell me?"

He scratched the comma of a beard under his lower lip. "Just that what happened to Jack, like, it never sat well with me."

"Did the police talk to you at the time?"

"Oh, aye. They talked to all his mates. Can I get you another drink?"

Annie had about a third of a pint left. She wasn't having any more. "No thanks," she said. "I'll stick with this."

"Suit yourself."

"You were saying. About Jack Grimley."

"I was the one saw him with that there woman, standing by the railings near the Captain Cook statue."

"And you're sure it was a woman?"

"Oh, aye. I could tell the difference." He smiled. "Still can. She might have been a skinny wee thing, but she was a lass, all right. Dark horse, our Jack. Not like him."

"What do you mean?"

"Jack was the serious type when it came to women. Couldn't look at one he fancied without falling in love with her. We used to tease him something cruel, and he'd go red as a beet."

"But he'd never mentioned this girl?"

"No. Not to me. Not to any of us. And he would have done."

"But she was new. He'd only just met her. They were getting to know one another."

"Oh, she was new, all right. She'd been in here once, a few days before, with a young lad. I recognized her. Not so much the face as the way she moved. And there she was, back again, outside with Jack."

"But she didn't come in the second time?"

"No. She must have been waiting for him outside."

"And you're sure he never mentioned anything about a new girlfriend, someone he'd met or talked to?"

"No."

"Did you ever see her again?"

"No. Nor Jack."

"I'm sorry about your friend," Annie said.

"Aye. The police said he must have fallen off the cliff, but Jack was too careful to do owt like that. He grew up here, knew the place like the back of his hand."

"I was just down on the beach," Annie said. "Do you think a fall would have killed him? There's not many rocks down there."

"It's hard enough if you fall all that way," said Kilbride, "but there's some has got away with a broken leg or two."

"There was a theory that he might have jumped."

"That's even more ridiculous. Jack had everything to live for. He was a simple bloke who liked the simple pleasures. Believed in a good job well done. He'd have made a fine husband and father one day if he'd had the chance." He shook his head. "No, there was no way Jack'd have done away with himself."

"So what do you think happened?"

"She killed him, pure and simple."

"Why?"

"You lot never tell the likes of us what you're thinking, so how would I know? Maybe she didn't need a reason. Maybe she was one of them there serial killers. But she killed him all right. He'd go anywhere with a pretty young woman, would Jack. Putty in her hands. The silly bastard was probably in love with her by the time she killed him." He stood up. "Anyway, I don't mean to bother you, love," he said. "I just recognized you and I thought I'd let you know that if you *are* investigating what happened to Jack Grimley, for whatever reason, you can take my word for it – someone did for him."

Annie finished her beer. "Thanks, Mr. Kilbride," she said. "I'll bear that in mind."

"And, young lass?"

"Yes," said Annie, far more flattered by that endearment than by all of Eric's attentions.

"You seem like the determined type. When you do find out, drop by and let us know, will you? I'm here most nights."

"Yes," said Annie, shaking his hand. "Yes, I promise I'll do that." When she got back to her room, she made a note to let both Kilbride and Keith McLaren know the outcome of the investigation.

Sophia was already waiting when Banks got to the new wine bar on Market Street, where they had arranged to meet. He apologized for being five minutes late and sat down opposite her. It was quieter and far less smoky than the pubs, a much more intimate setting, with shiny, round black-topped tables, each bearing a candle floating among flower petals, and chrome stools, mirrors, colourful Spanish prints and contemporary decor. The place had only been open about a month, and Banks hadn't been there before; it had been Sophia's idea. When she had been before, or who with, he had no idea. The music was cool jazz vocal, and Banks recognized Madeleine Peyroux singing Dylan's "You're Gonna Make Me Lonesome When You Go." It was a sentiment he could well share, because tomorrow Sophia was going back to London and Banks had no idea when, or if, he would see her again.

"Long day?" she said when he had settled down.

"I've had better," Banks said, rubbing his temples and thinking of the Templeton post-mortem, and the talk he'd had with Kev's distraught parents. "You?"

"A long run in the morning and a bit of work in the afternoon."

"'Work' work?"

"Yes. I've got a five-part series on the history of the Booker Prize coming up soon, so I have to read all the winners. Well, most of them, anyway. I mean, who remembers Percy Howard Newby or James Gordon Farrell?" She put her fist to her mouth. "Yawn. You want to eat?"

"Do they do burgers and chips?"

Sophia grinned. "A man of great culinary discernment, I can tell. No, they don't, but we might get some baked brie and garlic and a baguette if I ask nicely. The owner's an old pal of my dad's."

"It'll have to do, then," said Banks. "Any chance of a drink around here, too?"

"My, my, how impatient you are. You *must* have had a bad day." Sophia caught the waitress's attention and ordered Banks a large Rioja. When it came, she held her glass out for a toast, "To great ideas in the middle of the night."

Banks smiled and they clinked glasses.

"I've brought you a present," Sophia said, passing a familiar-shaped package across the table to Banks.

"Oh?"

"You can open it now."

Banks undid the wrapping and found a CD: *Burning Dorothy* by Thea Gilmore. "Thanks," he said. "I was going to buy it myself."

"Well, now you don't have to."

Already he could feel himself relaxing, the stresses of the day rolling off, the gruesome images and the raw human misery receding into the background. The wine bar was a good choice, he had to admit. It was full of couples talking softly and discreetly, and the music continued in the same vein. Sophia talked about her work and Banks forgot about his. They touched briefly on politics, found they both hated Bush, Blair and the Iraq War, and moved on to Greece, which Banks loved and Sophia knew well. Both felt that Delphi was the most magical place in the world.

When the baked brie and garlic had come and gone, towards the end of their second glass of wine, there was no one left in the place but the two of them and the staff. Their conversation meandered on through music, films, wine and family. Sophia loved the old 1960s stuff and its contemporary imitators, liked films by Kurasawa, Bergman and Truffaut, she drank Amarone whenever she could afford it and had a very large extended but close-knit family. She loved her job because it gave her a lot of free time, if she arranged things properly, and she liked to spend it in Greece with her mother's side of the family.

Banks was more than happy simply to sip his wine, listen to Sophia's voice and watch the expressions flitting across her animated features and behind her dark eyes. Excitement one moment, a hint of sadness the next. Sometimes he looked at her mouth and remembered the kiss, the feel of her lips, though neither of them mentioned it during the evening. He was also aware of her bare shoulders, and of the soft swelling at the front of her blouse, aroused without even really thinking about it. Everything about being here now with her felt so natural that he couldn't believe he had known this woman for only three days – and *known* was a gross overstatement. He still knew practically nothing about her.

The evening was winding down, their wine nearly finished. Corinne Bailey Rae, the Leeds lass, was singing "Till It Happens to You." Sophia insisted on paying the waitress and disappeared for a few moments to the ladies room. Banks looked at the framed Spanish scenes on the walls and let the music roll over him. Sophia came back and sat down again, resting her arms on the table. Banks reached across and took her hand. Her skin was warm and soft. He felt the slight return of pressure as she accepted his touch.

They sat like that in silence for a while, just looking at one another. "Come back with me," Banks said finally.

Sophia said nothing, but her eyes spoke for her. As one, they stood up and left.

16

"You've got a spring in your step, DCI Banks," said Superintendent Gervaise when Banks tapped on her door and walked into her office late on Tuesday morning. "What is it? Made a breakthrough?"

"You might say that," said Banks.

"Shut the door," Gervaise said.

"I want to show you something first. Can you come with me?"

Gervaise narrowed her eyes. "This had better be good. I was just settling down to last month's crime figures."

"I had a call from technical support earlier this morning," Banks said as they walked downstairs to the ground-floor viewing room. "I'd asked them if they could tidy up some CCTV surveillance tapes for me."

"The Hayley Daniels tapes?"

"Yes." Banks opened the door for her. The room was in semi-darkness, and Don Munro, from technical support, was already waiting for them. Gervaise sat down and smoothed her skirt. "You've got my attention," she said. "Let it roll."

"It doesn't exactly roll, ma'am," explained Munro. "Though, I suppose –".

"Oh, just switch it on, man," said Gervaise.

Munro fiddled with the machine, and the images of Hayley and her friends leaving the Fountain and congregating outside in the market square came into view.

"Here it is," said Banks, pointing to the flickering strip of light.

"Yes?" said Gervaise.

"Well, ma'am," said Munro, "DCI Banks asked if we could get rid of the flaring here."

"I see what you mean," said Gervaise. "Reminds me of the last time I watched *Casablanca*."

Munro gave her an admiring glance. "One of my favourites, ma'am."

Gervaise treated him to a smile. "Get on with it, then."

"Well, when I tried to correct the problem, I found that what I was dealing with wasn't a flaw, or a light flare, but a part of the actual image."

"A part of the image?" Gervaise glanced at Banks. "What's he talking about?"

"Well, if you look closely," Banks said, "you can see that it's actually a strip of light, flickering and flaring, of course, because of its brightness and the sensitivity of the videotape. But it only looks like a flaw."

"What it is, then?"

Banks glanced at Munro. "It's the strip of light showing through a partially open door," the technician said.

"Meaning?"

"Meaning," Banks took over, "that the door to the Fountain was slightly open while Hayley and her friends stood outside discussing what they were going to do and, more importantly, when Hayley announced she was going into the Maze for, well, to . . ."

"For a piss," said Gervaise. "Yes, I know. And?"

"Jamie Murdoch told us he closed the door as soon as they left and had no idea where Hayley was going, but this" – Banks pointed to the screen – "shows us that he was listening, and probably even watching them while they stood outside. Jamie Murdoch was lying. He knew exactly where Hayley Daniels was going, and that she was going by herself."

"I still don't see how that gets us anywhere," said Gervaise. "There's no access from the pub to the Maze without being seen on CCTV, and Jamie Murdoch just doesn't show up."

"I know," said Banks. "But that set me thinking."

Munro switched off the television and turned up the lights. "Will you be needing me any more?" he asked.

"No," said Banks. "Thanks a lot, Don, you've been a great help."

Munro blushed, gave a little bow to Gervaise, and left. "'This is the beginning of a beautiful friendship,'" Gervaise muttered behind him. His shoulders moved as he laughed. "So, DCI Banks, what were you going to say?"

"Just a theory I'd like to run by you."

She shuffled in her chair. "I'm all ears."

"As I said, Jamie Murdoch told us that as soon as the last customers left – Hayley and her friends – he locked up and got to work cleaning out the vandalized toilets."

"Well, maybe it took him a few seconds to close the doors, but that doesn't mean anything necessarily."

"It's more than a minute," said Banks. "And that's quite a long time. Also, during that period, Hayley announces her intention and goes off, while the others, who tried to persuade her against the idea, head for the Bar None. We know that Stuart Kinsey sneaked right out of the back and in all likelihood heard Hayley being attacked."

"So what are you saying? Or am I being thick?"

"No, ma'am. It took me a while to figure it out."

"Oh, that makes me feel a lot better. Well? I still don't see how Jamie Murdoch could have got into the Maze without being seen, raped and killed Hayley Daniels and then got back in again to clean up his toilets."

"Nor did I at first," said Banks. "Until I realized that nobody has conducted a thorough search of the Fountain. It's a mini-maze of its own. There's all sorts of rooms, upstairs, cellar, what have you, and it's an old building. Eighteenth century. When you think about it, it stands to reason that there *could* be another way in and out."

"A secret passage? You jest, surely?"

"It wouldn't be the first time in this part of the world," said Banks. "Some way of getting out quickly when unwelcome guests arrived, perhaps?"

"All right. I know my history. Priest holes and the like. Maybe you've got a point."

"And that made me think of something else."

Gervaise raised an eyebrow. "Pray tell."

"When Winsome talked to Jill Sutherland, the girl who works at the Fountain, Jill told her that one of the reasons she didn't like it there was because Jamie Murdoch dealt in smuggled booze and cigarettes, and that he had even tried to get her to bring back stuff when she went abroad."

"Everybody does it," said Gervaise. "I know it's a crime, but trying to stop it would be like sticking your finger in the dyke."

"That's not my point," said Banks. "The point is that when Kev Templeton had a look around the Fountain, he didn't find anything. Nor did Winsome and I."

" 'Nothing can come of nothing.' Didn't someone say that?"

"Shakespeare, ma'am."

"Clever bugger."

"It was just a guess. You've usually got at least a 49 per cent chance of being right if you say Shakespeare to every quote, maybe more."

"And the other 51 per cent?"

"Most – 49 per cent – to the Bible, and the rest . . . well, your guess is as good as mine. Oscar Wilde, probably."

"Interesting theory. Go on."

"Well, at first I thought that maybe all the police attention had encouraged Jamie to get rid of the stuff, or move it somewhere else, but then it struck me that if he had a good-enough hiding place from the start, and if the stuff's not in –"

"Any of the places Templeton searched, then it has to be hidden somewhere. A cubbyhole, something like that?"

"Exactly," said Banks. "And this cubbyhole may well lead out into the Maze."

"There's a great deal of speculation here," said Gervaise. "I'm not sure I like it."

"But we can check, can't we?" said Banks. "If you can arrange for a search warrant, first for Murdoch's home, so we can make sure he's not stashing the smuggled goods there, and second for a thorough search of the Fountain, walls, floors and all, then we've got him."

"I'm not sure we've got enough evidence for a search warrant."

"But we can try, can't we?"

Gervaise stood up. "We can try," she said.

"I've also been doing a bit of checking around this morning, and I have one more test I want to try first, with your help. Who knows, it might even add to our weight of evidence."

"At this point, a feather would tip the balance," said Gervaise. "But tell me anyway."

"Maggie Forrest went through a hell of a lot," Annie told Ginger as they ate a late lunch together in a pub on Flowergate. "It's bound to have affected her."

"That's what you get when you go around befriending sex killers," said Ginger, picking at her chips. "But if Liam's come through with the hair match, she's out of the picture anyway, isn't she?"

"Not necessarily. Maybe we should keep an open mind," Annie said. "Besides, there was some doubt as to Lucy Payne's role as a sex killer."

"You're not trying to say she didn't do it, are you?"

Annie ate another forkful of salad and pushed her plate aside. "We never really believed that she killed the victims," she said, "but she was certainly a willing participant in their degradation and torture. Terence Payne killed them, at least that was where the evidence pointed. But she helped him to abduct them. In my eyes it makes them both guilty of everything."

"People are less inclined to be wary of a woman, or a couple, approaching them."

"True enough," Annie agreed. "Sugar and spice, we are."

Ginger made a face and wiped the beer froth from her upper lip. The pub was busy, most of the tables taken up by local shop and office workers enjoying their lunch hour. "Anyway," she went on, "you're right about keeping an open mind. This hair business isn't conclusive. And just because we found it on the blanket, and just because it might match this Kirsten Farrow's, that still doesn't mean Maggie Forrest didn't kill Lucy Payne, right?"

"Right," Annie agreed. "Maggie Forrest doesn't have an alibi, for one thing."

"Maybe we should have a word with that shrink of hers?"

"Psychiatrists never tell you anything," Annie said. "They're worse than priests and lawyers. But I suppose we could always have a try. I want to talk to Kirsten Farrow's shrink, too. The one who hypnotized her. I've got a name from the files: Laura Henderson. I'll see if I can get her on the phone sometime this afternoon. What about Templeton, though? How does he fit in with all this?"

"Your mate?"

"No mate of mine, and a terrible copper, if truth be told. Poor sod, though. What a way to go."

"At least it was quick."

"I suppose so," said Annie. She felt a pang of sadness for Templeton, with his sharp suits, gelled hair and sense of himself as God's gift to women. The poor bastard had had blue balls for Winsome ever since she joined the team, and she never gave him a chance. Not that she should have; Annie wouldn't have either, even if he had tried it on with her. But even so, it had sometimes been painful to watch him suffer so obviously. There were some nights she bet he could hardly walk home.

"What's so funny?" Ginger asked.

"Nothing. Just thinking about Kev, that's all. Memories. They're having a wake for him at the Queen's Arms tonight."

"Going?"

"Maybe."

"That's all we're left with when it comes right down to it. Memories."

"That's a bloody depressing thought," said Annie. "What have you got so far? Are we any closer to the leak?"

Ginger ate her last chips and shook her head while her mouth was full. Then she patted her chest and took another sip of beer. Sunlight broke through the clouds for a moment and shone through the stained-glass windows. "Bugger all," she said. "But I still don't like Julia Ford, or that other one, the one we met first."

"Constance Wells?"

"That's the one. Another slippery little bitch."

"Now, now, Ginger. Claws."

"Well . . ."

"So neither of them will admit to telling anyone Karen Drew's real identity?"

"Of course not. Lips sealed tighter than a Scotsman's sphincter, if you'll excuse my language."

"Anything interesting in the background checks?"

"Nothing yet. The usual university stuff. I do believe Constance Wells was a member of the Marxist Society when she was a student, mind you. I'll bet she wouldn't want that to get around the firm."

Annie smiled. "You wouldn't, would you?"

Ginger gave a mischievous grin. "I might. You never know." She finished her beer. "I'm glad that had no calories in it."

"Anything else? Pudding, maybe?"

Ginger patted her stomach. "No, that's me done, guv. There was one thing struck me as interesting in all my digging around. Hardly relevant, mind you, but interesting."

"Oh?" said Annie. "What's that?"

"Well, Julia Ford was a late starter. She didn't go to university till she was in her early twenties."

"So?"

"Most people go straight from school, that's all. Law, medicine, what have you. Want to get the education over with and start earning the big money and pay off their student loans as soon as they can."

"Okay," said Annie. "That makes sense. I think they had grants back then, though, not loans. Still, it's an interesting point. If there's a chance that Maggie Forrest is really Kirsten Farrow, there's also a chance that Julia Ford is, too, isn't there?"

Ginger looked surprised. "That's not where I was —"

"Hold on a minute, though," Annie went on. "There is, isn't there? She's about the right age, she's slight enough in build, and if she hid her hair under a hat, downplayed the fancy clothes and the makeup . . . It could be her, couldn't it?"

"Julia Ford? Bloody hell! But she defended Lucy Payne."

"She also knew her identity and where she was. Okay, so we've got a bit of a problem with motive. There seems to be a conflict there. But perhaps there was a reason for that. Something we don't know about."

"I suppose you could have a point," said Ginger. "Want me to do a bit more digging into her background?"

Annie nodded. "Yes. See if you can find out where she was between 1985, which was when Kirsten would have started uni, and 1991 or 1992, which is about the last sighting of her. But be careful."

"What about alibis?"

"It'll be tricky without her knowing, but if you could find out where she was at the times Lucy and Templeton were murdered, it would be a big help."

"I'll see what I can do. But what I was going to tell you –"

"Yes?"

"Julia Ford did another degree before her law one. Not English lit. Psychology. At Liverpool."

"It still doesn't let her out of the picture. And the law degree?"

"Bristol."

"Kirsten Farrow was from Bath. It's very close."

"Our Ms. Ford shared a flat while she was there. First and second year."

"Students often do."

"It's just that I happened to get connected with a very chatty and helpful young woman from student housing, had all the records going back years. Anyway, Julia Ford shared the flat with Elizabeth Wallace, who was studying medicine at the time. Now, correct me if I'm wrong, but isn't Elizabeth Wallace your pathologist back in Western Area?"

"She is, indeed," said Annie. "Dr. Elizabeth Wallace."

"Just a point of interest, that's all," Ginger said. "They were mates, her and Julia Ford. And –"

"And what?"

"I did a bit more checking, and they both live in Harrogate now."

"Big place."

"Both members of the local golf club, too."

"Fellow professionals. Makes sense. But you're right, Ginger, it *is* interesting. Are you thinking Julia Ford might have told Dr. Wallace . . . ?"

"And Dr. Wallace might have let it slip elsewhere? Well, it's possible, isn't it? That is, if Julia Ford isn't the one we're looking for."

"I wonder if Dr. Wallace can tell us anything?"

"She's hardly any more likely to spill the beans than Julia Ford, is she?" said Ginger. "I mean, *doctors*. They're worse than lawyers. That's if there are any beans to spill."

"Perhaps not," said Annie. "But when we get back to the station, keep digging into Julia Ford's background. Discreetly, of course. Get back to your friend at Bristol and see if she can dig up any more names from around that time. Others who might have shared the flat, been members of the same societies, that sort of thing. It might be worth my having a word with Dr. Wallace later if you do come up with anything. I've met her a couple of times. She seems okay."

"What are you thinking?"

Annie grabbed her briefcase and stood up. They walked out onto Flowergate and joined the flow of people. "I'm thinking, you know, a couple of drinks at the nineteenth hole – there's been some decent enough weather for golf recently – the tongue loosens. 'Guess who's our client and what we've done with her,' says Julia. 'Oh?' says Dr. Wallace. And so on."

"Girl talk?"

"Something like that. And Dr. Wallace lets it slip somewhere else, another old university friend or . . . Who knows? What's Maggie Forrest's psychiatrist's name?"

"Simms. Dr. Susan Simms."

"Where did she get her education?"

"Dunno."

"Find out. Has she ever done any forensic psychiatry?"

"I'll check."

"Good. That could link her to Julia Ford through the courts. Dr. Simms is already linked with Maggie Forrest. So many possibilities."

"Right, guv," said Ginger.

"I don't know where all this gets us," Annie said, "but we might just be on to something here." She took out her mobile. "I should probably let Alan know, too."

"If you think so."

"And, Ginger?"

"Yes, guv?"

"Tread very carefully indeed on this one. Not only are we sniffing around the super's favourite kinds of people – doctors and lawyers –

there's also a killer on the loose somewhere, and the last thing you want to do is step on her tail and disturb her without knowing you've done so."

Banks walked over from Western Area Headquarters to the Fountain late that afternoon, mulling over what he had just heard from Annie on his mobile. Julia Ford and Elizabeth Wallace, old flatmates and golf buddies. Well, it made sense. If they'd known one another from their university days, and if both were professional single women living in Harrogate, they would probably be friends and members of the same golf club.

The Maggie Forrest connection was the one that really interested him, though. According to Annie, she used Constance Wells in Julia Ford's firm for her legal work, and she also knew Julia Ford slightly, so she might easily have overheard something about Karen Drew when she was at their office once, or seen a revealing document. Julia Ford had been Lucy Payne's lawyer, and Maggie had been her champion and her stooge. It had all gone haywire, of course, but there *was* a connection.

Then there was the hair. Annie had told him that their expert, Famke Larsen, had matched one of Kirsten Farrow's hairs, found in Greg Eastcote's house in 1989, with a hair on the blanket Lucy Payne had on when she was killed. It wasn't conclusive, of course, but it was enough to confirm their suspicions that Kirsten had somehow re-appeared and was involved in Lucy's murder. Who she was remained a mystery. The hair on the blanket, Annie had also said, would reveal a mitochondrial DNA profile that could further help them identify the killer. That would take a few days, though, and they would need samples from all their suspects for comparison. Still, it was definitely progress.

For the moment, though, he needed to concentrate on the Hayley Daniels case. He was getting close; he could feel it in his water.

"Hello, Jamie," Banks said as he walked in and stood at the bar. "Jill."

Jill Sutherland smiled at him, but Jamie didn't. A teenager in a long gabardine coat looked around from the slot machine he was playing and immediately turned away again. Banks recognized him from the comprehensive school. Underage truant. But he wasn't interested in that today. Maybe if he remembered, he'd give the headmaster a ring later. He got on well enough with Norman Lapkin, and they had a pint together now and again. Norman understood the problems of dealing with wayward youth.

"What is it this time?" Murdoch said. "Can't you lot leave me alone for one minute? I've got a pub to run."

"I won't get in your way," said Banks. "In fact, tell you what, I'll even put your profits up. I'll have a pint of Black Sheep, if that's all right with you."

Jamie glanced over to Jill, who took down a glass and started to pull the pint. "How's business?" Banks asked.

"Rotten," said Jamie. "Especially since last weekend."

"Yes, bloody inconsiderate of Kev Templeton to go and get his throat cut just around the corner, wasn't it? I mean, one murder might be quite good for business, brings in the curiosity seekers, but two . . . ?"

Murdoch paled. "I didn't mean that. You know I didn't. You're putting words into my mouth. I'm sorry about what happened to Mr. Templeton, really I am. He was a good copper."

"Let's not go too far, Jamie. Besides, nothing to do with you, was it?"

"Of course not."

Jill smiled when Banks gave her a five-pound note and told her to have a drink for herself. Jamie went back to poring over his books and menus, and Jill went back to cleaning glasses. They looked as if they had already been cleaned once.

The old music tape, or satellite station, was playing Dusty Springfield's "I Only Want to Be With You." Banks thought of Sophia and wondered where on earth things would go with her. They had listened to the Thea Gilmore CD that morning, and Banks had finally understood the reference Sophia had made to the song "Sugar" being a bit cheeky. The singer was saying that the person she was with could take her home and lay her on his bed, but *not* to call her "Sugar." Banks didn't call Sophia Sugar. If only he could have just dropped everything and gone off somewhere with her the way he had felt like doing. Now she would be back in London, back to her real life, friends, work and hectic social schedule. Perhaps she would forget him. Perhaps she would decide that it had all been a foolish dalliance with an unpromising future, best forgotten. Perhaps it had been. But why couldn't Banks stop thinking about her, and why was he suddenly so jealous of everyone who was younger and freer than he was?

He glanced around the pub. There were only about five or six people in the place, but the numbers would pick up soon when the town centre offices closed. Jamie Murdoch was right, though. A mood of gloom had descended on Eastvale since Templeton's murder, and it wouldn't pass completely until his killer was found. And if Banks didn't find her soon, various experts from all over the country would be arriving and taking over, just like Scotland Yard used to do in the old days. The press were already frothing at the mouth; one minute denouncing police incompetence, the next condemning a cop killer.

Banks sipped his pint. Dusty gave way to the Shadows' "Theme for Young Lovers," another bow in the direction of nostalgia. Banks had stolen his first kiss while that was playing down by the river one beautiful spring Sunday afternoon in 1964. Anita Longbottom was her name, and she wouldn't let him put his hand on her breast.

"Can you turn it down a bit, Jill?" Banks asked. "I can hardly hear myself think."

Jill turned the music down. Nobody complained. Banks wondered if anyone would miss it at all, but he realized that silence did bother some people. He sipped his pint and marvelled at the fact that even if DS Gervaise walked in right now, he wouldn't get into trouble. She had gone for his suggestion and had even agreed that he should appear as natural as possible. This was about the only good thing that had come from Templeton's murder, apart from the fact that Banks had had to postpone both his doctor's and dentist's appointments yet again.

"You're looking nervous, Jamie," Banks said. "Something on your mind?"

"My conscience is clear, Mr. Banks," said Jamie.

"Sure? Sure you don't have a room full of Spanish brandy and French cigarettes hidden away somewhere? I thought I could smell Gauloises a minute ago."

"Very funny. You are joking, right?"

"Not at all."

"Well, no, I don't." Jamie glared at Jill, who busied herself with the glasses again.

"There's something else that's been bothering me," Banks went on. "We have a witness who heard a snatch of music in the Maze around the time Hayley Daniels was killed."

"You mentioned that before. I didn't hear anything."

"We weren't sure where it came from," Banks went on. "A car passing by, a door opening and closing . . . something like that."

"Sorry, I can't help you."

"Then I had an idea."

"Oh?"

"Yes," Banks said. "The witness remembered that the music was 'Fit But You Know It' by the Streets, and I went on-line and found out you can buy it."

"I imagine you can," said Murdoch.

"As a ring tone."

Murdoch had no reply to that, and before Banks could say anything else, he heard "Fit But You Know It" coming from Murdoch's side pocket. DS Gervaise calling the number they had got from the mobile supplier, as arranged. The colour drained from Murdoch's face, his eyes turned back towards Banks, then he leaped over the bar and dashed out into the market square.

Banks ran after him. "Jamie, don't be a bloody fool!" he yelled as Jamie scattered a gaggle of elderly tourists getting off a bus near the cross. "You can't get away."

But Jamie ran across the square. The uniformed officers positioned outside the police station in case of just such an eventuality snapped into action, and seeing his escape route cut off, Jamie changed direction and veered towards the Swainsdale Centre. Once there, he bounded up the escalator, Banks in hot pursuit, breathing heavily, and ran into the arcade of first-level shops.

Women clutched their children and screamed as packages and people went flying. Banks became aware of a couple of uniformed officers behind him, and suddenly he saw Winsome coming in fast from his left side. She was an awesome sight, head tossed back, arms like pistons, long legs pumping like an athlete's.

Murdoch disappeared into the entrance of the Marks and Spencer's food department, knocking baskets out of people's hands as he went. A bottle of wine smashed on the floor, spilling red in every direction. Someone screamed, and Murdoch almost tripped over a small child who started to cry, but he caught his footing again and ran into the menswear department.

There was no way Banks was going to catch him. He was too out of shape, and he had never been a fast runner. Winsome ran marathons, though, and she moved gracefully and easily behind him catching up with every step. Murdoch glanced back and saw how close she was, then he knocked an old woman out of his way and put on a sprint towards the exit.

Banks could hardly believe what he saw next. Murdoch was about five or six feet ahead of Winsome when all of a sudden she launched herself through the air at him in something halfway between a dive and a rugby tackle, grasped him around his thighs with her long, powerful arms and brought him to the floor. A few moments later, Banks was standing over them, panting for breath, and Winsome had her knee in Murdoch's back and was doing her Christie Love act, saying, "You're under arrest, sugah," reading him his rights just like an American cop. "You have the right to remain silent . . ."

Banks couldn't help but smile, even through the pain in his chest. That wasn't the official caution at all, and surely *Get Christie Love!* was way before Winsome's time? "That's all right, Winsome," he said, still panting. "Well done. Pick the bastard up and cuff him. We'll deal with him back at the station."

17

Banks, Winsome and Jamie Murdoch sat in the bleak interview room, Murdoch in his orange police-issue coverall, picking his fingernails. The duty solicitor, Ms. Olivia Melchior, sat in the corner. She had already had a word with Jamie and explained the situation, told him it was best to answer simply and truthfully unless he was in danger of incriminating himself or having his rights violated – and she would be the judge of that. Banks turned on the tape recorders and video, went through the preamble about time, date, and those present, then gave Jamie his proper caution, the one about the disadvantages of not saying something now he might later rely on in court. Jamie kept on staring down at his fingernails.

"Right," said Banks. "Why did you run away, Jamie?"

"You were going to fit me up, weren't you?"

"What do you mean?"

"For the smuggling charge. The cigs and booze. You were going to fit me up. I've heard about things like that."

"This isn't about smuggling, Jamie."

"It isn't?"

"No."

"What, then?"

"This is about the rape and murder of Hayley Daniels."

Murdoch glanced back down at his fingernails. "I've already told you, I don't know nothing about that."

"You were just around the corner."

"The walls are thick. You can't hear much from inside."

"You can if the door is open, though, can't you, Jamie?" Winsome said.

Murdoch stared at her. "Huh?"

"When Hayley Daniels and her friends left," Winsome went on, "you left the door open a crack and were able to hear what they were saying. We think you heard Hayley say she was going into the Maze on her own."

"So what?"

"Do you admit this?" Winsome pressed.

"I might have. You know, it's bad manners to slam the door and lock it the minute your last punters are out in the street. You give them a few seconds. Somebody might have forgotten something. A handbag, a jacket."

"Very considerate of you, I'm sure," said Banks. "And I thought you were supposed to lock up fast to avoid a break-in."

"That, too. But . . ."

"Hayley Daniels gave you a hard time, didn't she?"

"How do you mean?"

"When you told her the toilets weren't working so she couldn't use them, she gave you a verbal mouthful, used bad language. Come on, Jamie, we've been through this before."

"It *was* vile," Murdoch said. He shook his head slowly. "I've never known such vile words coming from . . . from . . ."

"Such a pretty mouth? She was a good-looking girl, wasn't she, Jamie? Nice body, too."

"I wouldn't know about that."

"Don't tell me you didn't notice. Even I noticed, and she was dead when I saw her."

Melchior gave Banks a warning glance. She obviously knew that he had a tendency to go off on weird, almost surreal, tangents to throw his suspects off their predetermined stories.

"She was fit enough," said Murdoch.

"Fit and she knew it?"

"They usually do."

"What do you mean by that, Jamie?"

"What I say. Girls like her. They know they're fit."

"Is that why you like the song, have it as your ringtone?"

"It's just a bit of fun."

"Flaunt it, do they, these fit lasses?"

"You should see the clothes they wear – or don't." He gave an unpleasant, harsh laugh.

"Like Jill?"

"Jill?"

"Yes, the girl who works for you. Jill Sutherland. She's a pretty lass, isn't she? She used to take shortcuts to the car park through the Maze, didn't she? Is that where you got the idea?"

"What idea?"

"That it was a suitable place for an ambush."

"That's ridiculous."

"But it's enough to drive any red-blooded bloke crazy, isn't it?" Banks said. "The way they dress and the things they say."

"Don't answer that, Jamie," said Melchior. "He's leading you." She gave Banks a stern glance. "And you, stop it. Stick to the relevant questions."

"Yes, miss," said Banks.

Melchior glared at him.

"How long had you known Hayley?" Winsome asked.

"I didn't know her," said Jamie. "Just saw her when she came in the pub with her friends."

"But according to the records, you were both in the first year of college together before you dropped out," said Winsome. She adjusted her reading glasses and tapped the file on the table in front of her.

"Maybe I saw her around. It's a big college."

"Ever ask her out?"

"I might have done. So what?"

"Just that you have a history, that's all." Winsome took off her glasses and leaned back in her chair.

"You fancied her right from the start, didn't you?" Banks said.

"What's wrong with that?"

"But she wouldn't have anything to do with you. She was fussy about who she went out with. Preferred older men, professors, someone with a bit of experience, money, brains."

Jamie slammed his fist on the table.

"Calm down, Jamie," Melchior said. "Is this going anywhere?" she asked Banks.

"Oh, yes," he said. "Isn't it, Jamie? You know where it's going, don't you? Saturday, the seventeenth of March. St. Patrick's Day. What was special about that day?"

"Nothing. I don't know."

"Some yobbos wrecked your toilets, didn't they?"

"Yeah."

"What happened, did they find your peephole from the storeroom to the ladies room?"

Murdoch froze. "What?"

It had been a long shot on Banks's part – no one had mentioned such a thing – but it was turning out to be a good guess. It was exactly the sort of thing he thought someone like Murdoch would do. "We'll leave that for the moment," Banks went on. "Hayley was looking particularly good that night, wasn't she? The short skirt, low top. Looked a bit like a tart, didn't she?"

"DCI Banks," Melchior interrupted. "Fewer of those sorts of comments, if you don't mind."

"Sorry," said Banks. "But you fancied her, didn't you, Jamie?"

"She was very attractive."

"And you'd wanted her for a long time."

"I liked her, yes."

"And she knew it?"

"I suppose she did."

"And then this business with the toilets came up."

"She should never have said the things she did."

"She humiliated you in front of everybody, didn't she?"

"She shouldn't have called me those names."

"What names, Jamie?"

"Terrible names. About my manhood and things." He gave a shifty glance towards Melchior, who seemed enthralled.

"She called you impotent, didn't she? 'Limp dick.' That really got your goat, didn't it?"

"How could she say something like that? She knew I . . . knew I liked her. How could she be so cruel?"

"She was drunk, Jamie. And she needed a piss."

"Mr. Banks!"

Banks held his hand up. "Sorry."

"I couldn't help that, could I?" said Jamie. "It wasn't me that wrecked the fucking bogs!"

Banks heard a tap at the door. Winsome answered, came back and whispered in his ear.

"This interview is suspended at six thirteen," Banks said. "DCI Banks and DC Jackman are leaving the room, PC Mellors is entering to keep an eye on the suspect." Banks glanced at Melchior. "You coming?"

She seemed torn between her client and whatever new revelation had just come up. "You'll be all right, Jamie?"

"He'll be all right, ma'am," the PC said.

Jamie nodded, eyes averted.

"Very well, then." Melchior gathered up her papers and briefcase and strutted out after Banks and Winsome, across the market square to the Fountain. A brisk wind had sprung up, and she had to hold her lilac skirt down with one hand as she walked. There was already a crowd gathered outside the pub, and the two uniformed constables were doing a sterling job of defending the crime scene.

Once they had signed the sheet, Banks and the others were allowed inside the Fountain, where a thorough search had been in progress ever since they had taken Jamie Murdoch over to the station, all legal and above-board. The SOCOs were dressed in protective clothing and wore breathing filters against the dust, and an assistant handed out the same gear to Banks, Winsome and Melchior, who seemed a bit embarrassed in her hard hat, coveralls and face mask.

The pub was a shambles. There was dust and crumbled plaster everywhere. The landlord would go crazy when he found out, Banks thought, though with any luck that would be the least of his problems. They followed Stefan Nowak upstairs to one of the storerooms above the bar that abutted on Taylor's Yard and the Maze. Someone had moved a piece of the old wainscoting to reveal a hole big enough for a man to get through. Banks could hear voices and see the beam of a torch waving around on the other side.

"There's no light switch," said Stefan, handing out torches, "and no window." He bent and made his way through the hole. Banks followed. Melchior seemed reluctant, but Winsome held back to let her go first and brought up the rear. With all the beams of light, the room they found themselves in was more than bright enough. It smelled mouldy and airless, which it no doubt was, and stacked against one wall were cases of lager and cartons of cigarettes.

"Is this it?" said Banks, disappointed. "Is there no access to the Maze?"

"Hold your horses," said Stefan, moving to the other side of the room where he swung a hinged panel towards him. "Follow me."

They followed. The next room was just as cramped and musty as the first, but a steep wooden staircase led down to the ground floor, where a door with well-oiled hinges and a recently installed Yale lock opened into the anonymous alley at the back of Taylor's Yard, where no CCTV camera lens ever penetrated.

"Bingo," said Banks.

"It's like the bloody *Phantom of the Opera*," said Stefan. "Secret passages and God knows what."

"They were only secret from us," Banks pointed out. "Houses and storage areas cheek by jowl like this are often connected by crawl space or what have you. Murdoch simply found a way of removing the covering and replacing it so he could come and go as he wanted. Originally, it just made a great hiding place for storing the smuggled goods, but when Hayley Daniels pushed him past the end of his tether, it made the perfect way for him to get back at her. He knew where she was going, and he knew he could get there in seconds without being seen. How long would it take him to get from the front door to the Maze by this route?"

"Less than five minutes," said Stefan.

"Sir?" One of the SOCOs approached them, torch shining in a corner.

"What is it?" Banks asked.

"A plastic bag of some sort," Stefan said. He took some photographs, the flash blinding them all momentarily in the confined space, then carefully picked up the bag with his gloved hands and opened it. "Voila," he said, showing the contents to Banks. "Clothes. Condoms. Hairbrush. Cloth. Bottle of water."

"It's his kit," said Banks. "Templeton was right. The bastard liked it so much he was planning on doing it again."

"Or he'd been planning it for some time," Stefan added. "Possibly both."

"I don't think you should assume that," said a pale Ms. Melchior, who was clearly by now in duty solicitor mode again, just trying to do her job against all the mounting horror of her client's guilt that she must have been feeling.

"We'll see what the lab has to say," said Banks. "Good work, Stefan, lads. Come on, let's get back to the interview room. We don't want to keep Mr. Murdoch waiting too much longer, do we?"

After lunch with Ginger, Annie went back to the police station to see if anything had come in. She was hoping for more good news from forensics but had learned over the years that she had to be patient. In the meantime, she busied herself locating Dr. Laura Henderson who, as it turned out, was still practising in Bath. After a few engaged signals, Annie finally got through and introduced herself. Dr. Henderson was naturally suspicious and insisted on taking down Annie's extension number and ringing back through the automated station switchboard.

"Sorry about that," Dr. Henderson said when they finally got connected again, "but you can't be too careful in my business."

"Mine, too," said Annie. "No problem."

"Anyway, what can I help you with?"

"Do you remember a patient called Kirsten Farrow? This would be around 1988, perhaps early 1989. I know it's a long time ago."

"Of course I remember Kirsten," said Dr. Henderson. "There are some patients you never forget. Why? Has anything happened to her?"

"Not that I know of," said Annie. "In fact, that's the problem. Nobody's seen hide nor hair of her in about eighteen years. Has she been in touch with you at all?"

"No, she hasn't."

"When did you last see her?"

"Could you hang on a moment? I'll dig out the file. I'm afraid anything from that long ago isn't on the computer." Annie waited, tapping her pencil on the desk. A few moments later, Dr. Henderson came back on. "Our last session was January 9, 1989," she said. "I haven't seen Kirsten since then."

It wasn't what Annie had been hoping for. "Why did she stop coming to see you?"

There was a long pause at the other end. "I'm not sure I should be discussing this with you," said Dr. Henderson.

"I'm trying to locate her," Annie said. "Anything you could tell me might help. I wouldn't expect you to breach confidentiality."

"Why are you looking for her?"

"She might know something about a case I'm working on."

"What case?"

Annie felt like saying she couldn't divulge that information, but that would be playing the same silly game. Give a little, maybe get a little in return. "A woman has been killed in the same location Kirsten used to visit," she said. "We were thinking –"

"Oh, my God!" said Dr. Henderson. "You think he's back, don't you? The killer."

It wasn't what Annie was about to say at all, but she recognized a good opening when she heard one. "It's a possibility," she said. "They never did catch him."

"But I still don't see how I can help you."

"Why did Kirsten stop seeing you?"

There was another pause, and Annie could almost hear the argument raging in Henderson's mind. Finally, the pros seemed to win out over the cons. "The reason she gave me was that our sessions were becoming too painful for her," she said.

"In what way?"

"You have to realize that Kirsten had blocked out what happened to her on the night she was attacked, and that was causing her all kinds of problems: depression, nightmares, anxiety attacks. Along with her other problems –"

"The inability to have sex or children?"

"You know about that?" Henderson sounded surprised.

"I know a little," Annie said.

"Well, yes. Along with all those other problems, she was in, well, you probably also know, then, that she did attempt suicide. I'm sure it's in the police files."

"Yes," Annie lied. No point in letting Dr. Henderson think she'd given too much away. She would only clam up.

"I suggested a course of hypnosis, and Kirsten agreed."

"The aim of which was?"

"Healing, of course. Sometimes you have to confront your demons to vanquish them, and you can't do that if your memory is blocking them out."

Annie felt she knew a thing or two about that. "And did she?"

"No. As I said, I think it was becoming too painful for her. She was getting too close. At first, progress was very slow, then she started remembering too much too fast. I think she felt she was losing control, and she started to panic."

"What about confronting the demons?"

"It takes time," said Dr. Henderson. "Sometimes you need a lot of preparation. You need to be ready. I don't think Kirsten was. It would have felt like driving down a busy motorway before she'd learned to drive."

"How far did she get?" Annie asked. "Did she remember anything significant about her attacker?"

"That wasn't the point of the treatment."

"I realize that, but perhaps as a by-product?"

"I'm not sure," Dr. Henderson said.

"What do you mean, you're not sure?"

"That last session, Kirsten's voice was difficult to hear, her words hard to catch. Afterwards, when she came out of it, she seemed shocked, stunned at what she remembered. Even more so than usual."

"But what was it?"

"I don't know. Don't you understand what I'm telling you? I don't know. She left in a hurry, and she didn't come back, except to let my secretary know that she wouldn't be coming any more."

"But what do *you* think it was? What do you think shook her so much?"

Dr. Henderson paused again, then Annie heard her say in a voice barely above a whisper, "I think she remembered what he looked like."

"Where've you been?" said Murdoch. "I'm getting fed up of this. I want to go home."

"Not just yet, Jamie," said Banks. "A few more questions first. Let's start at the top. Maybe we can keep this short. Did you rape and kill Hayley Daniels?"

"No! How could I? You'd have seen me. There's no way out of the pub without being on CCTV."

Banks glanced over at Ms. Melchior, who appeared uncomfortable. She said nothing. Banks leaned forward and linked his hands on the table. "Let me tell you what I think happened, Jamie, and you can tell me if I'm wrong. Okay?"

Jamie nodded, still not looking up.

"You'd had a bad day. Been having a bad life lately, if truth be told. That miserable pub, always by yourself, the landlord sunning himself in Florida. Even Jill kept calling in sick. And she wasn't just a help behind the bar, she was easy on the eye, too, wasn't she? But she didn't want anything to do with you, did she? None of them did. I think maybe you entertained the fantasy of getting Jill alone in the Maze. You knew she used it as a shortcut. Maybe that's what you had planned for Saturday night. Finally plucked up the courage. But Jill called in sick, didn't she, and that spoiled your little plan. Until Hayley Daniels arrived. You'd seen her around for years, even asked her out when you were at college, before you failed half your first-year courses and dropped out. Isn't that right, Jamie?"

Murdoch said nothing. Melchior scribbled away on her legal pad and Winsome stared at a spot high on the wall.

"That Saturday night, after she called you names and insulted your manhood, you hurried them out and you heard them talking out front. Hayley had a loud, strident voice, especially when she drunk and upset, which she was. You heard her telling her friends what a useless bastard you were, a 'limp dick,' all over again, in the public market square, for anyone to hear, and you left the door open a crack so you could hear them. How am I doing so far, Jamie?"

Murdoch continued to pick away at his fingernails.

"You heard Hayley say she was going down into the Maze to relieve herself, though I doubt that's exactly how she put it. She had a foul mouth, didn't she, Jamie?"

Murdoch looked up for a moment at Banks. "She was very coarse and crude," he said.

"And you don't like that in a woman, do you?"

He shook his head.

"Right, so we have the friends dispersed and Hayley heading off by herself into the Maze. Well, it didn't take you long to figure out how you could get out there and give her what for, did it?"

"I've told you," Murdoch said in a bored voice without looking up. "I couldn't have got round there without being seen."

"Jamie," Banks said, "do you know anything about a storeroom attached to the Fountain, beyond the wainscoting upstairs?"

The pause before Murdoch said, "No," told Banks all he needed to know.

"We've found it, Jamie," said Banks. "No need to keep that lie afloat any more. We've found the room, the way out, the clothes you kept there, your 'assault kit,' the condoms, the hairbrush, the lot. We've found it all. Planning quite a career, weren't you?"

Murdoch turned very pale and stopped worrying the nail he was working on, but he said nothing.

"You'd been dreaming of something like that for a long time, hadn't you?" Banks went on. "Fantasizing. You'd even prepared that kit to wipe traces of evidence from the body, pick up all your pubic hairs. Very clever, Jamie. But you had no idea Hayley would be your first, did you? You thought it would be Jill. Maybe also you just wandered around there after closing time hoping someone, anyone, would come along,

but this was too good an opportunity to miss, wasn't it? What a beginning to an illustrious career. That foul-mouthed, sexy, tantalizing bitch
Hayley Daniels."

"Mr. Banks, could you tone it down a bit," said Melchior, but her
heart wasn't in it.

"Sorry," said Banks. "Would you prefer me to use euphemisms?
Make it all sound a lot nicer?" He turned back to Jamie. "You went out
by the usual way, and you saw Hayley doing her business there in the
alley like a common tart. I suppose it excited you, didn't it, the way
looking through that peephole into the ladies excited you. You probably
couldn't even wait until she'd finished. You knew about the leather
goods storeroom and the weak lock, and that was where she was squatting, wasn't it, right by the door? We found traces of her urine there.
She'd been sick, too. You took her before she could even get her knickers
up and dragged her in the shed, onto the soft pile of leather remnants.
Very romantic. But one little thing went wrong, didn't it? In all your
excitement, you'd forgotten to switch your mobile off, and it plays a very
distinctive ringtone quite loud, a real song, the Streets, 'Fit But You
Know It,' that you bought on-line. Very appropriate, don't you think?
Someone heard that, Jamie. He didn't recognize it at first, but someone
else heard it, too, a week later when you were leaving the Fountain. Who
was it, Jamie? Your boss calling from Florida, the way he usually does at
the end of the night? He couldn't reach you on the phone in the
Fountain, so he rang your mobile. Is that it? It would have been just after
seven in the evening there and he was probably just settling down to his
after-sunset, pre-dinner margarita with some bimbo in a bikini, and he
wants to know how his business is doing. What do you tell him, Jamie?
Not very well? I imagine you probably lie about it the way you do about
everything else. But that's another problem. You should have changed
your ringtone after you killed Hayley."

"How did it happen? I suppose you put your hand over Hayley's
mouth, then stuffed some leather remnants in, threatened you'd kill her
if she struggled or told anyone, then you raped her. My God, you raped
her. Vaginally and anally. Did that make you feel good? Powerful? And
what about when you'd finished? I think you felt guilty then, didn't you,
when you realized what you'd gone and done. Fantasy is one thing, but

reality . . . I should imagine it can come as quite a shock. There was no turning back now. She knew you. She knew what you'd done. One day, one way or another, it would get out. If she was left alive to tell the story. So you strangled her. Maybe you didn't enjoy that. I don't know. She looked too violated lying there with her legs open and her top pulled up. It showed you far too clearly what you'd done, like looking in a mirror, so you turned her gently on her side, put her legs together, as if she were sleeping, running in her sleep. That looked better, didn't it? Not quite so ugly. How am I doing, Jamie?"

Murdoch said nothing.

"It doesn't matter, anyway," Banks said, standing up and terminating the interview. "We've got all the evidence we need, and when forensics are through with it we'll be putting you away and throwing away the key."

Jamie didn't move. When Banks looked more closely he could see tears dropping on the scarred and scratched surface of the table. "Jamie?"

"She was so beautiful," Jamie said. "And so foul. She said she'd do anything. When I . . . when we . . . she said she'd do *anything* if I let her go."

"But you didn't?"

Murdoch looked at Banks, his eyes red with tears. "I wanted to, I really did, but I couldn't. How could I? You must understand I couldn't let her go. Not after. She wouldn't keep her word. A girl like that. A tramp like her. I knew she wouldn't keep her word. I knew I had to kill her."

Banks looked over at Melchior. "Did you get that?" he asked and left the room.

When Annie arrived at the Queen's Arms, Templeton's wake was in full swing, and she found out as soon as she got there that it was also being combined with a celebration of the capture of Hayley Daniels's killer, which made for a very odd sort of party indeed. Banks, Hatchley, Gervaise and the rest sat around a long table drinking pints and telling Templeton stories, the way you did at a wake, most of them funny, some of them bittersweet. Annie wasn't going to be a hypocrite and join in, but nor was she going to sour the mood by telling some of her own

Templeton stories. The poor bastard was dead, he didn't deserve that, let him have a proper send-off.

For some reason, Annie felt in a particularly good mood that night. It wasn't the occasion, of course, but something to do with being back in Eastvale, back in the Queen's Arms with the old crew. Eastern Area was okay, but she felt this was where she belonged. Winsome seemed to be enjoying herself, lounging against the bar talking to Dr. Wallace. Annie went over and joined them. Winsome seemed to stiffen a bit when she arrived, but she soon relaxed and offered Annie a drink.

"Pint of Black Sheep Bitter, please," Annie said.

"You know," Winsome offered, "you're welcome to stay at mine if . . . you know . . ."

It was part apology and part a reminder that she shouldn't drink and drive. "Thanks, Winsome," Annie said, clinking glasses. "We'll see how the evening goes. I'm not sure if I feel like getting pissed. How are you, Dr. Wallace? I'm DI Annie Cabbot. We met a couple of times before I was seconded to Eastern."

Dr. Wallace shook hands with Annie. "I remember," she said. "I'm fine. And it's Liz, please."

"Okay, Liz."

"I gather they're keeping you busy out there?"

"They are." Annie's drink came, and she took a long swallow. "Ah, that's better," she said.

Hatchley had just finished a Templeton joke, and the whole table roared with laughter. Even Superintendent Gervaise joined in. She was definitely looking a bit flushed and tipsy, Annie noticed.

"So how's the case going?" Dr. Wallace asked.

"Lucy Payne? Oh, you know, it's plodding along. Look." Annie touched her arm. It was only slight and momentary, but she felt Liz flinch. "We really must get together and talk about it sometime, compare notes." She gestured around the pub. "Not here. Not now, of course. Not an occasion like this. But there are some similarities with Kevin Templeton's murder."

"I'm aware of that," said Dr. Wallace. "I've spoken with Dr. Clarke, your pathologist. The blades used, for a start, seem similar."

"A razor, I believe you suggested?"

"Yes. At least that's most likely."

"Or a scalpel?"

"It could have been, I suppose. With that kind of wound it's often impossible to be exact. Very sharp, at any rate. Scalpels are just a little harder for the man in the street to get hold of."

"Or woman?"

"Of course. As you said, this is neither the place nor the time. Why don't you drop by the mortuary? You can usually find me there." She smiled. "If you'll excuse me, I need to have a word with Superintendent Gervaise before she falls down."

"Better hurry, then," said Annie, raising her glass. "Bottoms up."

Dr. Wallace smiled, walked away and took the empty chair beside Gervaise.

"Party pooper," said Winsome.

Annie looked at her. "Glad to see you're having such a good time, Winsome. Let me buy you a drink. How about something blue or pink with an umbrella in it?"

"Ooh, I don't know," said Winsome, clutching her half-pint of Guinness to her breast.

"Oh, go on. Let your hair down." Annie winked. "You never know what might happen." Annie leaned over the bar and asked Cyril for one of his specials. Cyril said it was coming right up.

"Look, about the other night –" Winsome began.

"It doesn't –"

"But it does. I'm sorry. I didn't mean to come across as such a prude. What you do is your own business, and I've got no right to judge you. I don't even have any right to judge Kev the way I did."

"What do you mean?"

"Well, I'm no angel. I kept a bloke tied to a bed naked when I should have been telling him his daughter was dead."

"Winsome, are you pissed?" Annie said. "What on earth are you talking about?"

Winsome explained about Geoff Daniels and Martina Redfern in the Faversham Hotel. Annie burst into laughter. "I really wouldn't worry too much about that," she said. "It sounds as if the bastard deserved it, no matter what. 'Black bitch,' indeed."

Winsome smiled. "You really think so?"

"I do. You just got me a bit confused when you started. I mean, I was trying to imagine *you* tying a naked man to a bed in a hotel room."

"*I* didn't tie him there!"

"I know that now. It was just a funny image, that's all. Forget it." Annie took another long belt of beer. Winsome's drink arrived. It was pink *and* blue. They were singing "Why Was He Born So Beautiful?" over at the table now. She could hear Banks's tuneless tenor mingled with the rest. "Cat's choir, hey?" she said.

Winsome laughed. "I mean it, you know," she said, touching Annie's arm. "About the other night. I'm sorry. I was insensitive."

"Look," said Annie, "between you and me, I fucked up. You were right to say what you did. It was a mistake. A big mistake. But it's over now. History. Sorted."

"Apology accepted, then?"

"Apology accepted. And I understand congratulations are in order for you? Nobody knew you could manage such a great rugby tackle. You'll be playing for England next."

Winsome laughed. "Can't be much worse than the team they've got already."

"Come on." Annie put her arm over Winsome's shoulders and together they picked up their drinks and walked over to the table, just in time to join in, "'He's no bloody use to anyone. He's no bloody use at all.'"

18

Banks enjoyed the drive to Leeds. The weather was fine, the traffic not too horrendous, and the iPod shuffle treated him to a truly random medley of David Crosby, John Cale, Pentangle and Grinderman, among others. A mild beer hangover from Kev Templeton's wake hammered away insistently in the back of his head, muffled by extra-strength Aspirin and plenty of water. At least he had had the sense to avoid spirits and sleep on Hatchley's sofa, though the children had awoken him at some ungodly hour of the morning. Annie had gone home early and said she would be coming back to Eastvale sometime to talk to Elizabeth Wallace. Banks and Annie planned to meet for a late lunch and compare notes.

Julia Ford had agreed to see Banks at eleven o'clock, sounding a little mystified by his request on the telephone, but perfectly pleasant and polite. In Leeds, he was fortunate in finding a parking spot not far off Park Square and arrived at the office in good time for his appointment. A young receptionist, messing with the flowers in the vestibule when he arrived, greeted him, then phoned through and led him to Julia's office.

Julia Ford stood up behind her large, tidy desk, leaned forward, shook hands and smiled. She was wearing a very subtle and no doubt expensive perfume. "DCI Banks," she said. "What a pleasure to see you again. You seem well."

"You, too, Julia. May I call you Julia?"

"Of course. And it's Alan, isn't it?"

"Yes. You don't look a day older than the last time I saw you." And it was true. Her chocolate brown hair was longer, curled at her shoulders, and there was the occasional strand of grey. Her eyes were as watchful and suspicious as ever, indicating a mind that never stopped working.

She sat down and patted her skirt. "Flattery will get you nowhere. What can I do for you?" Julia was quite slight in stature and seemed dwarfed by the desk.

"It's a rather delicate matter," Banks said.

"Oh, I think I'm used to those, don't you? As long as you don't expect me to give away any secrets."

"Wouldn't think of it," said Banks. "Actually, there are a couple of things. First of all, do you know a woman called Maggie, or Margaret Forrest?"

"The name rings a bell. I believe we do some legal work for her, yes. Not, I hasten to add, criminal. That's my area. The other members of the firm cover a wide range of legal services. I believe Ms. Forrest is a client of Constance's."

"Have you spoken with her recently?"

"Not personally, no."

"Perhaps I could talk to Constance?"

"I don't think that would help," said Julia. "My associates and part-ners are all just as discreet as I am."

"Somebody hasn't been," Banks said.

Her eyes narrowed. "What are you implying?"

"Your office knew from the start that Karen Drew was Lucy Payne. You arranged for the name change, the false reason for her quadriplegia, the transfer to Mapston Hall. Whatever else Lucy Payne was, she was your client. You took care of all her affairs."

"Of course. That was what we were engaged to do. I don't see what your point is."

"Someone found out and killed Lucy."

"But surely other people knew? You're not trying to blame the firm for what happened, are you?"

"We've talked to everyone else." Banks paused. "It comes back to you, Julia. You can help us out here."

"I don't know what you mean."

"We think that Lucy Payne was killed either by Maggie Forrest or by the same woman who killed two men in the same area eighteen years ago. Her name is Kirsten Farrow, though it's very unlikely she goes under that name now. A hair on Lucy's blanket has been matched with hairs taken from Kirsten eighteen years ago. The hair from the blanket has also yielded DNA, which is currently being processed. It would really help us a lot if we could find out who knew that Karen was Lucy, and where that information might have gone. Did you or someone else in your firm tell Maggie Forrest?"

"Well, *I* certainly didn't. I'm sorry, but I can't help you. Our lips were sealed."

"Come on, Julia. This is important. People are dead."

"They usually are when you turn up."

"A policeman is dead."

Julia touched her hair. "Yes. I was sorry to hear about that. I wish I could help."

"Have you ever heard of Kirsten Farrow, the woman I just mentioned?"

"Never."

"She'd be about forty now. About your age."

"I already told you flattery would get you nowhere."

"Do you know Dr. Elizabeth Wallace?"

Julia seemed surprised. "Liz? Yes, of course. We go back years. Why?"

"She's our pathologist, that's all."

"I know. She always was a bright spark. I'm sure she's very good at her job, especially if her golf game is anything to go by."

"Do you also know a psychiatrist called Dr. Susan Simms?"

"I've met her. For crying out loud, her office is just across the square. We've had lunch together now and then, when our paths have crossed."

"How have your paths crossed?"

"On occasion. I don't think it's any secret that she sometimes does forensic psychiatry."

"Does she also know Dr. Wallace?"

"How would I know?"

"Maggie Forrest was one of her patients."

"What can I say? It's a small world. I really don't know where you're going with this, Alan, but I can't tell you anything." She glanced at her perfect, tiny gold watch. "Look, I have another appointment in a few minutes, and I'd like some time to prepare. If there's nothing else?"

Banks got to his feet. "A pleasure, as ever," he said.

"Oh, don't lie. You think I was put on this earth just to stand in your way and make your life difficult. I really am sorry about that policeman who was killed. Was he a friend of yours?"

"I knew him," said Banks.

During the long drive over the moors to Eastvale, Annie spoke on her mobile with Ginger, when she could get a signal. It was too early for the DNA results from the hair, but Ginger had been burning up the phone lines, fax circuits and e-mail accounts. There was no way that Maggie Forrest could be Kirsten Farrow, she had concluded. Maggie was the right age, and she had been born in Leeds, but she had grown up in Canada, and in 1989, she had been attending art college in Toronto, specializing in graphic illustration. She married a young lawyer, and their relationship ended in a bad divorce a few years later. Apparently, he was a bully and a wife-beater. After her divorce, she came to live and work in England, staying at Ruth and Charles Everett's house on The Hill, and befriending Lucy Payne, until the notorious events of six years ago sent her reeling back to Canada.

But Maggie was working in England again, and according to Ginger, seeing Dr. Simms again. This in itself seemed odd to Annie. Why return? She could get book illustration work easily enough in Canada, surely? Maggie had told Annie that it was because she needed to be close to her roots, but was it really because she had decided to go after Lucy, get her revenge? Just because Maggie *wasn't* Kirsten Farrow, that didn't mean she hadn't killed Lucy Payne.

The main question in Annie's mind, given the links between the professional women – Maggie Forrest, Susan Simms, Julia Ford and Elizabeth Wallace – was had she had help from one of them? And if so, why? And where was Kirsten Farrow in all this? It was possible that someone *could* have planted one of her hairs on Lucy Payne's blanket, but how, and why? The hair could also have got there in Mapston Hall, for example. The Mapston Hall staff had been checked and rechecked, but she supposed it would do no harm to check again, dig even deeper, perhaps include the most regular visitors of other patients, delivery men, maintenance contractors, the postman, everyone who set foot in the place.

Annie parked in Eastvale market square rather than behind the police station. It was a bit of a walk down King Street to the infirmary, but the fresh air would do her good. Afterwards, she would call in at the station and see how everyone was recovering after last night's wake. Annie felt quite proud of herself for drinking only one pint over the course of the evening, then driving back to Whitby.

Reception told Annie that Dr. Wallace was in her office in the basement. Annie didn't like Eastvale General Infirmary, especially the basement. The corridors were high and dark with old green tiles, and footsteps echoed. The whole place was a Victorian Gothic monstrosity, and even though the mortuary and the post-mortem theatre had been modernized with the best equipment, the surroundings felt antiquated to Annie, associated with the barbaric times of no anaesthetics and unhygienic conditions. She shivered as her shoes clicked along the tiled corridor. The other thing about the basement that gave her the creeps was that there was hardly ever anyone around. She didn't know what else was down there other than storage and the mortuary. Maybe the bin where they dumped all the amputated limbs and extracted organs, for all she knew.

Dr. Wallace was actually in the post-mortem theatre, sitting at the long lab table mixing some chemicals over a Bunsen burner when Annie entered. There was a body on the table. The Y incision had already been made and the internal organs were all on display. The raw-lamb smell of dead human flesh hung in the air, mixed with disinfectant and formaldehyde. Annie felt slightly nauseated.

"Sorry," said Dr. Wallace with a weak smile. "I was just finishing up when I got sidetracked by this test. Wendy had to leave early – boyfriend trouble – or she'd have done it for me."

Annie glanced at the body. She could relate to boyfriend trouble. "Right," she said. "Just a few questions, as I mentioned."

"I'll get him closed up while we talk, if that's all right. Does it bother you? You seem a bit pale."

"I'm fine."

Dr. Wallace gave her an amused glance. "So what burning questions bring you all the way down to my little lair?"

"It's what we were talking about last night. Lucy Payne and Kevin Templeton."

"I don't see how I can help you. Lucy Payne wasn't my case. We agreed there were similarities, but that's all."

"It's not so much that," Annie said, settling on a high swivel stool by the lab bench. "Not specifically, at any rate."

"Oh? What, then? I'm curious." Dr. Wallace unceremoniously dumped the organs back into the chest cavity and prepared the large needle and heavy thread.

"You went to university with the lawyer, Julia Ford. You're still friends. Right?"

"That's true," said Dr. Wallace. "Julia and I have known one another a long time. We're practically neighbours, and we play the occasional round of golf together."

"What did you do before then?" Annie asked.

"Before playing golf?"

Annie laughed. "No, before going to medical school. You were a mature student, weren't you?"

"I wouldn't say I was all that mature, but I'd lived an interesting life."

"Did you travel?"

"For a few years."

"Where to?"

"All over. The Far East. America. South Africa. I'd get some low-paying job and support myself for a while, then move on."

"And before that?"

"What does it matter?"

"I don't suppose it does. Not if you don't want to talk about it."

"I don't." Dr. Wallace looked at Annie. "I had a disturbing phone call from an old friend of mine at university just an hour or two ago," she said. "She wanted to let me know that there had been a Detective Constable Helen Baker ringing up and asking questions about me. Is that true?"

"Quite the grapevine," said Annie.

"Is it true?"

"Okay. Look, this is a bit delicate," Annie said, "but Julia Ford was one of the few people who knew the true identity of the woman in Mapston Hall. Lucy Payne. Her firm made the arrangements to place her there, took care of all her affairs. As I just said, we know the two of you went to university together, that you're neighbours and friends. Did you know anything about this arrangement?"

Dr. Wallace turned back to her corpse. "No," she said. "Why should I?"

Annie felt that she could sense a lie, or at least an evasion. There was something about the pitch of Dr. Wallace's voice that wasn't quite right. "I was just wondering if, you know, during the course of an evening, she might have let something slip, and that you might have done the same."

Dr. Wallace paused in her sewing and turned to Annie. "Are you suggesting," she said, "that Julia would break a professional confidence? Or that I would?"

"These things happen," said Annie. "A couple of drinks. No big deal. Not the end of the world."

" 'Not the end of the world.' What an odd phrase to use. No, I don't suppose it would be the end of the world." She went back to sewing dead flesh. Annie could feel the tension rising in the room, as if the very air itself were thinning and stretching. She also felt even more nauseated by the smell.

"Well, did she?" she pressed on.

Dr. Wallace didn't look up. "Did she what?"

"Tell you about the arrangements her firm had made for Lucy Payne?"

"What does it matter if she did?"

"Well," said Annie. "It means . . . I mean . . . that someone else knew."

"So?"

"Did she tell you?"

"She might have done."

"And did you tell Maggie Forrest, for example? Or Dr. Susan Simms?"

Dr. Wallace seemed surprised. "No. Of course not. I vaguely know Susan Simms as a fellow professional and from the occasional court appearance, but we're hardly in the same field. I don't know any Maggie Forrest."

"She was the neighbour who befriended Lucy Payne and almost died at her hand."

"More fool her. But wasn't that a long time ago?"

"Six years. But Maggie's disturbed. She had a strong motive for wanting Lucy dead, and no alibi. All we're trying to find out now is whether she —"

"Knew that Karen Drew was Lucy Payne. Yes, I know where you're going with this."

"Karen Drew?"

"What?"

"You said Karen Drew. How did you know that?"

"I suppose I read it in the paper after the body was found, like everyone else."

"Right," said Annie. It was possible, of course. The body had been identified as Karen Drew's, but she would have thought that subsequent discoveries and all the publicity given to the Chameleon case and the House of Payne had driven that minor detail from most people's minds. Maggie Forrest had said she didn't recognize Karen Drew's name, only Lucy's. In the eyes of the world, Annie had thought, the dead woman in the wheelchair was Lucy Payne. Clearly not.

"I'm sorry, but I can't help you," Dr. Wallace said.

"Can't or won't?"

Dr. Wallace paused in her sewing and glanced across the body at Annie. "Well, it amounts to the same thing, really, doesn't it?"

"No, it doesn't. Either you don't know anything, or you're being wilfully obstructive, which I find very odd behaviour in a Home Office pathologist. You're supposed to be on our side, you know."

Dr. Wallace stared at Annie. "What are you saying?"

"I'm asking you if you gave anyone this information, for any reason." Annie softened her tone. "Look, Liz," she said. "You might have had good intentions. Perhaps you knew one of the victims' families, or someone who had been damaged by the Paynes? I can understand that. But we need to know. Did you tell *anyone* about Lucy Payne being registered at Mapston Hall under the name Karen Drew?"

"No."

"Did *you* know about it?"

Dr. Wallace sighed, put her needle and thread down and leaned on the edge of the table. "Yes," she said. "I knew."

In the silence that followed, Annie felt a growing tightness in her chest. "But that means —"

"I know what it means," said Dr. Wallace. "I'm not stupid."

Annie noticed that before she spoke Dr. Wallace had exchanged her needle for a scalpel and was moving away from the body on the table.

"Good to see you again, Alan," said DI Ken Blackstone, meeting Banks at the front desk of Millgarth and escorting him through security. "To what do I owe the pleasure?"

"It looks as if we've got Hayley Daniels's killer." Banks explained about Jamie Murdoch's confession and the hidden way out of the Fountain.

"Just one more to go, then," said Blackstone. "I was sorry to hear about Kev Templeton."

"We all were," said Banks.

"Anyway, what can I do for you?"

"Did you get the Chameleon files out for Annie Cabbot?"

"How are you two doing, by the way?"

"Better, I think. At least we're working together again. I'm still not sure what's going on with her, though."

"You're not . . . ?"

"No. That's been over for a long time."

"Anyone else?"

"Maybe. Ken, about those files?"

Blackstone laughed. "Yes, of course. Getting quite nosy in my old age, aren't I? Sorry. The files are in my office. Most of them, anyway. There isn't room for everything. Not if I want to sit in there, too. Why?"

"Mind if I have a look?"

"Not at all. It was your case. Partly, at any rate. Anything I can do?"

"A cup of coffee would go down a treat, Ken. Black no sugar. And maybe a KitKat. I like the dark-chocolate ones."

"Your diet's terrible. Anyone ever told you? I'll send down. Want me out of the way?"

"Not at all."

They went into Blackstone's office, and Banks saw immediately that he hadn't been exaggerating. They could hardly move for boxes.

"Know where everything is?" Banks asked.

"Not exactly." Blackstone picked up his phone and called for two coffees and a dark-chocolate KitKat. "After anything in particular?"

"I got to thinking about the Kirsten Farrow case," said Banks. "Anyway, I seemed to remember that the wounds were rather similar in both cases, and I wondered if that was what had set her off again after eighteen years. That and finding out where Lucy Payne was hiding out. It might have acted as a trigger."

"But what about the other woman you mentioned? Maggie Forrest?"

"She's not out of the picture yet. There could even be some connection between her and Kirsten Farrow. There are a number of odd links in this case, strange tangents, and I won't rest until I get them sorted."

"So you'll be wanting the pathologist's reports?"

"That's right. Dr. Mackenzie, I believe it was."

The coffee and KitKat arrived while they were digging through the boxes. Blackstone thanked the constable who brought them and got back to helping Banks. At last they unearthed the pathology reports, and Banks started reading through them while Blackstone left the office for a while.

It was as he had thought. Many of the bodies were badly decomposed, as they had been buried in the dirt of the cellar or the back garden. But Dr. Mackenzie had been able to identify slash marks to the areas of the victims' breasts and genitalia in all cases, probably made with the same machete Terence Payne used to attack and kill Janet Taylor's partner. They were similar to the wounds Kirsten Farrow had suffered, though the weapon was different, and they were wounds, unfortunately, not uncommon to vicious sexual assaults. They showed a deep hatred of the women men felt had betrayed, humiliated and rejected them all their lives, or so the profilers said. Of course, not all men who had been betrayed, humiliated or rejected by women became rapists and murderers, or the female population would be a lot smaller and the jails would be even more full of men than they already were, Banks thought.

Twenty minutes or more must have passed as Banks read the grisly details, most of which he remembered first-hand, then Blackstone returned.

"How's it going?" he asked.

"It's as I thought," Banks said. "Now I just need to find out how much of this was reported in the press at the time."

"Quite a lot, as I remember," said Blackstone. "Alan, what is it? Have you found something?"

Banks had let the last file slip out of his hand to the floor, not because the details were any more gruesome than any of the others, but because of a sheet of paper he had seen clipped to the end of the pile. It was simply a record of all those involved in the preparation of the reports and post-mortems, including the men who had transported the bodies to the mortuary and the cleaners who had cleaned up afterwards, initialled beside each name, partly kept to ensure continuous chain of custody. "I can't believe it," said Banks. "It's been staring me in the bloody face all along, and I never knew."

Blackstone moved closer. "What has? What is it?"

Banks picked the papers up off the floor and pointed with his index finger to what he had read. On the list of those involved with the Chameleon victims' post-mortems were several lab assistants, trainees and assistant pathologists, and one of them was a Dr. Elizabeth Wallace.

"I should have known," said Banks. "When Kev Templeton went on about patrolling the Maze for a would-be serial killer, Elizabeth Wallace was the only one who was as adamant as he was that we were dealing with a killer who would strike again. And she tried to convince us that the weapon was a razor, not a scalpel."

"So? I don't get it."

"Don't you see it? She was there, too. Elizabeth Wallace was keeping an eye on the Maze, and she had easy access to sharp scalpels. Much better to have us believe the weapon was a razor that anyone could have

got hold of. They were at cross-purposes, her and Kev. They didn't talk
to one another. Neither knew the other was going to be there. Elizabeth
Wallace thought Kev Templeton was going to rape and kill Chelsea
Pilton. She couldn't have recognized him from behind. It was too dark.
And there can be only one reason why she was there."

"Which is?"

"To kill the killer. She's Kirsten Farrow. The one we're looking for.
She was a trainee on the Chameleon victims' post-mortems. That
means she knew at first-hand about the wounds. They brought back
her own memories. She knows Julia Ford, and Julia must have let slip
about Lucy Payne being at Mapston Hall under a false name. It fits,
Ken. It all fits."

"She killed Templeton, too?"

"Almost certainly," said Banks. "By mistake, of course, the same way
she killed Jack Grimley eighteen years ago. But she did kill him. Her MO
is different now, but she trained as a doctor since then, so that makes
sense. And do you know what?"

Blackstone shook his head.

"Annie's going to see her today to push about her past and her
friendship with Julia Ford. Alone. She may be in danger." Banks took out
his mobile and pressed the button for Annie's number. No signal. "Shit,"
he said. "She wouldn't have turned it off, surely?"

"Why don't you try the station?"

"I'll ring Winsome on the way to Eastvale," said Banks, heading for
the door. He knew he could do it in about forty-five minutes, less if he
really put his foot down. He hoped that would be fast enough.

"Kirsten, what are you doing?" said Annie, getting up from her stool and
edging towards the door.

"Don't move. Keep still." Dr. Wallace waved the scalpel in her hand.
It glinted under the light. "Sit down again."

"Don't do anything foolish," Annie said, returning to the stool. "We
can work this out."

"You do speak in clichés and platitudes, don't you? Don't you realize
it's too late for any of that now?"

"It's never too late."

"It was too late eighteen years ago," said Dr. Wallace.

"So you're Kirsten," Annie whispered. Somehow, she had known it, at least in some part of her mind, since she had talked to Dr. Wallace in the Queen's Arms the previous evening, but that knowledge didn't do her a lot of good now.

"Yes. Elizabeth is my middle name. Wallace is from an ill-advised marriage that I should never have entered into. A marriage of convenience. An American student. At least I got the name from him, and he got his British citizenship from me. Needless to say, the marriage was never consummated. If you'd have dug deeper, you'd have uncovered it all. It's a matter of public record. All you really had to do was check the registry of marriages. I didn't even try very hard to hide it, really. When I went to medical school, I simply enrolled as Elizabeth Wallace. A new life. A new name. It caused one or two problems with my old records, but the university was patient, and we managed to get it all sorted out. I told them I was trying to avoid an abusive husband and would appreciate their discretion. But they would have told you in the end."

"So you moved on, changed your name, became a doctor."

"I didn't know what would become of me. I had no plans. I'd done what I set out to do. A terrible thing, really. A murder. No matter that the victim didn't deserve to live, was the worst kind of excuse for a human being you could imagine. And it wasn't my first. I'd also killed an innocent man and harmed a silly boy."

"I've talked to Keith McLaren," Annie said. "He's all right. He recovered. But why him?"

Dr. Wallace managed a tiny, tight smile. "I'm glad," she said. "Why? The Australian recognized me in Staithes, even though I was in disguise. I had to think fast. He'd been with me in the Lucky Fisherman, where I saw Jack Grimley. If they ever questioned him . . ."

"I've been there," said Annie. "The Lucky Fisherman. Why Grimley, too?"

"A mistake. Pure and simple. When I remembered what my attacker looked like, I found I had an even stronger memory of his voice, his accent, what he said. That was what led me to Whitby. Once I was there, I knew it was only a matter of time before I'd find him. Nothing else mattered. Grimley *sounded* like the man who attacked me. I led him to the beach. That part was easy. Then I hit him on the head with a heavy glass paperweight. That was hard. I had to hit him again. He wouldn't die. When he did, I dragged his body into a cave and left it for the sea to lick out. The tide was due in. Oh, I can justify it all to myself, of course. I was on a mission, and there were bound to be mistakes. Casualties. It's the cost of war. But I got there in the end. I got the one I was after. The right one. And when it was over everything felt different. Do you know St. Mary's Church, in Whitby?"

"The one on the hill, near the abbey?"

"Yes, with the graveyard where you can't read the names. Inside it's divided into box pews. Some them are for visitors, and they're marked For Strangers Only. After I pushed Greg Eastcote over the cliff, I went there and got into one of those pews, and I curled up in a ball. I was there . . . oh, I don't know how long. I thought, if they come for me now and catch me, it's okay, I'm not running, it's fine, that's how it's meant to be. I'll just wait here until they find me. But nobody came. And when I left that pew, I was a different person. I was calm. Totally calm. Can you believe that?" She shrugged. "I left what I had done behind me. I felt no guilt. No shame. So the name change seemed natural. I'd used different names all along, anyway. Martha Browne, Susan Bridehead. It was a sort of game as much as anything else. I was an English student. My name was Elizabeth Bennett for a while after that, but my husband's name just happened to be Wallace."

"But how did you find Greg Eastcote? How did you know who he was?"

"Like I told you, I remembered things. Partly it was the hypnosis." She paused. "He said things, you know. All the time he was doing it to me, he talked, said things. I remembered. He named places, the work he did. And there was a smell I could never forget. Dead fish. I put it all together in the end. I did make mistakes, but I got there. I got him. The right one. I made him pay for what he did to all of us."

"What did you do afterwards?"

"First I went back to Leeds, to Sarah, then back to Bath, to my parents. I tried to pick up the threads, but I was different. I was no longer one of them. I'd cut myself off by what I'd done. So I went away.

I travelled a lot, all over the world. In the end, I decided to put the past behind me and become a doctor. I wanted to help people, cure people. I know it sounds odd, after what I did, but it's the truth. Can you believe that? But in my studies I was drawn to specialize in pathology. Funny, isn't it? Working with the dead. I was always nervous around the living, but I never had any qualms about handling dead bodies. When I saw the wounds on the Paynes' victims six years ago, I couldn't help but revisit my own experiences. And then it just fell into my lap. Julia told me one night after dinner, when she'd had a few drinks. She had no idea, of course, *who* she was telling."

"Look," said Annie. "Please put the scalpel down. Let's stop this before someone else gets hurt. People know I'm here. People will come."

"It doesn't matter now."

"I can understand why you did it, all those years ago. Really, I can. I was raped once and almost killed. I hated him. I wanted to kill him. I felt such rage. I suppose I still do. We're not that different, you and I."

"Oh, but we are. I actually *did* it. I didn't feel rage. And I didn't feel guilt."

"Now I try to stop people from doing it, or bring them to the justice if they do."

"It's not the same. Don't you understand?"

"Why did you kill Lucy Payne? For God's sake, she was in a wheelchair. She couldn't move, couldn't speak, couldn't do anything. Why did you kill her? Wasn't she suffering enough?"

Dr. Wallace paused a moment and stared at Annie as if she were crazy. "You don't get it, do you? It wasn't about suffering. It was never about suffering. Certainly not about *her* suffering. I never cared whether she suffered."

"So what *was* the point?"

"She could *remember*, couldn't she?" Dr. Wallace whispered.

"Remember?"

"Yes. That's what they do. Surely you know that? That's the whole point. They remember every moment, every cut, every thrust, every feeling they experienced, every ejaculation, every orgasm, every drop of blood they shed. And they relive it. Day after day after day. As long as she could remember it, she had all she wanted." She tapped the side of her

head. "Right there. How could I let her live with the memory of what
she'd done? She could do it over and over again in her mind."

"Why not just push her over the edge?"

"I wanted her to know what I was doing and why I was doing it. I
talked to her the whole time, just the way Eastcote did to me, from the
moment the blade touched her throat until . . . right up to end. If I'd
pushed her, something might have gone wrong. Then I wouldn't have
been able to get down there and do what I had to. She might not even
have died."

"But what about Kevin Templeton?"

"Another mistake. Another casualty. I was trying to stop a memory
from being made, and I thought he was the one. He shouldn't have been
there. How could I have known he was there to protect people? I think
perhaps he'd sensed my presence there, and maybe he thought I was the
killer. When he started to walk towards the girl, he was going to warn
her to leave, but I thought he was going to attack her. I'm sorry. You've
got the real killer now. He's the same as Eastcote and Lucy Payne.
Perhaps at the moment he seems contrite, remorseful, but you wait.
That's because he's just been caught and he's scared. Even worse, he's
beginning to realize that he won't be able to do it again, to experience
that bliss again. But he'll still have his memories of that one glorious
time. He'll be sitting there in the corner of his cell running over every
detail. Relishing the first second he touched her, the moment he entered
her and she gasped with pain and fear, the moment he spilled his seed.
His only regret will be that he won't get to do it again."

"You sound as if you know what it feels like," said Annie.

Before Dr. Wallace could respond, footsteps sounded in the corridor and Winsome appeared at the door with several uniformed officers
behind her. Dr. Wallace lurched forward with the scalpel at her own
throat. "Stop! Stop right there."

Annie held her arm up and Winsome stopped in the doorway.
"Get back!" Annie yelled. "All of you. Get back out of sight." They disappeared, but Annie knew they weren't far away, working out their
options. She also knew there would be an armed response unit arriving
soon, and if she had any hope of talking Kirsten into surrendering, she

had to work fast. She checked her watch. It had been half an hour since Kirsten picked up the scalpel.

"Do you see what I mean?" Annie said, trying to sound calmer than she felt. "People know I'm here. They've come now. They won't just go away. Don't make things worse. Give me the scalpel."

Dr. Wallace glanced towards the door and, seeing no one there, seemed to relax a little.

"It doesn't matter," she said. "It's all over now anyway. I've done all I can do. God, I'm tired. Too many memories." She was leaning back on the blood-filled gutter of the post-mortem table, the half-sewn-up body behind her. Annie was about five feet away, and she calculated whether she could get over there and wrestle the scalpel out of Kirsten's hand. In the end, she decided she couldn't. The damn thing was way too sharp to risk something like that. She had seen what damage it could do.

"Look," said Annie. "There's still time. You can tell your story. People will understand. *I* understand. I do. We can get you help."

Dr. Wallace smiled, and for a moment Annie could see the remains of what had probably once been a lovely young girl with a brilliant future, one who would take the world by the horns and go as far as she wanted. Christ, she had almost been killed by a monster and had then taken her revenge, and after that she had reinvented herself as a pathologist. But she seemed weary now, and there were deep cracks in the smile. "Thanks, Annie," she said. "Thanks for being understanding, even though no one can ever really understand. I wish I'd known you before. This may sound weird, but I'm glad I got to spend my last few minutes on earth with you. You will take good care of yourself, won't you? Promise me. I can tell you've been damaged. You've suffered. We are kindred spirits underneath it all, in some ways. Don't let the bastards win. Have you seen what they can do?"

She opened the front of her smock, and Annie recoiled at the jagged criss-cross of red lines, the displaced nipple, the parody of a breast.

"Kirsten!" Annie cried out.

But it all happened too fast. Annie launched herself forward as Dr. Wallace drew the scalpel across her own throat. The warm spray of blood caught Annie full in the face, and she screamed as it kept pumping and gushing down the front of her blouse, all over her jeans. The scalpel fell from Dr. Wallace's hand and skittered across the shiny tile floor, leaving a zigzag of blood. Annie knelt beside her and became aware of movement all around her, soothing words, hands reaching for her, Winsome's voice. She tried to remember her first aid and press down hard on the bleeding carotid, but it was impossible. When she did, all that happened was that the blood spurted faster from the jugular. And Dr. Wallace couldn't breathe. Like Templeton, she had a severed carotid, jugular and windpipe. Annie didn't have three hands, and there was chaos all around her.

Annie screamed out for help. It was a hospital, after all; there had to be doctors everywhere. And they were trying. People milled around and manhandled her, bent over Kirsten with masks and needles, but when it was all over, she lay there on the floor in a pool of blood, her eyes wide open, pale, dead.

Annie heard someone say there was nothing more to be done. She rubbed her mouth and eyes with the back of her hand, but she could still taste the sweet metallic blood on her lips and feel it in burning in her eyes. God, she thought, she must look a sight, sitting on the floor rocking, crying and covered in blood. And after what seemed likes ages, who should come walking towards her but Banks.

He knelt beside her, kissed her temple, then sat on the floor and held her to his chest. People all around them were making various motions, but Banks's presence seemed to silence them and create a cocoon of peace. Soon it seemed as if there were only Annie, Banks and Kirsten in the room, though she knew that had to be an illusion. Kirsten's body was covered, and the lights seemed dimmer. Banks stroked her bloody brow. "I'm sorry, Annie," he said. "I should have realized sooner. I was too late."

"Me, too," said Annie. "I couldn't stop her."

"I know. I don't think anyone could. She'd come to the end. There was nowhere else for her to go. She'd already had a second lease on life. She didn't want to live any more. Can you imagine how terrible every day must have been for her?" Banks made a move to get up and help Annie out of the mortuary.

"Don't leave me!" Annie cried, clinging on tight, not letting him move. "Don't leave me. Not yet. Stay. Please. Just for a little while. Make them all go away."

"All right," Banks said, and she could feel him gently stroking her hair and humming a tuneless lullaby as she held on to him tight and buried her head deep in his chest, and for a moment it really did feel as if the whole world had gone away.

ACKNOWLEDGEMENTS

I would like to thank all the people who read and commented on this manuscript, in particular Dominick Abel, Dinah Forbes, Sheila Halladay, Carolyn Marino and Carolyn Mays, and the many copy editors and proofreaders who worked hard to ensure that the book you hold ends up as error-free as possible.